Copyright © 2013 by Chautona Havig

First Edition

Print ISBN

ISBN-13: 978-1494275693
ISBN-10: 1494275694

All rights reserved. No part of this book may be reproduced without the permission of Chautona Havig.

The scanning, uploading, and/or distribution of this book via the Internet or by any other means without the permission of the author and publisher is illegal and punishable by law. Please purchase only authorized electronic editions and avoid electronic piracy of copyrighted materials.

Your respect and support for the author's rights is appreciated. In other words, don't make me write you into another book as a villain!

Fonts: Times New Roman Alex Brush, Chocolate Box.
Cover photos: hillwoman2/istockphoto, EasyBuy4u/istockphoto, andhedesigns/istockphoto.com, and Fernando Eusebio /shutterstock.com
Cover Art: Chautona Havig
Edited by: Coyle Editing

The events and people in this book, aside from any caveats on the next page, are purely fictional, and any resemblance to actual people is purely coincidental and I'd love to meet them!

Connect with Me Online:
Twitter: https://twitter.com/ - !/Chautona
Facebook:https://www.facebook.com/pages/Chautona-Havig-Just-the-Write-Escape/320828588943
My blog: http://chautona.com/chautona/blog/
My newsletter (sign up for news of FREE eBook offers): http://chautona.com/chautona/newsletter

All Scripture references are from the NASB. NASB passages are taken from the NEW AMERICAN STANDARD BIBLE (registered), Copyright 1960, 1962, 1963, 1968, 1971, 1972, 1973, 1975, 1977, 1995 by The Lockman Foundation

~For Kevin~

All I can say is I'm grateful that I actually got to *spend* the last twenty-five years with you. It's been wonderful. I love you.

~Thanks to DJ~

In the process of writing, I couldn't remember where we'd gone to get our marriage license back in '88 (it was a quarter of a century ago!). After hours of searching, and discovering that they built a new complex in '95, I started calling. One operator transferred me to some deeds or something office, and I left a message asking for help. To be honest, I didn't think anyone would call back. But imagine my surprise and delight when I did get a call. DJ was amazing. She had already found what she thought I needed and didn't even whimper when I confessed that I realized I needed a different building. Within an hour, she called me back, all information right there. So thank you, DJ! Oh, and to all the Las Vegas City Government veterans who held off their retirement until DJ could ask the questions I needed to have answered, thank you too!

Chapter One

Thursday, November 13th

A few stray leaves crunched under her feet as Audrey Seever shivered her way home by streetlight. The brisk November air broke through her lightweight jacket, raising goose bumps on her arms. Several more leaves rained down on her as a gust of wind swirled around her shoulders.

Ahead, a young boy—Aiden Cox, if her memory of local boys' coats served her well—shuffled along the gutter, his shoulders and head drooping. Audrey waited until he almost reached her before she captured his attention. "Evenin'. What are you doing out here? Won't your mom be watching for you? Should be about dinner time…"

Aiden pulled a five dollar bill out of his pocket. "Mom told me to go to the store."

"Ice cream for dessert?" The minute she asked, Audrey regretted it.

The boy's expression answered before he did. "Nah… gotta get milk."

A new thought came to her and Audrey tried to keep her expression and her tone as nonchalant as possible. "Well, I'm glad I saw you. Can you give your mom a message for me?"

"Sure." The tone, while pleasant enough, still managed to indicate boredom.

"I ruined a batch of cookies—a special order. Can't sell them either. Who wants a bunch of blue baby buggies that say Zoe on them?"

Aiden grinned. "Supposed to be pink?"

"Lavender. I forgot to add some pink. Just got on a roll..." Audrey winked. "Sometimes I get in the zone and that's when I usually make expensive mistakes." Before Aiden could derail her, she continued. "So anyway, I started to toss them and thought maybe someone would come in and want them. Then I saw you. So, if your mom wants them for your lunch or snacks at home or something, tell her she can just stop in or send you down."

"Really?" The boy frowned. "You're not just saying that because Dad lost his job?"

"I didn't know he had. I'm sorry about that."

For whatever reason—one beyond Audrey's mental abilities after a long, hard day—those words brightened Aiden's countenance. "I'll tell Mom. She'll like that."

Audrey started to mention the day-old bread and occasional cakes she gave to the last customers of the day and decided against it. She could talk to Kelly Cox about that herself. "Well, I'm cold and tired, and your mom's waiting for you. See you 'round."

"Yeah. Thanks."

At Bramble Rose Drive, Audrey turned and leaned into the wind. Row houses lined both sides of the street, their small front yards bringing the neighbors closer together than the rest of the town. Lights glowed in windows and the unmistakable scent of coming snow mingled with Oscar Merkins' customary Thursday night chili.

"It's too early for snow," she muttered to herself as she trudged up her walk and to the steps. The old houses, reminiscent of those in San Francisco's Nob Hill, had once been large, grand affairs, but in recent decades, owners had converted them into two or four family condominiums. One street over, several had been chopped into six studio-sized flats. As much as it had made sense to save the money, Audrey liked the space of her duplex.

The scent of slow-cooked Italian chicken greeted her as she hung her keys on the rack by the door. That one ritual made her smile. Despite her inherent lack of order, she did have one die-hard, never-deviate-from-the-plan plan. Too many mornings of searching frantically for her key had taught her. Hang 'em first thing. *The office. I keep it well organized now, too. If I could just manage the rest of the house now.*

The living room almost swallowed her with disheveled décor. A basket of clean laundry, a stack of half-read newspapers—Audrey stepped back outside to retrieve the day's news and tossed it onto the pile—and several dirty dishes littered almost every available surface. Audrey's eyes slid toward the mail basket before she turned away again. "After dinner. Shower first."

She took the stairs two at a time—for the first two steps. Then, with a grunt of disgust at her rapidly dwindling energy, Audrey dragged herself up the remaining steps to the second floor. An unmade bed surrounded by a floor decorated with most of a week's worth of bras and panties, not to mention yoga pants and workout tops, greeted her. Why she did, Audrey didn't know, but she raked her hands through mostly-empty drawers in search of something clean. The dregs of her wardrobe offered little that was comfortable and nothing she wanted to wear.

Clean clothes awaited her—downstairs. She glanced at the stairs and whimpered. Grumbling about the insane distance between bath and living rooms, Audrey shuffled to the stairs and forced herself not to pout at each exhaustion-inducing step.

Though not soon enough for her, within minutes Audrey stood beneath the powerful spray of her new super-powered shower head. The water pounded her shoulder blades, kneading out the stress of the day's work. As always, the middle of October had ended the "back-to-school-lull" and begun the holiday influx, but this year's increase had been almost exponential over the previous years' orders. Her days began earlier and earlier and ended later and later.

As the water cooled, Audrey cranked it up once more, but soon only the cold remained and she shivered. "I really need one of those tankless heaters," she muttered as she briskly rubbed her skin, trying to re-stimulate the warmth that disappeared as the water heater tank drained.

She'd never do it, and she knew it. The guilt over removing the low-flow washer from her new shower head nearly ate her alive each time she thought of it. At least the water heater tank limited her in some way. Without it, she'd stand there until she fell asleep on her feet each night—not exactly the most eco-friendly decision.

Slightly rejuvenated, she half-jogged down the stairs and scrounged for a clean dish. A pie-plate and a workout water bottle later, she gave up and washed a fork before digging dinner from the slow-cooker and piling it on the plate. That sight gave her an idea. "Be good in the oven with biscuit topping—like a pot pie, almost."

She groped for a pen in the cup by the back door and grabbed an old envelope from a credit card offer and scribbled, *Make Italian chicken into a pot pie. Biscuit topping and*—a new thought occurred to her as she wrote–*make sure you add asparagus and maybe artichoke hearts.*

On the couch, Audrey shoved stuff out of her way and reached for the remote. Thursday night—best TV night of the week as far as she was concerned. The nightly news shared half a dozen grizzly stories about murder, armed robbery, kidnapping, and the encroaching human trafficking problem in Rockland. Audrey hardly heard it. She ate her dinner, closed her eyes, and fell asleep until the theme song for her favorite nighttime drama blared through the living room.

Audrey stretched, her hand whacking the lamp behind her and rocking it against the wall before it settled back into place. Bleary-eyed, she glared at the clock on the DVD player. "Midni—oh. Two o'clock. Ugh." She dragged herself off the couch and stared down at the dirty dishes on the coffee table. "Better soak that ice crea—oh no." A glance in the kitchen confirmed her dread. She'd left the ice cream melting in the container on the counter. "The good news—it is a great recipe. I'll sell it until I'm sick of it. Still, the Coxes would have liked it. The guys at the fire station would have loved it. How wasteful."

Dishes tempted her—taunted her. The pile of clothes by the washer outright mocked her. However, the call of her king-sized super-soft mattress won out over duty, responsibility, and even common sense. Scarlett O'Hara had it right. *"Tomorrow is another day."*

Friday, November 14th

The shop bell jingled, sending a wave of panic and a twinge of despair over Audrey. She peeked at the mirror that told her who had entered and relaxed. Wiping her hands on the damp towel before her, she hurried out front. "Kelly!"

"Hey there." Kelly glanced around the room before making eye contact. "So this is kind of embarrassing, but Aiden begged me to stop in for some cookies he said you were going to throw out..."

"I'm so glad you did—totally ruined them, and I can't sell cookies with someone's baby's name on them, y'know? I usually take stuff to the fire station, but I thought baby cookies..."

Kelly laughed, but the usual sparkle that characterized Kelly Cox never materialized. "That might be a bit much, even for hungry firemen."

"And at least you've got a baby baking in there!"

A protective hand rested on the swell of Kelly's midsection. "An active one, too. This little guy doesn't stop moving."

As Audrey retrieved the box of cookies, her mind whirled. *Jon's out of work*. There wouldn't be much in the way of treats in coming weeks if he didn't find a job soon. Kelly wasn't like a lot of Fairbury moms. She pinched every penny they had as it was. *Without income...*

"Hey, I have a question."

The woman dragged her eyes from a case of bread and smiled—again, her heart obviously not in it. "Oh?"

"Well, I've got this new flavor of ice cream I made up last night, and I wondered—" Something in Kelly's eyes forced Audrey to amend her suggestion. "—if you'd taste a bite and tell me what you think? I know *you'll* be honest. Too many people tell me that they love something and then they order something else every time they come in."

This time, Kelly's laughter reached her eyes. "I am, if nothing else, guilty of saying exactly what I think."

Kelly shook her head. "It's too sweet. It's too much like frozen pumpkin pie filling. It needs to be creamy with a lot of pumpkin but not a lot of sugar—flavor anyway. I get what you're going for, and it's really good, but it's just too sweet. Maybe less sugar and more vanilla?"

Audrey took a bite, rolling the flavors over her tongue as she considered Kelly's words. "I think you're right. I'll try to get another bit made tonight and—oh no. Not tonight. Maybe before I go home."

"Hot date?"

"Yeah... with a spray bottle and a cleaning rag. My house is a disaster." The expression on Kelly's face could have signified anything from disbelief to disgust. "What?"

Kelly had the grace to blush. "I just can't imagine how one person alone could have a 'disaster' for a house. My guess is that your definition of disaster and mine are very different."

Even as Kelly spoke, Audrey shook her head. "I have no clean clothes. These..." Audrey picked at her yoga pants and long-sleeved t-shirt. "—I just rinsed and hung them in front of the heater last night. I have no clean dishes, last night's attempt at ice cream is hardening on my counter as we speak, and I don't even want to use my own toilet for obvious reasons that I probably don't need to elaborate on..."

"And you're here until all hours some nights" Kelly hesitated before adding, "Maybe with all the extra holiday business, you could afford a housekeeper for a couple of months."

"Know anyone who does that?" The minute Audrey asked, she kicked herself. *As if they could afford something like that right now.*

"You might call Myra Scott. I think she does housecleaning, but you'd better hurry. I hear she fills up her holiday calendar fast. Alexa Hartfield has someone too... can't remember who." Kelly picked up the box of cookies and waved as she turned to leave. At the door, she paused. "You know, if you don't find someone and just get desperate, call me. I'd be happy to do it as a thanks for the cookies. I'm no professional, but I do get enough practice at my place."

Kelly was out the door and down the steps before the words fully registered. Audrey chased after her. "Wait! Kelly!"

"Wha—"

"Are you serious? Do you want the job?"

"I told you," Kelly insisted, "I'm not a professional. I—"

"But you know how to clean. That's all that matters." Audrey tried the one thing she thought might tip the decision in her favor. "Please? I need you."

"I'd be so slow..." Kelly demurred.

"I'll pay by the day instead of the hour then. How's that?" Audrey shivered for effect. It worked.

"I'll check with Jon. If he says it's okay, then I'll do it. I'll call you tomorrow."

Another customer hurried up the steps and reached for the door handle. Audrey opened it. "Welcome! C'mon in!"

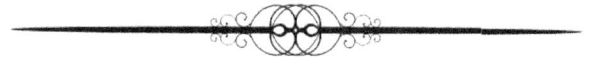

Jon Cox sat at the kitchen table, piles of bills,

receipts, and bank statements surrounding him. Kelly watched with amused interest. No matter how much she tried to convince him that a software program and paperless banking would save time and confusion, Jon insisted on doing stuff the "old-fashioned way."

Impatiently, and showing much more restraint than she knew she possessed, Kelly waited for him to close the checkbook. Once he did that, he'd be able to concentrate on the discussion she wanted to have. The boys were in bed *and* asleep—two important details—and she'd been hoarding hot chocolate for such an occasion.

He won't care, her rational side insisted. *He doesn't have that kind of false pride. But being out of work makes things different,* a quieter, more insistent part of her countered. *It forces men to accept what they don't want to **have** to—makes 'em feel like failures or something. I don't understand men any more than they understand us.*

The checkbook closed as Jon began assembling the bill-paying paraphernalia in the box. Kelly rose. "Hot chocolate and an episode of *Jeeves and Wooster*?"

"Sure. Gonna check the boys and then I'll be back."

Kelly piled a few of the Zoe cookies onto a plate as she waited for the water to boil. She found the marshmallows she'd hidden just for nights like this, and made a note to use a bit of her housecleaning money to keep them in hot chocolate for the winter. *It's his one semi-vice. The guy should get to have a bit of hot chocolate a couple of times a week if we can swing it. It's just too easy to call everything frivolous and strip life to beyond the barest of bones. I'm pretty sure that's **not** what Thoreau meant by "sucking the marrow out of life."*

Jon sat in his usual place on the couch looking more worn out than he ever did after a long, hard day's work. *Lord, I used to think he needed a few months off just to rest and rejuvenate, but this is worse than him being tired from overwork.* Lost in prayer, she almost burned him with the hot cup. "Ooooh, sorry."

"'Sokay. Cookies? Zoe?"

She hadn't intended them to be a subject opener, but Kelly couldn't have asked for a better one. "Audrey Seever botched a batch—was supposed to be purple or something. So, she told Aiden to ask if we wanted 'em."

After a thoughtful bite, Jon nodded. "They're good. Is that almond?"

"I think so. She makes the best sugar cookies I've ever had, and that frosting—thin enough not to be too much but still giving it flavor. Delicious." As he took another bite, she dropped the subject in his lap while he'd have a few seconds to chew on the idea as well as the cookie. "She also offered me a job."

Jon choked down the cookie. "In the shop?"

"No... cleaning her house. She says she doesn't have time to clean. I think she's probably exaggerating, but it would help with Christmas..."

He eyed her in that way that always made her feel as if she was lying, even if—if not especially when—she wasn't. "Is she making up work because she feels sorry for us?"

"I don't know," Kelly admitted. "I did think of that. I just figured I'd take a look and see. If it isn't really that bad, I'll clean it up a time or two and then tell her I can't keep doing it."

"Makes sense..."

"So... what do you think? Just tell her we're not interested or..." She tried not to push, but already Kelly had changed from mildly interested to eager to start. *Anything to bring in a little money.*

"How much did she offer you?"

Her eyes widened. "She didn't make it up for me. I just realized that. She asked me if I knew anyone first. She *asked* for a name, and when I suggested Myra, I also said if she didn't find anyone, that I'd be happy to do it as a thanks for the cookies. It's not a made up job."

"So how much..."

"I don't know. I think it's because she was planning to call someone who has established rates. She's probably looking up the going rate as we speak—unless she's perfecting the totally yummy ice cream I tested for her today. I mean, it was amazing. It would sell like hotcakes, but I told her to cut some of the sugar. I'm pretty sure it'll sell out every day if she does that."

Jon shook his head and took a sip of his chocolate. "If it was amazing, why did you tell her to change it?"

"Because she wants to know. I told her what would make it the best it could be—in my opinion anyway. Audrey likes honesty when she asks stuff like that. I'm honest, and she knows it." Kelly bit into the cookie in her hand. "Take this, for instance, I'd tell her not to change a thing. Not. One. Thing. Same with her carrot cake petit fours. Those things should be labeled a dangerous substance—to my hips!"

"Well, as long as you don't lose all your money paying for someone to watch Nathan, there's no reason not to."

Yes! Kelly screamed inside as she pumped an imaginary fist. *I was sure he'd think of a good reason I shouldn't do it—one of those brilliant things that are so annoying because of their obviousness.*

"I'll call her tomorrow then." She nudged his foot with hers. "Got the remote?"

Chapter Three

Wednesday, November 19th

A gust of wind pushed Kelly through the door at Audrey's house. Her eyes roamed the little entryway, taking in the small metal locking mailboxes, the door to another apartment, and the one with a shiny gold A as if for Audrey. *They did these up nicely. I bet a staircase used to be behind that wall.*

As she stepped into Audrey's unit, Kelly grinned. A staircase to her right seemed to prove her correct. But the mess in the room almost made her miss it. "I didn't believe you, Audrey. Really, I didn't," she mumbled to an empty living area. "This is pretty bad, though."

She'd spent the whole of her morning at home, struggling to decide just what she'd do first, and how to do it. Should she treat it as if it was her own home and do several things at once and risk running out of time with things half-finished? Should she do one thing at a time inefficiently, and risk having to come back due to wasted time? Now, standing in the house, Kelly realized that a combination might work best. "She said she needed laundry done. I can wash clothes—even if I don't fold. I'll start a load and then get cracking on the bathroom."

Kelly, in a fit of nervous energy and feeling quite out of place, began a running monologue with herself as she picked up laundry from every corner of the small home. A basket of laundry teetering on one corner of an ottoman made her hesitate. One carefully placed washcloth would send it toppling onto the floor—a thought that amused Kelly. "And at my house, it would have already hit and scattered."

The clothes looked clean, but she saw no evidence of a used dryer sheet to confirm her suspicions. An apron looked dirty, but it could also be stained. "You're wasting time. Just rewash. It's not a full load anyway."

Her genius plan nearly sent her screaming as she saw the tiny apartment-sized stackable washer/dryer combo. "I bet she can only fit five pairs of jeans in that thing. I'll be done before the laundry!" She tossed aside the temptation to run the clothes home and wash them in her own super-sized appliances and shoved as much as she could into the little front-loader. "There. Get clean."

From there, Kelly found it hard to know what to do next. She spun in slow, confused circles as she her pregnancy brain refused to divulge her previous plans. "Bathroom. I said bathroom."

Despite the apparent neglect of the home, it took little time at all to scrub down and squeegee the shower. Sink, toilet, walls, fixtures, and floor—only the trash sitting outside the door remained. She grabbed it and the one beside Audrey's bed and jogged downstairs. Her caddy held a roll of kitchen trash bags. However, as she returned the wastebasket to the bathroom, something struck her as not quite right. Her eyes roamed the six by nine room, trying to determine what was wrong—off. An empty towel bar sent her searching for towels, but there were none. "Towels next. She needs to be able to shower or bathe or something at the end of a long day."

Remove sheets, turn the mattresses, find a fresh mattress pad and clean sheets, make the bed. She stared at it, waiting. As she realized what she waited for wouldn't happen, she smiled. "No toddler ready to jump on the bed and mess it all up again." Her eyes slid back to the bathroom. "That's what's wrong. The lid's still down, there's no pile of clean TP at the base of the roll, it's still clean."

Mid-clean, Kelly discovered a flaw in the plan. Many things obviously weren't where they belonged, and she had no idea where they should go. "It's not going to look clean if I just leave it, but…" She eyed the phone and sighed. "I've gotta ask. I can't just put her stuff anywhere."

Audrey answered the phone a little out of breath. "The Confectionary—Audrey speaking."

"It's Kelly. Are you busy?" She shook her head. "Okay, I know you're busy, but do you have a second to answer a couple of questions?"

"Um… yeah, Stacy's got the front. What's up?"

"I have stuff that I don't know where it goes. I mean, shoes and jackets I can put in a closet and at least you'd find them, but there's a gift bag and a plastic bag from Walmart with stuff in it… there's—"

"Right. Good thought. I should have put stuff like that away, shouldn't I? I think that's what services expect. Sorry. I was just so—"

"Not a problem," Kelly assured her. "I just wanted to know if there was some place you wanted me to put it all so you'd find it." As she spoke, the washing machine buzzed to tell her it finished and prompted her second question. "And what laundry is priority for you? I've got towels going in next. You don't have any, but after that…"

"Underwear—that's for sure. Um, aprons, shop shirts, yoga pants. Definitely those, and just use a laundry basket and pile the random stuff in it. Leave it in the office. I'll look there if I can't find anything."

"Thanks! I'll get back to work then."

"Told you it was awful," Audrey teased.

"Well, it's worse than I expected, but you've got one major advantage." Kelly waited for Audrey to ask what before answering, "Yours *stays* clean after I get done. You'd never know I did half the stuff I have at my house. Nathan would have made it look 'lived in' again already."

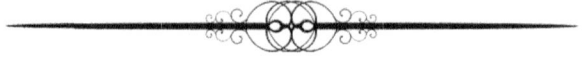

"Nathan would have made it look 'lived in' again already."

Kelly's words cut through Audrey with each reminder. Customers entered and distracted her for a moment. The mocha-skinned little girl with two fuzzy black tufts on each side of her head. *She could be mine. My daughter would have looked like her—if I ever had one.*

Audrey heard it often—little jabs about how lucky she was not to have pint-sized little marauders in her home, destroying her sleep. Tweens that are too old for their very young years, trying to live up to the teens they so long to be. Teenagers keeping their parents up all hours of the night for a myriad of reasons—none of which anyone would consider enviable. *Seems like parenting begins and ends with sleepless nights.*

Still, despite the visible disadvantages, one of which she forced herself to admit as she picked up the pieces of a destroyed gingerbread cottage that once was the pride of the shop, Audrey knew something those parents never could. *There are those of us who would risk it all if we could. Colic, potty training, temper tantrums, peer pressure, educational choices, chauffeuring them everywhere, trying to keep them safe from drugs and premature sex, college applications, and then an empty nest. No one considers that I have an empty nest. Mine doesn't count because it's never been occupied by anyone but me. People think I choose this—like I get a choice. They envy me sometimes. They're crazy—just as crazy as they think I am at times. It works both ways.*

The wrecking ball's mother led the sniffling child to Audrey's side. "Apologize, Serena."

"I'm sorry." Two dark chocolate eyes blinked away

tears and a little button nose sniffled again.

"It's o—"

"Don't tell her it's okay. Don't do that to her. It's not okay."

"Right," Audrey tried again, her thoughts jumbled. "I—I forgive you."

The mother tugged Serena's hand to lead her from the shop, but the little girl stared up at her, resisting. "How long does it take?"

"For what?"

"To make—that." Serena's little finger shook.

She knew it would annoy the mother—that it was probably rude and undermined all good parenting, but Audrey allowed herself the privilege of making the little girl smile again. "It takes a long time."

"See! See what you did? Just because—"

"But, can I tell you a secret?" Audrey leaned closer and ignored the expectant look in the woman's eye. *You are gonna be so ticked at me.* "I'm kind of excited to try a new idea I had. I wouldn't have gotten to do it, but now I can. Thanks."

A huff and a slight jerk of Serena's arm gave away the mother's indignation, but the gap-toothed grin on the little girl's face was worth the probable loss of Christmas business from that customer. As Audrey stood and reached for the broom, Stacy cleared her throat. "That's not what you told *me* to do when parents correct their kids."

"Yeah, well, sometimes kids need to see that not everything is the catastrophe their parents think it is."

Stacy crossed her arms and shook her head. "You were ticked. I saw it."

"Still am! I put a lot of work into it, but seriously? The kid was just spinning around to see her dress fly. She wasn't *trying* to punch it!" As Audrey shook the remnants of her gingerbread masterpiece into the garbage, she shrugged. "Besides. I'm not the mom. I don't have to read the kid the riot act. I said what she wanted until she wanted to push it too far and leave me holding the bag—or whatever metaphor works with that." She glanced up at the clock. "Time to close."

"Gingerbread house?"

The temptation hit hard. They'd worked all day so they could go home on time, but now… "No. Let's go. We'll do it sometime between now and Sunday, or I'll do it after church."

"Gonna try those heat-free lights you bought?"

"Yep."

"I'll bet it's up on the stand in the morning," Stacy insisted.

"You'd lose that bet. Now go home."

Despite her protests, the temptation continued all through backroom cleanup, taking out the garbage, filing orders, and end-of-day inventory. Even as she walked to the store for yogurt and salad greens, the pull back to her own shop nearly won out over her determination to let herself rest. *You're gonna wear out and then be too sick to have a successful holiday season. Now go home, re-watch last week's "Elementary," and go to sleep in your freshly-made bed.*

During the commercial break, Audrey carried her dishes to the sink, rinsed them, and stuck them in the dishwasher. "It's easier to keep clean when it is already."

The dryer buzzed with the last load of towels. "Kelly leaving those in the washer was a risk, but it's one I'm glad she took. Now I'll make it until she gets back here." She pulled the half-dozen towels from the little dryer and glanced around the room, looking for her laundry baskets. "Oh, right. Upstairs. Oh, well. Man, these feel good. I should take my shower down here on laundry days. Wow."

A body appeared on screen just as she plopped back down on the couch and began folding. "It's that guy with the art gallery. I can't believe Sherlock hasn't figured—and there he goes."

The next commercial break sent her rushing upstairs with the towels and back down again with her laptop. She flipped the screen up and waited for it to boot as a dancing dryer sheet promised to make her clothes soft and static-free. By the time the car commercial with the big red bow appeared, she'd deleted half her inbox—spam. She paused in her perusal of the rest of her digital correspondence and shook her head. "I do not understand how any wife would be glad to have her husband spend thirty-thousand dollars, even if he did call it a 'surprise.' I'd be seriously ticked." A familiar wrench in her heart forced her to add, "Not that I'll ever get to test that assertion."

The subject line of her sister's email, "Don't say no" gave away the contents long before she forced herself to open it. Audrey hit the pause button as her show resumed and double clicked the email. "Let me guess. There's this great new guy at church, he's single and not interested in a casual relationship, maybe even has a child who is missing his or her deceased mommy, and I'd be perfect for him because he loves short-term missions and Indian food."

As she skimmed the email, Audrey grinned. "Pretty close. No dead wife, but a dead sister's child. That's a heart-breaking new one. He sounds like any woman's dream." Three failed attempts later, Audrey typed out a short and poignant reply. "You... know... my... answer... Stop...doing...this... to... me." She stared at the words and added. "Love... you... for... it..., but... stop. Really."

Her finger hovered over the mouse button as she considered how her sister would take it. *Is it strong enough? Too strong? I guess we'll see. Why does she always have to do this near Christmas? Even Valentine's would be preferable.*

Audrey read it through once more, closed her eyes, and clicked the mouse button. The minute the blue progress bar disappeared, she closed the laptop and stood. "That's enough for one night. I'll finish the show some other time. Gotta find out if I'm right."

Chapter Four

Wednesday, November 26th

Arms laden with tote bags, grocery bags, and a box that had been leaning against the door, Kelly burst into Audrey's apartment and rushed to dump everything on the couch before she dropped it all. The box slid to the floor at a jaunty angle, as if to say, "I stand alone."

Kelly ignored the rogue package and grabbed the groceries. The fridge had a few new iffy containers of leftovers, but not the quantity of the first two weeks. "Progress... I guess. That's good."

The scent of slow-roasting beef and onions filled the room as she lifted the lid to the crock-pot. "That smells amazing." Kelly inhaled deeply once more. "I need that recipe."

Dishes in the sink were encrusted enough to make Kelly fill the sink with hot water and a little dish soap. She glanced in the dishwasher and relaxed as she saw food-free dishes waiting to be properly washed. "Either that, or she's eating out of the dishwasher."

A kick in her midsection seemed to jar her memory. "Laundry!" She grinned as she rubbed her belly. "You're right, little one. I forgot about laundry. Why is it that you little guys insist on sapping all my brain cells?"

All through the house, she chatted with the baby as she worked. Mopping, vacuuming, scrubbing, folding, dusting—every movement almost second nature as she worked clockwise through each room. Thus far, she hadn't had time to do much in Audrey's office, but on that Wednesday before Thanksgiving, she finished long before Aiden would be out of school.

While the rest of Audrey's home looked like generic arrangements from a furniture advertisement—simple shapes and neutral colors, contemporary but unremarkable—her office, on the other hand, appealed to Kelly's personal design aesthetic. Two bookcases with leaded glass doors held a set of classics. Curious to see if doors really helped keep the dust off books, Kelly opened one and pulled *The Picture of Dorian Gray* from the center of the top shelf. Her finger ran along the tops of the pages, but little dust transferred to it. "Works better than I thought."

The spine of the book showed a little wear, and the pages fell open easily. "Someone reads it—or did." She pulled out several others. *Dracula, Tales of Edgar Allen Poe, The Hounds of the Baskervilles,* and *Rebecca* all had the same well-worn but not abused appearance, while *Tom Sawyer, Pride and Prejudice,* and *Alice in Wonderland* showed no wear at all. "Someone likes mystery and classic horror." As she pulled *Lorna Doone* from the shelf, Kelly shook her head. "Either she and I have completely opposite tastes in reading, or she's never read these."

An open-faced bookcase held matching binders, and a liberal coating of dust covered it all. She pulled a disposable dust pad from her caddy and forced herself to start to the right of the door. It took little time to dust the three bookshelves, side table, two lamps, and desk, but the old secretary lay open with enough cubbyholes to ensure it would take forever to get all the dust out. "Wonder why she left it open—seems odd when everything else is closed up and neat."

The three plants got water and Kelly made a note to bring food. She turned them around to give the backsides a chance at light and smiled with satisfaction as she ran a dusty hand over her midsection. "Just that big ol' desk and we're done for the day, little one."

The desk looked like it belonged in a nineteenth century manor—a woman's writing desk. Only one narrow drawer for a few sheets of paper or pen kept it from being utterly useless in her eyes. "It is pretty..."

The papers and files scattered across the top looked important, so Kelly stacked them neatly on one side and ran her dust cloth over the surface of the desk. As she transferred them to the other side, the motion generated a breeze that flipped open the top file and sent a few papers fluttering to the floor. Exasperated, she collected the contents—tax returns from the previous year—and tried to sort them in order.

A name on the first page of the return sent her heart racing. Before she realized what she'd done, Kelly read the first lines of the return. Several times. Audrey Seever. She forced herself to close her eyes as they slid near the social security number. The next section sent her heart racing once more. Her eyes returned to the same checked box and the same name on the line—number three. Married filing separately. Spouse's name. Zain Kadir.

All through dinner, Kelly fidgeted. Between exhaustion after a long day of work with a baby that threatened to make her miserable in the final trimester, and aching to have Jon to herself so she could talk to him about what she'd discovered, she spent the evening trying not to snap at everything that happened and anyone who did it. Nathan earned himself a silent scolding for dragging out all of his toys. He'd have been astounded had she spoken aloud. Aiden, with the astute powers of observation that come with almost eleven years of avoiding "the wrath of mom" on days where he'd more than earned it, narrowly avoided added chores when he started to argue with her.

Jon gave her several odd looks but said nothing, which, of course, made her feel worse than ever. The boys' lights had hardly snapped off and Jon returned to the room when she dropped the dishcloth in the sink and whirled to face him. "Y'know, Audrey Seever—"

"Yeah? Something go wrong today? You've been, well, out of sorts since you got home."

"Have you ever seen or heard of her going out with anyone?"

Her husband's eyes narrowed. "Why would you care?"

"Just humor me, Jon! Have you ever seen or heard of her going out?"

"No." He pulled open the fridge door and retrieved an apple. "What's this all about, anyway?"

She rinsed the cloth, draped it over the faucet, and dried her hands. With a glance down the hall to be sure the boys weren't creeping out for some reason or another, she beckoned Jon to follow. Once he relaxed against the couch, she pounced. "So I was cleaning her office today and knocked a file on the floor. It was a bunch of tax stuff from last year."

Confusion flooded Jon's expression. "I don't get it. What does that have to do with her dating anyone?"

"I saw her filing status."

"So?"

Exasperated, Kelly leaned forward with a habitual glance toward the hallway to see if Aiden stood there. "Her last year's return was marked as 'Married filing separately.' It even had the husband's name and social security number on it."

Jon's jaw worked as he chewed the apple, but his eyes widened in shock. As he swallowed, he choked out, "What?"

"She's married, Jon! She has to be to file her taxes that way, doesn't she? How long has she been married? Who is this guy?"

"Maybe if she wanted us to know, she would have told people," Jon interjected as he stood. "I'm going to take a shower. Need anything first?"

"No..." Kelly pulled the laptop off the coffee table. "But thanks. I'll just see what's up on Facebook and check the email. Mom said she found a coupon for diapers."

With a nod, Jon sauntered down the hallway. Kelly waited, seconds ticking by so slowly she wanted to tear her hair out in frustration. At last, the sound of the shower released her reserve and sent her fingers flying over the keyboard. Facebook listed several Zains—and even more derivatives of the name—paired with Kadir, but only two in the United States were between the ages of twenty and sixty. She clicked on each one and hit the "about" link. The first, a man in Chicago, listed his relationship status as "complicated."

It's close-ish. Only six hours... A Christian. He's forty-five. That would be around the right age, I think. And complicated. Being married to a woman who lives as a single woman in this town. How much less complicated could you get than that?

Unwilling to leave things at that, Kelly right clicked on the other name and opened a new tab with his profile. Zain Kadir. In Santa Monica, California. Forty-five as well. Marital status. Single. This man listed no religious affiliation. *Probably not him. Right, Lord? I mean he says he's single; he's not even claiming to be religious at all. Surely if Audrey married, she'd marry someone who is at least saved, right?*

The more she thought about it, the less comfortable she was with looking at the mens' profiles. *It's kind of stalkerish, isn't it? And a bit inappropriate, I suppose. Married woman out there scrutinizing other men's profiles while her husband is taking a shower.* Her conscience added for her, *And hiding that fact from your husband. What's wrong with you?*

Kelly knew her actions weren't prompted by any inappropriate interest, but then again, wasn't being nosy "inappropriate interest"? Her mouse hovered over the tab's X, ready to close it. She hesitated as she heard their bedroom door open. *Just show him. It can't hurt and it removes awkward secrets.*

As Jon stepped into the room, she turned the screen toward him. "Look who I found."

"Tell me that's not who you think she married."

"Yeah. The guy's name was Zain Kadir and there are only two of them in the US. So, I looked at them, and this guy says his relationship status is "complicated."

"You're—" Jon shook his head and sighed. "It's not right, Kelly. If she wanted people to 'meet' her husband, she'd introduce him. Just let it go. We don't even know if she's really married or if that was some kind of joke for someone or whatever."

Kelly's eyes widened. "Hey, do people do that thing where they marry someone to help get or keep them in the country anymore? Did that ever really happen?"

"Seems like it has been done in the past, but it's not guaranteed. I know that. And it's harder now than it was. I've read that."

"I just wondered..." Kelly threw up her hands. "Okay, okay. I'm done with everything I need to do. Let's go to bed before you figure out that I checked out the other guy, too."

Halfway down the hall, Jon muttered, "You do know that you just told me what you don't want me to find out."

"Yeah. That's why I said it. No secrets and yet maybe I don't get in trouble because you're not 'supposed to know.' Win/win."

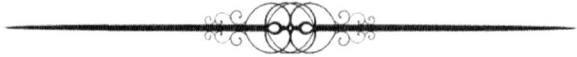

Laughter, and the occasional giggle, filled the kitchen as "the Seever girls" worked together on dinner preparations. Walt Seever, banished to the living room by the feminine element of the family, called out random trivia from the afternoon game. "Touchdown '49ers!"

"What's the score again?" Audrey strode into the family room, wiping her hands on a dishtowel.

"Twenty-one to thirteen, '49ers favor."

She grinned. "Someone's beating the Steelers, eh?"

But her father wasn't listening. He beckoned her closer. "I thought you'd never get in here," Walt hissed. "Tami's invited someone tonight. His name is Merritt or Mattox or something like that—has a nephew."

The pounding in her heart seemed to break her out in a sweat. Audrey leaned closer. "Not the guy who is raising—"

"Yes. She said you'd never give any guy a chance that you never met, so she invited him."

"Oh, ugh."

The doorbell rang and Tami dashed past to answer it. "I've got it."

"You're gonna get it all right," Audrey growled after her.

"Traitor!"

In a reasonable assumption that the accusation was his, Walt shrugged. "You asked for it with a stunt like that."

"Be civil."

What, because it is so civil of you to set a guy up with someone who has already rejected him—even if he doesn't know it? Unacceptable, Tamara Lee Seever!

Even as her mind chewed out Tami, her sister led a man and a four-year-old boy over to her side to be introduced. "Audrey, this is Merrill Tobin and his nephew, Jason." Tami beamed at the man before them. "This is Audrey, the sister I was telling you about." Walt stood as she added, "And this is my father—Walt."

Both guests murmured something about it being nice to meet everyone before being dragged into the kitchen to meet the rest of the family. Audrey stared at her father. "I thought Merritt or Mattox was the *last* name. I didn't know you meant first."

"Last names are popular first ones these days."

"Dad, he's got to be forty-five. That wasn't as common back then," she hissed.

"Who cares? He's a decent-looking guy, and he obviously is committed to family."

And I am not interested! her inner self screamed. "Well, I already told her no."

"And presented her with an even bigger challenge." Walt squeezed her hand and nudged her back toward the kitchen. "Give the guy a chance."

"Not you, too!"

"You're my only unmarried daughter. A man has to try…"

Audrey rolled her eyes and changed the subject. "Should I go down and get the guys and the kids?"

"Ask your mom, but probably." He grinned. "There goes my peace and quiet."

"Hey, at least they don't expect you to miss the game."

Merrill stepped into the room. "Know the score? We had to leave just be—" His eyes caught the score on the screen and he cheered. "They did it! I couldn't stay to see, but it looked like they might make it."

Audrey smiled and ignored the pleading in her father's eyes. *At least one of you could marry a guy who likes football! C'mon!*

Yeah, I could have done that, but I'm not in the market, so let's just drop it, she rejoined.

"So you're rooting for the '49ers?" Walt asked as he led their guest into the living room again, the upcoming meal forgotten.

"Not so much that—just rooting *against* the Steelers. On principle."

He would have to be perfect in that regard, Lord. Why do You do this to me? Will I have to pay for the sins of my youth until I'm ashes and dust?

Tami's voice called to her from the kitchen, snapping her out of her reverie. "Audrey, will you take Jason downstairs and introduce him to the kids? I have to mash the potatoes."

The words, "I'll mash 'em, you take him down" formed in her heart, but Audrey couldn't bring herself to speak them. Instead, she smiled at the little guy and beckoned for him to follow. "Most of the kids down there are a lot older than you, but Tanika is seven—not too many years."

"I have a Tamika in my class at school," the boy remarked.

"Almost the same name. C'mon down. They're playing Ping-Pong. Just don't let them talk you into a game. It's almost dinner time."

Once certain the boy felt at ease, Audrey rushed upstairs to help carry the dishes to the table. An argument erupted just as she arrived—an old, familiar, and most definitely unwanted one. Exasperated, she held her hands in a T. "Okay, time out. This is a holiday and we have guests. No fighting over whose ideas on culture are best."

"Fence-sitter," her oldest sister, Diane, snapped.

Audrey's mother spoke up, never taking her eyes off the turkey as she shaved piece after piece into a hot serving dish. "Peacemaker is more like it."

Before Audrey could thank her mother, Tami joined forces with Diane. "She's right. Audrey never makes a stand. She just sits back and says whatever she thinks will shut everyone up."

"I don't like conflict—especially on holidays and especially with company, so can you just shelve your political and social agendas until *after* all chance of indigestion has passed?"

Walt's voice interrupted before either woman could answer. "Phyllis, should I call anyone up yet?"

"Almost. Still cutting the turkey." Audrey's mother nodded at Diane. "Don't let that gravy burn. Did you heat the gravy boat?"

"It's in the oven."

Audrey stood back and listened, relieved to see the obligatory, "you're too obsessed with your black roots" and "you're too obsessed with ignoring them in favor of your white ones" argument tabled for a few minutes at least. Diane and Tami hadn't managed to be in the same room for over half an hour without arguing their individual positions since high school, although back then, they each held the opposite position. *We're just people. We've got good and bad in both sides of our family history. Isn't that enough? Why does one have to get any kind of preeminence over the other?* Audrey asked herself her usual question and as usual, felt relieved as she realized her sisters didn't hear it and wouldn't jump on her for it. *Same old. Same old.*

Tami had spent the past twenty some-odd years trying to set Audrey up with random men from church or work, but of late, she'd dropped all pretense of it being anything other than overt matchmaking. So, it came as no surprise when she suggested that Merrill and she take a walk after dinner to "settle their stomachs." As much as Audrey wanted to feign exhaustion and avoid the unpleasant task of warning off the man, she nodded her acceptance and asked if Jason would like to come or if he'd rather watch the game with her dad. To her delighted disgust, the boy opted to watch the game. *Could the kid be any more perfect? Could Merrill look any more interesting? Why can't Tami go back to finding men I couldn't be interested in if I wanted to be? It was easier then.*

They hadn't taken three steps outside when Merrill asked a question. Audrey, lost in how she'd warn him off without offending him, didn't hear it, but she did hear something in his tone that cut even deeper. *Oh, c'mon, Lord. This is just getting cruel. The guy knows how to start and hold a conversation too? I'm done with this!*

That thought gave her just the encouragement she needed to toss aside her usual deflection and tackle the awkwardness of the situation. "Merrill, it's really nice to meet you—"

"But you're not interested."

Well, he's not full of himself. I'll give him that. "I think a better way of putting it would be that I told my sister I didn't want to meet you, and she disregarded my wishes."

"Why is that better?"

Isn't it? It's not you, it's me, okay? Determined not to get sidetracked, Audrey tried again. "Because to say that I'm not interested an hour after I meet you implies that something about *you* disinterests me. Admitting that I did not want to meet you in the first place removes any personal rejection. I made a decision for me and my life, and my sister—" Audrey sighed, refusing to completely throw Tami under the bus. "As well-meaning as she is—"

"Ignored you. My sister would have done the same thing." He stopped mid-stride and faced her. "You're right. It's hard to feel rejected when I know that. Thanks."

She started to turn back, but Merrill tugged her sleeve. "Let's walk a bit more. I promise not to flirt."

"Then why walk more?"

"Let Tami learn a bit of a lesson. The longer we're out here, the better she'll think we're getting along."

Despite her best effort to control it, laughter bubbled over at the image of Tami's disappointment when they returned having *not* made a date for the following week or weekend. "Did she offer to watch Jason for you?"

"Yes. I turned her down."

Audrey hesitated, and turned back toward the corner, her hands shoved deep in her coat pockets for as much warmth as possible. "Why?"

"I have a friend with kids his age. He's used to them—likes them."

"I thought you were going to say you were going to bring him along. I almost agreed."

"I was going to bring him along," Merrill echoed.

"Very funny. You said no flirting."

She saw a twitch at the corner of his mouth before he said, "You started it."

See! It's just not fair. This is fun. I should be able— Audrey forced herself to change the direction of her thoughts. "He's just a cute kid. He said—" *You can't tell him that either. It's like asking for a compliment—flirting again. Since when do you flirt with your sister's setups? Knock it off.*

"He said you were pretty."

"He told you!"

Laughing, Merrill shook his head. "No. Didn't have to. He says that to all ladies who are nice to him. I can't figure out where he got it." Merrill sent her a sidelong glance before he added, "And he's right, of course."

"You said—"

"Again, you brought it up," the man protested.

"So, how about them Steelers?"

"They stink."

Audrey stifled a groan at the realization she'd just made talking with the man even more difficult. *There is no such thing as the perfect man. He has faults. His breath stinks in the morning like everyone's does. He passes gas after eating beans—just like everyone. If nothing else, he wasn't smart enough not to let Tami inveigle him into an introduction. This man is not amazing and interesting, so watch yourself.* "I agree. Why don't you like 'em?"

"Lots of reasons, of course. Obnoxious fans, biased refs, but I'd say the biggest one would have to be Stee—"

"—ly McBeam. Or the towel..." Merrill had the audacity to possess a deep, rich laugh that made her want to punch him and tickle him at the same time. *Lord...*

"Oh, the towel. My sister used to call it the "Shroud of Steelin. Her husband called her jealous."

"Wait. Back up. Did you just imply that your sister married a Steelers fan?" Audrey pulled her hands from

38

her pockets and crossed her arms over her chest.

"We tried to talk her out of it…"

"Tell me," Audrey insisted as she continued around the block, stuffing her hands back in her pockets. "Tell me Jason—"

"I think there's hope for him. He's just old enough to start paying attention now and then. I call him in when a good team has a chance at a good play." Merrill shrugged at her giggle. "Yeah, it's a bit indoctrinate but it works."

As if by mutual, silent agreement, they continued their walk down two more streets, around the block, and back up to the Seever house. Just as Audrey reached for the doorknob, Diane's voice reached them. "—as well contact Michael Jackson's plastic surgeon and get started, then!"

Merrill raised one eyebrow.

"How do you do that?"

"Do what?"

"Raise just one eyebrow," she said without any attempt to hide her frustration. "I never get how people do that. I can't."

"Dunno. Didn't realize I did."

"That's even worse," she began, but Tami's voice interrupted her as she neared the window, presumably to look out and see where the walking couple might be. "—need to remember that our identity is not in what happened to our ancestors! I'm just not willing to base who I am today on who my great, great, great—"

Merrill's eyes posed the question he seemed too polite to ask. Audrey sighed. "Diane's all about clutching at our African-American heritage and pretending Dad's not white enough to have been on the Mayflower. Tami's all about sweeping it under the rug and joining the DAR."

"And you?"

Audrey shrugged. "I'm the wishy-washy fence-sitter who won't take a stand."

"Why do I get the feeling that there's more to it

than that?"

She stared at him, grateful that he wasn't too tall or too short. *It doesn't matter since you're not going to see him again anyway. Stick to the topic, Audrey!* "You're right. I just think their constant debate—"

The voices escalated inside. Merrill shook his head. "That's one way of putting it."

"Fine, *argument* is proof of the problem. I don't think any of us should completely ignore the past—on either side of the family—but this obsession with our identity being caught up in what continent our ancestors ended up on after the flood is just stupid. It's why our country is still torn up about stuff." She couldn't leave it there, as much as she liked the approval on his face. "And to be honest, even if I didn't think that, I'd still want to smash their heads together, because more than anything, I hate conflict."

"Sorry."

Audrey leaned against the wall next to the door. "About what?"

"Tami bringing me here is just more conflict between you two."

"That's her problem, not yours."

As she spoke, Merrill's head shook. "Sorry. Not so. Because I just might show up at that little shop of yours someday. I wouldn't have without her talking you up for the past few weeks."

Oh, no. See what you've done. You should have come straight back. Stop him now. She blinked slowly, taking a slow, steadying breath. "Don't, Merrill. I'm serious. You can ask and I will say no. Every time."

"You didn't say no to a longer walk..."

And I should have. God, forgive me, I should have. "That won't happen again. I knew better and I ignored it." She reached for the doorknob. "I'm sorry, but I mean it. Don't ask unless you just really like rejection."

Chapter Five

Wednesday, December 3rd

The silence of Audrey's house drove Kelly crazy. Even the bouncing of the dryer didn't do enough to break up the aching silence. *I always want "peace and quiet." Well, this is driving me insane.*

Her eyes sought the window where she could see the hood of her minivan. *That CD Breanne gave me is in there. Is it unprofessional to use someone's CD player?* She glanced around the room to see if she could even find one. Nothing. A laptop tempted her, but she couldn't bring herself to open it.

The kitchen was half clean before she gave up and snatched up the handset for Audrey's land line. *Strange—so many people are giving up land lines. I wonder why Audrey hasn't. She's never here, and it's just her—I think.*

"—llo? Helllloooo?"

"Oh, Audrey! Sorry. I was thinking about you having a land line and—"

"As you're using it." Audrey laughed. "Got a problem?"

"Yeah, all that peace and quiet I've dreamed of isn't all it's cracked up to be. I don't know how to clean a house in total quiet. I think the first couple of times worked because I didn't know where things were and stuff. Now that I do, I'm going insane. Do you have a

CD player somewhere? I've got this new piano Christmas CD..."

"Just use my laptop. It should be on the end table or maybe on the couch."

Kelly hesitated. Audrey must have assumed it due to her reticence to invade some perception of privacy. She insisted that Kelly not worry about it. "I trust you."

Yeah, but I don't know if I trust me. "Thanks but—"

"Look, I've got an influx all of a sudden. I've got to go."

Kelly stared at the phone in her hand, still struggling with the idea of opening that laptop. She tried twice more to finish the kitchen before she gave up and dashed out to her van for the CD. "If she notices I didn't use it—how, I don't know—then that'll look weird."

A man passed her, his eyes shifting nervously. *Great, now I'm scaring her neighbors. Ridiculous.*

But it worked—just as she'd known it would. With the instrumental music serving almost as accompaniment, Kelly sang as she scrubbed down the fridge, washed out the garbage can, and mopped the floor. With a dust pad in hand, she worked her way through the house, seeing every item in a new light. Was the man in the photograph a cousin, a friend, a brother—or could it be Zain? She peered again. "Well, it's not the one on Facebook if it is. This guy isn't Middle Eastern."

The rhythm clock—had she purchased it herself, or was it an anniversary gift? Every item she touched as she eradicated the thin layer of dust from the room introduced a new question or idea until she thought she'd go crazy wondering.

However, much to her delight and astonishment, once she'd opened the laptop, the idea of looking for anything but the music player program revolted her. *At least I'm not **as** pathetic as I thought I was.*

Despite her electronic self-restraint, Kelly spent every minute of her cleaning time in search of something obvious to determine Audrey's exact marital status. The office, as she dusted each familiar item, became a ticking time-bomb of temptation. Her eyes slid to the same stack of papers and folders, glaring at them as if left there to test her strength of character.

"I won't do it," she said just after the line to "Santa Claus Is Coming to Town" informed her that "he sees" everything. "Well, Santa doesn't, perhaps, but You do, Lord, and I'm not going to shame You that way. I just won't." Temptation knocked again in time for her to add, "Or, at least, I'll *try* not to."

The washing machine hadn't finished washing its final load as she finished. And, despite her best efforts to find anything that might lead her to something that identified Zain Kadir, nothing did. Nothing. The house showed nothing at all that would indicate Audrey was anything but the single entrepreneur she appeared to be. "She doesn't even have Christmas decorations up."

That thought sparked a new one that flamed into a raging idea. "Closets. If I see even one thing in her closets that hint that she ever decorates for Christmas, I'm calling. Maybe she'll let me decorate for her, and if so, maybe I'll find an 'Our first Christmas' ornament or something with a picture. That's not too nosy, is it?" Her eyes stared at the ceiling as if the Lord would speak through the overhead light fixture and assure her that all would be well. He didn't.

The top shelf of the office closet was packed with boxes marked "Christmas ornaments" or "Christmas garland" or "Christmas linens." Kelly smiled as she raced for the phone. "That was almost too easy."

Audrey answered just before the phone went to voice mail. "Got a problem?"

"Not really. The laundry is still washing, and I noticed you didn't have any Christmas decorations up. I wondered if you'd like me to set up a tree or something. I'd be happy to do it for you—a thanks for being so generous to our family."

"Generous to pay you to do my work. Yeah, that

makes sense," Audrey laughed.

"Well, you pay well for not a lot of work—certainly not hard work. I'd like to say thanks."

"It's tempting," Audrey began.

Kelly nearly squealed with excitement. "Is everything somewhere in the house or do you have a storage unit or…" *There, that's technically not deceitful. I know some is, but she could have more. Right, Lord?*

"It's all in the office closet. Top shelf and then the right back corner." Audrey didn't speak for a moment and then added, "Y'know, don't bother. I'll decorate this weekend. You got done early; now go do something for yourself until you have to pick up Nathan. Just leave the clothes in the washer. I'll put them in the dryer when I get home."

"I really don't mind…"

"I appreciate it, I do. But I'll be disappointed if I don't do it myself. Go get yourself a coffee and relax for a bit. You deserve it."

Kelly thanked Audrey and disconnected the call, wincing at the use of the words, "Deserve it." *Mom would go nuts if she heard that. How many times have I heard her say, "We don't 'deserve' anything good. We 'deserve' hell. Only by God's goodness and mercy do we get anything but that."*

The washer buzzed just as she opened the front door. Kelly hesitated, trying to remember what had been put in there. The memory of a cotton shirt prompted her to pull the door shut behind her. "Better if she leaves it in the dryer to wrinkle beyond salvation than if I do."

Sunday, December 7th

Boxes of Christmas decor cluttered the corner at the bottom of Audrey's stairs. She'd awoken that morning with grand dreams of spreading a little holiday cheer across the mantel, over the windows, and on the door front at least. Instead, laundry, shopping, paperwork for her tax preparer, and a much needed afternoon nap had left her sitting on the couch that evening cheering as the Ravens celebrated their latest victory. "Way to go, guys! WOOT!"

Her eyes slid toward the pile of decor. "I could just put it away. One year without—" Before she even allowed herself to complete the thought, Audrey shut herself down again. She'd done that one year—left decorating until it was too late to enjoy the effort, so she hadn't done it. Her family had threatened her with a stint in Rockland's psych ward if she ever failed to decorate again. "So, I need the joy of the Christmas season around me. Sue me."

Despite her words, Audrey's back threatened that lawsuit if she dared to hoist one more box, no matter how light. "I could hire Kelly. She'd do it for me. It might be nice to come home and have it done. Or maybe..." Already her mind protested the idea of being left out of the fun of decorating. "Maybe I could have a decorating party tomorrow night. Invite Kelly and the employees. Have snacks. It would work. Might be fun to 'rock around the Christmas tree' with others. Maybe Diane and Tami would come. They're always wanting to meet my Fairbury friends."

Before she could stop herself, Audrey reached for her phone and slid her finger along the list of contacts. She tapped her fingers, stared up at the clock, and started to chew her nail before Jon answered the phone. "Cox residence..."

"Hey, Jon. It's Audrey Seever. Is Kelly around?"

"Yeah... just a minute. She was just tucking Nathan in bed. Actually, looks like they're ready to pray. Can she call you back in a few?"

"That'd be great. I'll be up for another hour or two, so no rush." Audrey said goodbye and closed her eyes. *How long has it been since Dad came in our room and prayed with Tami and me?*

Audrey's fingers hovered over the phone as she debated calling. Would he think it weird? Would he be concerned for her, or would he "get it?" *Maybe if I tell him about calling Kelly. That'd make sense to him.*

She slid her finger along the contacts and found her parents' number. Phyllis Seever answered the phone, a hint of concern in her voice. "Hello?"

"Hey, Mom. How are you?"

"Everything okay?"

Audrey smiled. After eight p.m., her mother always assumed any call was news of a calamity. "Great—never better. I just called to see how you guys are—"

"You saw us three days ago. What's wrong?"

Should've known she'd see right through you. "Nothing's wrong. I was just calling a friend to see if she wanted to help me have a decorating party tomorrow night, and—"

"Yeah..."

Feeling foolish, Audrey backtracked. "Never mind. Just wanted to call. I'll talk—"

"Hold on. Your father wants to talk to you." As Phyllis handed over the phone, Audrey heard her say, "Something's up with her. She won't tell me but I think she had a fight with a friend. You talk to her. She listens to you."

"Audie?"

Warmth flooded Audrey's heart at her father's childhood nickname for her. "Hey, Dad."

"What's going on?"

"Nothing—really. It's silly."

"What's that?"

Audrey knew he'd drive all the way to Fairbury and get it out of her face-to-face if she didn't open up. *That's why you called. You knew he'd make you talk.* "So I called to talk to a friend tonight—nothing important—and her husband said they were about to pray with their kids and could she call me back."

"Seems normal enough. What's wrong with that—oh. Sweetie, you can adopt. Single even. You don't have—"

"It's not kids, Dad. Really. I just started trying to

remember the last time you came in to me and Tami's room to pray with us, and suddenly I just wanted my daddy to pray with me again."

"Be right there."

Audrey laughed. "Silly. I meant over the phone."

"I can pray over the phone," Walt agreed, "but I can't tuck you in over airwaves."

"How about we save that for Christmas Eve. You know you hate driving at night, but I love that you offered to spend the next two hours in the car." Audrey smiled. "But I'll take that prayer. No way I'm refusing that."

As her father began praying, Audrey turned down the light and pulled the throw blanket up over her. Something about the cadence of her father's voice, or perhaps the nostalgia of falling asleep to it for so many years, pushed her out of consciousness and into slumber. The last words she heard him say were, "—bring the right man into her life. If it's not good for man to be alone, why should it be good for a woman?"

Chapter Six

Monday, December 8th

Nervous, Audrey watched the clock as six-thirty rolled into six-thirty-five and then six-forty. Nearly done now, and beautiful if I do say so myself. Ivory quilted tiers with gold candy balls at every intersection gave it an air of simple elegance, but the ecru roses with their gold dusted petals and leaves gave the anniversary cake every inch of elegance the client had requested. *This one gets a photo the minute it's done. I want this in my portfolio.*

A tray of white chocolate raspberry truffles sat chilling in the fridge, waiting for the cake to join them. *We'll deliver at four o'clock tomorrow afternoon and—* Her thoughts were arrested by the idea of a butterfly. "Oh, a filigree butterfly right on top there—perfect!"

Startled by her own voice, Audrey nearly dropped her pastry bag on the cake. "What's the deal? You talk to yourself all the time and now you get jumpy? Ridiculous!"

As she berated herself for her narrowly escaped catastrophe, Audrey added a square of wax paper to a small tray and thinned her Royal Icing. Within a couple of minutes, a simple butterfly waited to dry and be sprayed and decorated to fit the top of the cake. "Oh, you are a beauty. When I go home tonight and my feet ache and I don't want to have people over to decorate my tree, I need to remember this moment. This one right here."

Her phone rang. Audrey sprang for it, glancing up at the clock. "No one's supposed to come until seven-thirty! What—" She reached it before she could finish her thought. "The Confectionary, how may I help you?"

"Hello! I'm so glad I sent my husband to the market a minute ago. He said you're still there, so I'm calling." A few mumbles followed by the woman's hiss and then a start of surprise. "Oh, Ted says I didn't say who this is. It's Angie Taylor. You're doing the anniversary cake—"

"Yes! I'm almost done. I just decided to add a butterfly a minute ago, but I'll finish that in the morning—"

"Well, I remembered something a little while ago that I think we forgot to tell you."

"What's that?" Audrey stared at the cake with a nervous eye.

"It's for a twenty-fifth anniversary—silver anniversary. We should have that reflected in it somehow, shouldn't we?"

The gold and ivory confection stood proudly and all wrong for the occasion. "I think you're probably right." *And I'm staring at the perfect choice for a golden anniversary instead.*

"Will it work with what you're doing? The butterfly and everything?"

After I airbrush the whole thing white and replace a couple of hundred gold balls with silver ones... sure. "I think so. Would you like a silver twenty-five on it somewhere, or do you want that to be implied by the silver and white?" *Please say implied, please!*

"I suppose it might be nice, but only if it'll work with what you've done. I wouldn't want you to have to start over again."

"Oh, I will—be happy to do whatever you want. It's your cake, after all."

The woman—Angie—mumbled something to her

husband, listened, mumbled again, and then returned to the line. "Okay, well Ted pointed out that we chose you because we didn't want cliché, and you're so good at doing new things that are fresh and exciting without being ridiculous. So, only put it on if it's how you would design the cake. We trust you."

A new idea occurred to her—one that would take her hours, but save her cake design. "What about the truffles instead? We'll add twenty-fives to the hearts."

"Perfect! I knew you'd know how to make it work with what you've done!"

As she disconnected the call, Audrey began the debate of removing the gold balls versus painting each individual one silver. "It has to be faster to paint them because removing them means touching every one, replacing them means touching every one, and that's not including all the work of repairing every section I rip. Paint, no matter how tedious."

Another debate raged within as well. "To let them party and decorate my house for me while I stay and finish or to get up early or come in after the party tonight? Party or not, I suppose is the question."

Her phone buzzed with a text message from Tami. WHERE IS YOUR HOUSE KEY AND WHY ARE YOU NOT HERE YET?

"Looks like party for me. I'm not in the mood for Tami."

Audrey's party of eight had almost tripled. *Serves you right for adding that little bit about bringing a friend or two. Good thing you brought home those truffles to decorate. Now if you only had more hot chocolate.* As she scrambled to find something appropriate to serve, Audrey continued to berate herself.

Kelly stepped outside and returned within less than a minute, shivering. She hurried into the kitchen and thrust a jumbo-sized box of cocoa packets at her. "I just bought them today," she hissed. "I thought—" From beneath her coat she pulled a box of miniature candy canes. "Maybe to hang over the sides?"

"You're a life saver."

"I'm just excited that you invited me! This is wonderful. Your sisters crack me up!"

"That's one way of putting it." A voice from the living room asked where the lights were. Audrey groaned. "Just a minute! I'll get 'em."

"Can I get them for you? Or do this—"

"They're in my bedroom. They didn't fit in the closet in the office, so I stuck them in the top of my closet—to the right. Pink plastic tub. Thanks." Audrey pulled out a package of Styrofoam cups and began dumping packages of hot chocolate in each one as Kelly hurried from the room.

Decoration began in earnest once the tree had been liberally draped in white twinkle lights. Someone began singing and the rest followed. Off-key and out of rhythm jingles of a large bell ornament accompanied the singers, prompting giggles from different corners. Audrey rolled her eyes as Diane snorted and muttered, "Well, now that we have the percussion down..." She passed a photo frame to Kelly to hang on the tree. "Why is that a Christmas song anyway?"

Kelly, who had grown noticeably quiet, spoke up. "It wasn't always—just a seasonal thing. I remember reading *The Long Winter* as a little girl. I never liked the song before that. I was more into 'Away in a Manger' and 'Silent Night.'"

Audrey smiled as she tried to remember the book— one she'd read thirty years earlier. "What about that book made you like 'Jingle Bells'?"

"I was a romantic child—Anne Shirley kind of romantic. I was enamored with the idea of glistening snow, sleighs, friends singing wholesome songs as they slide across the snow."

"That was really the beginning of Laura and Almanzo's romance, wasn't it?" Audrey asked.

"I think so, but as a kid it was just about the setting—the old-fashioned beauty of it all."

"And the filthy horse tails in their faces, hooves tossing snow into their laps, pausing to take a dump on—"

"Tami!" Audrey shook her head. "Ignore my sister, everyone. Although an incurable matchmaker, she has no real romance at all."

"Speaking of matchmaking," Tami said loudly enough to ensure every woman in the room heard, "I hear my efforts have finally paid off!"

Audrey's head whipped around and she glared at her sister. "Not funny."

"Hey, Merrill is excited about your date."

"Date—" The room quieted to near silence as Audrey glared at her sister. "What are you talking about? I told him no."

"Right… but he said you guys made a date to meet at your shop, so… kind of a date to make a date, but it counts."

A movement to her right captured Audrey's attention. Kelly, half-hidden by the tree, looked panicked. *What's with her?* Before she could hope to answer her own question, several of her guests began making approving noises, including a couple of "oooh-oooh-oooh" sounds. "Whoa. Wait right there. I told him no. Said I was not going out with him or anyone else." A few confused expressions drove her to clarify a bit. "Hey, I was trying not to be too mean. It's not his fault. He's a nice guy. If I was interested in dating—which I am not and my sister knows it—I would absolutely have said yes. So, I made it clear that I wasn't interested in dating anyone—not just him."

"Why not, though? I mean, if you find him interesting," her friend Bentley asked.

Kelly spoke up before Audrey could. "Why? Why does she have to date anyone? It's like we've rewritten the opening to *Pride and Prejudice*. 'It is a truth, universally acknowledged, that a single woman with a lot to offer must be in want of a boyfriend.'"

Laugher filled the room and Audrey grinned. "Exactly."

Diane laughed too, but as the room quieted, said, "But she just said if she wanted to date, she'd be interested in him. Why doesn't she want to date?"

"When would she have time? She's busy—doesn't even have time to clean her own house. Why should she spend the little free time she has dating someone just because people assume that every single person out there is anxious to change their Facebook relationship status?"

As much as Audrey agreed with Kelly, she did wonder why the woman was so adamant about her remaining single. *Then again, my life probably looks pretty good on a day when everything she does gets undone before she can do the next thing. It probably looks freeing to have peace and quiet whenever I want it.* Her thoughts faded as she overheard someone else speaking.

"—she want to get married? I mean, singleness in today's world has its charms," Darla Varney conceded, "but who wants to grow old alone if there is an alternative?" She turned to Audrey and said, "Forgive me if you'd rather not answer. I won't be offended, but do you not want to get married or do you not want the process of getting to that point?"

You have no idea what you're asking. Aloud she said simply, "I think I can safely promise you that unless something terrible happens, I will never be sending out wedding invitations. Don't hold your breath—s."

"Why—"

"Y'know, I think I'm glad I'm already married," Kelly said at last. "I can't imagine what it would be like to have a bunch of women decide that my marital status was inadequate and therefore the business of anyone who thought it should change."

A cry of protest rose from the ladies around her,

but Kelly grabbed her coat, murmured an apology to Audrey, and rushed for the door. "Have fun. I'm sorry, but I need to go," she called as she left.

Audrey murmured something unintelligible even to her and rushed after Kelly. "Hey, are you all right?"

"Fine. Sorry. I just—" The woman stared at her feet. "I've spent a lot of time in your house lately. I've seen—" Eyes rose to meet Audrey's and then gazed upward. "—how you live. You seem happy—content. And I don't get why people wouldn't respect that choice."

"I suppose they mean well, but it's nice to have someone backing me up." *Which you can translate to mean, "You're way overreacting to this." They're just being women. All women like to play matchmaker from time to time.*

"Well, it was probably rude of me, but I kind of lost it there…" Kelly gave her a quick hug. "Have fun. I'll come tomorrow instead of Wednesday to clean up. Sound good?"

"Thanks. You don't have to go. I'm sure—"

Even as Audrey spoke, Kelly shook her head and interrupted. "I'm really tired, obviously grumpy…"

Audrey shivered as she watched Kelly hurry down the street and into her van. Once the lights came on, Audrey dashed up the steps and shivered her way into her apartment. Diane's voice reached her just as she stepped toward the living room. "—Mom thinks maybe Audrey is gay…"

Then again, maybe you're right, Kelly. Maybe they just need to mind their own business. Where do they come up with this stuff?

Chapter Seven

Tuesday, December 9th

Music spurred Kelly from one corner of the room to the next. How twenty women could leave such a mess, she couldn't understand. *Don't they know better? I don't get why women who claim they don't like the way their families just leave stuff out for them to clean up turn around and do it themselves.*

Seconds later, she gripped the counter. "Meow much? Wow. Talk about grumpy—"

The phone rang. Kelly dove for it, thankful for the distraction. "Hello?"

"Oh, you're there!"

"Audrey?"

"Yes, sorry." The woman began talking faster than Kelly could follow.

"Wait, what was that? I missed something."

"There's a box in the office closet—bankers box. I don't know which one, but it has a spiral-bound notebook in it—thick one. Inside are crazy things. Recipes, stories, songs. There's a table of contents of sorts at the front."

"Okay..."

Audrey mumbled something to someone in the shop and then returned to the conversation. "Sorry. We're insanely busy. Anyway, somewhere in that list might be a recipe for a chocolate log with marshmallows. I don't remember what it's called and I don't remember the ingredients. I know it had chocolate and marshmallows and maybe coconut. Can you please find me that notebook and see if you can find that recipe? I'm desperate."

"Sure, but wouldn't you like me to just Google it? I'm sure if I type those things—"

"No, no. Sorry. I want Grandma's recipe. I've had it at other times and hated it, but Grandma's was good. I just had a gal in here who needs one and I told her about Grandma's. Now I've got to find the recipe and my mom doesn't think she has it. She's looking for her notebook, too."

Kelly moved toward the stairs. "Okay upstairs, in the office, in the closet, in a box—got it. I'll call you when I find it."

"Thank you so much. That would be great! Gotta go."

She stared at the phone for a second before climbing the stairs. "Man, I'm glad we don't have stairs. This would be awful in a couple of months."

Twelve bankers boxes lined the floor, stacked three deep, in the closet. Each box was numbered but not labeled. "Could she have made it any easier? Lord, I'm gonna need help to mind my own business while I do this."

Box one—tax records. Below it, box five held medals, certificates of achievement, and a couple of running trophies. She found a box of sermon notes—pausing long enough to read an entire paragraph when she saw the line, *...were created in the image of God. God is love. We were created to love, so when we are unloving, we go counter to our design.*

Kelly stared at it, wondering if the words were true. They sounded good—had validity she couldn't deny—but then Scripture also said that the heart of man is deceitful and "desperately sick." *How do those ideas reconcile. Can they be?* She shoved the box aside and grabbed number nine.

In box six she found what she thought was the notebook, but closer examination proved to be a journal of sorts. From the line she read, Kelly decided it must be from Audrey's childhood. She closed it with a snap. *Mind your own business. Just find the right one.*

Those lofty thoughts lasted exactly forty-two more seconds. In box number seven, right at the top, lay a stack of folded letters bound together with a rubber band. She set them aside to dig deeper, but again, one line caught her eye. "*...marrying you was the best decision I've ever made...*"

She tried—Kelly tried to put them aside again. Several times she dragged her eyes from the words in the four inch section of a folded page, but eventually she managed to read the entire section, and being in the middle of the page, she drove herself crazy wondering what had come before and after—when it had been written. That thought killed all hope of self-restraint.

Minutes passed, slowly, as she read the first letters, one after the other. Each had been dated on Christmas day beginning back in the eighties. *She's been married that long? How...* Curious, Kelly began counting. Twenty-four letters—the latest dated the previous year. *Whoa. Twenty-four... maybe twenty-five years this year sometime.*

The first five years spoke of perfection—as if their life couldn't be any better—but sometime around year six, the tone of the letters changed. She hadn't made it halfway through the box when the phone rang. She jumped, the letters falling all over the floor. She nearly tripped over herself rushing down the stairs to answer it.

"Hello?"

"Yes, I am Anna Marx with the Tielbolt Research Group, and I wondered if you would—"

"I'm sorry," Kelly said, relieved. "This isn't my home and I'm supposed to be working." Without another word, she hung up the phone and stared at it, stunned to realize what she'd done.

Lord, I'm really sorry. I don't know what's wrong with me. I'm reading someone's private letters! I don't understand what got into me.

At the bottom of that same box, she found the notebook. She put all the boxes back and hurried downstairs, away from further temptation. As she dialed with one hand, she flipped through the notebook with the other. "Audrey, I found it. It's called Stained Glass Roll…"

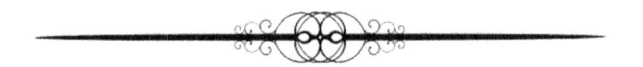

The minute Jon collapsed on the couch, Kelly pounced. "She got married at least twenty-four years ago—more like twenty-five."

"She told you?"

Kelly bit her lip and shook her head. "She had me looking for a recipe in some boxes for her and…"

"Oh, Kelly. What did you do?"

"Well, there was a stack of letters—all dated. Jon, she was so happy. Well, at first anyway. They had a great marriage but—"

"You read personal letters?" Her husband stared at her as if he didn't recognize her. "What possessed you! You can't *do* that!"

"Yeah. I'm gonna have to confess that one. That won't be easy, but, Jon! Her sisters don't seem to know any more about this husband than we do."

"And why is that any of our business?"

"Maybe," Kelly interjected, grateful for an idea that slightly exonerated her nosiness, "because she's living a lie? She's been married for twenty-five or near so years and no one knows about it."

"Maybe they got divorced—"

She shook her head as Jon spoke. "No, because that tax return. It was last year's. They were still married as of sometime in April when she did that tax return."

Eyes closed, Jon spoke in weary but resigned tones. "I still don't see why this is any of our business."

"If she's living a lie, how is that acceptable for a Christian?"

"Did she ever say she wasn't married?" Jon began unlacing his shoes. "Maybe she just doesn't like to talk about it. Maybe he left her."

"But her family doesn't know she's married if they're constantly trying to set her up with some man."

"I don't know, Kelly. I just know it's none of my business, and I don't feel comfortable talking about it. If you have a problem with your sister in Christ, take it to her, but leave me out of it."

Jon's words chastened her. *It is gossip, I suppose. But we're "one" aren't we? Isn't it different if I get my husband's opinion before I do things?* His words cut through her a bit. *Well, not now, of course. He's told me not to, but before I had to, right Lord?*

With his shoes off and set by the door, Jon got his glass of water from the kitchen and came to kiss her goodnight. "I've got to be at the farm early tomorrow. Willow said something about chickens, I think. Love you." He glanced at the unopened laptop in her hands. "Pray before you do something you can't undo. Just pray."

For an hour, she perused Zain-Kadir-the-complicated's Facebook page, looking for anything that might give away his feelings about his unusual marriage. The man enjoyed cycling, speculative fiction both on and off screen, and sushi. It also appeared that he was an ex-Muslim. *Is that it? Did she discover his faith too late or vice versa? Does she not trust his conversion?*

As Kelly did the math, she realized that Audrey had to have been young twenty-five years ago. *Eighteen? Nineteen? Surely no more than twenty. I always thought she was in her late thirties, but not if she was married that long ago. Wow.*

Her mouse hovered over the "message" button, but

Jon's words caused her to hesitate. *Tomorrow is soon enough—if ever. I shouldn't rush. I really should ask **her** instead of some strange guy. I mean, why would I do that? Why do I feel almost **compelled** to do that? This is crazy.*

With that thought, she snapped the laptop shut with more force than she meant to and stowed it on the bottom shelf of the coffee table. *Okay, Lord. I'll mind my own business until I find the courage to ask her. Maybe if I can't do that, it's a hint that I'm not supposed to.*

Friday, December 12th

Friday night Bible study on loving one another ended five minutes into the class. "Wow," Shannon said as she closed her notebook. "That was interesting. I thought it would take all evening. No one has anything?"

Heads around the semi-circle shook. Darla Varney flipped to the next page in the book. "No one studied the next section, I suppose."

"No... but we could toss out verses that we know apply to marriage," Kelly suggested. "Everyone could make a list for studying while we start the next section. It might help prepare us or something."

"I'll read the introduction to that section," Shannon offered. "We can't just quit after—" she pulled out a phone and glanced at it. "Ten minutes tops."

"Let's get those verses Kelly mentioned, and then we can read that before we go," Darla suggested.

The verses offered encompassed most of the usual Biblical references for marriage—loving your wife as Christ loves the church, submitting to your husband as unto the Lord, living with your wife in an understanding way, wives respecting their husbands—but Bentley said something different. "I would just like to remind us all of Jephthah."

"What the?" Shannon giggled. "Sorry. Couldn't

resist."

"Why would you bring him up?" Darla asked.

"He made a vow—to the Lord—and considered that so serious that he kept it even to killing his own daughter." She waved her hands as Shannon leaned forward. "No, I'm not saying that I think we need to make those kinds of vows, but when we get married, we make a lot of vows—vows to love, to respect, to honor, to stick with them through good, bad—everything. But we act like we promised to suffer together or something."

"I've never seen that," Kelly said. "Who acts like that?"

"I mean that when you hear people talking about the 'sanctity of marriage' or whatever, they always talk of it in terms of 'to divorce or not to divorce, that is the question,' but it's so much more than just sticking it out through thick and thin. I learned that the hard way. I almost missed out on the best our marriage has to give because of it."

As Bentley spoke, Kelly's mind raced with ideas. She made sense—Bentley did. Lots of sense, actually. *I've been as guilty as the next person in saying something about how a husband being a jerk about whether or not his wife works isn't an "out" or whatever. Why didn't I say something about the **other** vows they made?*

"Do you think we're reacting to the almost epidemic of divorce in the church?" she asked when a lull in the conversation came.

"Maybe. And, we don't take the idea of vows seriously."

"Wait a minute!" Darla waved her hands and then dove for it as her Bible tried to fall off her lap. "I don't think that's true. A lot of people stick out really hard marriages because—"

"But that's my point." Bentley blushed. "Sorry. I interrupted."

"Go ahead. I'm intrigued."

"Well..." Bentley glanced around the room as if trying to gauge her audience. "See we do give a lot of thought to 'for as long as you both shall live' and take that part of our vows seriously. But when our husbands aren't acting respectable or do things that make submission nearly impossible because they try to take out that element of choice, we blame them for our lack of keeping that vow. We say, 'Well, if he wants respect, he has to earn it.' That's not what our vows said. We didn't say we'd respect when they deserved it. We said we'd do it. Period. And the same goes for them too, of course," she added quickly as Shannon began a protest that would obviously point out the other side has responsibilities, too.

"Right. Good. I'm sick of being told how women have to do everything right and men get away with whatever." Her words came out in a huff.

"I don't think anyone really believes that," Kelly murmured, thinking aloud. "I think the wives are just the ones who usually ask, so they get the answer that applies to them. I mean, if Chief Varney came and said that his wife burned dinner every night and he'd had it with her lack of respect for his desire for a decent meal, I'd tell him he needed to forget what she's supposed to do and 'live with her in an understanding way.' It's all about who is talking."

"That's a really good point," Bentley agreed. "And I'm so sorry to hear the chief isn't getting decent meals."

The room erupted in laughter at the idea that famous cook Darla Varney could possibly ruin any dish. Darla flushed but shook her head. "I burned the beans every single time I made them for the first year we were married."

Kelly couldn't help but ask, "Did he eat them?"

"Didn't have a choice. We couldn't afford to throw them out. Even now, I have a hard time choking down a bean if it's even a hint over-cooked." Darla turned back to Bentley. "I think you make an interesting point. We do become a bit fixated on the 'ever after' part of the vows and ignore the day-to-day stuff. I wonder how marriages would change if people focused more on the rest and left the other thoughts for when they didn't think they could take another night of snoring or for when one spouse did something nearly unforgivable rather than using it to suck down every little irk that comes along."

"I can tell you how they would change." Bentley leaned forward. "You all know the first part of my story, but let me give you a hint to the rest."

"A Paul Harvey moment," Darla said with a smile. "Do tell."

"It can mend a heart full of shattered dreams and expectations. It can take a broken woman and make her a blessing to her husband, and if she has a good man, watch out when that happens. Just watch out."

Monday, December 15*th*

Monday morning, with Nathan in tow, Kelly drove out to Novak Landscaping on the outskirts of town. Bentley's little Corolla sat alone in the otherwise empty parking lot. "Yes!"

"What?"

Her eyes met those of her son in the rear view mirror and she smiled. "We're here!"

"We see dog?"

"I don't know if they have one—chickens maybe. I think she has chickens out here."

"Chickie!" Nathan grinned as she unbuckled him.

"You really need to learn to do this yourself. My belly isn't going to take much more of it."

Nodding solemnly, Nathan squeezed the button as hard as he could. "I do it. See!"

Kelly didn't bother to inform him that she'd already done it. *It's the attempt that counts.*

Bentley met them at the door, grinning. "Hey! What can I do for you?"

"I have a question." Kelly pointed to the half-dead looking plants. "Mind if we walk around so Nathan doesn't drive us crazy?"

"Sure. Lemme get my coat."

Nerves that she'd managed to squelch before she left home resurfaced and sent Kelly's mind zinging in a dozen directions. She called Nathan back from climbing a snow-covered pile of rocks, from climbing a wooden box holding a dormant—or dead—tree, and a dozen other adventuresome attempts. Between those rescue missions, Kelly tried to formulate her question again.

"I can't stop thinking about what you said on Friday night, and I have a question."

"Okay... you know I'm no expert, right?"

"Still, you had good insights and I wanted to be sure of something before I let myself think about it anymore."

Bentley pointed to a path to the left. "Chickens are in the shed there if he'd like to see them."

"Probably not a good idea if they're not where he can see and not touch. He's still a bit impulsive—" Truth made her adjust that thought. "Okay, a lot impulsive."

"So what was your question?"

Word it well. You can't start explaining and qualifying so get it right the first time, she admonished herself as she worked to find the right words. "I guess my question is if you think you can keep your vows while not living with your spouse."

Bentley's eyes narrowed. "As in gone on business or—"

"No, like if you separated—permanently. If you don't divorce, and you do it for loving reasons, can you choose not to live with your spouse and still be faithful to your vows?

Several seconds passed while, Kelly assumed, Bentley chewed on the question. When she did speak, Bentley asked one of her own. "What about children? How could that work with children?"

"What if there are none—and that arrangement

would probably ensure there never were," she joked. It seemed to Kelly that she'd just made the object of her question glaringly obvious. In an attempt to distract, she added, "Or what if they have an arrangement that works for them if they do."

"Well, with children, I don't see how that could be a healthy environment. At least children of divorced parents can eventually believe and understand that the problem was with the parents rather than them. I think that would be harder for kids where the parents are married, congenial, but not living together, and…" Bentley leaned closer, concern flooding her eyes. "I don't understand why anyone would choose to do something like that."

"Well, I just wondered if it *could* be Biblical. I know you've studied a lot about marriage and such, so I thought you might have an idea." *Well, it's true. It's not the whole truth, but it's true. And it would be wrong for me to give her an inkling about someone else's truth, so it's all the truth I can share. Right, Lord?*

"I can't say for sure in regards to women, but I suspect it's very interconnected, but men—I don't see how men can 'live with their wives in an understanding way' if they don't actually live with them."

That thought exploded in Kelly's mind. Different aspects bombarded her as she considered the ramifications of what Bentley said. "Wow."

"Yeah… I don't know that separation is any less serious than divorce unless it's for a safety issue. But I don't know. That's just a guess."

"I never thought of that. Men have to live with us in an understanding way, which means we can't be absent to make that possible any more than they can absent themselves. Whoa!"

As Kelly pulled out of the parking lot, Bentley stood, hands shoved in pockets, concern filling her. "Why would Kelly Cox be asking me about separation? Are things really that bad over there?"

Chapter Eight

"Live with her in an understanding way..."

Jon had gone to bed early, worn out from a long day at the Tesdall farm. Aiden slept in his room, fighting off a cold, and Nathan slept on the other end of the couch, no longer fighting anything—just miserable. And Kelly, her laptop open to Zain Kadir's Facebook page, wrestled within herself.

She was so happy. If something can be done to bring that back, shouldn't I?

That thought was all she needed. She punched the message button and began typing before she could talk herself out of it.

```
My name is Kelly and I am looking for a man,
Zain Kadir, who married approximately twenty-
five years ago. The Zain I need to contact is
still married but has not lived with his wife
for at least five to ten years. If you are the
correct man, I'd really like to talk to you
about something.
```

Kelly hesitated once more before hitting the reply button. As the message disappeared into the abyss otherwise known as Facebook, she switched tabs and hit the button to her mother's message board, but before the page loaded, the Facebook tab blinked, signifying a message. Expecting a request to get together with one of her sisters the next day, Kelly clicked over again, but instead a message from Zain Kadir flashed.

```
As much as I would like to be the man you seek,
I am sorry to say I do not think I am. I
married ten years ago and separated two months
ago due to religious differences. I hope you
find the man you seek. Something about your
message intrigues me.
```

She shuddered at the undertone of the message. What about it bothered her, she couldn't identify, but the words almost made her rethink sending an identical message to the second man. Almost. Within minutes she sent it off into cyberspace and returned to reading prayer needs, coupon deals, theological debates, and the latest thing someone's adorable child said.

Bed called to her. She went to log out of Facebook just as another message appeared. Excitement filled her as she clicked the little red bubble. But her stomach dropped as she read the words.

```
I'm sorry. I cannot help you.
```

Zain stared at the words and punched the reply button. "It's almost true. I technically can help her, I suppose, but I won't."

"...approximately twenty-five years ago...still married...has not lived with his wife..."

A glance at the time made him hesitate, but he pulled out his phone and his thumbs tapped out a quick text for his brother. **IF YOU'RE UP CALL ME**.

His phone rang immediately. "Hello?"

"Whassup?" His brother Yosef's voice sounded much too chipper for eleven o'clock on a Monday night.

"Joe, you annoy me."

"I can go. Night—"

"Knock it off. I've got a problem." Zain stood and

began pacing his living room. "I got a Facebook message tonight—about Audrey."

"She contacted you? You haven't spoken in years, have you?"

"Not since the audit in '02." Zain said. "She sent copies of her stuff and everything then. Pretty cut and dried. Didn't even have to meet." He sighed. "But she isn't the one who contacted me. As far as I know, she doesn't do Facebook."

"If not her, who?"

Zain rubbed his forehead and temple as he tried to think. "Just some woman—from Fairbury."

"Audrey's town? What did she say?"

He pulled his laptop up onto the bar and read. "'I am looking for a man, Zain Kadir, who married approximately twenty-five years ago. The Zain I need to contact is still married but has not lived with his wife for at least five to ten years. If you are the correct man, I'd really like to talk to you about something.'"

"Sounds like something serious happened."

"Joe..."

Yosef's exasperation came across the airwaves complete with mental imagery of his brother tossing his hands in the air in a perfect imitation of their mother. "What do you want from me, then? You call me when you are usually asleep and tell me that the wife you've hidden for a quarter of a century has surfaced—"

"I didn't say that. I said that someone from her town—"

"I think she's hurt. You need to talk to this person. You need to quit hiding your youthful in—"

"Don't say that. I hate it when you say that," Zain barked.

"Then quit treating her like one. You have regretted—"

"That's beside the point!" Zain lowered his voice. "I'm sorry. Shouldn't be yelling at you. I just don't know what to do."

"What did you tell the woman—anything?"

"Yes. I—" Justifications fizzled and Zain sank to the floor, his back to his breakfast bar. "I lied. I said I couldn't help her."

"Not exactly what a good Christian boy is supposed to do, is it?"

Just toss my faith in my face, why don't you? But Yosef was right, and Zain knew it. "I need to tell the truth—apologize. But I don't want to. If she's sick or dying, I will need to go." He swallowed the rising lump in his throat. "Joe, I'll need to tell Mama and Baba."

"Now I know you're upset."

"Why?"

Yosef's laughter filled the little space around him, relaxing Zain more than he would care to admit. "You called our father 'baba.' I don't think you've done that since you came home that day and told me about Audrey. You said, 'And of course, Baba will kill me.'"

After a promise to send a more truthful message, Zain disconnected the call, but he didn't rise for several minutes. Instead he prayed. In all the years since the day of his marriage, he hadn't prayed about it. Not once. "I didn't want to admit it, Abba. Yes, I knew You knew. I'm not that stupid, but as long as I kept it hidden in my heart, I hoped..."

Strange, awkward, and unfamiliar emotions flooded him. He forced himself to his feet while he had the mental and emotional strength to do what he knew he must. Uncustomary indecision attacked him as he tried again and again to write something that confessed the truth of his situation without disclosing anything too personal. When each attempt failed, he conceded defeat and wrote the next words that came to mind.

```
Kelly, I was not honest with you. If the
woman's name is Audrey, I am the Zain you are
looking for.
```

"There. That's sufficient." A glance at the clock warned of the inevitable and rapid approach of midnight. "And as one with an early appointment, I've got to get some sleep," he muttered as he closed the laptop and snapped off lights as he worked his way through his small condo to his bathroom. Toothpaste choked him as he scrubbed at each tooth with a ferocity that would earn him a scolding from his dentist if the woman ever saw it. *Relax, take it easy, one step at a time.*

Zain gripped the counter as he stared at his reflection. *I didn't have a beard back then. What would she think of it? She liked my face. Is that why I wear the beard now?* His hand shook slightly as he reached for the light switch. *That would be pathetic.*

Faint whiffs of salt air blew through his window as Zain settled beneath the down comforter that kept him toasty despite cooler outside temperatures. He liked his Santa Monica winters with low night temperatures that much of the country considered warm during the day. *It's probably below freezing there—maybe below zero. How can she stand it? She walked around Vegas when it was only fifty degrees—without a jacket. I froze!*

Memories flooded back as they always did when Zain thought of Christmas, mission work, Las Vegas, or the wife he hadn't seen since their wedding day.

December 18th—Las Vegas, twenty-five years ago

Zain sat in one corner of baggage claim, his suitcase at his feet and feeling as out of place as he suspected he looked. He hadn't seen another person wearing the obnoxious neon green t-shirts of the Las Vegas Outreach Center volunteers. Still, the church van was supposed to make regular rounds at four, six, eight, and ten o'clock. He glanced at his watch again. Eight-twenty.

Just as he decided to find a pay phone and call the mission, he spied her. Long curly hair—Cher hair—neon shirt. She had to be another from their group. *C'mon, turn around just enough… yeah! Thank you, God. Someone else is here, and she's **fine**.*

Guilt tried to carve a place in his conscience, but Zain had already started across the claim area. He wove between bystanders waiting for their suitcases to slide onto the carousels and stood beside her. "Just get in?"

He felt her response in the fraction of a second it took her to whirl to face him, ready to take on anyone cheeky enough to mess with her. "Oh! You're with—hi."

"Get a lecture on the evils of Las Vegas before you left?" He grinned at the chagrin on her face and added, "I'm Zain—Kadir."

"Audrey Seever from Rockland. You're from here?"

"Los Angeles. Got in a couple of hours ago, but neither the six nor the eight o'clock vans arrived." She reached for a suitcase—new, he suspected—one that looked like a Gucci knock-off. Zain grabbed it. "This yours?"

"Yeah. Thanks."

"Well, we might as well go grab chairs again while they have 'em. You're the only one I've seen since I got off the plane."

Audrey stared at him before giving her head a little shake and gesturing for him to lead the way. "I thought there were like two hundred of us or something. Shouldn't more of us be here by now?"

"You'd think." Zain set the suitcase at her feet and sat down again. "If they don't show up by ten o'clock, I'm gonna find a phone book and call."

Long fingers dug through a silver purse with an enormous bow tacked to one corner. He wanted to ask why—why the need for slapping bows the size of Rhode Island onto every feminine article of clothing or accessory imaginable—but he suspected he'd get an earful about minding his own fashion business. *She'd be right too, I guess*.

Her hands dropped as she murmured, "Oh."

"What?"

"I blew it. Big time. My dad is gonna have a cow if he finds out."

74

Zain waited for a second or two before asking again, "What?"

"It says p.m. I missed that. I talked them into the cheaper red-eye because I said we had to be here by ten in the morning."

"We're stuck here until four o'clock? In their dreams. C'mon. Is the address on that thing?" Even as he spoke, Zain regretted not bringing his paperwork— just long enough to remember that had he done so, he'd have left a good hour or two earlier. *Then she'd have been here alone. See, that's what Bro. Sykes meant by God having plans in the little things. Get some faith, man.*

"Yeah..."

"I'll get us a cab. Sitting here all day isn't going to help the mission at all."

"Taxis are expensive. I can't—"

"I'd have taken one already if I'd known," Zain insisted. "It doesn't cost anymore for two than one. Let's go. At least we can get out of this stupid airport."

She took one hesitant step. "I—"

She probably thinks you're gonna kidnap her or something. He ignored the suspicion on her face and glanced around him. "Want a drink? I'll get us something while we wait."

"I can buy a drink, I just—" She stared as he sat back down and shifted to get comfortable in chairs that seemed designed for the least comfort possible. "What are you doing?"

"Just thought I'd wait until you were thirsty or hungry or something. So what's it like in Rockland?"

"I thought you wanted to go to the mission."

Zain nodded. "No, duh."

"Why aren't you going?"

"Because if your dad is gonna freak out over you being in the airport twelve hours early, then I'm not going to leave you alone here. At least that way you can honestly say you were with part of the group."

She sank into the chair beside him and pulled her

feet up onto the seat, wrapping her arms around her legs. With her cheek resting on her knees and her hair hiding most of her face, she stared at him. "You think I'm stupid, don't you—a baby."

"I think you respect your father. Nothing wrong with that."

"Not everyone would agree with you. You turn eighteen and suddenly you're supposed to not care what your parents think. Well, I've had exactly twenty-four hours of being eighteen now, and I still care. I suck at being an adult already."

"Let me guess. This trip is your combination birthday and Christmas present."

"Yep. My sisters totally wigged out, but Mom and Dad were cool about it. Tami just doesn't want to have to wait another coupla days to open her presents, and Diane wanted to leave a day earlier to visit her fiancé's family." Audrey shifted again. "Okay, let's go, but I'm picking the cab."

"This'll be good."

"What?"

Zain grabbed both suitcases and led the way to the door. "You telling me what taxi to take."

Chapter Nine

Tuesday, December 16th—Fairbury

At five thirty-five, the alarm clock blared its first snooze warning. Audrey, wrapped in a cocoon of warm blankets, resisted even the effort to stretch her arm into the cooler air of the room. The clock continued its rude awakening chorus. Frustrated, and becoming well-aware that she'd never be on time if she didn't force herself out of bed, Audrey chose the "cold-turkey" approach and flung the blankets off her. "Ooooh... only in winter does a sixty-nine degrees room temperature feel freezing in the morning."

Within minutes, she stood in the doorway to her bedroom, brushing her teeth and glancing over the room. *She's made such a difference. It's so clean and clutter-free. I love it. Well,* she amended, *except for the mess of a bed I created and last night's towel on the floor.*

She grabbed the towel before returning to the bathroom to rinse her mouth. Then began the tedious task of de-tangling her hair and twisting the front locks out of the way and into a ponytail. Her brush, hair ties, toothbrush, and washcloth cluttered her small counter, and as she turned out the light, she noticed. Curious, she began counting. By eleven, each article had been put away. "Eleven seconds. It only took eleven seconds. That's crazy. Why do I just leave stuff there?"

Again, she started to leave her room, but the unmade bed stopped her. Though not perfect, she rushed through pulling the covers in place and plopping pillows against the headboard. One last glance at the room sent her downstairs satisfied. "It's a good life, Lord. There was a time I didn't think I'd ever believe that, but it is."

Kelly thought Nathan would never go to sleep. While he fought with dedication worthy of a soldier on the battlefield against somnolence, Kelly gave up any hope of a nap herself and cleaned the bathroom, dusted the pictures in the hall, and scrubbed grubby fingerprints from any surface three feet or lower. Nearly an hour into his prescribed nap time, the boy finally collapsed after one last squeak of protest.

She wanted her own nap—needed it—but Aiden would be home from school in just over an hour, and she preferred to be awake when he arrived. In what she suspected was a futile attempt to ward off a sleep attack, Kelly pulled out her laptop and decided to rest while looking for coupon deals. "First stop, the Facebook coupon page."

That never happened. The red message bubble caught her attention and she clicked it automatically. She'd read the short note twice before she realized who had written it—and why. "Wow. It is him. I was sure— well. So much for my idea that God closed that door."

That thought gave her a pang of discomfort. Jon wouldn't like it. God probably didn't either, but she consoled herself with the idea that she was encouraging a brother to reconcile with his wife. That she didn't bother to admit knowing about him to said wife, she opted to ignore as long as possible. *It's not like anything is likely to come from it anyway. Why make her feel awkward for nothing? But...* Her mind wandered with slightly romanticized ideas of seeing Audrey and her husband reunited their differences—whatever they might be—resolved.

She wrote, hoping her words would spark something in him—move him to consider his vows, as Bentley had so eloquently put it. She knew her reply would likely be jumbled and full of grammatical errors, but she chose to send rather than spend hours or even days trying to perfect words she didn't have to begin with.

```
Zain, I have a confession. I'm Audrey's house
cleaner. I was dusting her office a couple of
weeks ago and knocked over a stack of papers. I
couldn't help but see that you were listed as
her husband on a tax form. Considering she is
known in Fairbury as a single woman, I was
surprised.
I wanted to find out more or to ask or
something, but instead, I tried to mind my own
business. Then I saw a bundle of letters in a
box one day. (Yes, I was going through her
boxes, but she asked me to.) I admit that I
read some of them. I'm not proud of it, but I
did. You had such a wonderful marriage. She
writes of how much in love she was and how you
guys had nothing but you made it work. That
first fight was so cute!
Then the tone of those letters changed, and I
wondered what happened. I wasn't going to ask.
I kept trying to stay out of it, but I can't
let it go. Little things keep coming up that
make it even more curious to me. I can't stop
thinking about it, and I decided that asking
you made more sense than asking her. I don't
know you. I can't ruin a relationship with you,
but before I talk to her, I thought maybe.
Well, I don't know. Are you a Christian? Are
you guys still married? The tax form seems to
imply so. That's around twenty-five years. Her
family seems oblivious to her marital status. I
just don't understand.
I can't believe I'm even hitting submit. This
```

is so wrong of me, but I hope you'll write back. I hope you'll forgive me. I guess I invaded your privacy, too. I am sorry, but I admit I haven't exactly "repented" yet or I wouldn't still be typing.
Kelly Cox

The moment she hit that reply button, Kelly regretted it. She spent the next few minutes scouring the Internet for some way to get it back, but every site said the same thing. You can't. As much as she wanted to post a second note asking him not to read it in the hopes that he might see that one first, she didn't. "I deserve what I get for being a busybody. Mom will kill me. Jon's gonna be so disappointed in me. I'm disgusted with myself." Her eyes rose to the ceiling as if she could see the pain-filled eyes of Jesus telling her how wrong she was. "I think what bothers me most, Lord, is that I'm still not as convicted as I should be about reading those things in the first place. That's just horrible."

Weary, Audrey dragged herself up the steps and into her house. The extra few minutes she took that morning to move the dishes into the kitchen and toss the papers stopped her mid-stride to the kitchen. "It's just so nice. I get so tired of coming home to a mess, but especially this time of year—"

The truth halted that thought. She never felt like coming home and doing housework. By the time she finished after a long day at the shop, she was beat, regardless of season or holidays. Sure, Christmas and Valentine's were both busier times, but a full day's work and then some didn't leave much energy for things like scrubbing floors and washing clothes. "I wonder if she'd want to keep doing this. It would be nice to have time just to relax instead of change jobs."

Her hot roast beef that she now suspected was

lukewarm at best stopped her from charging upstairs to examine where she could trim her budget. "Dinner first, then budgets." That lofty thought lasted until after she'd dumped her sandwich on a plate, poured a glass of milk, and carried it as far as the living room. Instead of the comfy couch, she moved upstairs to the office, confident that if she didn't look right then, she'd collapse after eating and forget about it for another week.

A pile of papers occupied the space she'd intended for her plate. Audrey carried them to the secretary, shoved them in the proper drawer, and pulled her budget notebook from the shelf. A glance at her plate sent her in search of a damp washcloth and a page protector. "There. I can drip all I like."

Diane would flip if she saw it; she did every time Audrey pulled out paper and pen rather than her cheap laptop. "I think better with a pen in my hand," Audrey always insisted, but Diane had an answer for everything—an answer that always meant, "Go digital." She'd never do it. Something in putting words on paper, forming each stroke with a pen, helped her thoughts process properly. Even the blog posts for The Confectionary all started as pages in a notebook that she later transcribed into the weekly posts.

Audrey did not take her precautions in vain. Several drips of Mr. Goldberg's special sauce landed on the page protectors as she mentally shuffled dollars from one category to another. "A smaller clothing allowance, cut the gym membership from unlimited to three times a week, and two fewer lunches out each month—that's half the money right there. I could round down savings and take that extra twenty-five..."

Eventually, she managed a budget that allowed for Kelly every week and in a way she would hardly feel a difference. "Starting next year. For now, I'm sticking with household savings." As she chewed, she imagined a life where a few rinsed dishes and the occasional need to toss in a load of clothes would be the extent of her housecleaning. "I should've done this years ago. I owe Kelly." Her eyes rose as if to pray as she added, "And I'm glad I added a tiny raise in there."

By nine o'clock, she'd put away her budget book, stacked her dishes, and pulled on clean clothes for bed. Despite her desire for a shower, Audrey wanted nothing more than a "long winter's nap." She tried to convince herself that after a long day, sweating over the heat of the ovens, she stank and needed a shower, but Wednesday would bring Kelly and fresh sheets. "Forget it. I'll shower in the morning."

In the last few seconds before sleep consumed her, Audrey remembered the tax return lying face down atop the pile of papers she'd put away. Her eyes flew open and panic welled up in her. "Did she see? She didn't say anything." Her eyelids drooped again. Somewhere between consciousness and that wonderful world of dreams, reality blended into fiction and tax forms became soldiers keeping her prisoner in a cell of numbers.

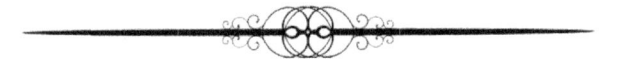

Zain spent half the evening ignoring the message and the other half confused by it. The clock ticked until his brother finally got off work at nine o'clock. Then it dragged until he thought he finally understood road rage. "And I'm not even driving. Where is he?"

At ten of ten, Yosef knocked. Zain unlocked the door and practically dragged him into the condo. "What took—you stopped for food."

"Um, yeah! I haven't eaten since one-thirty. I'm kinda hungry."

"I made you falafel. It's ready to fry."

Yosef pulled his Subway sandwich from the bag and carried it to the fridge. "Here's lunch for you tomorrow. Where's the food?"

Rolling his eyes, Zain turned on the burner and waited for the oil to heat. "Can you get the salad from the fridge?"

"I don't know why you insist on calling it a salad. Everyone says this is officially a slaw—shredded cabbage and lettuce. Slaw."

"Fine. Slaw. Sounds weird to serve falafel on slaw, but whatever makes you happy. Just grab it, will you?"

Only the sound of crackling oil broke the silence in Zain's kitchen. Yosef sat on a barstool, leaning against the counter top, and waited. As Zain plated the first falafel balls on the salad, Yosef said, "Why'd you call me here?"

"Joe, I'm wounded."

"We both know you wouldn't be cooking in the middle of the week unless something upset you."

"The woman wrote back."

"From Fairbury?"

Zain nodded. "She said the weirdest thing—well, wrote it. She said that she read some letters Audrey wrote to me and it bothered her that we had such a happy marriage back then."

"How—what?" Yosef cut into his food, blowing on his first bite before adding, "That doesn't make sense."

"Exactly my point. She talked about some fight we had and how 'cute' it was."

"Why is this woman reading private letters—"

"That I never got," Zain interjected.

"Right... that you never got. But—"

Zain grabbed his laptop and opened his messages to the one from Kelly Cox of Fairbury. "I admit; I searched everything I could about her. She seems like a decent person—Christian."

"Even I know it's not very 'Christian' to snoop into other people's private things."

"Joe! You're kind of missing the point. Audrey wrote me letters. She wrote about our great marriage. We never had a marriage! As far as I know, I'm the only virgin in the world about to celebrate his silver wedding anniversary!"

"TMI, bro."

"Well!"

Yosef stared at the screen before him as he took several more bites. "What'd you put in this? It's even better than ever."

"I added more sesame oil to the dressing. It brings out the sesame in the balls." He pointed to the plate. "Sorry. I was out of pita bread and too lazy to go get it."

"Too messed up at the idea your wife actually might have wanted to be a wife, you mean." Yosef took a sip of the glass of wine Zain poured him and sighed. "You should be with your wife. What woman wouldn't love to come home to a meal like this? You could be a house-husband and—"

"Enough. I'm serious."

"And she makes desserts! It's perfect!"

"Joe!"

"Fine," Yosef conceded. "So what are you going to do about it?"

"I don't know." Zain choked on his falafel and gulped down a glass of water to soothe his raw throat. "What if she's wrong?"

"Who?"

"The woman. What if she's wrong about the letters? Why would Audrey write me letters that she didn't send? Could this just be some teenager—"

"You saw her profile. That's no teenager. That's one pregnant woman there with a couple of kids and a husband."

"Yeah… and she's mentioned on a local church website as helping with some fundraiser last year. She's known in the town." Zain stared at the screen as he climbed up onto the barstool next to his brother. "Baba is gonna kill me."

"You're almost forty-six years old. Who cares what Dad thinks about something you did when you were twenty?"

"Obviously I do, Joe! Obviously I do. C'mon. Don't tell me you still don't get a bit nervous when you hear his voice boom through the offices at dispatch. I know you do. I can hear him, 'Yosef Kadir!' and you cringe."

"Not enough to hide a wife."

"You didn't have to hide yours. You weren't a Christian. You married a good Arabic girl. You didn't—"

"I get it, I get it. But, Zain. Maybe it's time. Maybe if your god is who you think he is, maybe he decided the lies and the deceit have done enough damage. You lost half your life with her because you were too proud—"

"I was too proud! She—" Zain sighed. "I don't even know anymore. It seemed right at the time. Honor our vows and our families both. It seemed right." Even as he spoke, Zain remembered the words in Proverbs, *"There is a way which seems right to a man, But its end is the way of death."*

Does that even work in context? I'll have to look it up. He speared the last bite of falafel and glanced at Yosef. "What if I ruined our lives because I was too proud or scared—whatever it was—to make it work?"

Chapter Ten

Monday, December 19th—Las Vegas

Two hundred six college students filled the sanctuary of a little church on University Avenue, all but half a dozen wearing the same neon green t-shirts. A young man—the director of the Las Vegas Outreach Center—stood at the front as he spoke to the group. From his place, Zain watched as the speaker, Jeff Lawrence, described the plight of the homeless and the goals of the LVOC. "We want to make an impact in the lives of these people, but to do that we have to meet their needs."

You might meet them better if you didn't talk about their misfortunes as if you won the mission lottery. There's just something wrong with shouting "homeless" in the same way you do "touchdown," Zain growled to himself. From the wrinkle in Audrey's nose, he suspected she agreed. *Lord, don't ever let this guy become an undertaker. He's better suited to be the next Og Mandino.*

"—always in pairs. I like to call it the Jesus Method, but it's really for everyone's safety. Where possible, we're going to pair men and women together. This has a dual purpose. First, sorry, girls. Not trying to be chauvinistic but let's face it, men are usually more intimidating than women. While I doubt anyone would actually try to hurt you, these are people in desperate circumstances and sometimes..." He shrugged off the ominous words delivered in a tone that sounded like Earl Scheib and his ninety-nine ninety-five paint jobs.

Audrey turned, glancing over her shoulder at him. Zain smiled and nodded. *That's just mint—totally mint. She actually **wants** to work with me.*

"—gather in the fellowship hall after a half-hour break and we'll start assembling the stockings."

Voices slowly filled the room as the volunteers made their way to the doors. Zain caught up to Audrey and a couple of other girls just outside. "Did you catch when they said lunch would be?"

"Hey, Zain. This is Brandy," she pointed to a girl with large pink-rimmed glasses. "And Amber."

Amber nodded and smiled. "You're the guy from L.A., right?"

To his surprise, Zain saw Audrey's cheeks darken a little. *So you talked about me. Interesting.* "Yeah. Where're you from?"

"San Diego. Brandy's from some hick town in Colorado." Amber nudged Audrey. "Lunch isn't until one o'clock. We're gonna run down to the mini-mart. Want anything?"

"Pepsi and a bag of Funyuns?" Audrey glanced at him. "What about you?"

"I'm good, thanks." The moment they were out of earshot, he added, "So are you going to protect me from desperate criminals masquerading as the less fortunate?"

Audrey laughed. "That would be a good way to hide, wouldn't it? Who would suspect? I'll have to tell Sam at the mission about that."

"What mission?"

"In Rockland—Sam Felton and a bunch of business people are starting a big one there. That's why I wanted to come. I'm going to help as much as I can, so they suggested this as a way to see how other places operate and to see if I like it."

"Nice."

"Why are you here?"

Zain didn't know how to answer the question. He hadn't known how when his father had asked the same thing. "I bet your parents are Christians, aren't they? Grandparents? Aunts? Uncles? Cousins?"

"Yeah—mostly."

"Well, with a name like Kadir, let's just say there aren't a lot of Christians in my family." He shuffled his feet as he tried to formulate his answer. "I wanted to help, of course. I mean, that's the point, right? I just also wanted to see what regular Christians do at my age."

"What do your parents think of it all?"

"My father didn't disown me," Zain muttered. "I consider that near miraculous."

Her eyes met his, searching his face for something he suspected he didn't possess. After a few seconds, she dropped them again and asked, "So are they some other faith? What is Kadir? Iranian?"

"Saudi Arabian—our family anyway. Over there, our family is mostly Muslim. Here, my parents are too 'enlightened' to be bothered with faith of any kind. Culture, however—" His eyes widened. "I guess that's it. I never realized it, but our culture is now their religion. Honoring family, marrying other Saudis, holding fast to the old ways while embracing the American Dream."

"My family couldn't be more opposite. My white dad married my black mom and created a multi-racial family. Took both sides a while to decide to be cool about it."

"Big blow up?"

"Nah…silent civility on Dad's family's side. Mom's family gushed with fake enthusiasm."

Zain listened with eager fascination. "Wow. That's like—"

"Weird, right? Totally nuts, but it's what happens, I guess. They're all good friends now," she added as an afterthought. "Mom found out that both sides of the family thought the other disapproved of them. So, now it's all peachy keen."

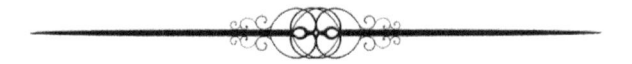

Several assembly lines filled the fellowship hall. The first person at a row of tables would pick up a long sock, shove a mate into the toe, and pass it to the next person. One by one, the volunteers added toiletry items like toothbrushes, toothpaste, hairbrushes, deodorant, and "soap-on-a-rope" bars. Thin copies of the four gospels were rolled around the contents and the tops tied with a rubber band. Zain and four other young men collected the finished stockings and shoved them into backpacks until each was as full as they could pack it.

At the front of the room, Jeff Lawrence turned on the mic and winced as overloud feedback nearly deafened anyone standing too close to the speakers. "Hey, that'll wake you up! Okay, so I've had a few people ask me why we're taking these out to the streets tomorrow, so I thought I'd like to explain our reasoning on that. I know stockings are generally for Christmas, but we want to show people that we want to help *them,* not just get them in the door. It's a trust builder."

"Makes sense," Zain mumbled as he zipped up another backpack.

A girl nearby sniffed. "Well maybe, but it's no fun for us. Stockings are for *Christmas*."

Audrey piped up from the next table as she shoved an orange into the heel of the sock. "We're here for people, not so we can have our traditions in a new setting."

"I'll say. I wouldn't want to try sledding in this sand. It's just *wrong* not to have snow at Christmas!"

Zain laughed. "A good portion of the world doesn't. How do they ever survive?"

The girl frowned. "I wasn't saying—"

"He's just joking," Audrey interjected. "No offense."

It took Zain a moment to see that the girl's

apparent pouting was actually her waiting for confirmation that Audrey knew what she was talking about. "Oh, sorry. Yeah. I was just joking."

"I never thought about it, but yeah. Sad."

As she walked away, Zain shook his head. "I always thought snow at Christmas would be fun—and we didn't really celebrate it when I was a kid."

Jeff's voice boomed in the background, rattling on about things like how to spot a genuine homeless person. "Why does it matter?" Audrey hissed. "Why should we decide who is 'worthy' of our help? Isn't that God's responsibility? Ours is to help one another—His is to determine if that help is abused."

"I suppose... hate to see crooks get what is meant for the truly needy, though."

"But how many crooks are really gonna want a sock of stuff they probably have. They want big stuff, not toothpaste. If one gets a sock and looks in those gospels while waiting for a bus because he's bored, who knows what could happen?"

Zain forced back an indulgent smile and focused on the possibility in her scenario. It *could* happen, but he doubted it ever would. *Still, why state the unfortunate obvious?* "Isn't there something about how one person planted an idea, another one watered it, and God made it grow? It never said anything about picking the best place to plant, did it?"

"Exactly! Who are we to decide that only the truly homeless are deserving of knowing Jesus?"

"Well, that is the point of the mission, though. They have to have a focus or they'd never get anything accomplished—just spend all their time talking about how they need to do this or that for whatever—" Zain stopped mid-sentence as he watched her twist her back awkwardly. "You okay?"

"Yeah... sleeping on the floor with no padding—not used to that. I don't know how these people do it."

"That's why we had you do it," a voice boomed behind him. Zain turned around and saw Jeff standing there. "We wanted you to get a hint of a feel for what it's like to be in their shoes so to speak." Then, as if oblivious to how it sounded he added, "I've got Tylenol in the first aid kit if you'd like to take something for that."

"Did he seriously say that?" Audrey muttered as the man moved on to the next table. "'We want to give you a semi-authentic experience but here's something to counteract it.' That's just crazy."

A guy behind Zain gave him a nasty look clearly designed to say, "Move along, you idiot. We've got work to do." He shook the full backpack in his hands and forced the zipper shut. "Better get another one."

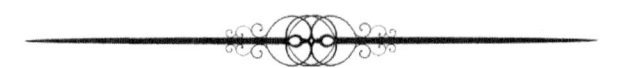

The church remained silent as the volunteers slept—well, as silent as rooms of snorers could be. Occasionally the heating came on, expanding metal somewhere with a resounding bang. Zain rolled over again and then sat up. His mind traveled at speeds that would make aeronautical engineers envious. *If I'm going to be awake, I might as well go outside and be comfortable.* He grabbed his jacket and tiptoed through the room, wincing as the door squeaked.

Built in a U shape, the church had a courtyard with tables for students at their little school to eat lunches at or for potlucks on the rare, pleasant afternoon. Zain paused at the door to the courtyard and hesitated. *Is there light out there? I could bring my Bible...* He pushed the door open and slipped through. *Not enough to read by. Oh, well.*

Traffic never ceased, something he hadn't expected. *It's not that different from L.A. Still a lot of people out. I wonder if it's safe to walk. Probably...* He crossed the yard and turned the corner when the creak of the side door stopped him. His neck craned around the corner and he stumbled back, calling softly, "Hey. You okay?"

Audrey's head snapped to his side of the building. "There you are."

Must not have worked if she's still awake. Bummer. She met him halfway across the courtyard. "You did it, didn't you?"

"What?" *You know what and she knows it. Dweeb.*

"The boxes under my blanket. You did that."

"After seeing a guy today, I thought it might help. Guess it didn't."

"But it does—not as comfortable as a bed, but it definitely makes a difference. I had to threaten girls with stealing their blankets if they touched my boxes."

"They're clean. I got 'em before that appliance place put them in the dumpster." *Just ask!* "So if they worked, what're you doing up?"

"My clock is all off. I should be exhausted, but I'm wide awake." Audrey stared at her shoes as she murmured, "Where were you going?"

"Just for a walk. Wanted to see what it's like here at night. Thought maybe I'd go down the Strip and see it. I've never been here."

She hesitated, and in that hesitation, Zain saw exactly what he'd hoped to see. *She wants to come.* "If you think it's okay—if we won't get in trouble—"

"We're adults, how can we get in trouble? We only agreed not to gamble, drink, smoke, swear, or fornicate. That's all the paper asked us to sign."

This girl's got spunk. Awesome. "Wanna come then?"

"Sure."

He glanced at her thin, long-sleeved shirt. "Need a jacket?"

"It's like fifty-five degrees. I've got long sleeves. I'm good."

"I'd freeze," Zain admitted.

"Wuss."

Chapter Eleven

Wednesday, December 17th—Fairbury

Kelly shoved the key in Audrey's lock and turned it, her mind on the argument she'd had with Jon that morning. *"You can't interfere like this! It's wrong. I don't know what's going on with you!"*

She sighed and pushed the door open. "He's right. It was so stupid. I hate when I do that—get all caught up in a neat idea that I forget that there are other sides to the equation. I don't know anything about this guy and I actually sent him a Facebook message! If any of my friends did that, I'd let them have it!"

Something felt off—what, she couldn't tell. Her eyes swept across the house, trying to discern any difference. It was a mess, definitely, but not much more than usual. A stain on the carpet by the entryway left her frustrated. "She should have put something on that. It's not going to come out easily."

After setting her purse on the kitchen counter and starting a load of laundry, Kelly grabbed a roll of paper towels and some Oxy-Clean. As she dabbed at it, Kelly shuddered. "Looks like blood. They should use this stuff in movies. It's—" She sniffed, gagging at the metallic scent that filled her nostrils. "Don't puke, don't puke, don't puke!" The stain widened as she scrubbed. "How do I get this out? I—Hydrogen peroxide. I need it— probably upstairs in the medicine cabinet."

She tried to race up the stairs, two at a time, and barely managed to half-jog up each step singly. As she reached the bathroom doorway, all hope at retaining the contents of her stomach dissolved at the sight before her. Audrey lay face down on the floor in a pool of blood—unmoving. Kelly retched. Tears streamed down her face as she stared at the horrifying scene before her. A bloody handprint—obviously Audrey's—showed where she'd tried to push herself off the floor. A glass vase lay shattered beside the woman's head.

"Audrey?"

She stepped around the breakfast remnants she'd deposited on the bathroom floor and leaned to touch the woman's face. "Please be alive, plea—" Words on the mirror arrested her words. **I'M COMING FOR THE HOUSEKEEPER NEXT**

Her screams ripped through the room, bouncing off the walls and echoing in her ears. Jon shook her awake. "What's wrong? Wha—"

She stared at him, around her, and back at him again. "Wha—"

"You screamed. It was horrible."

The sight of Audrey dead on her bathroom floor, the note on the mirror—it all flooded back at her. "Worst dream ever. Oh wow."

"Want some coffee?"

She closed her eyes and nodded. "I'd appreciate it."

Left alone, Kelly shuddered again. *Lord, what have I done? I don't know anything about this guy. She might be separated from him for a reason. Does he know where she lives? Did I just give away a location to a dangerous man? He knows me too. My name, my town. Jon's gonna kill me—and I don't blame him.*

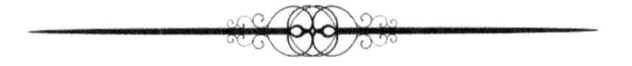

Once inside the door, Kelly hardly took the time to shove a few pairs of yoga pants and a couple of tops in the washer before rushing upstairs to the office and dug out the box with the letters. She'd spent all morning debating between telling Audrey everything before anything truly terrible could happen and discovering if she should hide her family from a madman. *It's probably nothing. After all, she probably would have divorced a truly horrible person. She's been married a **long** time—not just this year. Still, I've already broken her trust; I want to know what to expect before I tell her about it.*

Her thoughts sickened her. Never had she allowed her natural curiosity to do anything so reprehensible. *Forget Jon, Mom is gonna kill me when she finds out.*

With her new thoughts in mind, she began at letter one, scouring each page for hints of anything that should concern her. Instead, certain sections caught her attention anew. *...knew it would be hard at first. I remember Mom saying that she and Dad had nothing when they got married—nothing but love and a determination to prove to the world that their marriage was a good idea. That's what I want ours to be. We've made it one year. That's a big deal...*

"She was so happy. Oh Lord, please don't let him be anything but a guy my conscience warped into someone evil as a lesson in being a nosy busybody."

Near the end of that first letter, another line choked her. *...heard that when you fall in love so quickly, it won't last. I asked my sisters, and they say it has to be infatuation, but it's not. Infatuation doesn't get stronger after a year, love does. I love you. I love us. I want nothing more than fifty years of happiness together.*

Year two was another repeat of the first. Audrey wrote of an argument over what church they'd attend and the way she'd had to learn to trust his leadership and how he had to learn to trust her experience and knowledge. The way they worked through their problem, even in the highly abbreviated version in the letter, spoke of a determination to work together as they served Jesus. At the end of the section, she flipped back and reread one sentence. *You know, I never thought our first big fight would be over Jesus, but if we had to have one, I guess it was over something important like Him rather than the color of a couch or because I spent too much money on Christmas presents.*

"I wasn't that mature in our second year of marriage. That's back when I thought I knew it all and really knew nothing. I was pregnant with Aiden..." Her eyes widened at that thought, and she pulled the next letter out, eager to continue. "Lord, please don't let there have been a child. If that's why they split up..."

Three, four, and five all gave no indication of anything but happy years growing deeper in love and happier together. She noticed a shift in year six, again. However, instead of something about Zain that indicated a concern, it seemed that Audrey changed slightly. Her patience seemed thin and she wrote of his family with an edge that surprised Kelly. *...don't know what their problem is. I've done everything I know to be me without being offensive. It's not my fault I wasn't born in the right country or to people from the right country. I'm used to not fitting into cultures—not black enough for one or white enough for another. I slip through cultural cracks all the time. Some people still think worth has to do with the amount of pigment in a person's skin, but I've never been rejected because my extended family doesn't speak another language. I've never been rejected by an entire culture because my family serves Jesus. It gives new meaning to persecution for me.*

"Six years into marriage seems like an awfully long time for someone to reject a daughter-in-law—especially for something like her ethnicity." Her eyes scanned the rest of the page, looking for something to indicate what had set the annual anniversary love letter down such a negative path.

Year seven was worse. Audrey railed against forces that strove to pull them apart. She shared her fears, her dreams, her hopes, and asked repeatedly, *why do I still love you so much when it hurts like this?* Kelly read each one with a knife twisting deep into her gut.

"But it still doesn't even hint that he's anything but a wonderful man. She blames everything and everyone—even herself—but him for their problems. Surely if he was dangerous, she would say something, anything. She doesn't even act afraid of being honest with him."

Over the next ten years, the letters waffled between gratitude for a man who loves and cherishes her to anger that something always seemed to fight to drive them apart. At year twenty-one, however, her heart dropped into her stomach, and the knife nicked it. She read it twice, stopping to review several sections before reading each word one last time.

Zain,

I can't do it anymore. I can't write this letter again, telling you just how amazing you are, how wonderful our marriage is, how awful some parts are. I'll be honest. I resent you. I resent myself. I'm sick of this annual charade. What started as something cathartic to give me the chance to dream a little of what our life together should have been, it's become poison to me.

Why didn't you fight for me? Why didn't I fight for you? Why did you run out on me? We could have had a good marriage. Lord forgive me, but when I think of those few days in Vegas, I still feel that same overwhelming joy and love for you. We had every chance to make it work. Why didn't we? Why didn't we?

I've planned this letter for months. I was going to give us a long awaited child this year. I'm getting to the end of that possibility and I decided, why not? If these letters are going to be fictional accounts of our bizarre marriage, why not let them include all of my dreams? Instead, I finally write the truth to you—truth you'll never read. But maybe it'll help me accept that I'll always be married to a man I never see—a man who obviously didn't really want me after all.

*Happy Anniversary, Zain. I mean it. I hope this day is full of wonderful things for you—and I hope you don't remember what day it is. Well, not what day it is to **me**.*

Kelly felt betrayed. All the years of wonderful, if often painful, letters—and none were real. "What happened, Lord? Why? Why is she married to this man? Why didn't they get a div—they're Christians. Did they really stay together just for that? I don't get it. I really don't."

The next year shared a bit about Audrey's real life—the success of the shop finally, her week off doing mission work in Honduras, and her goal of a new year making new friends and accepting her life as it was rather than dreaming of one she had never and could never have. A tear ran down Kelly's cheek by the end of it. The next one both cracked her up and broke her heart.

Zain,

You jerk. I can't believe you. We had a silent agreement, and look at you. It's what I get for trying to see how you are doing. You're doing QUITE well, aren't you? Creep. Well, she's pretty anyway. I hope you're happy. You should be ashamed of yourself. Like it or not, you're a MARRIED man. If you want to get divorced, then say so, but otherwise, keep all your vows, not just the "till death" part or I'll be happy to arrange that for you.

It hurt, Zain. I guess I've spent these years picturing

you in L.A. just as sorry for what happened as I am. I just assumed you were faithful to our vows. You seemed like the kind of man who would be. Well, I won't be looking again. I can't stand the pain of it. I should have stayed off the Internet. I knew it, but I thought if I saw you again, I'd have the courage to find your number and call—see if you wanted to meet. To talk. That's not happening now.

I should file. I guess I have Biblical grounds for divorce now. My husband is an adulterer. I always wondered if I could forgive that. I don't know if I can or not, but I can't bring myself to call a lawyer, so maybe that's a kind of forgiveness. Maybe.

I hope next year is better. You ruined this one with that picture on Facebook.

Audrey

After twenty-two years of marriage, to discover her husband had a girlfriend—or just a date—how would she feel? Kelly didn't know, but a tiny, traitorous part of her heart wondered if it wouldn't have happened had they not been living apart for most of their marriage. "It doesn't make it right, Lord. I'm not saying that, but what if it was one date and then he repented. I mean, at least these letters don't make him sound like he's a jerk. She loves him still—or she did a couple of years ago. What drove them apart?"

As if driven, she read until she finished the last. Relief washed over her as she read the words, *...hoped you'd stop in when you went to Rockland for that missions conference. I saw your name on the list. I thought maybe, but I guess this answers the question I've had ever since that last afternoon in Vegas. Did you care as much about what happened as I did? Did it hurt you? Did you wish you could see me? Did you ever buy a* *plane ticket to fly out and talk to me like I did back in '97? If you came this far and didn't make the forty-five minute drive to visit the shop, I guess that answers the question. I almost wish I had gone to the conference— forced the issue. Then again, why? Would it be a good thing if you felt pressured to be a real husband if you didn't want to be?*

Later in the letter, Audrey expressed her happiness that missions were still important to him. She offered forgiveness for his indiscretion, and admitted she'd been tempted a time or two. *...I was just mad—hurt. Sounds strange to say that when we've been apart, but it just goes to show that whatever our families might have said, it was real—is real. As much as it hurts, as much as I'm embarrassed to admit it, I still love you.*

Merry Christmas. Happy Anniversary,

Audrey

"Oh... that really is twenty-four years. This is their silver anniversary. And she just catered that whole party! That must have stung. Lord... what do I do? I mean, I think she trusts him. At least, she's not afraid of him. He knows where she lives and works. That counts, right?"

A glance at the clock told her she'd spent an hour reading the letters. She reordered them to their proper positions, folded them, wrapped the stretched-out rubber band around them, and put them back in the box. Something in the letters still bothered her, but Kelly forced herself not to dig further. "I've done enough. It's embarrassing enough to have to admit that I read personal letters, but—"

As she closed the closet and turned around, a binder caught her eye—taunting her. *Personal Records.* As much as Kelly wanted to show the kind of self-restraint she knew she should, she also knew her limits had stretched beyond any use. She pulled the binder down and flipped through a dozen or two page protected sheets. Birth certificate, social security card, deed to her house and her lease for The Confectionary, but no marriage license. "Okay, now just get your job done and get out of here."

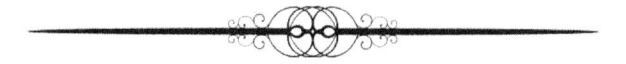

Coming out of the Post Office, Kelly bumped into Bentley. "Oh, sorry! I was kind of lost in my own world."

"I've been wondering how you were."

"Good—busy, of course." She rubbed her midsection. "Or, that's what I tell Jon when he's wondering why I'm fiddling on the laptop instead of doing the laundry or something. I say I'm busy growing a baby."

Bentley smiled. "Well, there's truth in that." She hesitated before adding. "Is everything else at home good?"

"Yep. Aiden gets out of school at the end of the week, so we'll be baking. I can do that now that I have a job. Makes things a lot easier." *Bentley might know what someone can determine from that message. Maybe ask her. She's got a lot of common sense.* Kelly glanced at her watch. "Oh, yikes. I've got to go—but..." She glanced around her. "Are you in a rush?"

"Not at all."

"Can you walk with me to my van? I had one more question for you."

"Sure!"

Kelly waited until they'd rounded the corner, slipping on a slick spot of the sidewalk. She clutched for Bentley in an attempt to keep from falling. "Whoa... thanks."

"I'll get them on that. Someone's gonna get hurt."

"Yeah, that'd be good, thanks. So what do you know about Facebook?" Kelly asked in an attempt to change the subject before she lost her nerve.

"Well, what do you need? I'm not an expert, but we use it for the business and—"

"Good. So if you were looking for someone for someone else and they could find *your* name and town, but you didn't give the other person's name or location—just something specific to them that would make it obvious who you were looking for..." Even as she spoke, Kelly knew it didn't make sense. "You know what, never mind. Sorry. I'm making it too complicated, and I can't be more specific, so I'd better just go. Thanks anyway."

Bentley stood with hands shoved in her coat pocket as the minivan drove away. *Lord, something is so seriously wrong there. I—*

The appearance of a man across the street interrupted her thoughts, sending her dashing between cars and waving, the ice on the sidewalk and her prayer forgotten.

Arlene Paulson bustled out of the Post Office, her arms full of packages. *You'd think they could just deliver them the next day instead of giving you that stupid pink slip. It's like getting fired every time you don't happen to be home when they deign to bring you the packages someone paid them to bring. It's ridiculous.*

She rushed to the parking lot behind the building, planning to take the narrow path between the Post Office and the building that housed the dentist and chiropractor's office. However, a voice made her pause at the corner. "—just talked to Kelly Cox."

Oh, did you? Arlene scooted closer to hear better.

"—other night we had a Bible study—remember? I told you about how we talked about vows?"

"Right—all of them."

Arlene frowned. *All of what? Vows? That makes no*

sense. Bentley, I always thought you married your intellectual inferior, and he's not doing a good job of proving me wrong.

"Well, a few days later Kelly came to the site and talked to me about vows and how it works if you're separated and what about children."

"What?"

Bentley's next words were obscured by a group of laughing women as they passed. Arlene strained to hear, but instead heard jokes about some ridiculous house in town with more lights on it than even Las Vegas would consider appropriate. *Would you shut up? There's trouble afoot in this town and you're worried about the excess lightage? Hush!*

Fran passed as well, back from her lunch break. "Hi, Arlene. How're doing today?"

"Fine—just too many stupid packages," she muttered. "You'd think your men could bring them back."

It worked. Fran got huffy and stormed into the building. *Good riddance. You're getting too easily offended in your old age. You really should know better.*

"—having an affair or something."

Arlene almost gasped audibly as she heard Bentley's husband say, "It sure sounds like it."

Shocked, revolted, and just a bit smugger than she would have cared to admit, Arlene turned the other way and went the long way around the Post Office, preferring *not* to be seen. She wove through town, her heart aching at the sight of Aiden Cox shuffling home from school. *Must be half day. Poor boy. He's a troublemaker, but children are a product of their upbringing. I suppose it isn't his fault, per se.*

By the time she made it inside, Arlene had worked herself into a state of combined indignation and panic. *This will rock the church.* A new idea occurred to her and she resolved to do something to stop the travesty of yet another broken family. She picked up her phone while digging through the church directory. "People keep talking about how we don't need these anymore—obsolete my eye. Not everyone lives on the blasted internet," she muttered as she finally spotted the name she sought. The phone rang and then went to voice mail. *I hate that thing. Just answer, why don't you?*

At the beep, she spoke, each word dripping with care and concern. "Shannon dear, this is Arlene Paulson—from church? We worked on the Christmas boxes together? Anyway, I learned some distressing news about your friend Kelly, and really think we all need to band together and pray for her and her marriage. I'm just distraught—" She choked back tears. "—to think of what a divorce would do to those children. So will you please pray and get Kelly's other friends to pray for them? I know I can count on your discretion with such sensitive information. One hates to have to be the one to share something so disturbing, but prayer is the only thing that can help at a time like this. Thank you. Bye."

As the phone sat back in its cradle, Arlene wiped a tear from her eye and collapsed in her kitchen chair, spent. "Those poor children. That poor man. Jon is too good for her. I bet Velma would pray too. She knows the importance of the home as the base of community. I better call her, too."

Chapter Twelve

Chili—the scent of Oscar's chili tempted Audrey to knock on the door and beg for a bowl. *What's the deal with chili on Wednesday? If I wasn't so tired, I'd go out and eat. I should have gotten something at the Deli.*

Instead, she unlocked her door and inhaled the scent of evergreen. "Wha—oh. Kelly. That woman is awesome—amazing. Totally rad, dude and all that stuff."

She found the source—a candle warmer with a brick of wax. "Tree farm—that's just what it smells like!" A card lay beside it. Audrey opened it and smiled as she read Kelly's note. *Happy Birthday. Your sister asked me what I thought you might like for your birthday, so since I knew it was, I thought I'd just say I hope it's a wonderful evening and that the day wasn't too hectic for you.*

Shouts of "Surprise!" behind her made her drop the note as she turned to see who was there. "Wha—"

Her family stood there beaming, a candlelit cake in her mother's hands. As the group sang, Audrey beamed, her eyes roaming the faces before her—right up to the moment where she saw Merrill Tobin standing just behind her father. She sent Tami a nasty look, but Merrill stepped forward. "Don't blame her. I invited myself."

"We're taking you out to dinner. There's a present upstairs. Go put it on."

"And now we all know what it is. Thanks, Mom," Diane muttered.

"She's not six!" Phyllis protested.

Despite her exhaustion, the idea of dinner with her family, a new dress, and—*God forgive me*—an interesting man to join them gave her a burst of energy as she climbed the stairs to her bedroom. A shiny pink bag with enough silver ribbon to save Santa a run for his money sat at the end of the bed. Her fingers deftly untied several knots and pulled a pile of tissue from the top of the bag. The dress inside—stunning. With illusion sleeves and neckline, the vermillion jersey had been created with every one of her favorite design features.

"For the record, I recommend your silver slingbacks. They'll look amazing."

Audrey glanced over her shoulder as she held up the dress. "It's gorgeous, Diane. But I know Mom did *not* pick this out."

"Actually, she did. She decided that she likes Merrill, so she wants to give him every reason to overcome your objections."

"Wha—" Audrey stared at her sister, disbelief filling her with dread, but Diane stood there, arms crossed over her chest, and nodded.

"Yep. Look," she continued, interrupting Audrey's protest. "I don't like Tami's meddling any more than you do, but I've got to say, this time she seems to have picked a real winner. Maybe you should—"

"I can't, okay?" Audrey closed her eyes, took a slow, cleansing breath, turned, and reached for her sister. Hugging Diane tighter than she probably had since they were children, she whispered, "Please—just help me with this. I know, without the slightest doubt, that the Lord does *not* want me dating any man. Can you just trust me on this?"

"Are you gay?"

Audrey rolled her eyes. "Honestly, I think I wish I was. I think you'd understand then and leave me alone. But I'm not going to lie. I'm not, okay?" *I've done enough lying over the years—lies of omission anyway— that I'm not about to start overt ones!*

Diane pulled back, gazing into Audrey's eyes. "You know I love you, right?"

"Yeah..."

"Then I'm gonna say something."

"Diane..."

"No, you listen. You've spent the last twenty years avoiding men. I never understood it, but it was obvious. Tami took it as a challenge, and that shouldn't surprise you."

"It doesn't."

"But Mom and Dad—they took it as a sign of failure."

The idea made no sense. "What?"

"That's right. So, listen. Tell me or don't, I really don't care. You've got your reasons, and we all have things we don't want to share. I get that. I kind of think I know what the problem is anyway. But—"

"What?" *If she nails it exactly, I'm telling her, Lord. I've got to do something before I burst.*

"You met someone there."

Audrey's heart raced.

"I think," Diane continued, "some guy in Las Vegas—probably not from there either, but how would I know where—still holds your heart. And I get that. You always were the most loyal thing."

"Goldie..."

Laughing, Diane nodded. "That's right. Dad used to call you Goldie—like a golden retriever. Loyal to the death." She brushed away a stray tear from the corner of Audrey's eye.

*C'mon, keep going. We were in **Las Vegas** for cryin' out loud!*

"But it's not like you're married to the guy. It's not a sin to let someone else try to win your heart." At the expression Audrey failed to hide, Diane added, "But you don't have to, of course. I'm just saying you should consider it. But if you decide you don't want to, that's fine. I get it. Just talk to Mom and Dad. It's eating Mom up."

Diane's words cut. *"It's not like you're married." Yeah, I am, Diane. What would you do if I told you that?* Audrey hugged her sister again and whispered, "I'll talk to them. Thanks for the support. I knew you'd back me up. Now if I could only convince Tami."

"I'll talk to her."

Audrey shook her head as she stepped toward the bathroom. "Don't. She'll get even more determined."

"Don't discount the power of reminding her that it's cruel to get a man's hopes up when your sister is too stubborn to see how great he is. She hates to see people with a broken heart."

"Could'a fooled me. She breaks mine on a regular basis."

Outside the door, Tami paused. Audrey's words ripped off blinders she hadn't known she wore and laid bare the pain she caused her little sister. *Okay then. I get it. Enough already. Now if I can just get rid of Merrill without hurting his feelings...*

Thursday, December 18th

With Nathan safely stowed at Jon's parents' house for the afternoon, Kelly sat outside The Confectionary from noon until two-thirty, waiting for a lull in business. It came almost at two-thirty on the dot. She hoisted herself down from the van and hurried to the store steps, acutely aware that she most definitely waddled the last several steps. *It's a bit early for that, Lord. Don'tcha think? Please? And while we're talking, I could use courage, honesty, and a huge, heaping pile of coals after what I've done. Please help her find a way to forgive me—eventually.*

Audrey waved from the back room as Kelly leaned over the counter, trying to catch the woman's attention. "You busy?"

"Always. C'mon back."

Kelly lifted the hinged counter and allowed herself the privilege of sniffing the spice-filled air. "What're you making?"

"Molasses cookies are baking, and I'm doing ribbon candy. Tomorrow is the annual elementary school field trip. Gotta have plenty for them to take home."

"They might like to see how it's made. That's amazing," Kelly remarked as she watched Audrey's hands pull, twist, and press hot colored sugar together. "Hey, it's getting shiny!"

"That's because it's satinizing. This one will be ready in a minute."

"Is it hot?"

"Yeah… really hot." Audrey kept moving, always moving. "Notice I don't keep my hands on it for very long?"

Kelly watched, her mind spinning with ideas. *If I talk to her now, she can't strangle me. Then again, she can chase me out the door with sugar that could do serious damage. On the other hand, she'd probably burn herself first. Or, she could throw it and—oh, quit whining and just do it.*

"I really needed to talk to you about something. Is your assistant gone for a bit?"

"She'll be back in about ten minutes. She's on her lunch break, why?"

The phone rang before Kelly could even start to speak. Audrey groaned but didn't move toward the phone. "Do you want me to get that for you?"

"The machine can do it. Sometimes you just have to keep working. So what's up? Oh, thanks for the candle warmer. My house smelled amazing last night."

"You're welcome." *Don't be nice to me. I'll never get through this!* Kelly swallowed, forcing her throat to relax again, and took a deep breath. "Well, I have a—well—confession of sorts."

"Decided you don't like cleaning?"

"No! I love it, but—"

Audrey plopped a chunk of sugar under a heat

lamp, turned two other lumps over, and grabbed a wad of amber-colored sugar and began pulling. "I think I should have done more white."

"White?"

She held it up, pulling, twisting, dropping onto the table, and then pulling again. "This one's white."

"Looks kind of goldenish."

"It'll whiten up as it cools. Anyway, you were saying—oh, wait. I was going to say that I hoped you weren't quitting. I just put you into my budget." Kelly's face dropped and Audrey spoke quickly. "I thought it might convince you to stay on if I'd already put you in."

"You might not want me to after I tell you—"

The shop door jingled. Audrey's lips pinched. "I'll be back—"

"Want me to see if I can help? That way you can keep going?"

"Please! Thank you."

By the time Kelly managed to find the right items, rang them up at the correct price, and made change, Audrey was on another color of sugar and Stacy walked in the back door. Audrey mouthed her apologies and said, "Maybe we can get together for coffee in a day or two? Stacy'll man the shop while I step out for a few minutes, won't you, Stacy?"

"I'd do it now, but you won't get me near that sugar. Ugh." Stacy wiggled her fingers. "I don't think I have fingerprints anymore after trying to work with that stuff. I'm sure it melted them right off."

Once in her van again, Kelly's eyes rose heavenward. "Really, Lord? I tried. You saw me try. Now let's pray Zain doesn't contact her and chew her out for my interference before I have a chance to tell her myself." Her forehead wrinkled. "Okay, not *let's* pray. I'll pray and You answer—how's that? Yeah..."

A boy about Aiden's age walked past, staring into the van window. *Great. Kid probably thinks I've lost my mind, talking to myself in public—sort of. Maybe I look like I'm singing. Yeah. That's more like it.* Kelly swayed for effect—just in case the boy was still looking.

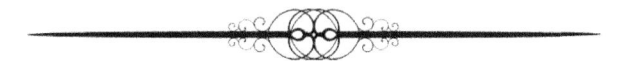

Zain stared at the screen before him. The woman's words made no sense. What fight? There was no way anyone would call their one and only fight "cute." *Horrible is more like it.*

He clicked in the reply box and began typing. "Maybe it's time." The words mocked him. "Okay, maybe it's long past time, I don't know. I'm just curious. What kind of letters are these? Were they addressed to me, or what? I've gotta know."

So Zain wrote. Several times he deleted a long message and tried again. As the message grew, it became impossible to see what he'd written at the beginning, so he copied his work, pasted into a Word document, and tried again. "Here goes… whatever, Lord. Let's see what we can learn."

```
Kelly,
I have a lot of questions. First, I want to
know if you've read the rest of the letters.
You'll get no judgment from me. As much as I
want to think I wouldn't have done it, here I
sit writing to ask more about them. That
doesn't make me any less at fault in my book.
How many letters are there? Are they addressed
to me by name, address, neither? What was the
argument that you spoke of about?
How is Audrey? Is she happy? I've only seen her
once in the past twenty-five years. I'm pretty
sure she didn't see me. I was in Rockland for a
missions conference and drove to Fairbury to
talk to her, but I chickened out. Still, she
looked good—happy—but I know looks can be
deceiving.
And I'm curious about what you said about not
being able to get it out of your mind. I'm
probably reading into things, but it felt like
there was something behind that. So I'm asking
```

again, and please be honest, is Audrey okay? Is she well? Does she need anything?
Thank you for your time,
Zain

He glanced at his clock. Seven. It would be ten in Rockland—or would it be nine? He'd never checked to see the time zone. His stomach growled, distracting him from the fascinating world of time differences.

Despite a refrigerator full of food he should cook, Zain slid his finger over the contacts in his phone and selected his favorite pizza. Woody's Italian Grill created and delivered the best pizza Zain had ever eaten. Perfect for a frustrating and chilly winter evening. "Hello, I'd like an order for delivery please…"

As he gave his order, Zain flipped through the mail, set aside a few bills, and dumped the rest in the trash. *Only junk mail comes as real mail. It's weird.* He tried the TV, but nothing interested him. The Thursday night football game, however, prompted an influx of new memories. *Audrey likes sports. She argued football with that guy—what was his name?—Barnett something. Argued with him for almost an hour on the superiority of the Cowboys to the Redskins. Poor guy never did figure out that she hated the Cowboys, too. Barney that was his name.*

He grabbed his laptop and settled into his chair. A scroll through his email found the one he sought. LVOC- Las Vegas Outreach Center. A receipt for a donation in the name of Audrey Kadir. "Happy Birthday—even if they sent it a day late."

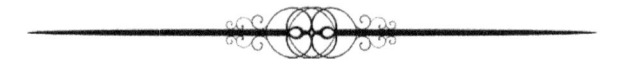

Jon slept beside her, snoring now and then if he flopped too far over on his back. Miserable, Kelly couldn't sleep. She stared at the clock. Just after ten o'clock. Frustrated with further failed attempts to get to sleep earlier, she slipped from the bed and tiptoed from the room. After a quick pit stop, she stopped in the kitchen and made a cup of chai tea. With steamy goodness filling her nostrils with scents that screamed "home and comfort" to her, she curled on the couch and reached for a book.

A chapter later, she snapped it shut, disgusted with the ending. *He chose the wrong woman. That other gal was twice the woman Denise is. Then again, she deserves someone better.*

Kelly had no other books—not "real" books. However, her laptop had a slew of eBooks in her account. She eyed the temptation warily. Once on, she'd be tempted to check her Facebook. If Zain had answered, she'd be sunk, and she knew it. *I can't stay off forever, though. Why did I do this! Audrey is never going to forgive me. Not that I blame her.*

As expected, the little red bubble showed she had messages—three to be exact. Kelly ignored the one from her sister and the one from a woman in town who offered her free canning jars and clicked on Zain's. *It's like an addiction. You can't resist no matter how much you know you should. I've got to tell him not to contact me anymore.*

But she didn't. His message said little but asked much. That he wasn't offended she'd read the letters became strangely comforting. *After all, they were written to him. Technically, you could say they're his. So, technically I have permission—after the fact.* She groaned. "You are so pathetic."

Her fingers flew over the keyboard, typing faster than she usually did and likely with mortifying mistakes, but Kelly felt driven to get the questions answered and sent out into cyberspace before she chickened out. A green dot appeared by Zain's name. Her mouth went dry as her index finger hovered over the mouse button. She clicked the X to close out of the tab, but the page popped a box up, asking if she was sure she wanted to leave the page. Defeated, Kelly clicked no and hit the reply button.

"I think I understand how David got in so much

trouble. One wrong move begets another until you can't stop—like a snowball, I guess."

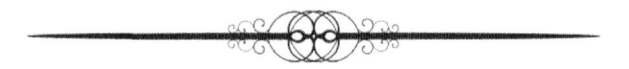

Kelly's reply appeared in his box just as his pizza arrived. He let the steam turn the perfectly crispy crust into a soggy mess as he left the box unopened on the breakfast bar. Instead, he sat down and read the response. Eagerly—much too eagerly, in his opinion.

```
Zain,
I tried to tell Audrey about finding the tax
return and the letters today. Everything was
against me. My nerves, customers, the phones,
her employee returning early. We're supposed to
have coffee this weekend. Let's hope I can find
a backbone somewhere by then.
Yes, I did read the rest of the letters. There
are twenty-four. They're all dated Christmas of
each year. Somewhere during years six to
seventeen or so, she became so frustrated with
your situation. I didn't discover until almost
the last letter that nothing in them—almost
nothing anyway—ever really happened.
She mentioned you coming to Rockland one time.
She hoped you were going to come see her and
was disappointed that you didn't. And then
there was the letter where she was seriously
ticked at you for going out with some woman.
She found a picture on Facebook with you and
the woman and it infuriated her.
Look, it's wrong of me to read her private
things. It's wrong of me to share them with
you. But since I've done it, I'm going to go a
step or two farther. I can't make things any
worse than I already have. She still loves you.
I wish I knew what happened to you guys,
because maybe I could make her see that there's
hope. Or, if there isn't, then I could make her
see that you obviously aren't worth it.
```

Zain grinned at those words. "She's nothing if not loyal."

And there's one other thing I want to share. If you're a Christian, and if you went to a missions conference I'm assuming you are, you made vows when you got married, didn't you? What were those vows? I'm pretty sure they weren't just, "I vow not to divorce you if we don't like being married." Even if they were, God has other things to say about your marriage. The Bible talks about how husbands are to love their wives. How is you living in California loving your wife? For that matter, how is it "living with her in an understanding way" or however that Scripture goes?

Then again, who am I to preach about what the Bible says? I'm the one about to lose a friend and seriously tick off my husband when I confess what I've done. Still, she loves you. And if you love the Lord, He can teach you to love her again. I haven't been married as long as you guys, but I've lived it longer. I recommend it—even though I'm about to make my husband regret it when I talk to him tomorrow. That's a pretty strong recommendation right there.

Just pray about it.
Kelly

The words blurred before his eyes as Zain absorbed all she'd written. Torn between fury at her presumption and curiosity at what it could mean for them if he listened, Zain absently reached for a now-soggy piece of pizza and took a bite. A slice of pepperoni dropped onto the keyboard, splattering oil all over the nearby keys. Zain hardly noticed.

Chapter Thirteen

Tuesday, December 20th—Las Vegas

Such a strange dichotomy—homelessness. As Zain and Audrey walked the "homeless corridor" three miles north east of the Strip, he saw groups of helpless people acting as happy as any family at a park picnic, and at the same time, they showed a hopelessness. Their moods changed quickly sometimes, and as Zain went from group to group he thought he knew what prompted it. The slightest hint of a threat spun their emotions into a new direction. *How else can they feel? They're vulnerable in a way I can't imagine.*

Watching Audrey, though. She inspired him with the way she encouraged people when he could see she was terrified. A few people snatched the stockings and ran, but most showed sincere gratitude despite being a bit wary. At lunchtime, he fought to drag her away from their task. "*They* don't get to take a break from ... from *this*," she choked out.

"And you won't have the energy to keep helping if you don't come."

"'Cause I'm a wuss. We're all wusses. This is bogus. We're not helping—not really. We're slapping a band-aid on a problem."

"Yeah, but a band-aid on a wound is better than it gaping and gushing if you can't stitch it yourself." Zain blinked. "I've been around Jeff too long. I'm talking like him."

Audrey snickered. "Yeah—but you're right. Let's go. Maybe I can sneak a few sandwiches back with us."

He winked at her. "That's the spirit." As they strolled back to the church, Zain tried to draw her out a bit. "So... you just turned eighteen. Does that make you a high school senior or a college freshman?"

"Freshman."

"UofR? Go Warriors?"

Audrey shook her head. "Not until after I'm done with my AA at NCC—Northside Community. It's cheaper that way."

"Smart. My brother's gonna do that."

"You have a brother..." Audrey gave him a sidelong glance. "What's his name?"

"Yosef." At her questioning glance, he added, "We call him Joe. Well, I do."

"And is he cute?"

Zain gave her a pointed look. "He's not a Christian, so does it matter?"

"Sure. I'm just trying to figure out if it runs in the family..."

He flushed. She laughed. Something about walking the streets of Las Vegas with this girl made him feel like they could do anything. "Thanks—I assume."

"Well, duh."

Tell her she's fine. Or at least tell her how awesome her hair is. Da—ng she's got awesome hair. But he couldn't do it. Instead he turned the subject back to safer ground. "So what are you studying at NCC?"

It succeeded and failed simultaneously. "Ooohhh I got yoooouuu... He's embarrassed to say what he thinks, which makes me think it's good. Thank you. Oh," she added, "I was studying nursing, but I changed my mind six weeks into the semester."

"Discover a fear of blood?"

"No... but I did discover that I'm too impatient to learn how to help people that way. I hated the classes,

I hated the professors, and I hated my fellow students. They all found legal principles in nursing, evidence-based practice, and patient education awesome topics. Me—it's all totally bunk. I wanted to know how to stop a guy from hemorrhaging to death or deliver a baby in a crowd." She glanced around her and swept her arm out. "So I want to do stuff like this instead."

"I doubt NNC—"

"NCC."

"Right," Zain agreed. "I doubt NCC has a homeless missions program, so what're you taking next semester?"

"Business. I took a look at my sister's old books and they seemed cool." As the church came in sight, she slowed visibly. "So, you? Are you in school? What year?"

"College isn't an option for me. I have to go. I have to take over the family business, so I'm a business major at UCLA, and I'm taking automotive classes on the side from a trade school."

"Why automotive?"

Zain led her around the corner of the building to the courtyard. "Like I said, family business."

"Which is..."

A sign sent them inside for their food, and he waited until a woman handed him a brown bagged lunch before saying, "Taxis."

Audrey stared at him for a moment before erupting in laughter. "That is like so cliché."

"Well, what can I say—every guy's dream."

"Bet it's good business in L.A.—not like New York, but still..."

"Yeah, we're right at the airport, so we have good business. Dad expects me to double our fleet within ten years. *That* is gonna be tough." Just the idea of it made Zain want to take up organic chemistry or some easier profession. Eager to drive unpleasant thoughts from his head, Zain led her back out into the courtyard where they could talk with relative privacy. "You sure you're still not cold?"

"Naw, it's awesome. Sixty-two according to that thermometer."

Her words made him feel like pansy. Just to reassure himself, Zain unzipped his jacket and sat with his back to the sun. "So we've got something in common—business. What'll you do with it?"

Audrey tossed him a not-so-amused expression and jerked her head at his jacket, chewing. Once she took a swig of her can of Pepsi, she said, "I'm so sure. Zip up the jacket. Jeez." She paused, thinking, and then said, "Oh, yeah. Business. Well, if my first semester is any indication, I'm kinda a control freak, so probably start my own—somehow."

How can she be so articulate one minute and so casual the next? It's cool in a weird sort of way. "What kind—"

Jeff stepped out of the door and beckoned. "We're gonna have a time of prayer while a few church members pack your backpacks again, so if you'd hurry up..."

Zain started to rise, but Audrey grabbed his arm. "Hold on..." Once the door shut behind Jeff, she hissed, "Zip your jacket halfway. I'll go get mine. We can fill them with the leftover bags while everyone's going into the sanctuary."

"Won't you be hot?"

"Like a little warm matters when people might need food," she snapped. "Fine, I'll—"

"Hey..." Zain stepped in front of her, blocking her flight. "It's not a crime for me to want you to be comfortable, too. I'm on your side, Audrey."

Her eyes rose to meet his. "Sorry. This stuff—it's getting to me." She turned toward the building. "Dad said it would."

Their jackets were half-stuffed with leftover lunches, creating noise that sounded like claps of thunder rather than the rustle of paper bags before Zain could say what he wanted. "I think—talking about it getting to you—I think that's good. Stuff like this *should* get to us."

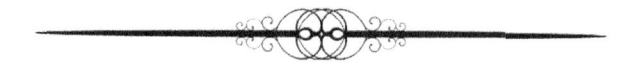

Raised voices at one corner of the courtyard sent Zain rushing to see what was wrong. At the sound of Audrey's voice, he kicked up speed, and then grabbed a tree to stop himself as he overheard one of the girls say, "Those people from over there are chauvinist pigs; they don't respect women. You can't trust 'em."

"Don't even go there. That's so bogus it makes me want to ralph."

I was right. She does get slangy when she's angry, but what brings on the articulation? Inquiring minds want to know.

"But I did a whole report on it. They—"

"He's not some pig! He's a Christian—"

"But he grew up influenced by it all," the girl protested. Zain peeked around the tree and tried to get a better look.

Shelli. Hmm... After flirting with me like she did yesterday, I wouldn't have thought she'd be against people of Middle Eastern descent.

Audrey caught it too. "You didn't seem to mind his ethnicity yesterday."

"That's before I found out his family isn't saved. He wasn't brought up to—"

But Shelli didn't get the chance to finish her thoughts. Audrey stormed off, right toward Zain, calling, "I'm glad *Jesus* didn't have the same kind of prejudice you have or I might not have a chance. You make me sick."

As she passed the tree, Zain reached out and jerked her behind it. "I heard that. Thanks."

"She makes me so mad—"

Clapping one hand over her mouth, Zain shushed her. "C'mon. Let's just walk it off. She's got a valid point in a way."

123

"What? You're gonna drag me off to some harem somewhere and beat me every day if I don't do your bidding?"

Before he realized he'd done it, Zain draped an arm over her shoulders and steered her around the building. His first instinct was to jerk back again, but at just the right moment, she leaned into him ever so slightly. *Okay, God. Help me here because I'm gonna totally kill this if You don't.* "But guys who just came here from traditional families with traditional expectations—different story. My dad says he's glad he doesn't have girls because it would make finding decent husbands hard."

"Finding husbands for daughters." Audrey stepped away from him and crossed her arms. "Now you sound exactly like what Shelli warned me about."

"That's what I'm saying. In the Saudi community, that's what's done. Parents do a lot of arranging for their daughters, but any sister of mine would be too Western to fit in, and there are other things..." Zain didn't want to get into it. "Joe and I had an American upbringing. We've never lived anywhere else, so American culture is interwoven in our heritage now, but some things don't change."

"Yeah. I guess that's probably true of any culture, isn't it? Still," she tossed a glance over her shoulder. "I think it's all a bunch of bunk." She smiled at him. "And, I think she's just jealous. You talk to me and not to her."

*I **like** you and not her is more like it.* "Yeah, well—" Zain couldn't think of a response. He mumbled something about going inside for the afternoon session and tried to ignore the sudden acceleration in his heart rate.

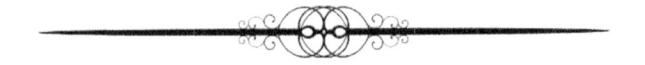

Never had Zain had so much trouble concentrating on prayer. Sermons, song services, memorization—they all gave him trouble at some point or another, but prayer had been natural and comfortable from the first moment he called out to the Lord for understanding the strange mystery otherwise known as Christianity. Sitting beside Audrey, one hand in hers and one in a guy's from Minnesota, he felt torn between attraction and misery. *Why do Christians hold hands all the time? It's just—ugh.*

The second the prayer ended, Manly Minnesota and he dropped hands faster than Jeff said "Amen." However, Audrey didn't let go—even when Zain forced himself to relax his grip a little. *Yes!*

"So a few announcements before we go. I know you've all been working hard and making friends, and here you are in a unique city and you're just trapped here working your butts off."

"Which is kind of the point," Audrey muttered.

"—but, no homonym intended." Jeff laughed at his pathetic attempt at a joke before continuing, "But, we want you to have time to invest in relationships too. Friendships like this can last a lifetime. And Christmas Eve and Christmas Day are going to be busy nights and days so…" He glanced around the room, his tone sounding more like Bob Barker at a "Showcase Showdown" than a preacher addressing a group of mission volunteers. "From noon on Friday until noon on Saturday, your days are yours. We do want to remind you of the code of conduct forms you signed. Please do not gamble, drink, use tobacco or drugs, and keep your hands in appropriate places, if you know what I mean."

"Way to make things awkward," Audrey hissed. "That guy should be a used car salesman or something. It's hard to take him seriously." She rolled her eyes as Jeff made another awkward joke about behaving themselves. "We're not twelve. We're adults for cryin' out loud!"

Several people glanced their way at Audrey's "shrieked whisper." *Yeah, but they don't call this place "Sin City" for nothing.* "Can't hurt to remember that people are probably waiting for us to blow it so they can blow us off."

The minute they were dismissed, Zain tugged her toward the door, looking for a chance to talk to Audrey about their "day off." *Just ask her before she figures you won't or gives up and asks herself.* "Wanna do something on Friday? We could see a show... have dinner... check out Cesar's Palace or play games at the Circus Circus?"

"Does that count as gambling?"

Zain popped his head in the door and called for Jeff. "Is the midway at the Circus Circus okay or is that gambling?"

"Not a problem. Just stay off the card tables and the slots—trying to avoid that 'appearance of evil' thing is all."

Zain grinned and waited for her answer. Audrey glanced down at their intertwined fingers and back up at him. "Guess I've got a date for Christmas Adam."

"Huh?"

Chapter Fourteen

Friday, December 19th—Fairbury

Nerves making her jittery enough to spill her coffee on her—twice—Kelly sat in the far corner of The Grind and watched for Audrey. The longer time passed, the more miserable she grew. Thanks to a night of guilt-induced insomnia, the only thing keeping her awake was the assurance that once she confessed, Audrey would be angry and let her have it. Then she could go home and cry herself to sleep with a clear conscience and burdened heart. *Anyone who says, "Confession is good for the soul," forgets things like the heart. If I live through telling her, remembering I did it at all is gonna kill me.*

The kid behind the counter couldn't meet her eyes when she asked for a refill, and the manager working on some kind of order couldn't take *her* eyes off Kelly. Mrs. Paulson gasped as Kelly carried her coffee back to her table, and whispers at the front of the building nearly drove Kelly crazy. *What happened? Who did what and to whom? This town is the worst for that kind of gossip. I mean, it doesn't get much opportunity, so I shouldn't complain, but when it does, watch out.* The obvious reason for sidelong glances her way hit her hard, and Kelly couldn't decide if she was happy or discouraged. *It's Aiden, isn't it? He got caught riding without his helmet again, didn't he? Well, serves him right, but it's nice to see him back to normal, I guess. Where we'll come up with the money for a ticket, especially now that Audrey is going to fire me, I do not know.*

As if the mere thought of her name conjured her up, Audrey opened the door, waved, and got in line for a coffee. It almost felt as if—but surely she imagined it—but it did seem as though Audrey couldn't quite meet her eyes. *If she somehow found out before I could confess, I'll cry, Lord. I—* A new thought slammed into her and rolled away again, taking her breath with it. *Zain. What if he—and she heard it from him rather than me? Oh, that's bad. Lord, please no...*

By the time Audrey reached her, the coffee shop had filled with enough customers to make a discussion such as she'd hoped to have impossible. "Busy today."

Kelly nodded. "I hoped for some privacy, but..."

"Me too. Why don't we see if the church is open? It's usually quiet in there."

Nerves tried to strangle her as she allowed her mind to race through various possibilities. *I didn't leave any trace of my snooping. She can't know unless Zain or Jon told her, and Jon wouldn't. I don't think Zain would either, though. It's so confusing.*

Step by slow step, they wandered up the sidewalks, each pointing at odd things in windows as if ignoring their respective topics would somehow make them more palatable when they finished. Just as Kelly worked up the courage to speak, Audrey asked a question. "What should people in difficult marriages do?"

"Difficult marriages?"

"Right." Audrey gave her an inscrutable look. "I mean, if family was interfering, or maybe someone else came along and showed how much better things could be right as times were tough. What should they do?"

Bentley's words came to her before she realized it. "Depends on if it's a man or woman, but I would hope that I would focus on my vows—all of them. When Jon and I married, we had very specific vows we took. I think at rough times, remembering *all* of your vows and striving to keep them should take the focus off the troubles, anyway."

"But that doesn't fix things, does it? It's just a Band-Aid." Her eyes shifted. "Then again, someone I once knew said that even with terrible wounds, Band-Aids are better than nothing if used right—at least until you can get the help you need."

"True. Speaking of marriage," Kelly began, but Audrey interrupted her again.

"I keep hearing things, Kelly. Things that I never thought anyone—it's hard to explain, but I'm worried."

"Audrey, it's my fault. I'm so sorry. I—"

"Don't you think you should be telling Jon this?" Audrey started to say more, but her phone rang. She excused herself and answered it, alarm growing on her face. "No! Okay, I'm coming right now. Oh, man this is bad." She shoved the phone in her pocket and took off at a jog. "The electricity is out—completely. Poor Stacy is in a dark store with customers wanting things and...We'll talk later," Audrey promised, calling over her shoulder as she raced back toward the store.

Kelly stared after Audrey, stunned. *Well that went better than I expected.* She glanced at her watch and smiled. *And I even have time for a nap. You're too good to me, Lord. You're much too good to me. I need to tell Jon, now. That won't be so easy, but nap first. I think I could sleep until tomorrow, but I'll be satisfied with until Mom brings the boys home.*

The truck door slammed shut—harder than Jon usually shut it. *Must be colder out there than I thought.* She glanced around the kitchen, smiling at the sight before her. Jon's favorite meal, a quiet house, clean and inviting. Everything was set to show where her true priorities lay and to soften the words she knew would shock and probably anger Jon. *I don't blame him either. I'd be furious.*

The back door opened and closed with more firmness than usual. Kelly turned to greet her husband and found him leaning against it, arms crossed over his chest. "What have you done?"

"Wha—"

"I don't know what it is, but I'm guessing it has to do with Audrey and that man. What have you done?"

"I—how'd you know?" Suddenly, the lofty ideas of confession and seeking forgiveness struggled to flee as the fight or flight response muscled into place.

"Well, other than the fact that the entire town is talking about how we're separating, you're trying to get custody of the kids, and you're having an affair with a man on Facebook?"

She laughed. The words sounded so ridiculous—something even a lunatic couldn't conjure—but Jon's expression choked her. "You're kidding. You have to be kidding."

"I'm not. First Gary Novak comes to me, tells me that Bentley has been talking to you about how to make separation work with kids, and then Audrey warns me that you know it's wrong but you seem to be justifying yourself."

"I—"

"What. Did. You. Do?" Jon didn't step forward—didn't wrap his arms around her and tell her he was furious but he loved her. Instead he stood there, resolute and immovable.

"I read her letters—all of them. She..." Kelly couldn't continue. She dropped the wooden spoon in the pot and fled the room. Even without looking behind her, she knew he hadn't followed—probably wouldn't for some time.

I've really done it now, Lord. I knew it was wrong, but I meant well. My heart was in the right place—truly. But despite her words, Kelly couldn't help but hear the prophet Jeremiah as if he stood next to her saying,

"The heart is more deceitful than anything else and is desperately sick. Who can know it?"

It's like when I was a kid and Dad would say it didn't matter how sincere someone was if they were sincerely wrong. Wrong is wrong. I did wrong. And now Audrey not only doesn't know it and hasn't forgiven me, she thinks I'm having some kind of affair! It's like every second this thing gets worse or something.

A thought came to her—as if handed to her by God Himself, although Kelly wouldn't have quite put it that way. It just seemed as if the Lord reminded her of the man she'd married, how he thought, and what demonstrated love and respect to him. She hated it; her flesh cried out against her as she shoved herself off the bed and forced her feet to retrace their steps to the kitchen. Jon stood over the pot of chicken noodle soup and stirred it. He didn't look her way, but she saw his jaw clench and his throat bob.

I hurt him. I knew I'd disappoint—even anger—but I never thought it would hurt him. Aloud, she forced herself to speak words that galled her pride. "It was wrong, Jon. I knew it, and I did it anyway. I let my curiosity and my desire to see something happen cloud my judgment and that hurt you. It hurt our reputation. I'm sorry." Kelly swallowed hard and forced herself to say the words that always resisted more than any others. "Please forgive me."

He continued to stir—continued to swallow wave after wave of emotion. After a long, agonizing minute, he turned off the stove and set down the spoon. His eyes met hers, pain etching both and making him look worn and haggard. "I forgive you."

Kelly's need for comfort nearly overpowered her resolve to respect his need to work through his emotions. She wanted a hug. She ached for him to hold her and tell her they'd weather the storm she'd created for them when she shook up the snow globe of their life. *I could have broken it. As it is, can he trust me? I mean, I violated someone's privacy. How can he know I won't be indiscreet with ours?*

Just as she began to mentally berate herself once more, Jon crossed the room and pulled her close. "I love you."

"I know. Don't know why, maybe, but I know."

"It's going to take a while for this to die down. This is Fairbury, after all."

"How does anyone know about anything? I never told anyone here what I did."

Jon led her to the couch and pulled her to him as he talked. "From what I gather from Gary, you talked to Bentley after a Bible Study—something about vows and separation and children. It made her nervous, but she didn't say anything to him that time."

"That time?" Kelly wrinkled her nose. "What other— oh. Yeah. I was trying to see if she thought Zain could find Audrey just by me asking if he'd gotten married about twenty-five years ago, but I couldn't say that. I bet it sounded weird."

"It did. She saw Gary across the road and went over to find out what he thought. Mrs. Paulson overheard—"

"And now it's on the front page of the Fairbury Gazette."

Jon gave her a rueful smile. "Almost."

"You know, I looked them up today—before I went to confess to her. I decided to see for sure that it was real."

"Looked up what?" Jon's hand toyed with her hair and his jaw still worked as he tried to deal with the remaining emotions. She felt it push and relax against the side of her head.

"I went to the Nevada website—Clark County it said. You just plug in the names and year and it spits out any marriage records."

"So you repented, decided to confess, and then looked up more personal information?"

She wanted to protest—to point out that marriages are a matter of public record, but she couldn't allow herself to do it. Not again. "I know. I'm not proud of it, but I figured I should confess everything." She reached for the laptop. "You should probably read our correspondencem too. I'll get food for us."

As Kelly fought her way out of the couch, feeling much more unwieldy than five and a half months pregnant, Jon asked, "Where're the boys?"

"Mom's. I wanted you to have the privacy to yell at me all you wanted."

"I wasn't going to yell, Kelly. Since when—"

She shook her head, trying to smile as she gazed down at him. "I know, but I figured if you ever were going to, this would be the time."

Left alone with her laptop, Jon found her Facebook page and eventually found the message link. He clicked on the bar with Zain's name on it and saw the end of their correspondence. Scrolling up, the first contact words hit him and churned his stomach. *It's just not like her. What possessed her to do something like this?*

By the time she returned with bowls of soup and cornbread, Jon had composed a reply. "I wrote him. I want you to read it—tell me if you think it's a good idea.

Kelly took the laptop and scanned the words. Her cheeks grew a little pink, but she nodded and passed it back to him. "That's good."

Halfway through the meal, she sighed and asked, "What are we going to do about this? How do we convince people we're not destined for divorce court?"

"We can't. They'll just have to see it's true."

"Well, our friends will stop rumors too—if they know." The phone rang. Kelly picked it up, and from what Jon could hear, the local gossip had reached the ears of her sisters.

Well, now things'll get even more interesting. Those Homstad girls aren't going to let people trash their sister's reputation. Yes, it's going to get very interesting.

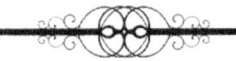

Zain read the message from Jon Cox, and as he did, a pit grew in his stomach.

```
Zain,
I am writing in place of my wife. She won't be
corresponding with you anymore and would like
to apologize for meddling in your private
business as well as ask forgiveness for such.
Her actions of late have been grossly out of
character and now have given rise to local
gossip. To the end of quelling such gossip, we
must take this step, not because we blame you
for it, but to protect our family's reputation
and privacy. We hope you'll understand.
Should you speak to Audrey in the near future,
I would appreciate if you did not mention
Kelly's discovery in case she has not yet been
able to confess to Audrey herself. Audrey
should not hear of this from anyone but Kelly.
I'm sure you can see why.
Regretfully,
Jonathan Cox
```

Immediately, he pulled out his phone and called his brother. "Joe, remember what I said this morning?"

"About how it's about time you faced the music and talked to your wife?"

"Well," Zain amended, "That's not exactly what I said—"

"It's the gist, why?"

"I might do it."

"Do what?"

He closed his eyes, inhaled, and let the air leave his lungs with a whoosh. "Tell Mama and Baba—then maybe go and talk to Audrey. If nothing else, maybe she'll forgive Kelly if I point out that I practically encouraged her to read more with my questions."

"Forgive Kelly—oh. She found out? No wonder—"

"Not yet, but she will. I'm thinking about asking

Kelly not to talk to Audrey until I do. I don't want Audrey taking off before I can talk to her—if I go."

"You're going," Yosef insisted.

"I am?"

"Even if Aida and I have to drag you there."

Zain smiled at the sight. "Considering she thinks that a picture of you and Aida is a picture of me with some woman, that might not be such a bad idea."

"What picture?"

"I don't know—a few years ago. I guess I put something up on Facebook and Audrey saw it. Kelly said it made her pretty ticked off."

"That sounds promising." Yosef remained quiet for a moment before he said, "Y'know, there's one thing I don't get."

"What?"

"Why you're not ticked off at this woman for digging into your personal business. That's not like you."

The question was one Zain had asked himself, but he didn't know if he wanted to admit the answer—not to his brother. He hesitated, but after a few threats of bodily harm, none of which he took seriously, Zain said, "Because she told me things I've wanted to know since the day I left Vegas."

Chapter Fifteen

Saturday, December 20th—Fairbury

Kelly stared at the screen before her, emotions confused. "Jooonnnn…"

After the third call, Jon popped his head around the corner. "You call?"

"Um, yeah! Can you look at this?"

She lifted the laptop and passed it to him. Jon sat on the arm of the couch, laptop in hand, and read Zain's message. His eyes met hers. "What do you think?"

"I don't know. I mean, I want to get it off my chest, but he makes a good point, and he is one of the 'injured parties' so to speak. I can't just do what I want because it makes me feel better, but is it right to wait?"

"Six days." Jon's jaw worked as he considered the words before him. "I don't know. Let me think about it. I've got to take a shower."

As she heard the pipes groan, signaling the beginning of Jon's shower, Kelly stared at the screen again. "What do we do, Lord?"

```
Jon and Kelly,
First, I would like to say how much I respect
and admire how transparent you've been about
this.  Jon's  protection  of  your  family's
reputation gives me hope that things can be
mended when things go wrong.
```

I think I must ask forgiveness as well. I requested information that wasn't hers to give. That, I am sure, led Kelly into temptation. I didn't think about it at the time, but in retrospect, I can see that I am culpable as well. I do hope you will forgive me.
I would ask a favor, however. Would you consider NOT talking to Audrey about this until after Christmas? Do you think it will further damage your reputation in town if you wait? If it would, don't delay. Do what is necessary to repair things or prevent further gossip. But if it won't make a difference, I think it would be nice for Audrey to have a Christmas free of discouragement and probable confessions of her own. Once she knows that someone else knows of our marriage, she likely will feel obligated to tell her family. I'd hate to see their holiday affected by this.
I should admit that I also have personal reasons for asking. I would tell you what those are, considering I'm asking you to accommodate them as well, but I haven't solidified them yet. I would promise to tell you once I do, but I can't. I just don't know.
I hope to get to meet you in person. My brother asked why I was not offended that Kelly dug into my past. I am usually a very private person. I wanted you to know what I told him. I said, "Because she told me things I've wanted to know since the day I left Vegas." I cannot be angry at you for doing what I would have if I had the courage and/or opportunity.
In Jesus,
Zain

I want to do it, Lord. I mean, I don't, but I do. He's right. It's not just her; it's her family. They'll pay for my actions, and does it make any difference to Audrey when she learns? I don't think it does. I want it over with. I need to get it off my chest. Now that I can see what has happened—really see it with blinders off—I am disgusted with myself. What do we do?

A new thought prompted her to pick up the phone. She hesitated, took a deep breath, and dialed her mother's number. "Hey, Mom. I have a scenario for you."

"Can't you just come get my card, do it for me, and I'll pay you?"

"What?"

Dee Homstad's laughter came over the phone. "I take it you're not talking coupons."

"No... different kind of scenario." Kelly swallowed, tossed out another quick prayer, and said, "So if you did something wrong against someone and they didn't know it or have any way to know of it."

"Look, I know you're not having an affair, so don't make—"

"Mom! No!" Kelly rolled her eyes. "That's part of the problem. Just listen. So if the person you wronged can't possibly know it, would it be wrong to wait five days to confess to him or her?"

"Why wait?"

"Christmas. Confessing will probably ruin their holiday and that of anyone related." She waited, fingers tapping and heart pounding.

"But waiting will hurt you, won't it?"

"How do you mean?"

"Well," Dee said with thoughtful pauses between words. "You said it was part of the problem, though. You said—" Again she paused. "Will your reputation be repairable if you don't clear it now?"

"Should that matter?" Dee protested, but Kelly interrupted. "Seriously. If I do wrong, should I get to choose the best time to confess for *me* or should I confess at the best time for the person I wronged."

"That is a good point."

"One last thing." She waited for her mother to ask and then said, "What if a second party was also wronged and that party *wanted* you to wait until after

Christmas?"

"Is that party your husband?"

"No."

Dee's relief came through the phone line quite audibly. "Then I'd say as long as it cannot hurt those you've wronged to wait, then I would honor that wish unless something happens that shows you otherwise."

"Like what?"

"I don't know, Kelly. But things happen. Don't lock yourself into, 'I'm telling on xyz date at 123 time.' Make a plan, but adjust based upon what happens between now and then if necessary."

"Is it bad that I just want to get it over with? I don't want to wait. It's almost a *week!*"

"If it was over a week, I probably would have said don't, but if it'll bless several people to hold off, then you probably should."

Kelly sat, phone in her hand, staring at it while she pondered her mother's words. Jon's voice startled her from the corner. "Your mom thinks you should wait."

"You heard?"

"Yeah."

She glanced over her shoulder to where Jon stood leaning against the doorjamb to the living room. "She said if I'm the only one hurt by waiting and Audrey, her family, and Zain will be blessed by the wait, then I should wait."

"That's what I was thinking in the shower."

Nathan staggered out of his room, awake from his afternoon nap. Kelly pulled the boy up on her lap and held him as she murmured, "Great minds think alike."

Jon shook his head. "I keep reminding you that the rest of that saying isn't quite as flattering."

"Yeah, well, I just pretend it doesn't exist, and then you're the genius we all know you to be."

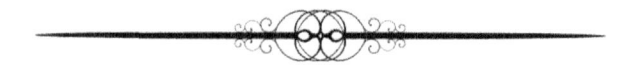

Zain had changed his mind four times in the space

of as many hours. The clock struck one-thirty, and still he hadn't decided. Hours of prayer had given him conflicting leanings. At first, he'd determined to confess all to his father and accept the consequences of disappointing the man Zain loved more than any other—risk destroying any hope of bringing his father to Jesus. That thought had changed his mind. He couldn't risk his father's salvation on something as unimportant as confessing a marriage he probably would never acknowledge in any other way. What would be the point? But the idea of continuing a charade and having something so big hovering over him, waiting to drop as it already had for Audrey, choked him. *What if something happens to Yosef? He knows. He could be injured and come out of it talking about stuff he's never told anyone. I've read about that kind of thing.* But once again, the thought of disappointing his father, proving that Christianity is no different than any other religion full of weak hypocrites, arrested his decision to drive to his parents' house and confess it all.

    Prayer had failed him. Usually, when lost in conversation with Jesus, Zain found Scriptures flooding into his mind. This time they'd remained silent. As a last resort, something that shamed him, he pulled his Bible from the table, opened it, and began flipping through the Psalms and Proverbs in hopes of finding something that spoke to his situation. Proverbs gave one indiscriminate jab to his conscience. Zain read it aloud, trying to burn any conviction the Lord might want to impress on him into his heart. "'He who conceals his transgressions will not prosper, but he who confesses and forsakes them will find compassion.' What does that even mean? I get it in regards to stealing or adultery or even lying, but I didn't do any of those things. I kept something private, private. How is that wrong? Still, it says if I forsake and confess, I will find compassion. But from whom?"

    He read the words again, guilt welling up in heart as he realized that he wanted compassion more from his father than from the Lord. "Is it because I know You've forgiven me if indeed it was wrong? Is it because I know that my sin is covered by the blood, but Baba..."

Frustrated, he flipped a chunk of his Bible and began reading in Mark. Always his favorite Gospel, he devoured chapter after chapter in the hunt for something Jesus said—something to tell him whether to keep quiet and preserve the hope of his father's eventual salvation or to share and somehow show that Jesus can change even a man's pride. Both seemed equally dangerous in eternal perspective.

Mark passed into Luke. Some portions he'd just read in Mark's concise writing style, but when Zain got to the parable of the lampstand, Luke's version spun new and uncomfortable thoughts in his mind. "'For nothing is hidden that will not become evident, nor anything secret that will not be known and come to light.' Well, there it is. That's probably talking about the Judgment, but it could mean now, too."

Before he could talk himself out of it again, Zain jumped up, abandoned his Bible and laptop, and grabbed his keys. Traffic on the 405 nearly sent him off onto side streets to return home, but he kept driving until he reached the Manchester Boulevard exit. "Too close to turn back now," he muttered as he navigated the streets to his parents' home. The closer he came, the stronger the temptation grew to talk to his mother first. "Mama would understand. I'm her favorite."

That thought made him smile. He and Yosef had a running joke about it. His mother always insisted her—albeit nonexistent—daughter was, of course, the favorite. "Forget it, Joe. I'm the favorite. I came first. Of course, I'm the favorite."

His mother greeted him excitedly. "Tariq, Zain is here!"

His father called for him to join him in the sunroom. "Sarah, can you send a new bottle of water with him?"

In the sunroom, Zain unscrewed the top and

handed his father the bottle. Without breaking his stride on the treadmill, Tariq downed half the bottle and shoved it into his cup holder. "What are you doing today?" he gasped as his feet pounded the conveyor belt.

"I actually need to talk to you." Zain back toward the door, sliding it shut behind him. "In private," he finished.

Tariq shut off the treadmill and grabbed a hand towel. "Is something wrong? Did we lose that appeal for the insurance?"

"No, actually, we got it. They've already cut us a check. It's something personal." He sat down in the nearest chair, his eyes unable to meet his father's. "I hid something from you, Baba. Right until this moment, I didn't think it was wrong, but now I think it was. My shame tells me so."

Seated at the end of the treadmill, Tariq mopped his forehead, guzzled the rest of his water, and waited. But Zain didn't speak again. "Am I so imposing? Have I been such a harsh father that you cannot speak to me?"

"It's a long-term secret."

"How long?"

Unable to elaborate yet, Zain whispered, "Las Vegas." Then he prayed for courage to say the words that would hurt his father.

"When you were what, twenty? Did you go back?"

"No."

Tariq tried a joke. "Well, the TV says that what happens in Vegas—"

"—stays there. I know. And this did... until recently."

"If you got a girl pregnant and are just now telling me I have a grandchild, I'll beat you."

Zain swallowed hard and forced himself to raise his eyes. "No grandchildren, Baba. But I do have a wife."

Feeling very much like a small child again, Zain found himself, head hung in shame, waiting for the ordeal to end so he could go home and lick his wounds.

So much for talking to Audrey, then. This is bad. I can't subject her to Baba's anger.

"You married a girl then? How do you see her? Why did you not tell us?"

"I haven't seen her since the afternoon we got married—well, I hid in her store once just to get a glimpse of her."

"Why, Zain? Why would you do this?"

"I didn't want to hurt you—anger you."

Tariq jumped to his feet, his voice booming as he railed against his son. "Hurt me! Anger me! Of course you have! Even more now than you would have then! She is your *wife,* Zain! How could you just abandon her?"

"I didn't—"

"No! You will listen to me. You shame us. You shame your god. You shame your religion and your friends. This woman—how can she not feel worthless? Why did you do this?"

"We argued—"

"I argue with your mother every other day. I don't leave her to fend for herself. I am her husband. She should be able to count on that much at least!" Tariq glanced over his shoulder and beckoned his stunned wife to enter. "Come in here, Sarah. You should know what your son has done."

Lord, where's that compassion? I need it now more than ever. This is worse than I thought. I thought he'd be angry I did it. I didn't ever imagine he'd be upset like this!

"What is it? What has happened? If you got a girl pregnant, Zain..."

"Mama!"

"He hasn't bothered with that—wait." Tariq glared at him. "Are you absolutely certain there is no child?"

He didn't want to admit it. Zain forced himself not to cover his head with his hands as he murmured, "I am still a virgin, Baba."

"What!" His parents stared at one another,

shocked, before beginning simultaneous verbal tirades against the folly that was their son.

Zain listened, took every accusation without protest, but his heart tried to harden. He found himself fighting the urge to justify himself and his decisions. He discounted their objections with reminders to himself that his parents weren't Christians. They couldn't know what God wanted him to do. But it failed. His conscience beat against his resistance until he was forced to hold back tears of repentance and grief.

When the rapid fire of their rebukes stilled, Zain found he could only whisper three words. "I am sorry."

"Why do you apologize to me? You should apologize to the wife you have abandoned. All these years we hoped for you, tried to find someone for you. You could have told us."

"She is not Arabic."

"Did I think she would be? Why would a good Arab girl be on a mission trip for Christians?" He frowned. "Why did you not divorce her?"

"Christians do not divorce for inconvenience. It isn't allowed."

"I don't suppose marrying someone and abandoning them is allowed either, but you have done that? What would your beloved English teacher say about this?"

The words sliced through an unscarred section of his heart, adding fresh wounds. "I—"

"Zain?" Sarah waited for him to focus on her before she said, "Tell us about it. What happened?"

Chapter Sixteen

Friday, December 23rd—Las Vegas

By eleven-forty on that Friday morning, Zain had perfected the "glance at your watch while handing out stockings" technique. He'd spent the last two days working at the mission building, setting up tables, unpacking boxes of food, prepping backpacks for those going out, and wondering if Audrey was safe with Barnett. *Hawthorne Barnett. No wonder he hates his name. That's just cruel.*

Now, tramping the far corners of their assigned areas in search of any ignored homeless, Zain eyed his watch at every moment he knew Audrey wasn't watching. *Twenty more minutes. I can do it.* He remembered her note she'd left on his pillow and used it as a personal distraction to pass the time. "Oh, I got your note..."

"Did you ask Jeff? I thought of it while I was out, but you were gone, so..."

"Yeah. He says most of the buffets are cheap and good, but I wanted a better one, so he suggested The Greek Shack. Says the food is amazing." He cast a sidelong glance at her. "So did you write the note yourself, or what?"

"Yes, I have terrible spelling," she growled. "Sue me."

"I wondered..." He pulled out the note and read it,

smiling.

> *Dear Zain,*
>
> *I was thinking. Maybe we should ask Jeff about a good resterant. I tried to find him but I couldn't. I just think there's probably alot of bad food around here. I'd hate to throw away alot of money on something not so good.*
>
> *Audrey ♥*

"Look, I knew I spelled restaurant wrong, but it's not like there's a dictionary on every corner waiting for me to use it. I can't just dial 4-1-1 and ask information how to spell something."

He didn't answer. After being drilled by Mr. Ahmed on the evils of combining the words a and lot into one nonexistent conglomeration of letters, Zain had developed a particular abhorrence for it. But it seemed a bit rude to bring it up, particularly after the heart at the end of her signature. Audrey, however, caught it. "Oh, great. What else did I misspell? You know, I like couldn't spell my own last name for years."

"A lot."

"I knew it had two Ls! I do it every time. Spelling just makes no sense—totally bogus. They should rewrite the spelling rules to be consistent."

"A lot doesn't have two Ls but it is two words—not one." He grinned and added, "And now you have to tell me about the last name thing."

"Seever. S-e-e-v-e-r. Simple right? But I knew how to spell sea—like the ocean. From a book we had with tongue twisters. I had read it with my dad so much that I recognized s-e-a. So, for years I spelled my last name S-e-a-v-e-r. My parents and teachers never noticed. Talk about total betrayal when I discovered it wasn't right."

As they approached another man, half-drunk and coughing by the side of a dumpster, Zain pulled a stocking from the backpack, checking his watch as he did. "It's five minutes after the last time," Audrey said as she took the sock from him. "Your watch should be glad you're not butt ugly or it'd be broken by now." She handed the sock to the man and explained that another one was inside, as well as a few other things. "Come down to the outreach center tomorrow night or Sunday morning. We're having food, music, everything but preaching. Not a single word of it."

"No prayers?" The man coughed again.

"Well," she admitted, "It's possible they'll pray over the food, but it won't be a sermon in a prayer. It'll just be a quick thanks for food."

Zain nodded. "And it's warm in there. Warm building, good food, people just wanting to make sure you get a nice Christmas and see what they have to offer the rest of the year—no obligation."

Between coughs, the man said, "Yeah... okay. Maybe. Got a coupla bucks?"

Audrey hesitated and then shoved her hands in her pockets. Zain's heart raced. They'd been warned against giving the indigents of Las Vegas any money. *"They'll either spend it on alcohol or the slot machines. Give them our address instead."*

"We're not supposed to," he hissed.

"Yeah, well, he asked and I'm giving." As she handed the man a wad of bills from her front pocket, she sank to her heels at the man's eye level. "Please use it for food or something you really need. Please don't throw it away in a machine somewhere."

A fit of coughing sprayed Audrey with whatever germs infected him, but Audrey just pounded his back and murmured reassurances that at the mission, they'd help him get proper medicine to help. "Just go down there—even now. It'll be okay. Want us to take you?"

"Yer boyfriend wants to go."

"Yeah, he's taking me out tonight, so he's kind of impatient, but he wants you to get better too, don't you, Zain?"

It took him a second or two to fight his flesh and

the frustration of having his plans thwarted, but Zain shook himself. "Sorry. Brain froze. C'mon, let's get you something for that cough."

"Need brandy," the man insisted. "It's the only thing that stops it for a while."

"They've got Comtrex liquid at the center," Audrey said. "I don't know what the alcohol content of that stuff is, but it's got a lot, I think. That's A lot, not one word. Zain'll quiz us later. Anyway," she gave him a wink as the man draped a rank smelling arm over Zain's shoulder and added, "it's also got actual medicine in it to help. When I have a cough, I take a coupla teaspoons of that stuff and wake up feeling normal again."

"Well, I'm never gonna feel normal again—got the AIDS—but feelin' better would be good." The man doubled over, hacking up half the contents of his chest cavity before he caught a full breath again.

Zain's eyes met hers and he mouthed, *"You wash up the minute we get back to the church."*

She smiled, and the concern that had begun to fill him dissolved into the windy—he checked his watch—afternoon.

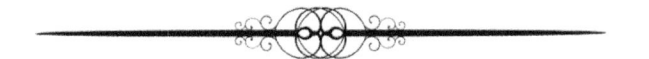

The mission's volunteer doctor reassured Zain that Audrey was at little to no risk of developing AIDS from germ-infested cough spray. "It's a bit harder to get than most people think. Recent research shows—"

"As long as she doesn't need to be seen..."

"If she was my daughter, I'd tell her to go take a shower and forget about it. She did a good thing. A man in his condition can't afford to be sick."

As Zain walked back to the church, he whistled just a little. Once inside, the place buzzed with activity. Groups of guys and girls chatted about where they'd go or what they'd do. Some of the guys stood around waiting for a specific girl. *Just like I would if I hadn't had to stay with Jimmy the Cougher. Now she'll be waiting for me. Why do I get the feeling she'll also be teasing me about that?*

Three guys waited ahead of him for a shower. The water would be lukewarm at best, but Zain couldn't imagine *not* taking a shower after the day's work and Jimmy's stench. A hand over his face reminded him that he hadn't shaved since he arrived. *Should do that too. Great. I need to hurry.*

Most of the group had disappeared into the streets of Las Vegas by the time Zain arrived in the foyer, ready to go. Audrey wasn't there. He stepped into the sanctuary and found her sitting in the last pew, her forearms leaning on the back of the one in front of her and her head resting on them. *Do I interrupt praying? That's kind of rude. Okay, God. What do I do?* Several seconds passed, but no answer came. Frustrated, he tried again. *Lord? A little help here?* Seconds ticked past. Nothing.

He adjusted his tie, wondering for probably the tenth time if it was too formal for a casual date. *Or is it a casual date? I mean, we're going to that restaurant, and we're gonna see Sigfreid and Roy.* He leaned forward to get a glimpse of her outfit—hoping for a hint as to whether he should remove the tie or not—but saw nothing. *Okay, here goes.*

In the dozen steps it took to cross from the doorway to her seat, Zain decided simply to sit beside her and wait. He did. She didn't turn, didn't pause in her prayer. Unsure what else to do, he began praying, eyes open to see if she moved, but praying nonetheless. After a few minutes, she sat back, her head still bowed. Another minute passed. She shifted but never looked up or at him.

Lord! What do I do? The answer came—or so Zain assumed—without any help of the Almighty. He reached for her hand. It worked. Audrey's head turned and she laughed.

"Were you waiting for me to be done?"

"Yeah."

"Me too." At his questioning gaze, she rolled her eyes. "I was waiting for you."

"Oh. You ready?"

Audrey nodded. "Yeah, you?"

"Lemme go call a cab then."

He made it five steps before she called out to him. "Zain?"

"Yeah?"

"Can you afford this? I've got some—"

"I'm good." Her uncertain nod sent his senses spinning. *Man she's just about as perfect as you can get.*

Zain retraced his steps and stood before her. With her three-inch heels, she stood taller than him, but to his astonishment, he didn't care. "I'm serious. Dad got me my own credit card for this trip—said it was time to start building a credit history. I'll have to pay him back, of course, but I'd say you're worth it."

"Gonna take a lot of fares to pay for it all."

"Like I said—" Audrey smiled, her eyes shining. *She looks like she should be an ad for toothpaste or something.*

"You're good."

He didn't allow himself to swagger across the sanctuary. He didn't look back, and despite the embarrassing and girly impulse, he didn't even touch his face. Still, he felt the soft, quick pressure of her lips to his cheek until he made the serious mistake of holding the phone up to the same side of his face. *Dweeb of the first order. Ugh, you're pathetic.*

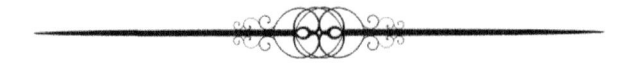

Sometime between the ride to the restaurant and the moment they found their seats at the MGM Grand, Zain realized something that terrified and excited him. *I'm totally falling in love with her. I wonder if she knows—if she can tell.*

Unaware that she nearly interrupted a premature and likely mortifying declaration of his feelings, Audrey bounced in her seat a little, grabbed his hand, and smiled into his eyes. "This is the best Christmas Adam ever."

"Okay," he said, forcing himself to focus on anything but her apparent appreciation for their date. "You said that before. What is Christmas Adam?"

"The day before Christmas Eve."

"I don't get it. I've heard of Christmas Eve—everyone has. But what's—"

"Okay, it's just this thing my Mom and her family say, okay? Adam comes before Eve, who comes before Cain and Abel. So in our family we have Christmas Adam—the twenty-third. Then there's Christmas Eve—"

"The twenty-fourth."

"Right!" She laughed at the look of incredulity he knew he'd failed to hide. "Then of course, Christmas Day. And, since candy canes are a big deal, if the day after Christmas has something go really wrong, we call it 'Christmas Cain." Then Dad always says, "But tomorrow we'll be *Abel* to put it all behind us."

"Seth who?"

"I didn't say anything about him. But he was the third—"

Zain shook his head. "Bad joke—like I was lisping and saying 'says who.' Ignore me."

"Dad would like you. You tried." She leaned back, resting her head on his shoulder. "Actually, I think he'd like you just because you're you—even without the bad jokes."

As the auditorium slowly filled with guests, Zain decided they might as well talk about the inevitable. "We're going to have to find a way to work that out. You know that, don't you?"

"Work what out?"

"Spending time together. I'm not walking away from this thing and totally forgetting about you."

A slow smile pushed up the corners of her mouth,

but Audrey didn't turn to face him. "I hoped you'd want to."

"But how..." He sighed. "That I don't know."

Audrey nodded as he spoke. "It's expensive to fly and busses take too long." Before he could offer any suggestions—not having any come to mind—she sat up straight and turned to face him. "One of us could switch schools—me for example. I could just move to UCLA after next semester."

"That's nine months." Even as he spoke, Zain realized he sounded like a whiny child. "Okay, so I don't want to have to wait that long to see you again. Sue me."

"Yeah. Phones are expensive, transportation is expensive, but what else can we do?" She picked at her cuticles as she murmured, "I didn't think it would be that big of a deal, but just thinking about it—ugh."

It seemed like the best time to admit he'd already begun to fall for her, but Zain couldn't bring himself to do it. He consoled himself with lofty ideas about it being too public for something so personal, but his inner self laughed. *You're just a coward—a great justifier, but a coward.*

They stood under the archway of the church entrance. Zain fought to try to say what he'd failed to all evening. *It's probably too early, but I don't care. She's exactly what I've always liked in a girl. She's a Christian—the first one I actually like. I'm even pretending with You, aren't I? I'm falling in love, I'm panicking over how we'll ever see each other, and I know all our ideas are gonna fail. Her parents aren't going to pay for her to come to California when she lives only a couple of miles from RU, and I'll never have the money to go there—Baba wouldn't pay for it. I need that education if I'm going to hope to ever get a decent job.*

Despite his more practical thoughts, Zain found himself stopping her as she reached for the door handle. "Audrey…"

"Yeah?"

"I—I'm falling—" *Don't say the L word! Not yet!* "—for you."

"Yeah…I know what you mean." A giggle escaped. "That was lame. I can hear it now. 'So what did she say when you told her you I—fell for her?'"

"Love works. It's crazy but it's true."

"Anyway," she continued, but Zain noticed a shift in her demeanor—a shift that could only mean she liked hearing it. "I can just hear it. 'Well, she said, 'I know what you mean.'"

"I think I *do* know what you mean," Zain said, tugging her away from the door and pulling her into a hug. "If I had the guts to kiss you—"

"There is something a bit revolting when you hear the words guts and kiss together. Kind of grody."

"Sorry."

"I'm not… I get the feeling I just might get a kiss out of it—to make up for it and everything."

Chapter Seventeen

Sunday, December 21st—Fairbury

Kelly sat shivering in the van, but Jon and Aiden still hovered near the entrance of the church. "Come on, let's go. It's freezing out there."

Jon waved at her, which Kelly took as a request to bring the van closer—why, she couldn't imagine. But as she neared the front of the building, Jon waved her on and began walking, Aiden by his side. A glance in the rear view mirror, once she turned out of the parking lot, sent a wave of panic through her. *What's wrong, Lord? Jon looks ready to blast the poor kid. Did he get out of line in Sunday School? Say something rude? Why would—*

"Why's Daddy not comin'?"

She tried to smile at her son in the mirror as she navigated through packed streets and into their neighborhood. "I think they wanted to walk."

"I could walk. I'm a good walker."

"Why is everyone always supposing that I am not a good walker?" The line from *Persuasion* tickled her, taking her mind temporarily off the questions surrounding Aiden.

However, once she had Nathan inside and changed from his little suit into more—she snickered at the thought—suitable clothing for play, Kelly didn't quite know how to handle the issue of lunch. *Do I wait for them? Feed Nathan and put him in bed? If Aiden is in trouble of some kind, it might be nice if Nathan wasn't in the middle of it all, trying to understand and distracting us from a serious discussion.*

That did it for her. She pulled the tamale casserole from the stove, scooped a bit out for Nathan, and replaced it, turning the oven down to just warming temperature. "Do you want some milk with that?"

"Juice?"

"Sorry, buddy. No juice, but we have milk and we have water."

The little guy propped his head on his hand, resting his elbow on the table, and considered his options with more forethought than many people do for expensive purchases. Just as Kelly was ready to decide for him, he sat up and grabbed his fork. "Milk, please."

"And there you have it. You are your father's son. Milk with spicy food."

"Yum! Can I have salsa?"

"Sorry. Don't have any." She took a slow, steadying breath and tried not to feel like a financial failure for not making the grocery budget stretch far enough for her son's favorite "condiment."

She waited half an hour after Nathan went to sleep before giving up and dishing up some food. Her blood sugar levels threatened her with revolt if she didn't, so she fixed a plate, sat alone at the table, and chewed with utter disinterest in the meal she'd been looking forward to for days. Even once she'd finished and rinsed her plate, Jon and Aiden hadn't appeared yet.

Busywork failed to keep her mind off whatever had delayed her husband and child. She hung Nathan's little jacket and pants, clipping the tie through the lapel buttonhole. She changed clothes, hanging her dress and brushing off both their shoes outside. One little task after another chipped away the minutes but still no sign of her menfolk.

Well over an hour later, Jon stepped inside the door and closed it firmly behind him. Aiden wasn't there. "Where's—"

"At Mom and Dad's."

"What'd he do?"

Jon's eyes flashed. "What did *he* do? You're serious," he added as his eyes searched her face. "I don't believe this."

"What are you talking about?"

"About," he said with an obvious attempt at self-control, "our *son* hearing in church about his parents' upcoming *divorce!*" He didn't yell—not exactly—but for Jon Cox, the emphasis, the slight raise of his voice, and the fury that he fought to control might have been equivalent to a tirade in a less self-controlled man.

Later, Kelly admitted that only the hormonal ditziness of pregnancy could have prompted such an obtuse question, but she quite seriously did ask, "We're getting a divorce?"

"Think, Kelly! Why on earth would our son think such a thing? How could he have heard something so disturbing at church? Why would any child have said something like that to him? This isn't incomprehensible."

"Oh." Her eyes widened. "Oh, no. He didn't really think—"

"What is he supposed to think? Some kid asks who he is going to live with, and the Sunday school teacher says, 'Oh, we don't discuss private family problems in class. We'll just pray for the family.' What's he supposed to think, Kelly?"

"But you told him—"

"Yes! I told him. You don't get it. You still do not get the problem. This is what happens when you involve yourself in other people's business. Other people start rearranging yours into this kind of garbage."

Her throat swelled, making it impossible to talk. She swallowed, took a sip of her drink, and swallowed again, her eyes never leaving Jon's face. Jon, on the other hand, seemed incapable of looking at her. The

159

longer she had to think about things, the angrier she grew. Once she did manage to choke out a few words, Kelly suspected they were not the contrite, repentant ones Jon expected to hear. "I'm not going to pretend that what I did was at all acceptable. We both know it wasn't. But you said you forgave me. You said that Jesus had covered it in His blood."

"I also said that the consequences don't—"

"—just go away because of that. I know that. But I just wasn't aware that one of those consequences would be you tossing my mistakes back in my face every time they affected one or more of us."

"So this is my fault."

"No, what happened is one hundred percent my fault and you know I've not pretended otherwise. But other people taking idle gossip and sharing it with their friends and families is not my fault. My fault is that I was nosy. I invaded Audrey's privacy. I read things I shouldn't have. I contacted a strange man because I was being a busybody and 'prying into other people's affairs.'"

"That sums it up pretty well."

"And your fault is going back on your word to forgive. You're angry because you're embarrassed. You're angry because you see this as a mark against your reputation. You are angry—with me—because people are talking about you. That's not my sin. Even when I think about it, there was nothing wrong with me talking to Bentley—"

"You shared private—"

"I did not!" Kelly stood as her voice rose. "Jon, I gave no names. I said nothing that should indicate it was me or anyone else. I asked her opinion on where her ideas could go. I was wrong to do what *prompted* that question, but the question wasn't wrong or sinful. Bentley talking to her husband about it wasn't even wrong or sinful. She should go to him. But Mrs. Paulson listening in on that conversation and then sharing it with anyone—both things were wrong and I am not responsible for that!"

Silence hung between them. Kelly began to wonder if she hadn't gone too far—even if perhaps she was wrong. Jon's tone cut deeper than his words when he whispered in ragged attempts to speak. "I can't believe you're standing there yelling at me. We've never done that."

"That was wrong," she admitted quickly. "I'm sorry."

He didn't look at her—didn't respond.

Kelly hated the way it would sound—like justification of her actions—but the words seemed to take over. They began in her heart and mind and flowed from her as if with wills of their own. "And I can't believe you're standing there in continual condemnation of what you said you forgave. You've never held my faults over my head before." When he didn't speak, her shoulders slumped and she asked, "Do you want me to go to Audrey? Do you want me to go to town and tell everyone I know that the rumors are bald-faced lies? What do you want me to do?"

Jon's only answer was to leave the room.

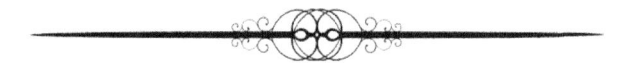

They ate dinner in relative silence, speaking only to Nathan when the boy asked a question or made a comment. Aiden didn't return home, opting to spend the night at his grandparents' house. She washed the dishes and put away the food. He cleared the table and cleaned up Nathan. The clock inched its way toward seven o'clock before Jon spoke. When he did, Kelly's face wrinkled in confusion.

"What?"

"I want you to go caroling with me."

"Where'd that come from?"

Jon tried to smile; she had to give him credit for that. With a lopsided attempt at a grin that came out more like a grimace, he repeated his request. "I want you to go caroling with me. It's what we normally would do. We'd normally take the boys, of course," he added thoughtfully, "but I think it might be best if we didn't this time."

"And why would we do that—sing with people like Mrs. Paulson?" Kelly stared at him, her hands dripping dishwater all over the floor.

"I just think we were planning to go with them anyway, so we should go. They'll expect one of us, or neither of us, or maybe even the whole family to put on a show, but just us there..." he shrugged. "It might make a difference. Maybe."

"I'm liable to say something if anyone even looks at us weird. You know that?"

This time, a hint of a genuine smile appeared. "That I well believe."

Nathan sing-songed all the way to the Cox Grandparents' home—silly songs about going to see the "goat grandma." Kelly rolled her eyes. "It's a good thing your parents are difficult to offend."

Their relationship still wasn't the same. Kelly didn't expect it would be. Of all things Jon disliked most, being the center of any attention—particularly the kind that attacks privacy—would top the list. However, the moment he opened her door, he didn't stop touching her. He held her hand as they walked to join the group of singers. He stood with his arm around her waist while the groups were divvied up evenly for each truck. Once seated on a hay bale at the back of the flatbed, his arm draped around her shoulder as he laughed and joked with those closest to him.

Each action, as normal and comfortable as it might look to others, was a deliberate act of love from a man much more comfortable with private affection and quiet camaraderie. Kelly's courage rose with each song, each murmured encouragement. The confused looks of several of their companions told her his decision had been a good one—the right one. *Not that I should be surprised. It usually is.*

Things seemed almost normal until the break at the church for warming and hot chocolate. Audrey pulled her aside almost the minute they stepped down from the vehicle and dragged her to the far corner of the fellowship hall. "I'm going to ask you flat out. Is everything okay with you and Jon?"

"If you mean am I leaving him for some other man, the answer is no. The rumors are one hundred percent false."

"I figured they had to be, but then you did say you needed to talk to me—"

"And I still do. Got time the day after Christmas?" Kelly wanted to dump it all right there, but the relief and happiness on Audrey's face told her to keep her mouth shut and stick with her agreement with Jon and Zain.

"Sure." Audrey leaned forward and whispered, "I have to admit. I'm relieved. Mrs. Paulson said something to me before you guys got here and I kind of went off on her. I am so glad I wasn't wrong."

Kelly giggled. "Man, that I would have liked to see."

"I'll make an effort to straighten people out if I hear any more. With you guys here and obviously not at odds, I think that'll die a natural death."

"That was Jon's opinion. I think he'd rather have stayed home, but he loves me."

Something flitted across Audrey's face—an expression she'd seen before, but this time she thought she knew what it meant. *She wants a real relationship. Would she take one with Zain or is she against it now, even though she says she still loves him?* The realization that she still based thoughts and opinions on information she wasn't supposed to know, prompted her to smile, hug her friend, and walk away before the temptation to speculate further created an even bigger mess.

Chapter Eighteen

Monday, December 22nd—Santa Monica

Tomorrow is our twenty-fifth anniversary—of our first date anyway. First and only, but could it have been any more perfect? Doubt it. He gnawed on the inside of his lip. *I could go. Baba thinks I should. Joe thinks I should. Aida and Mama think I should.* He gripped the desk, ready to shove back his chair and bolt, but pride forced him to hesitate. *She might hate me. I mean, Kelly said the letters say she still loves me, but that doesn't mean she doesn't hate me, too. I didn't fight for her. I was a coward.*

Those words squeezed his lungs until he felt like he had to fight to breathe. *All these years, I've blamed her for leaving, but did I give her a reason to stay? Did I go after her? No, I just answered a letter with a string of numbers and let her go. This was my fault.*

Zain picked up the phone and dialed his brother's extension. Through the glass windows of their offices, the two men's eyes met. Yosef picked up the phone slowly, as if aware that something had changed. "Yeah?"

"What if I go?"

"Go where?"

Just as Zain opened his mouth to tell Yosef not to play stupid, he realized his brother's meaning. "Go back to the beginning—try again." He swallowed hard and added, "Tomorrow is our anniversary."

"I thought—"

"Of our first date," he clarified. "I could get a flight tonight or in the morning."

"Why haven't you made the reservation yet?"

There's the answer you wanted, so why are you still hesitating? "Do I bring a gift? I should, shouldn't I?"

"You're going for your anniversary and at Christmas. C'mon, you bring a gift or three. Maybe that one you got her in Vegas?"

"Joe!"

Zain shook his head and hung up the phone. His eyes met Yosef's again. After a few seconds his brother pretended to pick up the phone as he mouthed, *"Call Baba."*

*I should. He won't tell me what he thinks I want to hear. He'll tell me what I **need** to hear. Lord, I really wish he would become a Christian. Can you imagine his wisdom influenced by Your Word? What else could a son want?*

Tariq answered on the first ring, out of breath and the faint hum of the treadmill adding white noise to the conversation. "If you tell me you've started a harem, I'll ship you overseas and let the family have you."

"Very funny." Zain swallowed his nerves and forced himself to ask the question. "Should I go?"

"Go where? Go to this little town where your wife lives all alone and tries to keep busy without her husband there, yes. You should. You should go beg her forgiveness. You should go tell her that you are her husband and you failed her, but you are here now and you *will* be the man she deserves to have."

"You don't know anything about her, Baba!"

"I know she did not divorce you. You abandoned her—"

"Technically," Zain protested, "she abandoned *me.*"

"You are the man. You have the responsibility. You did not do your job. You did not try to salvage your marriage. You did not even release her with a divorce.

You deprived her of a marriage—of children—"

"Okay, okay. I get the point. I should go."

"And bring her a present. A nice one—really nice. What do women love?" He called for his wife. "Sarah, what should Zain buy his wife to show he is sorry? She needs a good gift. What?"

Zain couldn't hear his mother's response, but the ensuing argument made him roll his eyes at his brother. Yosef laughed, tears running down his face as he struggled to type something. A message popped up on his open Facebook page. YOU KNEW THIS WOULD HAPPEN. BABA WANTS A CAR OR A GADGET. MAMA WANTS JEWELRY. WHAT'LL IT BE?

Zain hesitated before he typed back, IF THIS WORKS, BOTH. IN A MANNER OF SPEAKING.

"I have to go, Baba. I'll let you know when I'm going to be gone."

"Go big—an iPad maybe."

Zain disconnected as his finger hesitated over the mouse button. He stared at the URL bar and tried to remember the name of any travel site he'd ever seen, and his brain froze. His eyes rose again and met his brother's through the glass once more. Without a thought for what their employees would think, he shouted, "Where the heck do I go? I can't think!"

Yosef sauntered into his office and leaned against the doorjamb. "I think the nearest airport is Rockland..."

"Yeah, but what's the name of that travel site where you can book tickets? I can't remember!"

Laughing, Yosef took over the keyboard and typed "airfare rockland" into the Google search bar. Instantly, a dozen sites popped up. "Pick one. It's not rocket science."

Zain rubbed his chin, his beard distracting him. "Should I shave?"

"What?"

"I didn't have a beard back then. What if she hates it? She didn't sign up for a husband with a beard."

"Are you for real?" Yosef cracked up. "Like she

hasn't done anything at all since then? You think she's never cut her hair? You think she's never changed her makeup style or maybe her clothing style? C'mon!" He leaned forward and added, "And Baba would say she didn't sign up to be a single spouse either."

"Rub it in, Joe. Man!"

But Yosef ignored him. His finger pounded the down arrow key until he found something he liked. "There. That one. It's not crazy expensive like the others but you still get in tomorrow in time to relax, have something to eat, and then see her before the store closes."

The words struck a fresh wave of disappointment over him. "Oh. I didn't even think. She'll be busy. It's Christmas!"

"So you show up near the end of the business day, you go in—"

Zain didn't hear anything else Yosef said. New thoughts swirled until he got dizzy. "I just thought of something."

"What's that?"

"I might have to move."

"Aren't you getting a bit premature?" Yosef clapped a hand on Zain's shoulder. "You know she might just send you right back home. You know this, right? You just can't—"

"I'm not coming right back, even if she sends me home. If we have a good conversation and agree mutually to keep things how they are, then fine, but otherwise, I'm not coming back until I know there's no hope or until I know that it'll take longer than I can stay, but if I have to move..."

"Because you don't want to bring her here?"

Zain swallowed as he stared at the screen. After a moment he murmured, "Because I'm not going to make that kind of expectation. If I go, I have to be willing to *leave father and mother and be joined*' to my wife."

The row of clothing before him he found singularly uninspiring. *You're not twenty anymore. You wouldn't want to look like you did back then. She'd laugh at you. And Joe is right. You need to be careful not to expect too much. Because this is probably not going to work.* That thought hit him hard. Frustrated, he jerked the suitcase from his bed and shoved it in the closet, closing the door.

"Why am I doing this? It's not going to work. She'll send me right home, and I can't blame her. I did this. I blew it over twenty years ago. Maybe after college I could have gotten her to consider trying again, but now?" Zain dug into his wallet. Under a stack of business cards, a well-worn photo tried to tear as he pulled it from the pocket. Audrey smiled back at him, her curls tumbling around her shoulders. "Did you ever order pictures?" His younger self stared back at him. "I bet you didn't. Maybe you didn't care as much as I did. Maybe you didn't remember or know how."

A fire safe file box at the bottom corner of his entryway closet held the rest of the package. Zain pulled out the sheet of wallets. "Maybe she'll want one. That might be a good way to gauge where she is on this. Yeah..."

Resolved, all doubts and uncertainties gone, Zain strode into his room, pulled out his carry-on bag, and began filling it with the warmest clothes he owned. Jeans, sweatshirts, dress sweater, slacks, blazer, dress shirt, tie. The bag filled quickly. After several repacks, he managed to squeeze in socks, underwear, sweats and a t-shirt for sleeping. He started to pack a toothbrush and toothpaste, and hesitated. *Gotta buy shampoo and stuff like that when I get there anyway. I'll just leave it. Stupid Patriot Act. They oughtta take lessons from the Israelis instead of all this nonsense.*

He remembered his Bible just as he finally managed to force the zipper shut and latch the cover clasp. *Laptop case. It'll have to go in there. Should I take our marriage certificate? Would I need it?*

"Now you're just getting ridiculous. Grab the life insurance policy papers though. She should have 'em if you're going to see her." At second thought, he grabbed the marriage certificate, too.

Zain gripped the handle of his suitcase and jerked it from the bed. There was something unnerving and final about seeing it sitting beside the door. As a reminder, and possibly a way to hide it from himself, he dropped his heaviest coat over it. Laptop, power cord, and phone charger made it into the laptop bag and sat by the door as well. He dumped the perishable contents of his fridge in his trash can and carried it out to the dumpster. The sight of the bank of mailboxes popped a flaw in his carefully constructed plan, so he sent a last minute text to Yosef. **FORGOT ABOUT THE MAIL. CAN YOU PICK IT UP EVERY FEW DAYS?**

The reply came within seconds. **WILL DO. YOU NERVOUS?**

"How could I not be," he muttered as he strolled through the narrow walkway to his door. A neighbor eyed him curiously.

"What's that?"

"Talking to myself." He paused. "Look, I'm going out of town for a week or two. My brother'll be stopping by to check on things like mail and such. Can I give you his number in case something happens?"

The man, Austin, nodded. "Sure. That'd be good. Save me calling the cops if your smoke alarm goes on the fritz again."

Fire department would be more effective, but you call whoever you like, Zain growled to himself. "Excellent."

Within the hour, he lay in his bed, hands behind his head on the pillow, staring up at an inky black ceiling. Sleep refused to come. A glance at the clock told him he had seven hours before he had to walk out the door. Another glance, seemingly hours later, showed six and a half hours to go. Frustrated, he propped his extra pillow against the electric blue glare of the clock numbers. *Joe would say it's what I get for still using an alarm clock instead of my phone.*

In the space of the next two hours, he revisited the idea of a gift commemorating their first date. *Maybe I should. I mean, not everyone has only a single date before they get married—not when their parents aren't involved. Not in America.* He revisited the idea of waiting to buy a gift in Rockland. *What if they don't have anything good left? I could be really risking things. But I don't want to carry anything of value through security, and it's not like I'll have time now. I could overnight something tooooooo...where?* His brain paused there. *Her shop! I could send it there. Maybe. Would they do same day delivery an hour away? Surely they could.*

And, he revisited the idea of the trip altogether. *It's crazy. I'm getting all worked up over this like some stupid teenager. I wasn't this nervous and eager back when we were in Vegas. It was all so matter-of-fact then. It made sense. If we were married, we'd **have** to find a way to make it work. Simple as that.*

Sometime between the decision to stick with just a combination Christmas and anniversary present, and the decision to go at all, Zain slept, and as he slept, he dreamed of a wedding party of homeless bridesmaids and groomsmen, cheering and waving stuffed white socks instead of throwing bird seed or blowing bubbles.

Chapter Nineteen

Christmas Eve—Las Vegas

Audrey's denim jacket didn't look like it kept out much cold at all, but she insisted she was perfectly comfortable. "Your blood's too thin or something," she'd insisted after he tried to talk her into something warmer. He'd also tried to talk her into a cab, thinking she'd at least be out of the stiff breeze that threatened to become a strong, windy morning. She'd said no to that, too. "Too expensive."

So they walked north, following the route to the Strip from University Avenue and Maryland Parkway to Flamingo. But as they turned onto Paradise Road, the wind now at their backs, Audrey reached for his hand. "Two more days. I can't believe it's almost over."

"Yeah..." *As if you couldn't say something stupider. Dufus.*

"I keep wanting to say bogus stuff—like I can do any of it."

"Like what?" *Like **your** ideas? Get more jobs, move home and take the bus to school and ask Baba for the savings. I can hear it now, "You want me to pay you to live in my home so that you can fly halfway across the country to see a girl you met somewhere? She's not one of us, so what could you possibly have in common?"*

The closer they came to the Strip, the more

agitated she grew. "I can just see me trying to explain it to my mom and dad. 'He's a really cool guy, and we really hit it off, and I want to fly to Los Angeles so we can go on a date.' Yeah, like that'll fly."

A billboard caught his attention, and he tried to make a joke of it. "There's our answer."

She stopped in the middle of the sidewalk and stared at the advertisement for a cheesy wedding chapel. "That's not funny."

"Sorry."

"Another thing," Audrey added as she began walking again, "I'm not into the whole getting down on one knee thing, but when I do get engaged, I want it not to be something so generic that I have to wonder if it's real. So don't joke about it."

"What if it was real?"

She gave him a sidelong glance and then pulled her hand from his, shoving both of hers in her pockets. "I'd have to be able to tell it was or I'd just get P.O.'ed." A second or three later, she added, "Besides, it's not like we're going to do anything like that anyway, so the whole conversation is just bogus."

However, the idea had taken root. "But we could. I mean, it's fast—crazy fast—but it's one way to be sure we actually get to *see* each other. I mean, if we're married, who can stop us? Are your parents going to insist on some kind of annulment or divorce?"

"Don't believe in divorce outside of adultery." She kicked a Coke can. "But I'd divorce a guy who hit me anyway. God'd have to understand, because I'm no man's punching bag."

"Seems reasonable to me." His heart tried to pound its way out of his chest as he continued. "Then they'd want you to see your husband, right? We could find a way." The moment he said the words, Zain realized how ridiculous it sounded. "You're right. I'm being stupid."

He felt her fingers lace through his again half a block later. "I like that you want to see me, though. It means something."

They passed The Chapel of the Bells, and Zain forced himself to talk about anything but the growing idea that maybe, just maybe, it wasn't so crazy to want to get married. *We're adults. We're Christians. We have similar interests. We get along and haven't had a moment where we didn't have something to talk about. I've never been so comfortable with anyone. Why wouldn't it work? Why does it have to be a big long thing where we write and write, call once in a while and tick off our parents, and then finally get to see each other? Why do we have to wait a year or two or four? I can't imagine wanting to marry anyone else now that I've met Audrey.* He shifted his eyes just slightly as he saw her glance over her shoulder. *And I think she's feeling the same. It's just—*

"I wonder how hard it is."

"How hard what is?"

She hesitated, stopping in the middle of the sidewalk again. "To get married here. Like, I mean, people talk about it like you just decide to do it and bam. Done. Just like those weird romances my aunt reads about those people in England who ran away to Scotland, said, 'I'm married to Lord Runnaway' and bam. They're married because they said they were.'"

"Never heard of it." He followed her eyes to the silly bells hanging over the sign. "But they wouldn't have the reputation for making it easy if it wasn't."

"Bet you still have to get a license, and you know they'd be closed on Christmas Eve."

Zain glanced at his watch. "Well, unless they stay open until noon or something. Maybe in a town like this. Or maybe the chapels have people who can issue them. Probably do. That'd make sense." Even as he spoke, his mind screamed, *Do you hear yourself? Do you hear her? You're talking like it's going to happen. She's not running. Marriage isn't something you do to say, "Yeah, I had the full Vegas experience. Helped some homeless, ate at a great restaurant, saw a cool show, got married—"* It just doesn't work that way.

Her high tops became objects of extreme fascination, or so it seemed by the intensity with which she studied them. "I can't even believe I'm going to say this, but, like, it wouldn't hurt to ask. I mean, even if we decided we wanted to do it sometime down the road—Easter Break or something. We could meet here—"

"Let's ask. Like you said, it can't hurt."

Ten minutes later, they stood in front of the building again, indecision plaguing him and nerves making her as jittery as a two year old on a pot of coffee. "It's good for a year," he murmured.

"And they're open three sixty-five. Wow. What government offices are open on Christmas? That's almost wrong!"

His watch told him they'd have to hurry if they wanted to eat and get back to the mission by noon. Even hurrying, they'd have to take a taxi. "Let's find someplace to eat."

"I bet the Sahara has a buffet. It's close." Audrey waited until he turned to head back to it before adding, "Did we really just go into a wedding chapel and ask what you have to do to get married here?"

"Yeah..."

"Why does it sound less insane all the time?"

Zain didn't know how to answer her. The same question kept spinning in his mind. The rational side of him pointed out that he had no steady source of income—no way to feed a wife, much less give her a place to live. She also had no way to help out. They'd be a couple of minimum wage people living in one expensive city or another. But a romantic side he hadn't known existed had taken over his mind and heart, insisting that people had done similar things before and made them work. *Why shouldn't it work for two people committed to one another and to Jesus?*

"I don't know. I just know that every time I tell myself that we can do it at any time—we don't *have* to do it right now—I panic as if I know that if we don't, we never will."

They navigated through the parking and into the casino, skirting the gambling areas in search of food. Neither spoke until they sat behind menus and stared at them in silence. Audrey dropped hers after a moment and said, "That's exactly how I feel. And I hate it. The idea makes me want to ralph."

"Is it real?"

"What?"

He shrugged and tried again. "This—us. Whatever you call it. Is it real?"

Zain's heart sank as she shook her head. "Nuh uh. You're not doing that. If you want to ask me what I think or feel or whatever, then ask me, but don't put everything on me. Don't make me have to read your mind, too."

"Why does it all have to be on me?" The moment he spoke the words, Zain tried to drown them out with something less pathetic. "You're right. I want to know, so it's on me. Fine."

"Zain—"

"No, really. That was just totally wussy of me. Sooo… I guess what I want to know is, do you like—love—care about—something me as much as I—you can't answer that either. You don't know. Man this is hard."

"So I take it you like me." Her smile told him she was going somewhere with her question.

"No duh."

"Right. Then," Audrey added, a smile sending his heart racing in new directions. "What about the care thing? You care about me."

"No." Her shocked eyes made him laugh. "What I mean is that I'm just being a dufus about this. I told you I was falling for you. Well I am—or did—or—"

The waitress appeared in time to save him from making an awkward moment unbearable. He ordered an omelet and grinned as he listened to her order her Belgian waffle with strawberries and whipped cream.

Love that about her. She enjoys everything to the max. That thought echoed in his mind until he only heard *"Love her"* repeatedly.

"So what are we going to do, Mr. I'm-falling-for-you-or-maybe-more?"

"Can you love someone you've known less than a week?"

She didn't meet his gaze but her head nodded, albeit a bit hesitantly. "I guess. I mean, my aunt swears she fell in love with my uncle in six and a half minutes."

"Why that long—or short?"

"That's how long it took him to give his testimony at church." Audrey took a sip of her water and winked. "I always asked how she knew how long it took him to give it. It's not like she timed him or anything."

"There's this old couple at my church—been married for almost sixty years. He says they met and married in two weeks."

Her laughter sent curious looks their direction, but Audrey didn't seem to notice. "Well, they say everything happens faster these days."

Their plates arrived. They prayed. They ate, and they ignored the subject as they focused on the one thing that didn't require a decision—their food. Long after they finished, they took turns watching one another, Zain playing with her hands or Audrey squeezing his at just the perfect moment. She spoke first. "What's the worst thing that would happen if we got the license?"

"We throw thirty-five bucks away?"

"Am I worth it?"

His heart thudded at the question. *She's coming around. Wow.* "Let's walk." He tried to hide the deliberate choice to continue north past the chapel again, but her giggle told him he'd failed.

"Okay, I answered the first question; you answer mine."

"Deal."

Audrey grabbed his hand and moved a little faster in what appeared to be an attempt to keep her talking. "So what's the worst thing that happens if we actually do it—get married?"

"We find out we hate each other?" The moment he said it, Zain shook his head. "Nope. Not possible. Ummm... we find out we don't know how to do this marriage thing and it drives us apart?"

"So we get a new map and drive back together. I hate it when people say that." Audrey dropped her voice to a deeper, low-pitched tone. "'Oh, we just drifted apart, so we're getting a divorce.'"

"No divorce. And get out your oars and row until you're back in the same boat again—sticking with your analogy or metaphor or whatever that was." Zain flushed. "Not my best subject. Good with spelling and basic grammar, not so good with story structure and stuff."

"Right. Okay so we'll probably have problems. So we work on them and fix them. We go into this expecting them so we're not shocked when we find out that waking up to halitosis is grody." She shuddered. "Can we make an agreement to always keep Certs by the bed so we don't gag when we say 'Good morning' to each other?"

"Deal." His sub-conscience told him to rewind what she'd said. "Wait. Did you just say what I think you did?"

"What?"

Maybe you shouldn't say it. You don't want to pressure her. That's just wrong. But he did. "You just asked for an agreement after we're married. Does that mean we're doing it?" He held up his hands, waving her off. "No. No. Don't answer that."

Audrey's face fell. "Okay."

Lord, what do I do? I mean, the least I could do is ask. Should I? Is this wrong? Right? Crazy but doable? Crazy and certain to fail? What is this? As he expected, no answer came from the heavens, telling him exactly what he should do.

However, Audrey said, "You know that verse about how a guy who finds a wife finds a good thing?"

"Yeah. What about it?"

"Is there an equal one for girls? I mean, is it good if we get married or just guys?"

Zain shrugged but his mind raced through every scripture he'd ever read, heard, or prayed. "All I can think of is about widows and that one about how so you don't fall into sin, get married. Every wife have her own husband, husband his own wife—that one."

"Okay. Good."

"What?"

The wind tossed her hair into her face, but Audrey adjusted her jacket, pulling it all under the collar and out of the way. "I just thought if there wasn't any—and I couldn't remember any so you know, I thought maybe there was a reason for it—anyway if there wasn't any that told women, 'get married' then I wouldn't even consider it. Just to be on the safe side."

The logic seemed skewed to him, but as they neared West Charleston Boulevard, Audrey smiled up at him and all his uncertainties fled. "I want to do it."

Her eyebrows drew together, but a smile formed on her lips. "What?"

"Get married. I don't want to go home without you—or you to go home without me. Whichever. We'll make it work. I just know that if we don't do this, something's gonna happen."

"I thought that too," Audrey admitted, "but then I thought maybe that meant we shouldn't. I mean, if being separated like that is enough to keep us apart, then is it real enough to make it worth the risk?"

"Even people who have good marriages for years, if they never spend time together, will discover life without the other. They can live in the same house and not know each other anymore. Why would we deliberately put something in our paths to make it harder to do what we want to do?"

"Yeah. True. Kind of like it doesn't matter how great the seeds and soil are, if you don't water 'em, nothing's gonna grow." Audrey giggled. "My preacher uncle gets to me sometimes. I've heard that one a lot in regards to friendships. Why not marriage?"

Zain didn't speak again until they reached their next turn. "Is that the street? Left on Bridger?"

"Yeah. They said turn right there and right onto South 3rd."

They hadn't expected the enormous line of people waiting out the doors and onto the sidewalk. Surprisingly enough, it moved quickly. They found themselves inside the building within a matter of minutes. *We're really doing this. Of course, "this" is just getting the license—one we'll probably never get the guts to use after all, but still. We're doing it.* Her demeanor shifted and he smiled. *No, we're actually **doing** it. We're going to get married. This is totally cool.* "Did I ever ask you if you'd marry me?"

"Nope."

"You said you wouldn't do it if I didn't—ask that is."

Audrey tried to stifle a smile, but he saw it nonetheless. "I decided not marrying you was worse than not being asked."

"So, I'll probably have to spend the next twenty-five years polishing my romantic skills after this pathetic proposal, but since we're standing in line for a license, um—" Zain glared at a woman nearby who gave a shocked gasp. "*Will* you marry me?"

"Yep. Just as soon as they give us the okay, because we're already so late it isn't funny."

His watch told him it was just past eleven. "We're not late yet."

"And," Audrey insisted, "there are a hundred people ahead of us. I don't care how fast this line goes, we're never going to make it."

"We could make it a Christmas present—tomorrow between the dinner and cleanup—just get a cab and go for it."

The bored voice of the woman behind the desk at the back of the room startled them. "Next."

Audrey leaned closer and whispered, "I feel like I'm in a cattle drive or something."

"Okay, good."

"What!"

Chuckling, Zain whispered back, "I thought it was just me."

The couple ahead of them answered the questions with almost as indifferent a tone as the woman who asked them, "Date of last divorce finalization."

"November twenty-second," the woman said.

Zain and Audrey's eyes met, somewhat horrified by the timing. *That paper says you have to wait thirty-days. It's been almost exactly that long. Wow.* Once the couple walked away and they were called with the same monotonic "Next," Zain pulled Audrey back and whispered, "No divorce, right? We make this work. I won't cheat on you. I won't verbally or physically abuse you. You won't either. We stay married no matter what."

"Agreed."

Together they stepped up to the woman's desk and handed over their driver's licenses.

Chapter Twenty

Tuesday, December 23rd—Rockland

Zain stood at the Avis counter, waiting to hear the verdict. After one company failed to produce the car he'd reserved, he'd tried three others—with no success. Avis was almost his last shot before he'd have to dash to make the Fairbury shuttle.

The man, Rich, behind the counter winced. "I'm afraid I can't help you." Zain's face fell and then grew resigned as Rich continued saying, "All I can give you is a twelve passenger van."

"I'll take it."

"Really?" Rich's eyes flitted back and forth between Zain and the screen. "If you'll be anywhere around here tomorrow, you could come in and exchange sometime after four o'clock, but you'd have to make a reservation."

"Let's do that."

Rich glanced around him and leaned forward. "If you wait an hour or so, one of the companies will have something, I'm sure. We don't tell people that, of course, but if you leave your number, the minute something unreserved comes in, they'll call you. On holidays, we don't usually offer—"

"Can you reserve something for me tomorrow? I'll just take this. I really need to get on the road."

Fingers clicked over a noisy keyboard as he worked

to type in Zain's license number. "Phone?"

Minutes passed as he waited for confirmation on his card, as he signed on every line and initialed every box, and as he chose to accept the additional coverage on a vehicle he suspected would be a deadly weapon in his hands—and feet. *If you thought you were going to ride into town and impress her and her neighbors with your trippendicular car and lookin' all fly, you're trippin. You're gonna show up now lookin' like a total barney poser.* He smirked as he accepted the keys and thanked Rich for his help. *And if you interject one more freakish 80's slang into your thoughts, I'm like gonna deck you myself.*

At the van, Zain froze. Wedged between two other big SUVs, in rows that looked too narrow to back a Prius out of, the vehicle mocked his driving skills. Frustrated, he unlocked the passenger door, stowed his bags on the seat, and locked it again. "Gotta find an employee."

Half an hour later, as the sun sank behind him, he whizzed down the highway to Fairbury. "Bet they'll be mocking me for a month. Probably have a pool already—how much damage will it return with?" As a car pulled out from a rest stop and Zain slammed on his brakes to avoid hitting it, he growled, "And why didn't they let me in on it?" To the car ahead of him, he shouted, "Um, hello? I know it's nearly impossible to see such a tiny vehicle, but I'm here, I'm actually much bigger than you, and I could have killed all of us. Pay attention, Sherlock!"

Zain enjoyed the catharsis his outburst provided a bit more than he suspected he should. As he neared the town, his nerves bundled and knotted into a nightmare that would make even the most dedicated Christmas light detangler cry "Uncle!" He tried singing, but his nerves took his barely on-key voice and turned it into a squeaky nightmare. He tried reciting every Scripture he could remember—and managed two, one of which was "Jesus wept."

"Zain Kadir, you are pathetic." He gripped the steering wheel tighter. "Lord, I need some help here. I keep putting a lot of hope into this thing, but it's entirely likely that she'll just tell me to go home and deal with the consequences of our decision." That thought galled. "But we didn't *make* a decision. We just—" He snickered. "One could say we just 'drifted apart.' Ohhh, I might have to use that. It might make her smile." A thought, one he'd never considered, made him pull to the side of the road, holding the steering wheel in a death grip. "What if she's changed—I mean a lot. We haven't had years to grow together so that changes are normal and natural. She's not going to be the same girl. I mean, she's not eighteen anymore. I'm not the same idealistic kid. What if she can't stand me—or vice versa? I did not think this out."

He pulled out his phone and dialed his father. "Baba?"

"Are you there? Have you seen her? Did she forgive you? Will—"

"Baba, please. Is this right? I have to know before I go any further, is this really right? I feel like I'm eight again. I don't know what to do. She probably despises me. If I show up, I'm going to disrupt her entire life. Is it wrong? Selfish—"

"Zain. Stop." Tariq waited a moment and said, "What does your Bible say?"

"About what?"

"About what a husband should be. Surely there is something in there about providing her food or protecting her from men who would steal her away. What does it tell you as a husband to do?"

That, Zain could answer. "It says to live with her in an understanding way. It says to love her and give myself up for her. It says to show her deference as a 'weaker vessel,' whatever that means."

"So you do that. How is it selfish to try to do that?" Tariq's voice dropped almost to a whisper. "I've never understood your fascination with Christianity, but you've been true to it from the beginning. I respect that, and I've defended you to friends and family who thought it was some kind of rebellion thing. I saw that it grieved you to hold fast to things you knew I didn't support."

With his head resting on the steering wheel, tears filled his eyes as Zain struggled to find his breath. "Baba…"

"What? Did you think I despised you?"

"Not me, but my Jesus, yeah. Maybe."

"Zain, you've always taken things very seriously—a little too seriously at times. I can see it with this marriage thing. You took your vows seriously enough. You didn't divorce her, and I read online that this is good. But you've missed out on years with her, and Mama says she thinks it's because you didn't want *me* to be angry." Tariq cleared his throat in that familiar way he always did when he tried to hide emotion. Zain waited, a bit nervously for what would come next. "All you did, my son, is truly anger me in seeing how you treated her. It was wrong. Go try to make it right. You can't, but try. Then you can go to your god with a clear conscience and say, 'I failed. I tried to make restitution. Please forgive me.' Right now, you are asking for cheap forgiveness. It's wrong, Zain."

All through his father's lecture, Zain wept. *Lord, the fear of one man—my father—kept me from seeing how wrong I was. I blamed her, and it made me feel justified.* Aloud, before he realized he'd said it, Zain murmured, "Oh, Baba. I wish you were a praying man. I wish you knew Jesus. I need—" He jerked his head off the steering wheel. "Oh—Ba—"

Laughter filled the phone. "I don't think my prayers will do you much good, but I could try. Maybe I'll call that teacher of yours. He will pray for you. His prayers would mean much, I'm sure."

"That you're willing to," Zain insisted. "That means a lot."

"Still, I'll find the number for Mr. Ahmed—"

"I have it. I'll text it to you." He swallowed the rising lump in his throat and added, "Thanks, Baba."

"You've got to get this settled. I don't think you've called me Baba this much since you were three. It's disturbing—nice, in a way—but also disturbing."

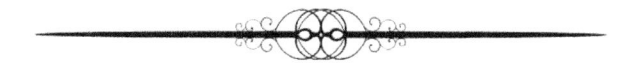

He hadn't noticed it on his last trip, but as he stood across the street staring at her building, the sign for Audrey's store made him smile. It had taken three passes before he finally read the store hours. *Holiday hours—close at eight.* He glanced at his watch again. Just past seven. Zain shivered. For the first time all evening, the store was empty and the streets nearly bare. *Why stay open so late if no one comes?* The answer came with a customer's arrival. The man dashed in and out of the store so fast, Zain hardly got a glimpse of Audrey at all. The moment the door closed behind the man, she stretched and disappeared into the back again. *She's probably finishing orders. Makes sense. Stay open since you'll be there anyway. Let people get last-minute gifts or pick up orders after work. Good business sense. Those classes must have been good ones.*

After another five minutes of shivering, and not another customer nearing the street, much less the shop, Zain crossed and started up the steps. Nerves hit. Desperate for some kind of support, he called Yosef. "Send good vibes—something—because I'm going in."

"You could call Jim. He'd understand. He'd pray and all that stuff."

Zain just groaned.

Yosef laughed at Zain and added, "Look, I'll vibe you all the way to the renewal of your vows if you like, but just text your friend and say, 'Got problems that really need a prayer or two—' Or however the lingo goes. Surely your god is big enough to figure out what he means, right?"

"You're right. Here goes nothing—but a text and a thanks to my little bro. You're a good guy, Joe."

"Tell Aida that. She expects something big for Christmas. I think she's figured out something's up and is milking it."

"Got it. I'll contribute. Go to Jared or something. Isn't that what all the women like?"

"She'd probably prefer a little blue box, but I can't afford anything worth buying from there."

He laughed. "Joe, I think the saying goes that 'it's the thought that counts,' but I think when you're talking Tiffany's, it's the 'box that counts.'"

"That should be their new slogan." Yosef sighed. "You're procrastinating. Get it over with—and call me. I'm doing that worrying thing now."

After a quick text that probably made even less sense to his friend Jim than it did to him, Zain forced himself up the steps and jerked open the door. The warm air hit him full-force. *That's better... so much better.*

"Be right with you—sorry. I let Stacy go home early and I've got my hands stuck in dough."

"Take your time." *Might as well take advantage of the opportunity to talk before she comes out.* "Nice store you have here."

"Thanks—you in town for the holidays?"

The sound of water told him she'd gone to wash her hands. *Showtime—or whatever it is this is.* "Sort of."

She appeared, her hair pulled back into a ponytail and tied up in a net. He smiled, his nerves probably turning it into a freakish-looking grimace, and said the only thing that came to mind. "Still having trouble with spelling, eh?"

Audrey reached for plastic food-service gloves and froze as the words reached her ears. "Wha—?"

"Surprise?"

"What kind of surprise? Wha—" Her eyes widened and her jaw drooped in a decidedly unflattering way.

Lord, don't let her know she did that, or she might kill me. "Happy Anniversary."

"That's not for two more days. What are—I didn't even recognize you."

"I think this is where I'm supposed to say you don't look any different at all or something, but you do—"

Her eyes flashed. "Gee. Thanks for reminding me. What are you doing here, Zain?"

"That was the beginning of a compliment," Zain insisted. "I was trying to say that you're more beautiful than I remembered."

"Yeah right. Seriously, why are you here?"

Right about now you should have had that gift Joe and Baba tried to talk you into. See what you get? "And I'm serious, too. It's the twenty-fifth anniversary of our first date, and—" A new thought occurred to him. "—I thought maybe we could have an anniversary dinner and talk."

Tears pooled in her eyes and trickled down her cheeks. "Why—why now? I don't get it."

"That's part of what I want to talk to you about."

"You can file for a divorce if you want it, Zain. I won't contest it, but—"

He leaned against the candy case as he shook his head. "I don't want a divorce."

"Then—"

His eyes slid around the room, lingering at the door. "Do you really want to talk about this here where anyone can walk in?"

"No!" Audrey crossed her arms over her chest and struggled with emotions that he could see but not decipher. "You're right. Later, okay. Um... no restaurant."

"I could make us something if you'd let me use your stove. I'm a decent cook."

Audrey nodded as she pulled a ring of keys from her pocket and worked one off it. "Four o' eight Bramble Rose Drive."

"How do I—" The door jingled as several women

burst into the room, laughing. Zain took it, allowing his hand to linger on hers long enough to see if it still sent the same electricity through him that it had all those years ago. *Wow. Is that just anticipation? Hormones? What?* "Thanks. I'll get directions."

As he reached for the door handle, she called out, "Wait. You didn't tell me about the spelling. What are you talking about?"

He gave the group of women a pointed look, but she nodded anyway. "The sign above the door. Some things never change."

"What's wrong with it?"

She's going to kill you for embarrassing her, his inner critic warned. *Then again, she didn't have to bring it up now.* "It's —ery, not —ary." An idea hit him in time to help her save face. "You should probably get a refund from the guy who made that thing."

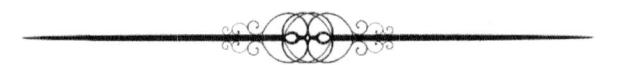

The women couldn't leave fast enough for Audrey's taste. Though twenty minutes early, the moment they disappeared from view of the windows, she locked the doors and turned out the front lights. She crawled through the steps of turning sweet dough into cinnamon rolls, her mind trying to process, to calm her, to pray. All three failed, repeatedly. *I haven't seen the man in twenty-five years. What is he doing here? Why? I don't get it. And what is wrong with me in that all I can think of is how good he looks? It's ridiculous.* She tried praying again and failed again. *I don't know what he wants, but if I make a fool out of myself, I'm blaming You. How's that?*

She scrubbed and prayed, mopped and prayed, ranted and prayed, and watched the clock until the moment she could pull the rolls from the oven and set them on the cooling racks. "Ten minutes in the oven in the morning and they'll be perfect. Nice."

Just past eight-thirty, Audrey locked the back door

behind her and hurried out into the frigid night air. *Should have driven this morning. Always seems so invigorating to walk **before** the day starts, but after, not so much.* Despite her sherpa-lined boots, long parka, scarf, and thick gloves, the cold rattled her bones until she realized it was nerves as much as degrees and wind-chill. A giant white van sat parked in the street at an awkward angle as she neared her house. *Poor fool's gonna get a ticket for that if one of the guys or Judith sees it. Bad—* The Avis sticker on the back window gave her pause. *If he brought his whole family, so help me they're gone. Out. I'm not doing this. Not at all. What kind of idiot comes back after all this time with a huge family in tow?*

Oscar must have been hovering near his door, because the moment she opened their common entryway, he pounced. "There's a man in there."

"I know."

A furrowed brow created the uni-brow of the century. "You do?" He leaned close as if to sniff her breath. "A man—in your house. He looks like one of them terrorists—Middle Eastern."

"Well, he's not. And he has my key because I gave it to him." *I'm allowed to have men over if I want. It's not a crime or a sin, so back off, buster.* Her conscience pricked and Audrey forced herself to give the man a reassuring smile. "He's an old friend who's making dinner for me. He's not a terrorist. He's a Christian, actually."

"Oh." The uni-brow began to separate. "That's good—I think. If you're sure. I could call Joe or one of the guys."

"If I need anything, I'll call or come get you. Thanks."

The scent of something beefy and spicy hit her nostrils the moment she entered the door. Zain stood in her kitchen, chopping something, but his head rose and he smiled at her. "Hey, it's almost done—maybe ten—fifteen minutes tops."

Audrey's mouth opened, but the only words she could formulate she refused to say. Instead she nodded and pointed upstairs, as if he could understand her pathetic attempt at sign language. Zain waved a knife in the same general direction. "Go change or shower or whatever you usually do. I've got this."

Within minutes, she stood gripping the bathroom sink with water dripping all around her and stared at her reflection. *Hi honey, I'm home? Seriously?* She shook her head as she glanced heavenward. *Lord, I owe you for that one. You stopped me just in time.*

Chapter Twenty-One

Man, she looks good. The moment the thought registered in his consciousness, Zain wanted to thrash himself. *You weren't that obsessed with her looks back when you were a kid with hormone issues. How shallow can you get?*

"—looks good."

"I was just thinking the same thing." Zain saw a flicker of irritation flash in Audrey's eyes and tried to salvage the discussion before it died a premature death. "Then again, I already said that. Sorry."

"What are you talking about?"

Confused, Zain carried plates to her table and returned to the kitchen to retrieve glasses and silverware. *Deep breath and try again.* "I'm sorry—"

"Stop apologizing. Just tell me what you already said, because I didn't hear anything." Audrey gripped the back of her chair. "Okay, now I'm sorry. No need to snap. I'm just—taken aback, I guess."

"I was just noticing your hair. You didn't change it. Baba thought you would have by now. But I already said you looked nice, so that's probably just annoying."

Her laughter relaxed him a little. She shook her head, pulled out her chair, and seated herself before he remembered that it might be a nice gesture for him to do something like that. "I said the food looks good—not you. Although," she added with a twist of her lips, that if he remembered correctly, meant she was annoyed with herself. "You do."

"I almost shaved."

"I'm glad you didn't." She waited for him to sit, asked him to pray, and picked up her fork before she added, "It was fun freaking out the neighbor. He thinks you're a terrorist. I promised you wouldn't bomb the building until he had a chance to get out."

The calm way she spoke, her deadpan expression—Zain almost fell for it. This time that hint of a wink he remembered gave her away as joking. "I forgot about your killer humor."

"Good pun."

Zain blinked as he tried to remember what he'd said and then grinned. "Can't take credit. Unintentional."

Half a dozen bites later, she spoke again. "Why are you here?"

"I told you."

She dropped her fork in her plate and grabbed her water glass, taking a swig as if it was a shot of whiskey to steady her nerves. "Fine. You're here for our anniversary. Why?" Before he could answer, her eyes met his and held them. "Did you say your father said I would have cut my hair?" Zain nodded. "You told him?"

"Finally, yes. Look, can we eat first? I fully expect to be thrown out on the street where I also expect a ticket for my pathetic parking job—"

"Oh, yeah. You'll get one, too. Where're your keys. I'll fix it."

"Eat first—"

But Audrey stood and held out her hand, her middle finger rubbing her thumb in a "Gimme" fashion. "If we've missed it already, it'll be a miracle. I saw Chad on beat tonight, so either Joe or Judith'll be in the car—both are sticklers for good parking."

He stared at his plate as she took his keys and disappeared through the door, pulling on her coat. A slow smile formed on his lips. *She said "we," Lord. "We've missed it already."* Why does that feel like *success somehow?*

Alas, his hope lasted only as long as the meal. The moment he stood to carry their plates to the sink, Audrey pounced. "Okay, so what the heck are you doing here, and don't give me that, 'I thought we should celebrate' garbage. After twenty-four other ignored ones, I don't see why this one makes any difference."

The phone, mail, airways, roadways—they all work both ways, Zain's heart protested. How he managed to say the right thing—the thing he wanted to be his only thought—he didn't know, but he heard himself murmur, "That was wrong of me. I'm sorry."

She moved to the couch and balled herself up in the corner—almost protectively. Zain followed and took the other corner, reminding himself to stay as relaxed as possible. Once he managed to get comfortable, she asked again, "Why are you here?"

"I told you—"

"Yeah, but it doesn't follow. There's something going on. Just tell me. If you're dying and need a kidney, then ask. It's yours if it'll help."

"As much as I am glad to know that, I'm not dying and my organs are perfectly healthy." He swallowed and tried to find a way to explain while keeping Kelly's name out of it. *Lord, why didn't I think of that? I don't know how to explain without ratting her out. Help.*

"Then what?"

"Something happened a few weeks ago," he began. "Anyway, what it was really isn't my story to tell—yet. I will, though—later, that is. What's important is that I started thinking about us—a lot."

"Is that one L or two?" Audrey shook her head and waved off his reply. "Sorry. I get stupid when I'm upset. Go on."

"Anyway, I finally got the courage to tell my father about us." Again, he realized he'd used the wrong words. "Look, I was a coward. I admit that. It was so wrong, but I kept justifying it. I have no excuse and not much of a reason."

"So your dad wants you to get a divorce."

"No." *It's too soon to tell her I want to make this work. I don't know what else to do, though.* "A lot of things happened before I told my parents, okay? I started seeing all these scriptures about vows and what married people are supposed to do and be for each other, and I failed you in those. I convinced you to marry me—secretly, no less—and then I broke those vows."

"I knew it. That girl on Facebook, huh?"

He had to force himself not to smile at the slight quiver of her upper lip. *She still cares about it in some fashion. That's promising.* "What girl?"

"You and some girl on Facebook a few years back. I was so mad. The one thing we said before we did this—the one thing—was that we'd stick it out no matter what. Then you went and found some other woman and—"

"I know the picture." He waited for her to meet his gaze, but she wouldn't look at him. "Audrey, that's my sister-in-law, Aida. That isn't even me in the picture, it's Joe."

Her eyes now flew up to meet his. "What?"

"Got a laptop or a wi-fi password?" He rose to retrieve his laptop bag, but she reached beside her and retrieved hers. "Here. Why?"

He pulled up the Facebook page, typed in his password, and navigated through the site until he found the picture he thought she meant. "That one?"

Emotions flitted across her face before she nodded and slid it back across the couch. "I can see it now. I just hadn't seen you in so long, that I assumed—"

"We look a lot alike. Always have." Zain tapped the screen before closing the laptop. "I don't post pictures of myself often—just once in a while if it's all of us or something." A new thought sent his hand digging into his pocket for his wallet. "There's one I'd *like* to post, though." He pulled out their wedding picture and passed it to her.

The tears he'd seen earlier resurfaced and cut him. Before he could apologize, something he'd begun to feel had become a new punctuation option for him, she whispered, "Where'd you get it?"

"They gave us that form, remember? I filled it out when I got home—had the basic package and our certificate sent to my dorm."

"Why?"

Of all the questions she might have asked, "why" wasn't one he'd prepared to answer. "I loved you. I really thought we'd work things out. I wanted to have that memory."

"When did you stop?"

Zain watched as new emotions took up the dance and drove off the old ones. "Stop what?"

"Loving me." The words came out in a choked whisper.

"I didn't." Before she could protest, he added, "But I sure acted like it. I broke our vows."

"Who was she—is she?" Audrey now met his gaze, eyes flashing. "You've got some nerve coming here, telling me you just want to spend our anniversary together and then springing some affair on me."

He leaned forward, reaching for her hand, but she pulled away. He sank back against the couch cushions trying to hide his disappointment. "There's more than one way to break your marriage vows, Audrey. You don't have to commit adultery to disobey what the Bible says to be as a husband."

"I don't get it. Is there another woman or not?"

"Not. I've never been interested in anyone else since I met you."

Audrey rose, looking weary and defeated. "You know what? Just go. I'm done. I don't know what you're doing here, and I don't know what you're talking about, but I do know you need to leave. We failed at being married, but we at least honored those vows."

"We didn't, Audrey. We didn't. That's—"

"No. Don't talk to me about it anymore. I can't do

this. Just go."

There was nothing else he could do. Zain stood and crossed the room to retrieve his coat and laptop case. "I'm sorry, Audrey. I still want to talk. We *need* to talk, but I guess after a long day of work wasn't the best time." He reached for the doorknob. "Oh, where's the nearest hotel?"

She'd started toward the kitchen, but at those words, she turned, her eyes wide. "You have *got* to be kidding me. You showed up here without reservations at the B&B?"

"I thought one of the towns nearby—"

"Wouldn't be booked solid for the holidays? You've got a shot at a skeezy room somewhere in Rockland at best, but there's not a hotel or motel around the rest of the loop that'll have a vacancy on Christmas Adam. Geez!"

Before he realized what happened, he smiled. Her angst rose half a dozen notches, but he preempted her rant. "Sorry, I've heard a few people say that over the years and it always makes me think of you."

"Not enough to call. Not enough to write. Just enough to show up here twenty-five years too late."

His heart sank. "I'll say it again. I'm sorry."

"Sorry doesn't fix things, Zain. Sorry is just a word that people use to get a clean slate. Well it doesn't work that way with me."

She's right. It's too much all at once. Maybe now that you've already destroyed Christmas, it might be good to see if Kelly can talk to her first. This would all make a lot more sense if she could see how I got to this place.

"You're right. I'll call tomorrow." She started to protest, but he grabbed the doorknob and said, "Oh... and where's the nearest Walmart? One that might be open this late?"

"What do you need a Walmart for?"

He dropped his bags and began ticking off items on his fingers. "Toothbrush, toothpaste, deodorant, soap, shampoo, conditioner—"

"I've got it here. Hold on."

"And a sleeping bag."

"What?" Audrey froze with the door to a closet beneath her stairs half open. "Why a sleeping bag?"

"I'll try calling around, but if I don't find a hotel soon enough, I'll just park that van behind your shop or over by the police station and sleep in it. I'm kind of glad that's all they had now—more room."

She didn't respond—not that he'd expected her to. Instead, she dug through the closet and returned with her arms full of toiletries. On the kitchen island—such as it was—she set them down and retrieved a "green" shopping bag from beneath the sink. Halfway through filling it, she gripped the edges of the counter top and took a visible breath. "Fine. Sleep on the couch. What do I care?"

Zain slung the laptop bag over his shoulder and met her on the other side of the island. "I care. I won't destroy your reputation that way. People will see. They will talk. Small towns like this—"

"Don't I know it. My housekeeper's marriage is apparently in jeopardy—ruined by some online affair, if you listen to the gossip. We've been trying to crush it for days now. Stupid people."

And that's partly my fault. Will you forgive either of us when you hear? "I appreciate it, though."

At the door, she stopped him again. "Don't. Just don't. It's not like people aren't going to want to know who you are now anyway."

The truth of her words hit him hard. "I should have called first—talked over the phone or through email—your website at least." His Adam's apple bobbed, and seeing it in the reflection of the kitchen window almost made him smile again. *On Christmas Adam, no less.* "I didn't want to chicken out. I wanted you to see my sincerity. I wanted you to have the chance to tell me what you think of me—face to face."

"Do you hear yourself? Every sentence was 'I

wanted' or 'I didn't want.' What about what I want?"

"Okay. Fair enough," Zain admitted. "We'll talk about that, but I promised no more tonight, and I've got to keep a promise to you, if only to prove I can. So, I'm going to leave you with one question to consider—a question about what you want."

Audrey skirted the island and returned to the closet. "Fine—but you're not leaving. You're not sleeping outside tonight. It'll be fourteen below." From within she called, asking, "What's the question?"

"Is this—what we've been doing for the past twenty-five years—is it what you want your marriage to be or do you want something more?"

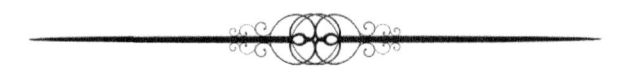

Audrey lay in bed, her mind on high alert as she listened for any hint of snoring or Zain moving around downstairs. As each second passed, she regretted telling him to stay. *But what else could I do? I mean, he'd freeze out there.* She rolled over, punching the pillow for comfort. *But if Tami or Diane stop by before he leaves, things are going to get awkward.* Her fists balled up the sheets and pulled them to her chin. *He told his family. I never thought he'd do that.*

Illogically and much to her chagrin, she wondered, not for the first time, if his beard was soft and silky or rough and scruffy. *That night after our date—standing out by the door making out in the shadows—* She swallowed hard. *If I hadn't already decided I was in love with him, I might have chalked it all up to hormones. I might have called it infatuation or even lust, but it wasn't—was it?*

The memory of her new friends teasing her about her chapped chin the next morning. *They knew and I didn't care. If I didn't love him, I would have cared. I always cared if someone teased me about a guy I thought I liked. With Zain, it was different. Mom and Dad could have come right that minute and known I'd been making out with a guy, and I still don't think I would have cared.*

Her chest heaved with suppressed emotion as she fought back the same feelings that had kept her in the clouds—all two of them—that Christmas Eve in Las Vegas. *"Is this—what we've been doing for the past twenty-five years—is it what you want your marriage to be or do you want something more?"*

Of course I want something more. Who wouldn't? But can I actually have it with the man who abandoned me? I don't think so. I'll have to forgive if he asks— probably should regardless— A new thought sickened her. *Probably should have long ago, but that doesn't mean I have to move to California and be a normal wife.* She closed her eyes, squeezing them shut. *Do I?*

Chapter Twenty-Two

Christmas Day—Las Vegas

All through the morning, Audrey flirted. Even the others noticed and teased her, but she didn't care, and from the look on Zain's face, neither did he. Plate after plate of food passed through the assembly line, and each time she took one from him, Audrey tried to ensure their fingers touched. Before long, he did it too.

"Barney" Barnett—as they now called him—shuffled past and murmured just loud enough for both Zain and Audrey to hear, "Your fingers are making out in public."

She giggled. "Well, if *we* can't—"

Laughter around them startled her. She blushed, but as she glanced up, all attention was on Jeff dressed as the scrawniest "Santa" anyone has ever seen. Audrey leaned close to Zain and said, "I thought I'd embarrassed us both."

"I'm not complaining."

She eyed him. "No, you're not, are you? Good." A second later, she glanced back, her lashes lowered.

Zain nudged her. "Two more hours…"

"Forever, you mean."

The smile that had become a signal for her emotions to take over her and set her heart racing and her imagination soaring appeared as he said, "Better be."

How does he always say the right thing? The

203

memory of his bumbled declaration of his feelings prompted her to amend, *almost always, anyway.*

Jeff waved their row off for a ten minute break. "Dishes after. Dish folks will rotate in then."

Most of the volunteers grabbed a plate and went to eat with their guests, but Zain tugged her outside. "We can eat—after."

Tami had once walked her fiancé to the door, running her fingers through her hair at just the right moment. Audrey hadn't seen Tami's expression, but she'd never forgotten the look on Tyler's face. *Make it smooth—fluid. Natural.* Then she remembered the hairnet and nearly cheered as she pulled it from her head, shaking out the curls she knew Zain admired. "So—"

Whatever she'd planned to say, Audrey forgot as she lost herself in his kiss, and when it finally ended, she leaned just a little closer and murmured into his ear, "Now I know the next two hours are going to crawl by."

"You know we'll have to get practical about this tomorrow."

She smiled. "Yeah... but today I'm just going to enjoy my wedding day. I'm pretty sure somewhere in the Bible it says that tomorrow will take care of itself." Audrey's finger traced a tiny scar at the corner of his eye. "Diane told me there'd be a ton of cute guys here."

"Yeah?"

"She was wrong. Just one—and in a few hours, he's mine."

The door opened and Barney stuck his head out. "They're about to call for us. Thought you'd wanna know."

"Thanks," Audrey called out. "We'll be in after he tells me how amazing I am or something equally awesome."

Once the door closed behind Barney, Zain kissed her again. "I love you."

"That's awesome enough for me." She started for

the door, but he pulled her back again.

"Got anything to amaze me with?"

"I'd tell you how much I think I love you too, but that wouldn't surprise you at all."

They shuffled back to the door, huddled together in an attempt to keep out the cold that she thought felt wonderful and nearly froze Zain, but at the door, he hesitated. "I don't think I'll ever *not* be surprised to hear you say that. I'm pretty lucky."

"Blessed."

"What?" His eyebrows drew together in evident confusion.

"When you have an uncle who is a preacher, you get it drilled into your head. No luck—only blessings from the Lord."

Not until they were in the kitchen, taking over dish duty, did Zain lean close and whisper, "I think he's right—your uncle. That's exactly what I've been feeling like all week. I just couldn't describe it. It's totally cool. I'd say wicked cool, but that just sounds wrong."

"How about 'Righteous' then," she tossed back as she plunged her hands in dishwater.

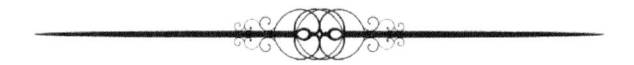

Zain snapped her backside with a damp towel. "It's time."

Audrey glanced around her, guilt hitting hard. *We have so much more to do. Is it right to leave it for everyone else—*

"If you're having second thou—"

"No!" Several eyes glanced their way as Zain inched her to a more private corner of the room. "I just feel guilty. Not everyone is done eating and the dishes aren't done."

Disappointment filled his eyes before he managed to say, "We can wait an hour or two. The place stays open until eight tonight, right?"

That was just too cool. He'd change for me. He

wants to go now, but he'll— Audrey shoved her thoughts aside and shook her head. "No, let's go. You go get what you need and wait out front. I'll be there in a minute. If we go at the same time..."

"I feel like we should just tell everyone what we're doing, but then—"

"I know. We could spend all night listening to everyone try to talk us out of it. Jeff might even try calling my parents. Yeah, I'm not a minor anymore, but barely."

Concern filled Zain's eyes. "Would they try to stop you?" He shook his head. "Of course they would. Stupid question."

"What you mean is would I let them." Her hand rested on his chest and she smiled at the steady but strong beat of his heart beneath her fingers. "No. I'd do it anyway."

"Five minutes?" he asked as he backed away.

Audrey nodded.

It took fifteen. A taxi waited out front by the time she arrived. "Sorry. There were girls in the room and they kept asking questions. Drove me crazy." She shoved her suitcase across the seat and climbed in. "Where's yours? Trunk?"

"I didn't get it."

"Oh." *I thought we were getting a room for the night. What if—*

"Had a hard enough time getting *past* our room, much less into it, so I just came straight out."

"But the license!" she squealed. The driver's eyes met hers and he smiled.

"I've had that on me all day. Wasn't letting it out of my sight."

They arrived at just after five. The receptionist added them to the list, offered a notebook of available packages, and visibly sniffed when they admitted they didn't have different clothes to change into and wanted just a simple ceremony. "That's fine. It'll be seventy-five dollars."

Audrey choked at the amount, but Zain pulled out his wallet and passed the bills across the counter. "We can get pictures taken though, right?"

Once more, the receptionist pulled out a few laminated options and passed him an order form. "You can pay now or order when you get home."

He started to pay and then paused. "I don't know what we'll need. If your parents or mine want more than just—"

"Order later then. That's fine," the woman interjected. "If you just wait over there, we have two couples ahead of you. One will take about twenty minutes and the other is like you—about five. So, give us about half an hour."

They sat in chairs, their hands intertwined. Though their place gave them some privacy, they spoke little. A bridal party appeared, girls in shiny teal satin dresses with enormous bows covering their backsides and flopping awkwardly with each step. The bride's dress looked like a replica of Princess Diana's. *Probably cost less than one of the bows on the real thing, though.*

As the doors closed behind the party, Zain turned to her. "You should have had a nice dress. I didn't think of it."

"Those are for big weddings with lots of guests."

He pointed to her suitcase beside him. "You've probably got a dress in there. You could—"

But Audrey had no interest. She only wished for one thing, but she found herself shy of admitting it. Something in Zain's demeanor—uncertainty, or perhaps discouragement—prompted her to add, "The only thing I wish I had was something nice." She leaned her head on his shoulder. "You know, for later."

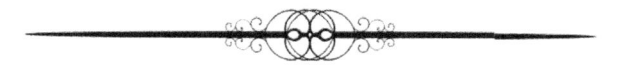

Before he led them to the altar, the pastor spoke to them, explaining what would happen and asking what they wanted for the service. "My name is Pete, and you are?" They introduced themselves, and Audrey offered her hand, but the man didn't seem to notice. "Now, we'll begin with me asking if you'll love and honor and respect—"

Her mind wandered as she reveled in the surreality of standing in a wedding chapel in Las Vegas of all places with a man—one her mother would call a boy— she'd known for just a week. *You know that "speak now or forever hold your peace part?"* she asked the Lord. *Well, maybe You won't speak, but do something to stop me and do it fast if I'm not supposed to do this.* Her eyes bounced back and forth between Pastor Pete and the man she was about to marry. No warning bells rang—even at the "Chapel of the Bells." No uncertainty blossomed. Instead, a slow, steady surety that God would bless them simply because they were His people took root in her heart and held fast.

"—you'll give me the rings, and—"

Zain shook his head. "We don't have rings." He glanced at her with a panicked look on his face. "I didn't even think—"

"That is fine." Pastor Pete scribbled something on the paper in his hand and smiled. "Shall we, then?"

Two women sat in the front row, one on each side of the short aisle. Audrey and Zain stepped up front together. The photographer snapped a couple of pictures, and Audrey couldn't help but wonder what he thought of them—Zain in his Levis and polo with the collar turned up like the preppy he was, she in her acid washed jeans and over-sized paint-splatter shirt. *Diane would freak that I wore this shirt. I can hear her now, "I mean it's cute and all, but by design or not, it's still spattered paint. Not exactly wedding attire."* But Zain had liked it the first day she wore it, so instead of the cheesy Christmas sweater her mother had bought her to "brighten the day of the homeless," she put on the one thing Zain had complimented the strongest.

They'd chosen simple vows from a stack of options, from the *Book of Common Prayer,* or influenced by it, if

Pastor Pete could be believed. The words filled her mind as she listened to the pastor ask Zain if he would take her to be his wedded wife to live together in marriage.

Live together in marriage. Wow. Everything really is going to change. We're going to need lots of help, Lord.

As she prayed, Zain promised to love, comfort, honor, and keep her. Audrey met his gaze as Pastor Pete added the familiar words, "For richer or poorer, in sickness and in health, forsaking all others, be faithful only to her so long as you both shall live."

Zain didn't hesitate. "I do."

And Audrey as well, promised to love, honor, and be faithful only to him, but a part of her disliked the wording. *It sounds like I can be unfaithful to anyone else that I want, just not him. Which works out to be the same, I guess, but still. Sounds weird.*

"May I have the rings?"

Audrey snapped from her reverie and Zain's eyes widened. "We don't have—"

"Ah yes, the ring is but a symbol..."

Seriously? It wasn't five minutes ago that you asked about them. This is still a cattle drive, she decided. *They just dress it up with a different sign on the door to disguise it.* But Zain's lips caught hers and tore her from her disillusioned thoughts and back to her new reality. A part of her regretted missing the words, "Pronounce you man and wife," but Zain's kiss proved, beyond any doubt in her mind, that it had been said.

The photographer snapped three or four more pictures and then disappeared behind a curtain. Disillusionment returned as pen and clipboard were thrust into her hands for her to sign. "It'll be filed next week and you can request a copy ten days after that. Good luck and congratulations."

Audrey waited for the word, "Next" in a bored monotone, but to her immense relief, it never came.

Outside the chapel, Zain carried her suitcase in one hand and held her hand with the other. They stared at each other a bit shell-shocked. Smiling, he murmured, "Hungry?"

"Starving."

"We can walk to the Sahara again, or we can go back inside and call a cab."

"Sahara," she insisted. "I don't want to go back in. I feel much happier now that it's just us again."

"Was a bit rushed, wasn't it? I guess it had to be. We didn't have anything to do but promise to do exactly what we wanted to—live together, love each other, be there, comfort and all that. That was the best part."

Audrey kissed his cheek. "Thank you. You're right. That's exactly the part I loved most. I needed to hear that, because that ring thing—"

Zain laughed. "Can you believe that? I guess with as many as they must do every day, it's probably just so rote for them." He tugged her toward the corner. "I feel sorry for him. He's probably lost the wonder of seeing two people choose to spend the rest of their lives together."

"And here I was thinking it was just a cattle drive with bows on the cows' butts. I like your version better."

Chapter Twenty-Three

Christmas Eve—Fairbury

The morning began innocently enough—if a complete disaster could be considered innocent. Audrey awoke, stretched, and tossed aside her covers, feeling remarkably refreshed considering the bizarre dreams that had plagued her for half the night. She dressed on auto-pilot, each action sparking the next until she stood in front of the bathroom mirror ready for the day and satisfied with the results. In her room once more, she hesitated beside the bed. *Make it? Wait? Nah,* she decided at last. *Kelly's gonna change the sheets anyway. How did I ever exist without this luxury? She's my new best friend—and all because I never have to wonder if I have clean underwear anymore!*

Down the stairs, with light feet and heart, Audrey sang, "...children laughing, people passing, meeting smile after smi—"

The sight of a body on her couch made her trip on the last few steps and sent her sprawling at the bottom of the stairs. "Aaaak!"

"Whaaa—Audrey!"

"Yeah," she tried to stand, but a glance at her clock sent her flopping onto her back. "Oh, no!"

"Wha—"

"It's eight-thirty! I was supposed to open the shop half an hour ago! I overslept—forgot to set the alarm—

something." She shoved herself up and collapsed again with a cry of pain. "Yikes!"

The phrase, "leaps tall buildings in a single bound" came to mind as Zain practically vaulted the coffee table and landed at her side. "What?"

"I think I jammed or sprained my wrist," she admitted as she tried to move it. "Probably jammed. That's good."

"Ice?"

Audrey nodded. "Yeah, thanks. Can you hand me my phone? Stacy's gonna have to open."

Zain reached for the phone and passed it to her before hurrying to find ice—of which she realized she had none. "Probably have to get peas or something," she called just as Stacy answered the phone. "Hey, Stace. I overslept. Any chance you're ready and can run over to the shop? People are probably thinking I skipped out without filling their orders or something."

"Sure. I was just reading until time to go. See you when you get there."

Audrey disconnected and stared at her wrist, willing it to cooperate. When Zain arrived with a kitchen towel full of peas, she muttered, "Thanks. Can I beg another favor?"

"Sure."

"Upstairs bathroom off my bedroom—Jack and Jill thing—anyway, bottom drawer on the left. Ace bandage. Can you get it?"

He was half up the stairs before he answered. "Be right back. Keep ice on that thing."

Her agitation grew with each passing second. Zain helped her to the couch, examined the wrist, and concluded in his "not eligible for malpractice suits" opinion that it was not broken. "Gee, that's helpful."

"I aim to please. Want me to wrap it?"

Let's see, do I want you to spend the next minute or two holding my arm and hand, touching me, making me go even crazier than I already am? Yeah, sure I do. Just like I'm dying for a colonoscopy. "Yeah, thanks. I

212

never wrap them well enough by myself."

Each gentle touch of his hands as he semi-immobilized her wrist sent fresh zinging electro-currents through her, which in turn made her even more cranky and irritable. *Traitor. This guy is not a white knight here to rescue you. He's not even a cool black knight with all kinds of excitement in store. He's the man who walked out of your life in Las Vegas and now thinks he can just waltz back in and pretend to have ever cared. Well it's not going to work, so get a grip, woman.*

A key in the lock sent her heart racing and her hand shaking. "Oh, no! I—"

Kelly stepped into the entryway and froze at the sight of them on the couch. "Audrey! Zain! I didn't—I just thought—I would have knocked—"

"That's all right. You didn't know I'd be here—" Something Kelly had said stopped her. "Wait. How do you know Zain?" Her eyes snapped over to the man beside her and she leaned back, jerking her arm away. "What the—on earth—is going on here?"

"Um…" Zain's eyes seemed to question Kelly, but the woman didn't see. Kelly stood, tears filling her eyes and her hands wrapped protectively around her middle.

"Audrey, I didn't mean—"

Zain interrupted. "Can I tell her?"

Choking back tears, Kelly nodded. "Please. Well, no." Her head shook as she changed her mind. "I need to—" She swallowed and dropped her purse to the floor. "Zain is here because of me—sort of."

"Sort of?" Audrey stood and backed away from both of them, her arms crossed over her chest. "What do you mean?"

Zain pointed to the chair. "Why don't you sit, Kelly. I keep expecting you to drop."

Then Audrey saw it. Kelly had gone almost gray. "Yeah. Sit. Need some water? Soda? Tea? Coffee?"

"Water. Thanks."

Zain offered to get it, but Audrey moved quickly.

"I've got one good arm anyway, but thanks." As she worked, Audrey's mind visited a million possible scenarios for how Zain and Kelly could possibly know one another, but only one—the most improbable of all— actually was a possibility.

Kelly accepted the glass and drained half of it before she set it on the coffee table and clasped her hands together. As Audrey watched, she noted, albeit a bit illogically, that the woman looked like Megan Follows in *Anne of Green Gables,* as she stood before Marilla to make her "apology." *What does that have to do with anything? Lord, tell me she didn't. It's the only thing possible, but I can't see—*

"—second week, or was it third?" Kelly frowned as she thought. "Pregnancy brain. I can't remember what week. Anyway, I cleaned your office and accidentally knocked off a file. In it was—"

"My tax return. You saw Zain's name and our status as married."

Kelly nodded. "I didn't mean to. I saw it before I could get bent over to pick it up."

"Accidents happen," Audrey forced herself to say, "but how does Zain enter the picture?"

"Well." She stared at her feet for a moment and then raised her eyes once more. "Then you asked me to find that recipe journal for you, remember?"

"Grandma's chocolate log." Audrey still didn't understand how that explained anything.

"Going through the boxes, I found a bundle of letters..."

Audrey felt the blood drain from her face. *Oh, Lord no. No, no no! This cannot be happening.* "You read my letters."

"I saw a few words—" emotion choked Kelly as she tried to continue. "—so sorry. Really. I can't believe I did it. I tried to tell you once—to apologize, but then the electricity went out—"

With each word Kelly spoke, Audrey's anger levels doubled until she'd nearly exploded her thermometer.

"Okay, back up. So you read the letters."

"Well, not all. I got about five or six into them and realized what I was doing, so I put them back." Tears fell freely now. "Then I went to this Bible study where they talked about vows and I remembered how much in love you guys were from those letters and I thought maybe he'd left you—"

"I do not believe this."

Zain stepped in. "She read the rest, Audrey, and told me about them—at my request. It was wrong of me to ask, and it was wrong of her to do it. Neither one of us are proud of how we got to this place today. She wanted to come and confess days ago when it really hit her how wrong she'd been, but I asked her to give you a good Christmas."

"And you showing up was that 'good Christmas?' Are you kidding me?" Audrey rose, grabbed her phone, purse, and coat, and strode to the front door. "Since you've already invaded my privacy and gotten me used to having someone clean up after me, you can finish today," she snapped. As Kelly nodded, pain filling her eyes, Audrey continued. "But you're fired. You can pick up your check after three. Don't put me down as a previous employer anywhere. You won't get the job, I assure you."

"Audrey—" Zain began.

"As for you, be out of here before I get home. Don't come back without an invitation, or I'll call the cops. They're pretty good friends of mine, too."

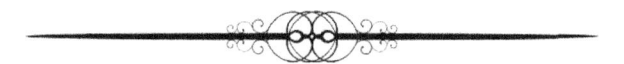

That afternoon, Bentley saw Kelly coming out of The Confectionary and the look of utter misery on the woman's face sent her rushing down the sidewalk. "Kelly! Wait up!"

A flash of anger—one she could have missed with a blink at just the right moment—crossed Kelly's face before resignation covered it. Kelly forced a smile and nodded. "Merry Christmas."

"Thanks to me, you're not having much of one."

Kelly didn't deny it. "Well, I opened myself up for it, I suppose."

"I don't know how anyone overheard us talking, Kelly. I was just asking Gary if I should talk to you about how your questions sounded. I mean, they really did make it sound like you were having an affair, and I knew you wouldn't do that. But someone had to have heard us."

"You—wait, what?" Kelly glanced around them and beckoned for Bentley to follow. "Let's talk in my van."

Kelly started the engine the moment they climbed inside and turned to Bentley. "So what happened again?"

Realization struck Bentley hard. "Oh, no! You thought I—well, I guess you would. I didn't tell anyone anything—not intentionally. Gary and I were talking in the breezeway between the Post Office and the dentist's office. I thought we were deep enough in that no one could hear us, but I guess not. I just told him how you'd come to me about the whole separation and children and vows thing. I didn't think much of that until you asked about Facebook. I was so rattled, as the two ideas kept spinning, that after you left, I saw him and just asked him if he thought I should tell you how it sounds so that you could be careful. You know how people can be if they misunderstand."

"I do now."

Remorse hit anew. "I am so—"

"Don't be sorry." Kelly met Bentley's gaze with tear-filled eyes. "This is all my fault, okay? I did something really wrong and now two people are hurt and my family is being raked through the mud."

"I think you should go tell Tom Allen whatever has happened and let him address it with the church."

"I can't, though. I'm wrong, but doing that gives private information to Tom—information I shouldn't have." She hung her hands on the wheel and rested her head on them. "I've never done anything like this before, and man, I'll never do it again."

The helplessness of Kelly's situation, as ambiguous as it was, left Bentley unsettled. "Well, then I'd tell him your part—like you told me. And ask how he would recommend straightening things out. There is some nasty gossip going around, despite those of us who keep saying that it isn't true, and it feels like it's coming from the church. I keep hearing, 'We need to pray for their marriage.'"

"Well, if Jon wasn't the man he is, that might be true by now."

"This other situation," Bentley asked, praying as she spoke. "Is there anything I can do to help that won't mean more trouble for you or the other party?"

"Pray. Pray that my repentance prompts forgiveness. I don't expect no consequences, but I would like to be forgiven—for the other person's sake as much as mine. I've lived with unforgiveness and it rots your heart until you finally let it go."

Zain paced the car rental hub at the Rockland International Airport, stopping occasionally to reply to a text from someone in his family. The latest came from his mother. OF COURSE SHE IS ANGRY. GIVE HER TIME. DO NOT LEAVE. TRUST ME. SHE WILL BE MAD THAT YOU DIDN'T BUT HURT IF YOU DO. ANGER IS BETTER THAN PAIN.

He eyed the counter where Rich the Avis guy shook his head again. *Two hours. I've still got two hours before they're supposed to have it. If a car comes up before that time, I'm taking it, even if it's a 1985 Yugo.*

Yosef sent another text before he could begin pacing again. AIDA WANTS TO KNOW IF YOU GAVE HER THE GIFT YET?

No, and if I don't get a car—Rich beckoned for him to come. He typed out a reply as he walked, nearly running over a couple of children in his haste. "Sorry."

Her words haunted him as he stared at the family leaving the airport. *"Sorry doesn't fix things, Zain. Sorry is just a word people use to get a clean slate. Well, it doesn't work that way with me."*

He signed for his car, smiling at the free upgrade for his "trouble." *A Mustang will look a little less pathetic, but I doubt anyone linked that van to Audrey's house. This might,* he mused as he tossed his bags in the back seat and climbed behind the wheel. *No one can hide a canary yellow 'stang.*

Google Maps gave him directions to Boutique Row and the fine shops nearby. He parked in the garage near the row and strolled through the streets until he stood in front of the one store he had never imagined shopping in at all. "Not having breakfast here, that's for sure."

The doorman instantly made Zain feel both at home and completely out of his element. *Lord, I do not shop at stores with doormen. What am I doing here? There's no way I can afford anything they have—well, nothing more exciting than a key chain with a T&Co. on it.*

He circled the store twice before finally accepting help from an assistant who introduced herself as Erin. "I need to be frank. I don't think I can afford anything in here I'd like, but on the off chance I can, here I am."

"What is your budget, and what are you looking for? We have a variety of price ranges." The woman smiled at him without the slightest hint that she might be disappointed in his news. *Maybe they don't work on commission. I sure hope not.* Aloud he said, "I shouldn't spend over five hundred dollars and I really don't want a ring."

"Come with me. I'm sure we can find just the right thing."

As they passed the counter where another assistant showed the classic blue box to a customer, Zain nodded in that direction. "Why the red ribbon?

Christmas?"

"Yes."

"Would it be possible to get the white one instead? I'm not a fan of that color combination."

Erin smiled. "I agree. If I got a gift from here, I'd like the white myself, but the customers do seem to appreciate the red—most of you, anyway." She pulled out a tray of earrings and pointed to several options, explaining the metals and designs. "I'll be honest, in your range, we're looking primarily, if not exclusively, at sterling, but it's a lovely look and good quality, of course."

"Sterling is fine." Zain pointed to a pair with a leaf and vine design. "Those are pretty."

"They have a matching necklace. I'll show you when we get to those if you like."

It didn't take him long to decide against earrings—unless he decided he could afford both earrings and their coordinating necklace. At the bracelets, he pointed to one before she could. "Now if I could afford that, I'd consider myself done."

"But you can. That's a little under half what you decided on." She leaned forward, glanced from side to side to be sure no one could overhear, and whispered, "But why that in particular?"

"It's for my wife. I've never bought her any jewelry before, but she wore a cheap piece of costume jewelry the day we got married—looked just like that, except the heart was gold-toned and dark in spots. The 'pearls' were chipped in places. It just seems like the perfect idea for her—give her one that won't tarnish or flake."

"Would you like to keep looking, or shall I have it wrapped?"

"I suppose it can't hurt," Zain said as his eyes skimmed over the rest of the bracelets she showed him. "I didn't look at necklaces, although those are probably a bit pricier too, I suppose."

"Some, yes." Erin led him past stones large enough to likely rival the cost of the car he'd driven there and over to a few collections and several other necklace options. One collection showed the olive leaf earrings, another pair that looked more like a vine, and the matching necklace Erin had mentioned. "That is what I was talking about. Isn't it pretty?"

Zain hated to ask. "And—"

"Less than the bracelet." Erin laughed at the confusion he knew must have shown. "Does she wear more earrings, more necklaces? Bracelet or watch perhaps?"

How do I admit that I don't know? Thinking aloud, he considered his options. "She owns a candy shop and bakery—spends a lot of time with her hands in messy stuff, so she couldn't wear a bracelet often."

"Something like that wouldn't be every day wear, for sure. Pearls are porous. You don't want to get them wet or dirty if you can avoid it."

Though he hadn't expected she would wear anything like it to work, he did realize that she also did little else *but* work. *Maybe you should do something she could wear more often if she wanted.* "Great. Now what to do. Both have meaning—"

"Oh?"

Zain nodded. "I—" *How do I be honest without giving TMI? Maybe if she knew what I am thinking she'd tell me what to do.*

"You don't have to tell me. Perhaps something non-jewelry might be in order then? We have lovely crystal, we have sterling frames—"

"I really did want to do jewelry but—wait, frames?"

Laughing, Erin led him to a display near the center of the store. "These are lovely and timeless."

"I could give her our wedding picture in it."

"That would be very meaningful, I'm sure."

He jerked his head toward her as he realized he'd spoken aloud. "You must think I'm crazy. Look," Zain backed away to a semi-deserted corner of the store and murmured, "Awkward situation. We've been separated for—well, a long time. We don't want to divorce, and I do want to show her that I know where I've been wrong and I'm taking responsibility for that. So, I could do the frame with the picture to show where we made those vows in the first place, or I could do the bracelet that reminds me so much of what she had that is probably rotting at the bottom a landfill now for all I know."

"Or, you could do that necklace—an olive branch. What better way to call a truce and work towards peace than that?"

"Exactly." Zain hesitated before asking, "Do you see a flaw with any of them?"

One finger stroked the side of the glass case before Erin turned. "Don't do the frame. The picture has meaning, yes, but the frame isn't quite personal enough. I agree with the jewelry option and," she leaned a bit closer as one of her associates came close, "that frame is actually more expensive anyway."

"Lead on, then. Let's look at the necklace and the bracelet again."

Erin brought both to the same counter and allowed him the chance to see them side by side. His heart tore in equal pieces, one side of him leaning toward the nostalgic while the other loved the symbolism of the olive branch. *She obviously liked bracelets at one time, and it would show I remembered.* His eye traveled to the necklace and he sighed. *But I do like that better, and it has greater meaning to now—today. Lord? What do I do?*

"May I offer my opinion?"

"Please."

"As lovely an idea as the bracelet is," she began, "you say she works with her hands a lot. If she works long hours like most business owners I know, she won't have much time to wear it."

"I thought the same thing. I just couldn't decide if showing that I remembered mattered more than how often she got to wear it."

"Well, what I was thinking is that the more often she can wear it, the more she will remember you—"

"That's right. I want the necklace. Maybe for her birthday I can do the bracelet."

Erin nodded as she began putting away the bracelet. "When's her birthday?"

"Last week."

The woman laughed. "Okay, I wasn't going to say this, because I don't do well pushing for a sale." She leaned forward and added in a whisper, "Which probably means I won't have this job after the Christmas rush, but hey. I have to live with myself."

"But…"

"But you said your absolute maximum was five hundred. You can afford, even with tax, to buy both if you wanted to do a belated birthday gift as well. Maybe you'd get the bonus of showing you remember the past while bridging a path to the future."

Indecision held Zain in a silver-chained grip. *If she does forgive you and you have to move, you won't have a job. You'll have to start a business or use the money from selling out to Yosef to live on until you find a nine-to-five. But then, all the money you've saved on birthday, Valentine's Day, Christmas, Anniversary—isn't it time to do a little pampering?*

"Okay. You sold me."

"Really?"

Zain nodded. "I think, after the week she's had and the one to come, I owe it to her."

"She's a lucky woman—not just because you bought her presents," Erin insisted. "She's lucky because it means something to you to give them. A lot of guys just buy them because they're expected to."

"That's not much of a gift in my book."

Chapter Twenty-Four

Four o'clock came and to Audrey's relief, every order had gone out the door by three. She locked the door behind the last customer and sagged against it. "Another Christmas season complete—ish."

Stacy grinned. "Best one ever, I think. Even if it's a ghost town next week, we still did better than last year."

"The week after Christmas is usually pretty good, though, but man, I can't wait until New Year's. One whole week—all to myself." The words mocked her. *Unless Zain sticks around. Then it's a week of avoiding him. Jerk.*

The shop looked disheveled, tattered, and a bit forlorn as most cases sat nearly empty and some completely so. She began straightening things as she made her way toward the register. "Why don't you go home and be with your kids. They should be back from Jim's by now, right?"

Stacy glanced at her phone. "Yep. Got a text saying they got here forty minutes ago. They're probably lost in some video game or a movie, but hey."

The cash register beeped as she punched the key to open the drawer. Audrey lifted out the tray and pulled out an envelope with Stacy's name written on it. "Merry Christmas."

"I told you—"

"And I said that you don't get to decide if you get

gifts or not. That's not how it works. Now go home."

"You sure you don't want to come to our house tonight?"

"Nope. I was going to go to Mom and Dad's, but I think I'll just drive over in the morning. I'm really not in the mood for squabbles amongst the nieces and nephews—or their mothers."

"Then you made the right decision," Stacy admitted, "when you decided not to come to my house. I bet Elle and Jimmy are already fighting over something. It's their mutual hobby."

With Stacy gone, Audrey finally relaxed. Her wrist noticed and screamed for relief, but she had perishables to salvage for the next day's celebration. As she worked, she mulled over the events of the morning and the previous night. Whatever mellowing that may have occurred during the day dissipated as her anger grew into even greater proportions.

*Lord, she read my private papers. She **read** them. He asked her to! It doesn't get much lower than that. I thought she was a friend. I thought she had integrity. Everyone always talks about how the Cox family has such strong values and a solid reputation. Jon married badly if he wanted that. Poor guy. She's made a mess of things for him. I wonder if it'll hurt his chances of getting a good job.*

The thoughts spiraled and grew until they became a tornado of emotions and hurts. *I know it's supposed to be until death do we part, but do I have to keep this up? How on earth can I keep this private? People are going to find out now. Look how they found out about Kelly's mess. That's what it was, right? Someone found out about her contacting Zain and assumed it was personal? What else **could** it be?*

No white van sat parked in front of her house as she passed. Audrey rounded the corner and inched down the alleyway to her parking place at the back of what was once the house's back yard. Now only a common yard remained—one that she rarely used and

Oscar practically lived in. The moment she pulled out her keys, Audrey remembered that Zain had it and Tami had apologized the week after the decorating party for taking her spare home. *Locksmith or Zain? Tami?*

Tami she ruled out immediately. Too complicated to explain why she didn't have her key. *I'll have to tell them now, but that's not how to do it.* A locksmith would be easiest, but the cost on Christmas Eve, combined with knowing that Zain would have to bring back the key sometime, sent her back to her vehicle in search of Zain's number.

Google failed to provide the cell number, but it did give her the name of Coastal Cab Company—COO, Zain Kadir. Taking a deep breath, she dialed the number and waited. Three failed attempts to make the dispatch operator understand that she didn't need a ride occurred before the woman said, "If you need the business line, try this number, but I don't know if anyone is in the office."

"Can you give *my* number to one of the owners. This is kind of an emergency."

"The owners don't drive, lady."

"I don't need a ride," Audrey snapped. She took a quick cleansing breath and said, "Sorry. Like I said, this is kind of an emergency, but I had no right to snap at you. I need Mr. Kadir or Joe to call me immediately. It's about Zain."

Those words seemed to connect in a much more positive way. The woman took her number and promised to call immediately. "Merry Christmas. May your rides be safe and your fares be cheap!"

Well, there's something to be said for habits, I suppose. Audrey waited. In the back of her mind the faint tune of the Jeopardy theme played, growing louder with each quarter minute. At last, a phone number with a 310 area code flashed as her ring tone assured her that it was "beginning to look a lot like Christmas."

"Hello?"

"Audrey? Zain's Audrey? Is he okay? Did you kill him?"

She couldn't help but laugh. "No, but he nearly killed me this morning when I saw him on my couch. Fell down the stairs."

The man laughed. "I always said my son would have girls falling for him."

Oh, why couldn't he have been a Christian? I think I would have liked him. This whole thing is a mess because of this man. I want to hate him, but instead, he makes me laugh.

"—wrong?"

"What?" Audrey frowned. "I missed that."

"I asked if something is wrong. Marla said it was an emergency."

"Oh, not that kind of emergency. Zain has my key, Mr. Kadir—"

"Tariq—unless you're speaking to him now. Then Baba works."

He doesn't sound like he thinks I'm beneath him. I don't understand. Audrey jerked herself out of her thoughts and returned to the conversation. "I'll talk to Zain before I go with Baba, but thank you, Tariq. That's a cool name."

"I think my son chose well. Too bad he's such an idiot. Anyway, what do you need, my dear?"

"His number? He has my house key. I can't get in, and a locksmith on Christmas Eve—"

"Expensive. I will text you the number. I do that now, text. Zain made me learn how. It is very efficient when you want self-control but don't have it. I have yelled at Zain for days now and no sore throat."

Another voice came through the phone, a softer, feminine one. "He's trying, my Zain. I hope you will give him a chance to explain. And I hope you like your anniversary present."

"Thank you…"

"That was Sarah," Tariq explained. "She is excited to have another daughter. She regularly tells me that I failed her in that department, but I assure you, it was from no lack of trying."

Audrey stifled back hysterical giggles as she heard Sarah blasting her husband for his "indelicacy." "Well, I'll let you go. It was nice to 'meet' you—sort of. I really need to get Zain to come before I freeze."

"I am sure he can help warm you up." Tariq laughed and added, "Now my Sarah plans to murder me quietly. Consider this her confession. You may be called to testify. Goodbye, Audrey. Visit us soon—or invite us there. I've never been to that part of the country."

"You've never been outside of California, you fool—not since you left Medina," Sarah's voice interjected.

"That doesn't make my words any less true. Leave me alone so I can convince her that we're not freakish people and she doesn't go into Witness Protection to get away from us."

Audrey was still laughing as Zain picked up her call. "Wha—Audrey? Are you okay? I'm so—"

"—parents," she gasped, "—are hysterical."

"They're mad, huh? I don't know what we were thinking. I really—wait. Are you laughing?"

"Yeah, what else?" A fresh round of giggles exploded from her. "Seriously, they are hysterical. Your dad is proud of himself for knowing how to yell at you with text, oh, and if he dies in the next few days, he wants you to know that your mom did it."

"Oh, no. You called—of course you did. My number." Silence hovered until Zain asked, "Does that mean you'll talk to me? I really—"

"I understand you have a present for me. But I'll be honest; I just want my key before I freeze in my car."

"On my way."

"Where are you?" she demanded, hoping he hadn't disconnected yet.

"The Grind." A scream of pain followed. "Gotta—aaak. Go."

"Wha—"

"—guy just spilled coffee all over me. Burns. Bye." Zain's voice disappeared into the abyss of disconnected calls.

Sooner than she would have expected, a yellow Mustang pulled up in front of her house where Audrey waited, shivering in the brisk wind. "Sorry. Stupid guy wouldn't let me leave. I finally had to stalk off as if I was mad just so he wouldn't keep trying to get me to go to the clinic." Zain's hand shook as he tried to unlock the door. "Sorry. Surprisingly cold now that I'm wet—and sticky. Ew."

"You smell like chai."

"I don't suppose you'd let a homeless—so to speak—man use your shower?"

Say no. Tell him he can suffer. Go ahead. "Upstairs—you know where it is."

She waited until he disappeared up the stairs before she hurried out to carry in the ice cream. *Just leave the other stuff until tomorrow.* As she stowed the ice cream, the sight of a bag of peas wrapped tight and wedged against the side of the freezer hit her hard. *Is this how it's going to be now? Every time I turn around, something in my own home is going to remind me of him. I can't live like this. I just can't.*

The spotless house, smelling both fresh and Christmassy thanks to Kelly's cleaning and candle scents, stung her anew. *I can't believe he lost me a new friend. I could have forgiven her that first glance at the letters, but going back? I don't even remember what was in most of them. And now Zain knows. Did he come in last night and go right up to the box and read? Did he laugh at my silliness? Probably. Jerk.*

She'd planned to pack the car with gifts and be ready to go first thing in the morning, but her wrist ached. Instead, she removed her apron and hairnet, kicked off her shoes, and plopped herself onto the couch, grabbing her laptop as an afterthought. *Email. I should make sure I'm not supposed to bring something I've forgotten.*

But she never got to email. Zain's Facebook page stared at her as she typed in her password and the computer loaded the screen. One word on the left called to her. Messages. She listened intently and thought she still heard the shower water running. *He'd never know. He did it to me—well, he tempted Kelly, anyway. That's bad enough. At least she stopped herself at first.* Her conscience spoke up before she could continue her justification process. *If you asked him, he'd show you.* No matter how true the words were, Audrey didn't like that idea at all. *No one bothered to ask me.* Her conscience laughed. *If you hadn't played a false part, Kelly never would have thought a thing of seeing your tax forms. You tempted her with your deception.*

"Well, it doesn't make it right," Audrey muttered. She glared at the screen and then found the logout button. "And at least I had the character to resist it."

Email forgotten, she sat stewing on the couch, waiting for Zain to arrive for another opportunity to kick him out. The last time she'd waited for him to get out of the shower, someone had doused him with alcohol in the Sahara—on their wedding day. *It got us a discounted room, sooooo that was cool,* she mused. *That was the **only** cool thing about the rest of that day.*

Chapter Twenty-Five

Christmas Day—Las Vegas

They hadn't taken more than five steps away from the chapel door when Audrey froze. "Wait, hold on."

Zain waited outside while she dashed in and found Pastor Pete. "That paper—with our vows—do you need it? Can I have it? The one where you made a note about the rings and everything?"

The man flipped through a few papers and shrugged. "I think I tossed it." His eyes slid to a wastepaper basket.

"Mind if I look?"

"Uh, sure?" Pete got confirmation from a woman behind the desk before handing her the can. "Here, but you can have a new one—"

"I want that one, but thanks." She found one marked "No rings" near the beginning of the ring ceremony. *Too bad you can't read your own writing or something.* She waved it in triumph and backed away. The astounded look on the man's face prompted her to add, "I know it's cheesy. I get sentimental about stuff like this."

"For the album?"

Audrey nodded. "Right. For the album." Suddenly, she felt a little silly and folded it up, stowing it in her pocket. "I really want to say thanks. We appreciate it. Have a great rest of your Christmas."

Outside, she grabbed Zain's hand and tugged him toward the hotel. "I'm starving."

"What was that all about?"

Her conscience protested as she said, "Thanked him for the service and told him to have a Merry Christmas." Another protest rose, but she stifled it down. *Well it's true!* Another thought pounced before she could direct her mind back to the fact that she was now a wife. *A half-truth. Great way to start a marriage.*

"—eat or should we try to see if they have a room first?" He paused at the end of the entrance drive. "We don't have to do this now—I mean stay. We have to eat," he hastened to add. "I just mean that if you want to go back and talk about how to tell our parents and everything like that at the mission—" Zain shuffled his feet and kicked her suitcase. "I just mean that this whole thing—getting married. It wasn't about making it okay to—well, to get a room."

"It may not be *about* that, but I—well, I've got no objections if you don't."

Their first true awkwardness settled between them. Audrey felt an undercurrent driving them closer together than ever as they ordered, ate, and avoided each other's eyes while chatting about nothing and everything. They hadn't made it five steps out of the restaurant before a man came staggering toward them, calling out "Omar!" in a drunken voice. Zain tried to steer her around him, but the man stepped in front just in time to slosh his drink all over Zain. "Whoa, there, Omar."

"My name," Zain insisted with an obvious attempt at civility, "is not Omar. I'm sorry, but you've got—"

Vomit spewed all over Zain's shoes and the corner of Audrey's suitcase. From seemingly out of nowhere, two hotel employees arrived to escort the man back to his room. Another beckoned for maintenance to take care of Zain's shoes and the suitcase, and upon hearing they'd hoped to check in, the man picked up a house phone and called the front desk. Audrey heard the words "discount" before he asked their name. "Audrey— Kadir. Zain and Audrey Kadir."

I like the sound of that. Audrey Kadir. I wonder if that's with two E's or one. I can't remember how he spelled it. I hope it's two.

Their room, three floors from the top, was nicer than anything she'd expected. Zain dashed for the shower almost without hesitating. Audrey grabbed his jeans and rinsed his shirt, the bottoms of the legs, his shoes, and his socks off in the sink. "Well, it'll be a bit before they dry, but it'll work," she said as she inched out of the bathroom.

"Be right out. Sorry. That was pretty gross."

"I'm gonna go down to the gift shop and get a sweatshirt for you. Everything I have is too girly."

"Thanks."

Nerves grew taut and raw as she hurried downstairs, wove through smoke-infested slot machines, and found a gift shop with an overpriced sweatshirt. It took almost all her cash to do it, but she knew he'd freeze without it. *Guy needs to thicken up his blood. Rockland would do that for him—if he comes home with me instead of the other way around. I wonder what it's like in California. It can't all be like the movies, can it?*

She found Zain sitting on the bed wearing just his damp-legged jeans. Seeing him without a shirt sent her pulse racing, but she tried to act as nonchalant as possible. "Got it. Stupid thing was crazy expensive."

"You didn't have to, but thanks. It's kind of chilly in here."

And you're kind of crazy. It's perfect. "So I'm thinking we're going to be one of those couples where our bed is all lopsided because you've got extra blankets on one side and I've got almost none."

"Maybe." Zain ripped the tag off the sweatshirt and pulled it over his head before grabbing her around the waist and pulling her onto his lap. "Now I was thinking..."

She waited. "And you were thinking what?"

"We should figure out what we're going to do in case we need to make calls and find different flights or something. Besides," he murmured into her ear. "I think we'll be more relaxed if we don't have that hanging over us."

Audrey had begun to protest that they'd decided to save the discussion until the next day, but his argument made sense. "Okay, I think you're right. But…" She kissed him. "That doesn't mean that I can't find out if you're ticklish, does it?" She tried tickling him, sliding off his lap, but he caught her hands.

"Nuh uh. No way." He grinned. "So, um," Zain flopped back on the bed, his hands behind his head. "I don't even know what to think—where to start. We did this thing, but now what? Where are we going to live? How do we tell our parents? What are yours going to think?"

"I'm nuts. That's what they're going to think. Dad will worry about my education, about how we will eat, and things like medical bills, if I'll get pregnant too soon, and if you will take me away from Rockland."

"Reasonable," Zain agreed. "Don't you think? I don't suppose he'll take, 'God will supply all our needs,' as an answer, will he?" As Audrey curled up beside him, he brushed her hair from her face. "What about your mom?"

"Mom's emotional. She'll flip out. She's gonna cry." A tear trickled down her cheek. "I didn't give her a wedding to plan—no memories and stuff. She's gonna be worried about you, too."

"What's wrong with me?" Zain wiped at the tear before kissing her.

At least he wasn't offended at that. "It's just that your family isn't Christian, and you're a 'baby' in her mind. How can I 'learn from my husband at home' if I know more than him—or so she'll assume." Audrey shrugged. "It's a mom thing."

"Because it's not okay for us to learn together?"

"It's a maturity thing, Zain," Audrey explained. "Mom's really big on not being 'unequally yoked.'"

"We're both Christians. What's unequal about that?"

She tried to explain, but Audrey found herself stumbling. "It's just that Mom says there's more than one way to be unequally yoked. She says that we can be unequally yoked by marrying someone with big theological differences—like a Catholic marrying a Baptist. And if one person's a big theologian type and the other barely knows the names of the sixty-six books of the Bible."

"There are sixty-six?"

She almost fell for it. "Very funny."

"I just don't see what the big deal is. No one can know everything from the day they get saved, but c'mon, Audrey! Do you really think I'm that pathetic?"

"I didn't say *I* did. I said Mom would think that. We're talking about how they're going to handle the news. I was honest." She laid a hand on his cheek. "So, what will your parents say?"

Zain shook his head. "I've already broken their hearts."

"So I'm just another footprint on it, huh?"

"Poetic way of putting it," Zain murmured. "You're not Arabic, Audrey. They don't know your family. You are a Christian. You couldn't be more wrong for me in their eyes if you tried."

Though he said, "You're not Arabic," she heard, "You're half-black." Her eyes narrowed and she sat up. "So your foreign parents who have been here what, forty years—"

"Dad's been here around twenty-five or so, why?"

"They think they're better than me because they're pure-blooded Arab and I'm just a mixed black/white girl whose family has lived here for a coupla centuries? Really?"

"That's not what I said," Zain protested. "You could be as white as the president's daughter and it wouldn't matter. Dad expects me to marry a girl with Saudi parents who knows the value of culture and family."

"Why is white as the president's daughter better than black as—MLK Jr.'s daughter?"

Zain stared at her and sat up as well. "Does he have one?"

"I—" she shook her head. "I don't know! That's not the point. This is about race, and when you're half-black, that means it's about being black."

"Not when you're from the Middle East. It's a cultural thing. You marry within your culture. You do it because it's expected. Okay? It's like the unequal yoke in their minds. It has nothing to do with black or white. Who cares about that? I don't see color or lack of it when I see you. They won't either. They'll just see what isn't there—history that meshes with theirs."

"That's just bogus. You're in America now. If you wanted to be all Saudi, your family should have stayed over there where you could marry a Saudi girl to appease his royal haremship."

Zain jumped to his feet and began pacing the room. "No, *that's* bogus. I married *you.*"

"Why? So you could take me back to Saudi Arabia in a few years and marry a couple of other more suitable women to make up for sullying his good name with tainted blood like mine?" She crossed her arms over her chest and glared at him. "That makes me sick."

He stared at her, his head shaking in disbelief. For just a moment she regretted her words. But he spoke, and what he said hurt. "So all that stuff you said to Shelli—lies, huh? Do you remember? Do you remember what you said?"

Audrey swallowed hard but didn't respond.

"You said, 'I'm glad *Jesus* didn't have the same kind of prejudice you have, or *I* might not have a chance. You make me sick.'" His lip trembled with repressed emotion—hurt or anger, she couldn't decide. "I could never forget those words. But you didn't mean it, did you? You just think—"

"I think your *dad* means so much to you that you can't see that you're caught up in his weird culture—afraid to disappoint Daddy. You're a *Christian* now! Act like it!"

"I did. I married a Christian girl, Audrey." Zain gripped the back of a chair and held onto it. Audrey wondered if it was to steady himself or to prevent himself from doing something ugly.

He wouldn't hit me. He wouldn't! She swallowed again, leaning away involuntarily. *Would he?*

"I married you. I love you. And I *chose* you over what my dad would want. I chose the first thing that *Jesus* would want in a wife for me. A Christian." He dropped his head, covering his face with his hands. "Dad's probably going to disown me. I may lose my entire family over this."

"That's better than me sharing you with a coupla other wives," she muttered. At least losing family for Jesus is biblical."

"True, but just remember I'm giving up a lot of dreams for this too. I always wanted two or three wives. When I became a Christian in America, I pretty much lost that dream in one swoop."

Panic tried to well up in her heart. *He's joking, right?*

Her mouth went dry as she heard him add, "I've always loved a woman in a burqa. Do you think your parents would object?"

"Maybe," she spat out, shaking with repressed anger at the ridiculousness of the argument and the tastelessness of what she had to hope was a joke. *He's gotta be kidding me, but it's just not funny!* "We can use our firstborn in a suicide bomb and offer him as a sacrifice to God. We can name him Isaac. Or will your family require him to be Ishmael?"

The look on Zain's face as he stared at her in shock—anger—sucked every ounce of breath from her. He glared, almost growled. "Don't *ever* speak to me about harming a child again. It's not funny." Audrey's eyes widened as he added, "I'm done. That's it. This is over. You disrespected my father, me—but worse, you disrespected my faith in Jesus. Yeah, I'm done." He pulled on his jacket, shoes, and socks and muttered something incomprehensible as he snatched the room key from the dresser and jerked open the door. As he pulled it shut behind him, Audrey thought she heard him whisper something, but what, she couldn't tell. She started to rise—to go after him and apologize, but her father's words came to her.

"Don't chase a man when he's angry. Talk to him when he has calmed. You'll provoke them to deeper anger, and it's wrong. Give him time to calm himself."

Tears filled her eyes as she curled up on the bed to wait for Zain to return.

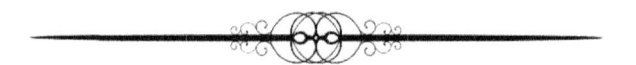

His hands shook as Zain walked the streets of Las Vegas—hands shook and his toes froze as the wet shoes grew colder with each second in the frigid desert air. He started up at Sahara, made his way down South Las Vegas Boulevard, and onto the strip. Signs flashed lights, beckoning him into stores selling tchotchkes with the name of the town splattered over them—spoons, thimbles, gaudy plastic coin purses, along with the usual hats and shirts. *Garbage. This whole place is garbage.*

As he walked, his anger boiled, roiling higher with each step until he thought he'd lash out at the world for the injustice of it all. *How could she? What are we going to do now? This is my wedding night, and I'm walking around the streets of Las Vegas to cool off. That's just wrong.* His conscience tried to correct him—tried to remind him that he'd made snarky comments that sparked her hurtful ones. Zain brushed it aside as he remembered the nasty words, *"Use our firstborn in a suicide bomb..."*

Several hours passed as he continued to wander the streets, trying to calm himself as well as try to decide what to do. *The Bible says to leave father and mother. I should go to Rockland—at least at first. Oh, God tell me we won't always be like this. I want to scream at her for all she said. Can't she see it's the same thing? I'm not spiritual enough. She's not cultural enough. Her mother should know better though—she has Jesus. Dad only has culture and family to cling to. He doesn't even have Islam anymore.*

A sight—one he'd seen often on the seedier streets in L.A. on street mission trips—broke his heart. A woman sidled up to a man, offering herself to him. *Lord, she needs help. How do we help these people?* But the answer to that question didn't come. Instead, he watched the man back away, revulsion showing in expression and words. The vile racist filth that spewed from the man's mouth earned him a few choice words from the prostitute, but as she turned away, Zain saw the pain in her eyes.

"Ignore him," Zain murmured as he passed. The woman tried to shift her proposition to Zain, but he shook his head. "Not interested, sorry. Look, there's a mission over on University. They'll help. I promise. Just tell them Zain sent you."

"Yeah, I'll take my chances here. Plenty of men like a darker-skinned companion—oops, better get moving before that cop decides I'm workin' this corner too long."

He watched the woman stroll past the oncoming police car as if without a care in the world. The officers in the car slowed and stared at him. He met their gaze frankly until they zoomed past again. *I guess,* Zain thought as he sauntered back down the street, *I guess she might have mistaken wrong nationality for wrong race. I see it differently, but if that's how she's been treated—ever—how else would she take it?* This time he listened as his conscience added, *And your barbs about the other wives and burqa just fueled her pain. You already broke the honor part of your vows. You dishonored her with those words. Go back, apologize, and start over.*

Her words in the chapel came back to him as he went in search of a taxi. *She wanted something pretty for tonight. I could get that, if I could find some place open, that is. Where do I look? Maybe she'd see that I'm trying.*

Sign after sign alerted him to everything but the one thing he sought. He found a small shop tucked away at last—closed. Frustrated, he began a different kind of search. *There's got to be a phone book somewhere!* As if summoned by his thoughts, there one hung from a pay phone near a street corner. After trying to remember names of streets, Zain gave up and did something he never thought he'd do. He ripped the pages from the book and went in search of a taxi.

Six stores later, Zain exited the only one open on a Sunday Christmas night, with a black and silver box—gift wrapped as a courtesy from an understanding and helpful clerk. *"She'll love it. You're a good guy. She's lucky."* The woman's words soothed his spirit as the cab crawled through an obscene amount of traffic.

We still have to talk about this stuff, Lord. She can't throw things out like that. It's just—bogus. She knows better, and now I do. I didn't think about it. I've lived most of my life in the shelter of a sub-culture. People like Shelli say things now and then, but I think Audrey's runs deeper somehow. We've got to see how it is from the other side. We've got to work it out, or we're going to be the most miserable couple ever.

As he rode the elevator, he practiced his apology. Each step to their room became a fresh attempt to choose each word with precision. Even as he opened the door, his mind retraced every possible way to apologize without compromise. *We can't tear each other or each other's family down. We're all united now. We have to act like it.*

"Audrey? I'm back. Sorry it took so long. I—" His

eyes scanned the room. Empty. The bathroom door stood open and empty, the light off. The end of the dresser where he'd grabbed the room key—right next to her purse—empty as well. No purse. The floor beside it. No suitcase. *Where'd she go? Is she coming back? Why would she bring the suitcase with her if she is? But where would—* "The mission."

His feet pounded the pavement as he ran through the streets. When his lungs wouldn't let him go another foot, he paused to catch his breath and walked again. Each time he felt able, he ran, weaving through the occasional crowds coming out of shows or walking in groups to something or another. The three miles back to the mission felt like five. By the time he'd nearly arrived, he amended that number to five hundred. He stumbled up the steps, jerked open the door, and went in search of Jeff, but "Barney" Barnett stopped him.

"Hey, where've you been? Is Audrey with you? Saw you guys slip off earlier."

"No. She's not here?"

Barney shook his head. "Haven't seen her since around four when you guys left."

Zain's mind whizzed through possibilities before asking, "Any girls still up?"

"A few—out in the courtyard. They're having a singing before everyone starts taking off tomorrow." Barney jerked his head. "I've got a red-eye in a few hours, so, I'm going to get a couple hours' sleep."

"Nice meeting you." Zain didn't want to take the time to ask, but he forced himself. "Got my address?"

"Yeah. I'll write. And if I ever get to California, I expect you to take me to Hollywood."

Stifling back the temptation to roll his eyes, Zain nodded. "Will do. Bye."

The girls didn't find Audrey in their room. She wasn't in the courtyard. Jeff didn't know where she'd gone or what time her return flight actually was, but he chalked it up to one of the red-eye flights. "She came in on one, so maybe."

"Shouldn't we look for her? Call the police? She's just gone! Suitcase and all." The moment he said it, Zain regretted it.

"Did the girls say that? Then she must be going home. You could try the airport, but I doubt she's there now."

But he tried anyway. With a cash advance on his credit card, he replenished his wallet and jumped in yet another taxi, this time to the McCarran Airport. He walked through each terminal, read every flight on the arrivals and departures split-flap board, and even stalked the bathrooms until the time for his own flight drew so near that he had to return to retrieve his suitcase. Jeff offered to call and let him know that she'd arrived—offered to give her his contact information. Zain opened his mouth to say yes but found himself shaking his head. "Nah. If she didn't want to say goodbye or give it to me herself, it's probably better if you don't. If she ever asks for it, though, just give it to her."

"I thought you guys really hit it off," Jeff added as Zain carried out his suitcase to the waiting taxi.

"Yeah, well, so did I."

Chapter Twenty-Six

—Fairbury

Zain found her asleep on the couch, the laptop open beside her. The open Facebook page offered to allow him to login, confusing him. *I don't remember logging out, now that I think about it. Weird.*

He pulled the little box from his jacket pocket and hunkered down on his heels, ready to offer it, but his plans to awaken her failed. He couldn't do it. The box lay in sight on the coffee table, and the laptop, he stowed beside the couch again. The kitchen beckoned him to make *something* for dinner, but he knew she'd be unlikely to sleep through it, so he removed his jacket, draped a throw over her, and settled into the other corner of the couch.

As he waited, Zain prayed. He prayed for forgiveness, for compassion, and for clarity in all and for all. *And a place to spend tomorrow would be nice as well. Maybe the Rockland Mission is having something I can help with—be like old times with Barney again. Still weird that he ended up here, Lord. I should have too, I suppose. I should have let Jeff ask her to call me. I shouldn't have been so stubborn.*

At six, the clock on her wall spun in beautiful motion as it played a short tune. Audrey shifted, her eyes resting on him for a moment as she murmured, "You left me." But before he could respond, she slept again.

I did leave, I suppose, but what else was I supposed to do? I was angry—okay, I was royally ticked off, to be precise.

Her eyes fluttered open a few minutes later, and she sat up, staring at the blanket as if trying to discover how it had gotten there. "Thanks."

"You looked exhausted."

"I am. Busy day." The moment Audrey saw the box on the coffee table, she jerked her head toward him. "Is that what your mom was talking about?"

"Yeah."

"You do know I'm not going to be bribed by something so cliché as Tiffany?"

Zain's throat went dry but he managed to choke out, "It's not a bribe, Audrey. It's well, it's symbolic of how I really feel."

"You can't feel much of anything as far as I can tell. You haven't spoken to me in twenty-five years. You walked out on me, Zain. You left me less than two hours after we got married. Seriously? You bring that—" she kicked the little rectangular box off the table and onto the floor. "—and expect me to believe it means anything?"

His heart constricted and his throat ached as he listened. "You thought I left you?"

"Um, yeah. Ya did. You said you were done. You walked out of that room and didn't come back, and—"

"But I did. You were gone."

"No you didn't," she snapped, standing. "I'm not stupid. I waited there for hours—three or four at least. You didn't come back."

"I came back. Your purse was gone, your suitcase—no sign of you anywhere—and I had the key. I didn't look around the hotel, but I went to the mission, I searched the airport for hours."

Audrey stopped pacing and stared at him. "You searched the airport?"

"Yeah. I think I had security called on me a couple

of times for stalking the ladies' room."

"That's where I was too. Spent hours in there crying. I thought my parents were going to kill me." She shuffled back to the couch and pulled the blanket back over her. "Why'd you come back?"

"I said I would."

Even as she spoke, Audrey shook her head. "No you didn't. You said you were done."

"Done with the conversation. I was hurt and angry and I knew I'd say something I regretted. So I went to walk it off—froze my toes, too."

"Good." Despite her words, Audrey smiled—the first one he'd seen that reminded him of the old Audrey.

"Yeah. It took a while," Zain admitted, "but I figured out that I'd set you up for what you said. I didn't get it, but I had an inkling by the time I got back."

"And I was gone."

"And you were gone," he echoed. "I thought you'd call—write. But I never heard a word until February."

"My letter about dependents and taxes."

"That's when I found out you didn't tell your parents either." Zain nudged her foot. "I was so wrong to reply like that."

Audrey's lips twisted as she struggled to fight back emotion. "When I got my letter back with your social written across the bottom like that's all that you cared to have to do with me, I was so glad I hadn't told my parents. They would have wanted us to get counseling—all that stuff."

"Mine would have wanted a divorce."

Surprise flashed in her eyes. "They didn't seem like that when I talked to them."

"Now—not so much. Then, yes. They would have considered it the right thing to do. Now they see me as having abandoned you—failed you as a husband. They are very ashamed of me." He leaned forward, not touching her but trying to be nearer in some fashion. "I'm ashamed of me. When I think about our vows and how I have trashed them—" He sighed. "I don't remember all I promised, but love, honor, and sickness and health were in there."

The blanket flew against the back of the couch as she rose and hurried upstairs. Zain heard a muffled, "ouch" and followed. In the room that must be the "office" Kelly had described, he found her pulling out banker boxes, wincing each time she reached for another. "Here. Let me—what are you doing?"

"I have those vows. That's why I went back into the chapel—to get them. I wanted to frame them." She shoved one box aside and pulled the lid off another. "It's in the envelope that our confirmation stuff from the outreach center came in. None of this stuff is organized, unfortunately."

Zain reached for the lid of one box. "Mind if I look? I'd really like to see that." She didn't answer. Zain tried again, "Audrey?"

She nodded. "Go ahead. Sorry, I'm still reeling from hearing you came back. I waited for what seemed like forever."

They worked in silence after that, Audrey working faster than he did, but he being able to move box after box. When he pulled the lid from yet another box, a packet of letters stared back at him. He reached in. "Are these *the* letters?"

Audrey took them from him and stared at them. "Yeah. I can't believe she read these."

"Why'd you write them?"

"The first year—I just remembered everything and I was still so hurt. So I just pretended everything was how it *should* have been. Each year, I kept doing it—still don't know why. Then it became a habit. Now it's kind of a tradition."

He wanted to ask to read them but couldn't do it. Papers, envelopes, photos—a large conglomeration of things filled the box, but he still didn't find it. A Bible caught his eye, though. "I remember this. It's the one you had there."

"I never used it after that. I bought a new one. Every time I opened this one it reminded me of Vegas, so I just put it away." Audrey started to set it back in the box and froze. She flipped through it, and pulled out a folded half-sheet of paper. "And I moved the vows into it a few Christmases ago. I forgot. Here it is."

Zain started putting boxes back, but Audrey stopped him. "Just leave them for now. Who knows what else we'll end up needing."

That's promising. She's not kicking me out yet. At the base of the stairs, she handed him the paper. It was well worn for something she'd implied had been tucked away since the day she returned home. He read the words, smiling at the note of no rings and their names written over brackets that said "Groom's name" and "Bride's name."

"'[Groom's name], do you take [Bride's name] to be your wedded wife, to live together in marriage? Do you promise to love her, comfort her, honor and keep her, for better or worse, for richer or poorer, in sickness and health, and forsaking all others, be faithful only to her so long as you both shall live?'" He sighed. "Well, I was faithful to you. And I have always loved you, but I haven't shown it well." He risked angering her further by adding, "I might not have realized that without Kelly. What we did was so wrong, Audrey. I hope eventually you'll forgive us, but I have to say—"

"Zain, don't. I was just relaxing, and now I'm getting all ticked off again."

"Haven't you ever done something that you later looked back at and thought, 'What was I thinking? I know better than that?'"

Dark eyes—the very ones that had mesmerized him so long ago—clouded with pain. "That's called our marriage."

I guess I deserved that. "Okay, so you know that temptation and then the remorse and determination to do what—"

"That's the thing. I didn't. I never felt real remorse.

I never repented. I always wanted it to work out. Only recently, when Tami finally found a guy I thought I could be interested in, did I ever even have a hint of regret."

His heart plummeted to the bottom of his empty stomach and struggled to beat again. *Be honest but be understanding. It's been a lot of lonely years for her.* "I—I can understand that. It's what I mean, though."

"Zain?"

He couldn't bring himself to meet her gaze. "Yeah?"

"I didn't write letters about how I wanted our marriage to be because I regretted doing it in the first place." Her voice dropped to a whisper. "But usually Tami finds men that are so wrong for me. This one actually wasn't—except that, of course, *any* man is wrong for me."

It took him a moment to realize the unstated codicil. *Except you.* One after another, he raised ideas and tossed them aside again, nothing saying what he wanted to. *Try the necklace again. It can't hurt.*

The little blue box looked out of place, upside down and on the floor. Zain retrieved it and once more hunkered down on his heels, handing it to her. "Will you open it? I have to admit, I had a hard time choosing. I kept thinking of other ideas, and it's not easy to find things in my budget in there."

Her hand brushed his as she took it, the gesture reminding him so much of filling plates in Las Vegas with their deliberate touches every few seconds. Audrey's lips turned up at the corners. "It was so long ago. Why does it seem like it just happened?"

She thought of it too. "Because for us as a couple, it *is* the last thing that happened."

As he spoke, she tugged the edge of the bow that tied the box together. His patience stretched until he thought he'd snap as she hesitated. The words came in a ragged whisper. "I don't want to give you—I mean, I don't want you to think that if I open this and like it that everything is just perfect now and we'll live happily ever after."

"I'm not the fatalistic guy I was back then," Zain assured her.

Her eyes met his and she laughed. "We were pretty fatalistic, weren't we? 'If we don't do this now, we never will. Our hearts will be broken.'" The lid lifted, the tissue folded back, and Audrey fingered the olive vine. "It's beautiful."

"I mean it, Audrey. I want to make peace. I know I'm risking you throwing me out for reminding you of it, but if Kelly hadn't spoken to me about how I ignored what the Bible says about what a Christian is supposed to do and be in a marriage, I might never have seen just how wrong I was. I know two wrongs don't make a right—"

"No they don't," she murmured.

Something in Audrey's tone made him pause before continuing. "I—"

"I know I have to forgive." Her eyes flitted in his general direction before dropping to the necklace again. "It's just not that easy. But—"

"I'm not asking for overnight forgiveness. I know broken trust must be re-earned."

"Zain," she interrupted, "I understand a little more than I want to admit."

As he waited for her to continue, Zain prayed harder than he had since his father's heart attack ten years prior. *Lord, if she will just listen. Will just give it a chance. We could be good together. I know we could. We've managed apart well for all these years, why couldn't we do well together now? I mean, we're older. Less immature, at least.*

"—almost did it. It terrifies me how close I came to clicking that link."

"Wait, what link?"

"To your Facebook. It sat there and glared at me as if ordering me to see what she wrote."

Without a second of hesitation, Zain retrieved her laptop and logged into his account. "Here. Read it. If I thought about it, I would have suggested it this morning. Maybe you'll see her intention behind the wrong actions."

"I'm afraid I'll just get angry again. Right now, I'm struggling to forgive, but at least I'm in a place where I can do that much. If I read—"

The words spoke themselves before he had time to consider the ramifications of them. "It's a risk I'm willing to take. It's that important." He stood. "I'll find you something to eat. You read." Then, looking much too nonchalant for the crazed panic that washed over him as he did it, Zain covered her hand with his. "We can work this out—if we're both willing."

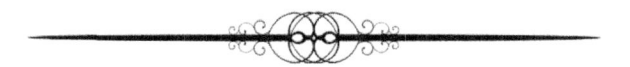

Words swirled on the screen before her like one of those obnoxious cursors with the trailing words behind it. Audrey blinked often as she read, convincing herself that it was to clear her vision rather than force back irritating tears. Illogically, she found her heart softening and her resolve not to yield hardening at the same time. *Lord, what do I do? I have to forgive. I don't want to. Why don't I want to?*

The answer came in a single thought. *Ask.*

I am asking! I'm sitting here, trying not to cry and I'm asking. What do You mean, "Ask?"

Again the reply came. *Ask.*

A pan rattled on the stove and she heard something sizzle seconds later. A glance his way showed Zain smiling back at her. "Can I ask you a question?"

"Shoot."

Audrey shifted so she could see him easier, setting the laptop on the table. "Okay, laying it all out there."

"Okaaay..."

"I know I have to forgive. Okay? I know that. I just don't want to. I've never not wanted to forgive something. Sometimes I want to and have a hard time with it, but this time I don't want to. Why?"

He snapped off the burner and crossed the room. Audrey started to protest but forced herself to be quiet—to listen. Zain perched on the arm of the couch beside her and waited until she'd met his gaze. "Forgiveness makes you vulnerable. It takes down a wall of stone, leaving only a thin layer of glass. The wall is still there, but now it's much easier to breach."

"Why glass?"

"That's the vulnerability," he explained. We can now see you—see the raw you left in the wake of our offense. Before forgiveness, you're not just blocked; you're invisible. Once we can see you, we also can see how easy it is to get to you. Forgiveness isn't just the acceptance of someone else's wrong and the choice to put it aside because it's right. It—well, like I said, it makes you vulnerable."

"You're not making this easier."

Laughter—deep, quiet, rumbling laughter—caught her unaware. Some women found buff bodies or backsides in a well-fitting pair of jeans attractive. Others liked glasses or a great smile. Audrey's weakness—that exact laughter. Before she knew she'd spoken, she whispered, "You didn't laugh like that in Vegas."

"Like what?"

With a dismissive shake of her head, Audrey returned to the topic. "I think..." She swallowed as the realization of what she was about to say hit her full force. "I think my problem is that I want to forgive *you,* but I don't want to forgive Kelly. And that's pretty hypocritical." She gave him a weak smile. "You know, why isn't it as easy to make this kind of life-changing decision as it was the last time?"

"We're not kids playing at adults this time." Her eyes closed as he brushed the back of his knuckles across her cheek. "We also know what kind of pain we're capable of causing each other."

Her phone rang, startling both of them. Zain

returned to the kitchen and his food preparation, while Audrey answered and promised her sister that she'd be there early. "I just need time to myself right now—well, and I've got something to talk to you guys about and I have to work through that, too."

"What is that supposed to mean?" Diane sounded beyond annoyed.

"Just that. Okay? I'll tell you when I'm good and ready, but it means I can't handle a houseful of kids and sisters bugging me. I'll see you around seven or so."

"Kids are going to want to start opening at five."

"They can wait," Audrey snapped. "Goodnight. Record Dad reading Luke for me, will you?"

"If you were *here*—"

"Bye." Audrey tossed her phone on the couch and went to help Zain. "Sisters."

He nodded and tossed a few vegetables into the pan. "Don't have any—just Aida—but I remember you talking about them arguing all the time. Trying to bring you into it now, eh?"

"No. She just likes everything to be exactly the same every year, and it can't be." A few pieces of leftover meat from the previous night followed. Audrey started to ask what he planned to make, but their previous conversation returned. "Is it true forgiveness if you decide to forgive—choose to do it even though it's hard not to still be upset?"

"I think so. I think some things almost require that, y'know? I mean if someone willfully murdered someone I love, I'd have to do that seventy times seven thing—maybe every day."

"I guess I've never had to forgive anything like this. It's always been relatively easy. Even you leaving—or so I thought," she amended. "I loved you so much. I just found it easier to forgive."

"And you don't love me anymore." Zain nodded. "I understand."

"That's not what I said."

"Look, Audrey. You thought I left you. Then you find out I didn't. Then you—well earlier you find out—or rather—" He shook his head. "The fact is in your mind, I betrayed you and our vows repeatedly. Of course that's going to damage your love for me. I don't expect it not to."

"I read Kelly's message, Zain. I know you know that I wrote about how much I still love you, okay? It never went away. Man, Zain, I *prayed* to make it go away."

"And there," he insisted, "is your problem. Never pray for something you want not to care about. You'll care even more."

"Tell me about it."

He pulled rice from the microwave and shook it onto plates before dumping the veggie-beef mix over it. "Here. Can I read the letters?"

"What?"

"Sorry, had to ask while I had the guts to do it. Can I read them?" He filled his own plate as he spoke, never looking at her.

"I—I guess. Maybe while I'm gone tomorrow." She stamped down rising panic at the idea and changed the subject. "What are you going to do for Christmas?"

They sat on her couch, eating in near silence until he finished his plate and set it on the coffee table. "I was thinking about going to the mission around noonish—see if they need any help. Might go there tonight and see if Barney will let me sleep on the floor of his office or something. I should have thought about that last night."

As he spoke, she shook her head. "You can sleep here—stay here until you go." She grabbed the plates and carried them to the kitchen, hiding a wince as her wrist complained about holding the weight of the plate.

"Go where?"

"To the mission tomorrow. I'd invite you to my parents' but I don't think tomorrow is the day to spring a son-in-law on them."

He followed, gently nudging her onto a stool while he rinsed plates and filled the sink with dishwater. Audrey protested as she pointed out the dishwasher, but Zain shook his head. "Not enough dishes to make it worthwhile."

They talked as he worked—not about their past and the problems they had to overcome. They just talked. Zain told her about his niece and nephew, his father's retirement, and the growth of the business in recent years. Audrey talked mainly of her business, the town, and added a few dreams she'd put on the back burner to make it all happen.

He helped her carry the pile of gifts under her tree to her car, and he teased her about having a PT Cruiser with her misspelled business name plastered on the side. She pulled out an air mattress and helped him blow it up between funny stories about their respective customers. Twice she thought he'd kiss her, and the second time a twinge of disappointment made her wonder if things might actually work out for them after all.

Just before she rose to say goodnight, Audrey turned to him and asked, "How long are you staying?"

"Where?"

"Here—with me, in town, wherever—how long?"

Feathers should have filled the room with the kind of pounding he gave his pillow, but Zain didn't answer until he'd finished making up his "bed." He offered his hand, pulled her to her feet, and once more she held her breath in anticipation of a kiss that didn't come. "I'm not leaving. I'm here indefinitely—not necessarily here in your house. That's up to you. But I am not leaving this town unless I become convinced that you will never consider a real marriage between us."

Chapter Twenty-Seven

Christmas Day—Fairbury

Her alarm bleeped, and on auto-pilot, Audrey slammed her hand in its general direction, effectively shutting it off. *Muscle memory—genius thing, Lord.*

She peered through one half-open eye and saw the numbers. Five-thirty. Something else caught her attention. An envelope. Audrey rubbed her eyes and tried to read the writing on it. *Audrey. Well, that's genius. Who would have thought that an envelope on my nightstand might have my name on it?* She stifled a snicker and reached for it. *Oh, you're in fine form already. This is gonna be one bizarre Christmas.*

A Tiffany box lay on the stand, once hidden by the envelope. She frowned and rolled over, forcing her eyes to focus on the dresser. There it lay—the box with her necklace in it. Audrey's heart raced as she opened the envelope. A copy of their wedding picture fell out and dropped on the comforter.

> *Dear Audrey,*
>
> *I know this looks crazy, but I hope when you see what's inside, you'll understand why I found it so hard to decide what to get you. I stayed under (barely, I admit) my budget for both, and so used that to justify getting this as well. In my mind, it was a belated birthday gift,*

but I didn't like not having something for you on Christmas. So, Merry Christmas. It's the second we've "spent" together in a sense. I hope it's the second of many.

Thank you for your understanding. Thank you for not kicking me out without hope. I hope you have a wonderful day with your family. I suspect they don't know how blessed (see, I learned that lesson) they are to have you.

Love,

Zain

P.S. I did dig through your desk for pen and paper. I didn't see anything personal. Just in the interest of full disclosure and everything.

Though she reached for it, Audrey hesitated over opening the box. *Should I wait? Maybe he'd like me to open it with him?* She shook the box and smiled at the hint of a rattle. *Then again, he did bring it up here. Why don't I find that creepy?* Her uncertainty refused to abate. With a frustrated sigh, she put the box inside her nightstand so he wouldn't know she hadn't opened it if he came upstairs. *Later. I'll explain later. He'll understand.*

She dressed in a hurry, pulling on jeans and a sweater she'd purchased months ago especially for Christmas morning. *Lord, I wish Zain could see it. Is that crazy? I mean, he is my husband. It's not wrong for me to want him to like what he sees, is it?* Her own reply came almost instantly. *It's wrong that you have to ask that question. You blew it—big time.*

Boots, clip to pull her hair out of her face, earrings, light makeup, and only a split-second of hesitation before choosing not to put on the necklace. *They won't understand, and I've told enough half-truths and concealed enough others to last a lifetime. I'm not going to play the "we're one, so if he buys it I buy it and vice versa" like Tami does.* Her conscience kicked in and hit hard. *Yeah, and she knows everyone knows it. She's not pretending it's real. That's the difference.*

Once ready, she crept downstairs, every move designed not to wake Zain. He shifted, his foot sticking out from under the blanket. Audrey remembered his propensity toward cold and retrieved the couch throw. It looked odd draped over the lower third of Zain's body, but it would keep his feet warm.

He's still good looking—scary good looking. Then again, guys like him always look even better when they hit about fifty or so. He's probably got a few years to go before he hits his prime. That's just not fair.

Purse in hand, Audrey started to leave and then remembered the letters. *If I don't get them, he won't read them, and I did say he could.* That thought hit her hard. *I know this and still I hesitate to trust him. Why? He came back. Sure, he should have come back sooner, but if we had had cellphones back then, this wouldn't be an issue. I would have sent a text, he would have clarified, and we would have made up.*

She crept upstairs, trying to make as little noise as possible, and retrieved the packet. There on the desk lay the paper and pen he'd used to write her a note. As quick as possible, she scrawled her own.

Zain,

I got your note this morning. Make sure I talk to you about it later. Meanwhile, thank you.

Here are the letters. You should know something before you read them. At times, I was in a bad place when I wrote them, and sometimes that meant that I said things that were wrong. I usually repented right away, but a year would pass between writing them, so that's not always reflected in the next. Let's face it, December has been a very hard month for me since Las Vegas—particularly the last two weeks of it. I just wanted you to know that when you read me write how much I love you, that isn't any less true because at other times I focus on being hurt or angry with you.

I'm going to tell my parents—sometime between tomorrow and New Year's. I'm also going to make it clear that we're going to work toward a real marriage, so you'd better tell me fast if you're not serious about that.

Audrey paused as she stared at the line she'd just written. *Do I mean it?* Her heart screamed "yes" while her sense of self-preservation hesitated. *He left you.* Before she could stop herself, Audrey penned the last line.

I'm glad you came and that you're here. I have to say that while I can bring myself to admit it. It might take me a while to be more open with you. I hope you can deal with that.

Merry Christmas,

Audrey

She snatched the packet of letters, her note, and hurried from the office. *Yeah, well, he may have left you, but from his perspective, you left him. You both blew it. Now suck it up and straighten out.*

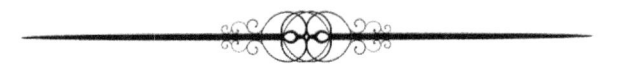

How Christmas has changed, Audrey mused as she watched her nieces and nephews argue about what movie they were going to go see after Christmas dinner ended. *I can't imagine what we would have thought about seeing a movie on Christmas Day back when we were kids.* Her sisters joined the argument, making Audrey ready to lose all patience with the so-called festivities. In his chair, Walt sent her a plea to do something, and in hers, Phyllis looked ready to bang heads together.

I could shake this up big time. I wonder what

would happen if I did. She eyed her father. *Would he be relieved or furious? There's one way to find out.*

Audrey inched her way over to her father's chair and knelt beside him. "I have news for this family—big news. It's going to create a massive amount of drama," she whispered. "Do you want it today where we can stop the usual bickering about this stuff or do you want me to save it so I don't ruin Christmas?"

"Like they didn't already? Let's have it." He started to call the room to attention, but Audrey hushed him.

"Let me talk to Mom first, and I need to make a phone call."

"Wait." Walt cupped her face in his hands, searching for something in her expression—her eyes. He didn't find it, but she saw he still remained uncertain.

She leaned close and hissed, "What?"

"If you're going to come out of some closet—"

"Not the kind you're thinking of," she assured him. "But it's big like that."

Walt nodded. "Then talk to your mom. She's about to blow a gasket."

To her surprise, her mom also chose a new kind of drama over the current offering. Phyllis hugged her, thanked her, and begged her not to wait to do "whatever it is that you're going to do to fix this. I don't think I can take much more of this. I always thought they'd get better after they were married and living on their own. It just gets worse every year!"

"What, Mom?" Tami glanced over. "Are you guys coming?"

"No," the three remaining Seevers muttered.

"Be right back." Audrey kissed her mother and grabbed her jacket. Diane called after her, but Audrey just waved and shuffled down the walkway to the sidewalk where she knew she couldn't be overheard. *Lord, please don't let him feel used. I mean, I am technically using him, but it would be nice if he didn't **feel** like it.*

He answered after several rings—just before she gave up and tried the house phone. "Zain?"

"Yeah, everything all right?"

"Sort of. Everything is normal, which means everything is stressful and even my parents have had it. We have a great family, but when there's a decision in the offing, you can forget it. Things get ugly. So, I wondered how you'd feel about being the star of Christmas dinner. I have to admit," she nearly kicked herself for doing it, but her conscience wouldn't relent, "it's totally using you and us and everything as a way to diffuse one kind of conflict and just get our own over with, but—"

"What do you want? I'll do it, just tell me."

"I want you to come here for Christmas dinner. Will Barney let you off?"

"I'm not at the mission. Barney asked if I could come Sunday instead, so I was about to go figure out if any restaurants are open in this town." Zain's voice dropped. "Are you sure?"

"I want to introduce you. I want to tell them everything, and I want—actually kind of need—you here for that."

"I'm on my way."

"Great. Um, call me when you get here and I'll come out. I'll text the address. Got a GPS?" Her nerves kicked into overdrive. Just as he said he'd be there within the hour, Audrey thought of something else. "Hey, Zain?"

"Yeah."

"Can you bring my necklace? I left it on my dresser. I think I'd like to have it for this. Feels like a good luck charm or something."

Zain's laughter sent familiar ripples through her heart. "We're going to have to talk about this luck thing. You've got to make up your mind."

"Very funny." And don't you dare laugh or I'll melt and well, um, now's not the time.

"I'll bring it."

By the time she returned to the house, dinner preparations had kicked up a notch, and half the kids were in the basement with a new Wii game, battling it out in front of the big screen the three sisters had chipped in to purchase for their father. Phyllis called her daughters into the kitchen and handed out orders. "We might be able to eat a little early—"

Audrey protested. "We can't eat before four."

"Why not? It'll give us more time to get to the cinema," Tami insisted.

"Because seeing some stupid movie on Christmas Day is more important than having a calm, family dinner."

Tami's shocked face almost made Audrey capitulate, but when Tami said, "Why can't we have a calm, family dinner thirty minutes earlier?" her frustration level boiled over.

"Because we always eat at four. We do that for a reason, Tami! We don't eat breakfast until almost noon! If we eat too early, we're not going to have room for a decent meal and we're just going to get hungry earlier later."

"That doesn't even make sense!" Tami would have said more, but Walt called his agreement from the living room.

"Audrey's right. I refuse to get out of this chair before four o'clock for any reason other than a quick trip to the latrine."

"There you have it," Tami whined. "Dad won't get up unless he's gotta pee."

The three girls relaxed and giggled as Phyllis muttered automatically, "No potty talk in the kitchen."

However, the argument resumed a few minutes later when Phyllis stopped Tami from mashing the potatoes yet. "It's too early. They'll get cold."

"It wouldn't be," Tami groused, "if Audrey wasn't being so ridiculous."

Something in her expression must have given away her near desperation, because Diane gave Audrey a questioning look and then said, "Oh, what's the point of having Christmas dinner before four? It's not dinner then. It's lunch. Besides, we'll never get the rolls done even by four. Yeast is unyielding in that respect."

"Now we know where Audrey gets it," Tami muttered. "She spends too much time with the fungus stuff as it is."

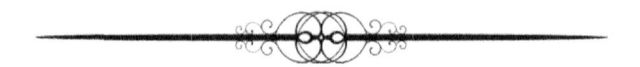

As he waited at a red light two blocks from the Seever home, Zain sent Audrey a text. **THERE IN LESS THAN TWO MINUTES**.

She stood outside, gesturing for him to park in front of a blue house of a bizarre shade. *Looks like it belongs in the Caribbean rather than here. I can't see Audrey living in a house like that—even as a child.*

He'd hardly put the car in gear when she climbed into it. "Whew. I just took the rolls out."

Something in her voice made him uneasy. "If you're not sure…"

"I'm sure." She gave him a smile that, if somewhat tentative, was definitely genuine. "Did you bring the necklace?"

"Yes." He pulled it from his pocket.

"I was thinking about it. Did you buy silver deliberately?"

"In that it was the only thing I could afford," he admitted. "Well, not knowing what my finances will look like moving here and all."

She looked disappointed until she lifted the lid. "It's so pretty. Well, intentional or not, silver for our silver anniversary is still pretty amazing." Audrey removed the necklace from the box and offered it to him. "Will you?"

Without waiting for an answer, she turned and pulled her hair out of the way. Zain found his hands shaky and clumsy as he fumbled with the clasp, nearly dropping it twice. Once secured, his hands dropped to her shoulders. He closed his eyes and forced himself to admit his unease. "I'm so afraid I'm going to blow this."

"They're not that—"

"No," Zain interrupted. "This—us. I was content before I got that message from Kelly." His throat constricted and his heart thundered as she turned, her face so near to his. "At least I thought I was. Now—not so much." Zain pressed his forehead against hers and murmured, "I don't know if I can stand another heartbreak."

"Did it hurt you that much?"

He nodded. "Dad tells everyone that I left my brains in my Bible in Las Vegas. I almost flunked out of my second semester that year."

Expressive eyes searched his face for an answer before she leaned back and crossed her arms over her chest. "You got a few Bs didn't you?"

"Guilty as charged. Barely missed a C, but he doesn't know that."

"Which is just how you like it." She opened the car door. "C'mon, they're going to come find me if we don't hurry. Dinner'll get cold."

To his surprise, the more nervous she acted, the calmer he felt. And to his utter relief, she led him to a house two doors up the street on the opposite side—one with a calm, gray-blue and stone exterior. *I don't know why it matters to me, but it gives me hope somehow.*

Inside the door, they shed their coats. Voices reached him—chattering, bickering, exasperated voices that made him understand her mood just a little better. Audrey led him to where a man sat in a recliner, reading. "Dad?"

The man stood and offered his hand before she could introduce them. "I'm Walt—Seever."

"Nice to meet you, Mr. Seever."

"Dad, this is Zain Kadir. He's—an old friend, you might say."

She's going to chicken out. Can't say that I blame

her. How many times did I almost turn around?

Audrey led him to the kitchen, sending her father a look that Zain couldn't read. When Walt followed, he suspected it was akin to "Rescue me."

The voices stopped at their arrival. "Mom, Diane, Tami, I invited someone very special to me as a surprise guest. This is Zain." She finished introductions and started to lead Zain downstairs, but Phyllis stopped her.

"I'll call everyone upstairs. You just find a chair for Zain."

The area became miserably quiet to him, but Audrey seemed happy. Once she'd dragged a chair to the table from somewhere down the hall, she whispered, "If I'd known that would work so well, I would have called you hours ago. I should have brought you this morning."

"No, you did the right thing. Christmas morning is for family."

"Which you are!" she hissed.

Introductions to the nieces and nephews buzzed in his head. *Tami, Kammi—double whammy! I'll never get 'em straight.*

Audrey leaned over and murmured, "I don't want to tell them everything until after we eat, so try to evade anything too obvious."

"Gotcha."

The moment Walt said "Amen" after thanking the Lord for blessing them for another year, the air around the table changed. Audrey's sisters looked to their parents to open what he expected to be an interrogation worthy of any crime drama, but one of the nieces—Carly, if he remembered correctly—asked the first question almost the moment heads rose from prayer.

"So, how did you guys meet?"

Audrey choked despite not having eaten a bite yet. Determined to keep her as out of the line of fire as possible, he answered for them. "We met in Las Vegas."

Diane whipped her head around and mouthed, "*Is that him?*"

Zain's confusion flickered and burst into flame as Audrey's face went ashen before nodding. *I thought none of them knew! What on earth is going on?*

"And just which Vegas trip was this?" Tami lost no time ignoring the previous unspoken agreement to let the parents do the interrogating.

"I've only been there once, Tami. You know that."

"So you've known this guy for twenty-five years, and you're just now telling us about him?"

Audrey nodded. "I figured better late than never."

Tami's voice raised a notch. "So you've been writing? Visiting? What—since then?"

Zain stepped in. "Nothing. We—" he fumbled for an honest as well as ambiguous explanation. "We knew how to get in touch but didn't really. I saw her once, though," he added as Diane's face fell.

"And so seeing her once brings you back here—why?" Tami leaned in to say more, but Walt cleared his throat in an obvious attempt to stifle the awkward line of questioning.

Diane glared at Tami before asking, "Where are you from, Zain? I assume we'd have seen you before this if you lived close..."

"Los Angeles."

Walt jumped into the fray with a typical fatherly question. "And what do you do in Los Angeles?"

"Zain's family owns a taxi service, Dad. I intend to make him promise to give us free rides if we ever go to Disneyland." Audrey's hand slipped under the table and squeezed his. Zain didn't know if it was in thanks or warning.

"Yellow taxis like in movies?" The little girl to his right—obviously the youngest of them all—stared up at him with curious eyes.

"Well, ours are all black, but we have yellow lettering," he hastened to add as she gave him a look that clearly indicated her displeasure with black taxis.

Phyllis noticed Audrey's necklace just as Tami opened her mouth. Zain found himself blasted with two questions at once. "Where'd you get that, Audrey? You weren't wearing that necklace earlier."

"How often do you guys get together then?"

Zain ignored Tami and answered the easier question. "I bought it for our silver anniversary."

That earned him a kick from Audrey and a unified cry of surprise from around the table. "What—" Tami waited for a dozen other questions before she finished. "—did you say?"

Again, Audrey kicked him, but Zain reached over and patted her leg. "It's been twenty-five years since we spent our first Christmas together. It was a pretty special day for us, too, so—"

Diane turned to Audrey, eyes wide, and started to ask, "Wait, are you—"

Audrey shook her head. "Can we talk about this after dinner?" She turned to Walt and added, "He has a big flaw that we'll have to overcome."

"And that is?" Walt asked. Zain's mind asked it as well.

"He loves the Steelers."

How do I respond to that, Lord? I could care less about the Steelers or any other football team for that matter.

It worked, however. The room erupted in arguments over the team, but unlike Audrey, who looked utterly miserable, Zain found the discussion stimulating. *It's a little like home. Baba and Mama battling out who is the best all-time singer or Joe and I fighting over UCLA versus USC. It's cool.* A glance in Audrey's direction made him amend that thought. *It's not cool for her, I guess. I wonder why she hates it so much. It just seems like good-natured fun.*

At the end of the meal, Audrey stood to help her sisters clear the table and bring out dessert. As she did, she murmured, "As soon as I get back, I'm going to tell 'em."

"Let me." She started to protest, but Zain added, "Trust me."

Her eyes met his and a part of him saw the scene from outside himself. He smiled. *This looks much more intimate than it really is. I wonder what they're thinking.*

Zain waited. Diane squeezed his shoulder as she set a slice of cake before him, which Zain took for confirmation that she'd figured out what was coming. A bowl of ice cream—he'd never seen anyone move ice cream from the container to a serving bowl—appeared on his right and the little girl, Tanika, pointed to Audrey. "It's hers. She makes the best."

"Thank you." Zain waited until Audrey seated herself, squeezed her hand in warning, and said, "I actually have something to tell all of you." Though he spoke to the room, his eyes rested on Walt.

Walt grinned as if he thought he knew what Zain would say. "Well, tell us then."

"This isn't just the twenty-fifth anniversary of our first Christmas together." Zain's eyes panned the faces before him before resting on Walt's again. "It is also our twenty-fifth wedding anniversary."

The smile faded from Walt's face.

Chapter Twenty-Eight

The room erupted in a cacophony of protests, but Tami's, being closest to him, was loudest. "That's not funny, Zain."

"Tami, shut up!" Diane glared once more at her sister. "He's not joking."

"How do *you* know?"

Diane's head shook as she rolled her eyes. "We've said for years that she came back so different after that trip. She never went out with another man—even one like Merrill whom we both know she *should* have found irresistible—no offense, Zain."

"None taken."

Audrey's brothers-in-law stood and began ushering kids from the table. Tami's husband grabbed plates and carried them to the kitchen. "You can finish later. Let's get to the theater. We want good seats."

"But Dad," one of the teen aged boys protested, "we'll be waiting for almost—"

"Go!"

They went. The table became eerily silent, marred only by the occasional clink of a fork hitting a plate too hard. Audrey choked down her cake and seemed to choke back tears. Tami and Diane exchanged eloquent glances. Walt looked like he'd aged instantaneously. Phyllis alone watched him.

"Zain?"

He smiled at Audrey's mother, unable to answer

with a mouth full of cake.

"Do you really expect us to believe that you and my daughter have been married for twenty-five years? That's a bit—far-fetched, don't you think?"

Audrey started to answer, but seeing him pull out his wallet silenced her. He tugged their wedding picture from it and passed it across the table to Tami. By the time it had reached Phyllis and Walt, it became evident that doubts had already formed in Tami's mind. She shook her head. "Probably one of those souvenir shots—like those things where you stick your head in a cutout. Vegas *is* the wedding capital of the world or something like that."

After a glance at Audrey for approval, he reached in and withdrew his cash and the certificate he'd stashed with it. Wordlessly, he passed it across the table and reached for Audrey's hand. "I know you probably have questions—"

"No duh," Tami muttered.

"Let's go in the living room," Phyllis suggested. "I don't feel like eating anymore."

Zain held Audrey back and hugged her as the room emptied. "It's going to be okay. If nothing else, they're Christians. They *have* to forgive us—eventually."

"I guess. I knew it would be hard, but I didn't expect that look on Dad's face. I feel like I punched him."

In a sense, we did. No use mentioning that, though. Just get her through this. You can do it.

They sat side by side on a loveseat that left little space between them. Taking his cue from Audrey, Zain sat looking as relaxed as possible, one arm draped over the arm of the couch, his ankle resting on the opposite knee. But he kept his hand ready to take hers, to pull her close—anything to show both his support and his genuine affection for her. *Is that what it is? Genuine affection? Do I love her like I think I do? I don't know. I never felt like it went away. Any time I thought about us, it hurt. So, I tried not to think about us. I was happy—content. But I wasn't complete.* That thought hit him the hardest. *I guess that makes sense, though. We are supposed to be one as a couple. We weren't. We were split and for no good reason.*

Diane spoke first. "I always thought something happened there. Why I didn't think of marriage, I don't know, but it makes sense."

"What?" Walt's voice thundered through the room with unexpected strength. "You think getting married at eighteen and never telling your family makes sense? You think it makes sense that they haven't seen each other since? I don't think that makes sense at all."

"No, I just think that things that have happened since make sense now." She tried to explain further, but the others bombarded the couple with questions, drowning out Diane's words.

Beside him, Audrey grew visibly agitated. He pulled her close, murmured assurances that he could handle the discussion, and kept his arm around her as he spoke. "Can I tell our story?"

"Why isn't Audrey telling it?" Tami snapped.

"Because I am trying to accept responsibility for failing my wife."

"You don't know what it means to have a wife."

He nodded as Walt's words sank into his heart. "That is true. And that is my fault."

"Can he just tell the stupid story?" Diane glared at the rest of her family after sending Audrey a reassuring glance. "I'm dying to know what could have happened to make goody-goody Audrey do something like elope, okay?"

He began at the airport, describing his amusement as she chose their taxi to be sure he hadn't concocted some elaborate scheme to kidnap her and sell her into slavery in some far-distant country. Even Walt managed a hint of a smile at that. "By Wednesday, I was falling hard and fast. Audrey was—is still—just everything I could have hoped for. Our first date—"

"On Christmas Adam," Audrey interjected.

"Right. Best night of my life. We talked for hours—well after two or three in the morning."

"Did more than talk," she muttered. At Diane's raised eyebrows, Audrey admitted "Nothing immoral! Sheesh!"

Zain smiled. "Yeah, I admit we were a bit...affectionate."

This time Audrey snorted. "Okay, fine. We totally made out at the door to the church, okay? Nothing I would have done in a group of people but nothing I would have been ashamed to get caught doing either, okay?"

To bring the topic back on track, Zain described their Christmas Eve trek across Las Vegas. "We walked for hours. Something about seeing the wedding chapel just brought out the—"

Audrey snickered. "Fatalistic. That's what Zain called it last night—fatalistic. We totally had this attitude like if we didn't do it before we left town, we'd lose all hope of ever seeing each other again."

"Looks like it worked the other way around," Phyllis murmured. "But why didn't you tell us? Why didn't you bring him home? Why did you two live separate lives? How is that right?"

"It's not." Zain begged the Lord for guidance as he began to explain how they'd gone back the next day, how they'd made vows, and then within less than two hours, he'd broken them. "She thought I left—for good. Now that I hear my words through her ears, I understand why. I mean, I did say I was 'done.' How was she to know that I meant with the conversation?"

"But I left, Zain. I didn't even go where you could find me. I ran away and hid in the airport. That's *my* fault."

He tried not to laugh and felt guilty about failing—well, until she leaned closer. That closeness buoyed his spirit. "Since I got here, we've been at odds over this. We each blamed the other. Now look at us."

"That doesn't answer why you didn't tell us, Audie."

Walt didn't look at Zain. His eyes riveted on his daughter as he added, "We would have helped. We—"

"I thought I'd blown it. I thought I'd married a man who didn't love me like I loved him. I mean, part of me knew it was an immature love. I wasn't *that* naive, but if he left, that meant he didn't really want me. We said ugly things to each other that night. I'm not proud of what I did." Audrey sighed. "But while I sat here justifying my anger, he arrived asking forgiveness and not making any excuses."

"What took you so long?" Phyllis' eyes swept back and forth between Audrey and Zain. "I mean it. Both of you. What took so long?"

Audrey fidgeted and said nothing. Zain swallowed his pride and laid it all bare for them to examine. "Lots of reasons. At first, pride. I felt like I'd been rejected. I didn't want to admit that. Then fear. My father would have been furious—was furious when I told him. But between all that, each day becomes another opportunity to say, 'Tomorrow. I can't deal with it today. It's not like another day will make any difference.'"

"But—"

Zain interrupted Tami before she could derail his thoughts. "And the more you do that, the less you think of it. You just get caught up in working and family and fixing meals and hobbies. I mean, I doubt a day went by that I didn't *think* of her, but that doesn't mean that I thought of the need to *fix* things on those days. Then a year is gone—two—ten—twenty. At that point, you wake up and think, 'Even if we could make it work, at this point, why? She'd probably hate me more then. We might have nothing in common anymore. We haven't grown together in our likes and dislikes.' It's just easier to let it go."

As he spoke, Audrey nodded. "I didn't tell you because I knew what you'd say. You'd want us to get counseling. You'd want him to come here, and I didn't think he would. Then you'd urge me to go there and I'd be all alone in a place where I really thought his parents would hate me. Why do that? He seemed fine with being apart, so we stayed apart."

"So what changed?"

Audrey and Zain exchanged disconcerted glances before she answered. "My friend saw my tax form with his name on it. Everything spiraled from there."

Diane's eyes widened. "Kelly! That's why she was so upset about us pushing you to go out with someone! Wow!"

Nodding, Audrey agreed. "Yeah. I was pretty mad at her at first—still am working through some of that," she admitted. "But she told Zain something that one of our mutual friends has learned."

"What's that?"

"There's more to being married than 'for better or worse.'"

Zain nodded. "Even of that, we tend to hear only the 'for worse' part. I didn't live together with her. I didn't leave father and mother. I didn't love her and live with her in an understanding way. I wasn't faithful to *all* my vows—only to the not committing adultery. Otherwise, I pretty much broke every single one." His hand reached for hers as his arm pulled her closer. "I plan to make the next twenty-five years a picture of how to reverse that."

Tami jumped up and fled the room. Audrey started to follow, but she returned with their picture in hand. "This was your wedding picture. You wore that shirt—of all shirts, that one?"

"That was Diane's line," Audrey joked. "We all know how much she hated it. But, Zain liked it, so I wanted to look nice for him."

"And that cheesy bracelet. It was shot when I gave it to you."

"I liked it—it broke in the bathroom at the airport that night."

Zain waited for her to mention the bracelet he'd given her, but she didn't. Disappointed, he whispered,

"I remembered that bracelet. That's why—"

Walt stood and sank back down again. "I can't believe my daughter has lied to me for so long."

"Daddy..." Audrey pulled away from Zain and knelt at her father's feet, her head in his lap. "I'm sorry. It was wrong, I know."

"And yet you did it anyway."

"Tell me about it," Tami snapped. "I've been an obnoxious jerk all these years, trying to help my sister find happiness when she's already married."

"And she asked you not to." Diane drew back as the other Seevers glared at her. "What? I'm not saying what Audrey did was right. I'm saying that she told us over and over again that she didn't want us setting her up with anyone, and even I tried a couple of times, knowing she didn't want me to. We all did."

"But you're acting like it's no big deal—like this is no different than saying, 'Oh, I forgot to share the souvenir I bought while I was in Vegas that time.'" Tami glanced at Zain. "No offense."

What do I say to that? The answer came quickly. "If I say that to you, will this be over for us? If I apologize, confess my wrong behavior—which I have done—and say, 'no offense,' does that make it all fine now?"

"Zain..." Audrey warned.

"I don't mean to be rude, and I actually wasn't offended at what you said, Tami, but we can't change what we did. It's past. We can only change what we do now. We can only ask forgiveness. So the question becomes, will this family forgive us?"

Diane spoke first—almost before he finished speaking. "I do."

Phyllis stood and pulled Audrey to her feet, hugging her daughter. "I'll try, honey. I'll try. But I have to admit, I feel like you kicked me in the gut. The daughter I know wouldn't hide something like this—not this long. I don't know this Audrey."

"Mom—"

"Just give us time to adjust."

"Mrs. Seever?" Zain waited for Audrey's mother to look his way before saying, "Thank you for trying." He turned to Diane. "Thank you."

"What, so Dad and I are the bad guys because we're having trouble accepting that what we thought we knew isn't so? Yeah. That's rich."

"Tami—"

"No, Audrey. No. You *lied* to me. You broke my trust. I can't just pretend like that's okay."

"I never asked you to," Audrey whispered. "I just asked you to try to forgive me."

"Us," Zain corrected. "We both failed, although my parents pretty much blame me exclusively."

Walt leaned forward, watching Zain closely as he asked, "How *do* your parents feel about this? What did they say?"

"They pretty much let me have it in every way possible for failing Audrey as a husband. I denied her the protection and support of a husband. I denied her children. I did not even give her the release of a divorce or annulment." He smiled at the shock on the Seevers' faces. "My parents are not Christians. They do not understand why I should not have given her the opportunity to marry someone else at the very least."

"Audrey grew up in a Christian home. She knows—"

"As do I, Mr. Seever. I know. I made the mistake. If either of us had ever contacted the other, this could have been cleared up, but I think as a husband, it was my responsibility and I failed her. She seems to have forgiven me. I just hope you will too."

"Well, he says all the right words, doesn't he?"

Even Walt, as visibly upset as the man still was, glared at Tami. "What kind of nonsense is that? If you aren't prepared to forgive, fine. Work that out between you and the Lord." Tami began to protest, but Walt shushed her. "But do not trample a man's apology because your pride is hurt."

"What!"

"That's what it is, Tami. I don't like it any more than you do, but we're struggling because our pride is hurt. *We* weren't told."

"She betrayed our trust!" Tami's cry of protest echoed in the room and acted as an emotional whip, slicing through Audrey's last remaining armor.

Zain couldn't stand anymore. "We'll go now. You need time to process, and Audrey's hurting enough as it is."

Another protest began, but Phyllis' words silenced it. "That might be best. We can talk in a couple of days—when we've had time to get used to the idea."

It took a couple of trips to Audrey's car to fill it with the food and gifts Audrey had to take home, and by the time she finally pulled away from the curb, Zain wanted nothing more than to be away from Tami and her sarcastic comments. With a heavy heart, he walked back up to the front door with Diane and followed her inside. He shook hands with Walt and returned Phyllis' hug as he said, "I just wanted to thank you for a delicious meal and for not kicking me out. If I could undo the wrongs we did, trust me I would."

It took great effort on Walt's part—that much was evident—but the man followed him back to the door and said as Zain turned the knob, "We're going to love you. We're going to forgive. We have to. We just need a bit of time to get there."

She'd locked herself in the office within minutes of arriving home. Zain promised to put away the food—promised to give her space. Audrey sat, head in her hands, half-open boxes surrounding her on the floor, and tried to decide how much of the damage she'd done to her family relationships would be irreparable. Every answer discouraged her. She tried prayer. She tried reading her Bible—the one she'd used in Las Vegas, no less—but her mind refused to concentrate.

As the clock downstairs chimed nine o'clock, she realized the day and pulled several pieces of copy paper from the printer tray. Four false starts ended up in the wastepaper basket, but at last she decided what she'd write for her anniversary letter.

Zain,

You're here. Even as I sit at this desk and write this, I'm amazed to think that I could call your name and you'd be beside me within seconds. I never expected ever to spend an anniversary in the same house. Well, at least not for the past fifteen or more years. In the beginning, I did often hope we'd find a way to fix our mess.

What you did today at my parents' house means more to me than I know how to say. So I'll just say thank you instead. I also learned an even deeper lesson on forgiveness. I'll be calling Kelly tomorrow. Yes, what she did was wrong, but I feel a bit like either the 'he who is without sin' thing or the 'take the plank out of your eye' thing fits here. I broke trust with my family. I want forgiveness. I'm still bothered by what she did, but if I don't forgive, how can I hope to be forgiven? That's in the Gospels somewhere. 'But if you do not forgive others, then your Father will not forgive your transgressions.' I should look it up.

I need to thank you for the necklace. It's beautiful. Just the kind of thing I'd buy if I saw it and was looking for something to buy myself. That's pretty impressive. I need to take this letter downstairs with my other box so I can see how else you spoiled me. I want to thank you for that too. I mean for spoiling me. I would have said it wasn't important, but honestly, right now I needed that.

There's so much to say. So much to plan. So much to

decide. I can't seem to find words. For years I've poured out my heart on paper and now that you're here, I have no words.

Audrey dropped the pen as she realized why. She started to rise but ordered herself to find a way to end the letter. Her hand hovered over the paper, lowered, raised, and lowered once more as the words came to her again.

I know why now. It's BECAUSE you're here. Because you're here, I want to talk, not write. So, I'm going to end this letter and go spend time with you. But before I do I want to say something I might not have the courage to say. I needed you to come back. I needed you to force me to confess to my family. I needed to see how I'd wronged them. I also needed to forgive you. I still do when I think about you asking Kelly about those letters, but I'll get past that. WE'll get past that.

And I love you. I know we're still in a pretty immature stage of loving right now. I mean, what else could we be? We haven't had years to mature and grow together. But we will. And at least we didn't learn to hate each other. That's a good thing right there. It could have been so easy. God was good to us. God IS good to us.

Happy Anniversary, Zain.
Audrey

With a quick detour to her room to grab the other blue box, she hurried downstairs and found Zain on the couch typing way on his computer. He smiled up at her. "Just a second. I want you to meet my family. I'll tell Joe to get on Skype."

Her eyes widened. "I didn't think of that. Is this going to be another Seever thing? I don't think I can do two in a row."

"No. Remember, they've known for a week or two."

She set the box down on the table and handed him the letter. "Let me run upstairs and make sure I don't look pathetic after the crying jag. I should have done that before I came down here. Ugh. I have to think about stuff like that now."

"You look fine!" he called after her, but she dashed upstairs anyway. A makeup wipe took care of a few mascara smudges and a swipe of lipstick gave her face a little polish without making her look like she was trying too hard. She adjusted the necklace to hang straight and reached for her perfume.

I know they can't smell it, but he can. We'll be close if we're on Skype. That thought brought a smile to her lips. *Lord, is it real? I never imagined I'd have this. I—*

Zain called her from downstairs, insisting that she couldn't look better if she tried. She hurried down and settled in beside him, a smile in her heart. "That's not true, but it's nice to hear it."

"Don't argue with my son," a voice insisted. "He'll make you rue it."

She stared at the screen, smiling at the face before her. "Now are you Mr. Kadir or Joe?"

"Oh, this one is good, Sarah. She asked if I was Yosef or me."

"I can hear as well—no, better—than you can." A smiling woman with that distinctive aristocratic Saudi nose filled the screen. "Ignore him. He is just so happy to meet you—as am I." She backed away again as if to leave the screen to her husband and then leaned in closer. "Is that the necklace? You did well, Zain. Very well. I think Audrey approves?"

"Very much. It's beautiful and very meaningful to me."

"Good—good. You talk to my husband before I have to hit him with a frying pan. He's very pushy tonight."

And so the visit began. She spoke to Tariq, Sarah,

Yosef, and Aida. Two children, both just entering their teens, waved curiously and each asked Zain a question about snow and skiing, before disappearing to do their own thing. By the time Zain closed the laptop, she thought she had a sense of his family's personalities. "Whew. I like your family."

Zain reached for the unopened gift box. "They like you—as much as they can from a Skype visit." He shook the box. "You didn't open it."

"I wanted to do it with you, so I waited."

"Well, you're with me. Open it."

She sighed. "I don't have a gift for you."

"I'm here, aren't I In your home, not sent away to try to find a way to get to talk to me—" He pushed the box at her again. "That's more than I hoped for at this point. I thought it might take weeks."

His eagerness became contagious. She jerked at the tail of the ribbon and pulled the lid from the box. Emotions flooded her as she stared down at the little pearl bracelet with the silver heart. "Zain—"

"I would have bought it without even looking farther, but the woman helping me said pearls are porous and something about not getting them dirty, so I kept looking. Then I couldn't decide."

"It's perfect. I always regretted not saving the pieces of that bracelet. At the time, all I could think of was that they were all over a nasty bathroom floor."

Her heart warned her that everything would change if she looked at him. A part of her resisted, still unready for the swirl of emotions that barreled toward her. But another side of Audrey pushed her forward, easing her closer and closer to a doorway to the unknown. As a compromise, she reached up and unclasped her necklace. Dangling it over their heads, she whispered, "Our family's never really done the whole mistletoe thing, but I think I'll start hanging olive twigs on special occasions. Same idea—deeper meaning. For me, anyway."

Zain's kiss did suggest that perhaps it held a

deeper meaning for him as well. *Or that's how I'm taking it, Lord. I forgot how amazing this is. I didn't think I had, but yeah. Totally forgot.*

"Happy Christmas-versary?"

Audrey nodded. "Something like that."

Chapter Twenty-Nine

Friday, December 26th—Fairbury

The shop bell jingled—again. Zain glanced at Audrey, her hands busy creating more mouth-watering chocolate, and called, "I've got it."

"Thanks."

A woman scanned the displays, the shelves, and the glass cases before smiling at Zain and pulling a ziplock baggie from her purse. "I thought this would be easy. I'd come in, ask for a pound of these, and voila! Done. Yeah. Not so easy. This is amazing." She leaned closer to a cake plate piled high with ribbon candy. "Are those made here?"

He started to nod and then hesitated. "I think so, but I'm new. Better let me ask."

"Audrey? Do you make the ribbon candy?"

"Every food item in the shop is one hundred percent made on site."

Zain grinned at the woman's astounded expression. "There you have it. Every item is made right here. She's working on chocolate right now. Would you like to see?"

Eyes widened and a smile brightened the woman's otherwise plain face. "Yes! Wow! Thanks!"

While Audrey explained her process, Zain went to answer the phone and then to help yet another customer. *Telling Stacy to take a long lunch might not have been the most genius idea. I am so lost here.*

"Audrey? Is there a difference in price on the truffles versus the salted caramels?"

"Nope. I keep the price the same on everything for everyone's ease."

"Perfect." Clumsy fingers tied a decidedly *im*perfect bow. He stared at it. "Are these a gift?"

The man standing before him winced and nodded. "Yeah."

"Hold on, I'll see if Audrey's hands are clean yet. I haven't mastered the art of bow-tying yet. Hey, I can barely tie my shoes." He carried it to the worktable in the back and sighed. "Any pointers? This looks like something a kindergartner would sneer at."

The woman coughed—an attempt to hide a laugh, he suspected—and Audrey shook her head. "Okay, untie it. Now, start with the middle of the ribbon flat on the top of the box. Flip the box. Criss-cross over the back and flip again."

Zain barely managed not to flip the box onto the floor. "Okay, now tie?"

"No, slip the tails under that center ribbon—one going each way. Right. Good. Now tie a super tight knot right there."

It looked pathetic to him. "Yeah. It's there but—"

Audrey shook her head at the woman observing and said, "Men. Now, rabbit ears—"

"Ra—what?"

After a glance at chocolate covered hands as if somehow that look would wash them, Audrey tried again. "Make a loop with each side. It looks like two long rabbit ears. See?" She waited until he had the floppy loops in place. "Now just wrap one around the other and pull through like you would any bow. See?"

It did look a little better, but not much. "Okaaaay..."

"Now just hold the center and pull the ends a bit to make them a little less big—more perky."

"If you tell Joe that I tied a 'perky' bow, I'll find out what tortures you most and be sure to do it," Zain warned as he hurried back to the register.

"You do that—and cut those tails." Just as he picked up the scissors she added, "Make sure you do dove-tails."

"Dove what—"

The man laughed. "This one I know. I've heard Lily describe it before. It's when you fold the ribbon over and cut at an angle so you get that little V in it."

"See, even Pastor Allen knows what a dove-tail is," Audrey said behind him.

Zain whirled and nearly got a chocolate-decorated shirt. "Aaak."

"I'd recognize that laugh anywhere." Audrey smiled at the man and said, "Tom, I'd like to introduce you to my husband, Zain."

"Nice to mee—what?" The man shook Zain's hand, but his eyes remained riveted on Audrey. "You got married and didn't invite me? I'm wounded."

"I didn't know you back then. We've been married a long time. Just reconciled, so to speak."

As Audrey spoke, Zain's mind spun wildly. *Why is she doing this? People will talk. Look what they did with Kelly!* However, while the pastor looked properly stunned, the woman seemed only mildly curious. Audrey chatted, left the chocolate abandoned in the kitchen area, and made suggestions for the woman while the pastor asked questions and welcomed him to the community. Zain nodded at the right places, smiled at others, expressed his appreciation for the town, and admitted looking forward to finding new business opportunities in the area.

The moment the shop emptied, he pounced. "Why did you do that? You know people are going to be talking inside an hour."

"Now that I told him he can share it, yeah. Of course they will."

"What about the woman?"

"Never saw her before. She's probably a tourist. I'll bet she never forgets this shop, and adding that ribbon candy to the top of the package—genius!" Audrey kissed his cheek and hurried back to her candy making. "Argh. Lost that batch. It seized. Great." She began scraping the chocolate into the trash and started again.

The door jingled again, sending Zain out front, but this time his sisters-in-law stood there, grinning. Tami rushed up and hugged him. "Hey!"

"Audrey..." Zain gave a weak smile as he added, "you might want to wash your hands and wait on the chocolate."

"Why—oh." He couldn't help but notice that Audrey's eyes went directly to Diane for reassurance before she smiled at Tami. "What's up?"

"We have a plan," Tami said. "But first, I need to apologize. I was ticked, but Dad's right. Mostly because my pride was hurt. Forgive me?"

That was easy—too easy? Is that how she always is or what?

Hugs—hands-free for Audrey—told him the sisters were used to this kind of up and down from Tami. Diane whispered as she hugged him, "If you really hate the idea, just make sure I know. I'll stop it."

"So what's this plan?" Audrey asked, beckoning them all into the kitchen. "I've got to keep working. We're almost completely out of soft-centers."

"You need to renew your vows. Even Dad thinks so," Tami added, as if saying as much would prevent the protests she expected.

Not a bad idea, I guess. Kind of a reminder for us of what we set out to do. Hmm...

"I've always hated the idea—as if the first time wasn't good enough. It bugs me, but—" Audrey glanced at him. "We've never even had a chance to live our vows."

"We had one. We blew it," he corrected. "Still, it would be nice if people we actually know could witness them and hold us to them this time. If we had invited the mission group in Las Vegas, do you really think we could have spent twenty-five years apart? The secrecy of it all is what hurt us."

He watched Audrey grow wary. His eyes flitted between the three women, trying to see what she saw, but only Tami's excitement seemed a bit overblown. "What?"

"Tami's making me nervous."

"Well, we do kind of have a crazy idea to go with the plan."

"*You* have a crazy idea—" Diane corrected, but Tami cut her off.

"Which you *love!*"

Grinning, Diane nodded. "I do. I love it. It's genius, really, but it's crazy and it's hers. She gets all fault or all credit. I'm hoping for credit."

That's when Zain saw it—that strange and wondrous thing that is the sister bond. The girls might fight, argue, bicker, push each other to do things they'd never otherwise do, but the love there and the connection reminded him a little of that special bond he had with Yosef. *That's why Audrey was hurt but not broken last night. She was weary of the bickering, not upset about a broken relationship. It's amazing.*

"So what is it?" Audrey began molding and dipping again as she spoke, but Zain saw the action for what it was—a chance to think without her sisters watching her reaction.

"New Year's Eve," Tami said, beaming. "It's so perfect. We could have a mini-ceremony. We'd actually get to be bridesmaids. We never got to do that for you, and we were all each others' in ours." Tami looked at Diane and shook her head. "That didn't make any sense, did it?"

Audrey shook her head in sync with Diane. "Yeah, but I know what you mean. But New Year's? Impossible!"

"No it's not. Diane and I have talked all morning about it and we think we can do it. If you can make a cake, we'll do the rest—all of it. Trust me."

"But why so fast? What about Zain's family? I

mean, if we do this, they should at least be *able* to come, right?" Her eyes pleaded with him, but Zain didn't know for what. *Does she want me to say yes if they can? No? What?* Without any other way to ask privately, he pulled out his phone and sent her a text. **IS THE DATE A PROBLEM FOR YOU OR JUST BECAUSE OF MOM AND DAD?**

She punched her pinky on her phone and read the message but answered aloud. "I don't care about the date, really. If they want to do it all, then now is great—while I don't have to do the work." Audrey winked at her sisters. "But I don't get why the rush and I don't like the idea that we might have to exclude your family because they can't wait!"

"Let me call them—"

"But I want to know why it has to be now," she objected. "It feels so much like Vegas all over again—like we're just pushing to do something before we can't anymore."

Tami crossed her arms over her chest and glared at Audrey. "You keep asking but you won't let me answer. Do you really want to know or not?"

"I really want to know."

"Then I'll really tell you," Tami muttered. "Look, New Year's is the time for new beginnings, right? Resolutions and all that stuff? Well, we thought—"

"You thought," Diane clarified.

"Fine, I thought it would be brilliant to time the vow thing so that your Barney could say 'you may kiss your bride' just as the clock strikes midnight. I mean, it's meaningful, it's romantic, it's everything you'd want in something like that!"

Zain couldn't help but like the idea. He watched Audrey as she processed her sister's words but couldn't read her thoughts. "Would it help if I called to see if they could come? Would that make it easier or harder to decide?"

"Would you? I mean, I don't want to lose free labor—"

"See, we're just grunts to her," Tami objected, grinning with the look of one who knows she's one step away from victory.

"The other advantage," Diane interjected, "is that we knew you'd have the week off after that. It just seemed like a good chance for you guys to get away. You won't get great deals on a trip, but Mom and Dad said they wanted to provide a week somewhere or to pay for the 'wedding.'"

While the sisters talked bridal shop, Zain stepped out the back door and into the alleyway. His father answered on the first ring. "So, how are you? What is going on? Is everything good?"

"Everything is *very* good. I need a big favor, though—really big."

"What is it? Do you need money? We can—"

"Not money, you. I need you and Mama—Yosef and the family, too, if they can." Zain realized as he spoke, that it still didn't answer the question. "I want you to come this weekend or early next week. We're going to renew our vows—affirm them anyway—but only if you can come."

"Mama and I—we will come." Zain grinned as Tariq called for Sarah to "make reservations right away. We're going to Rockland."

"Well, that was easy. I thought I'd have to convince you."

Tariq laughed. "You are married. I've wanted that for so long. I'm not about to miss the chance to meet her. And she should come here—maybe in a couple of months."

"She can't, Baba. She has the business. Maybe you could stay a few weeks. She has an air mattress. We could get a room for you or something."

"We'll talk about that later. I'll call Yosef and then call you back. But we're coming. You tell Audrey that. I like your Audrey. She's very pretty—reminds me a little of my sister."

Six eyes bored into him the minute he stepped in

the back door. Zain tried to keep his face as deadpan as possible. Three voices asked, "Well?"

"Mama and Baba are coming. He'll get back to—" Zain's phone chimed, alerting him to a text message. "Correction. They're all coming. Yosef, Aida, Hana, and Tomas too."

"Just like that?" Audrey crossed the room and gazed into his eyes, looking for something he couldn't imagine. "Why?"

"Because I asked them to?" *Why wouldn't they?*

"So we can get started?" Tami inched toward the front of the store.

Zain and Audrey exchanged glances before she nodded. "Go ahead."

"Fine. I'm going to your house to measure your best fitting dress. Which one is it?"

"That one I got for my birthday—but it's stretchy. Maybe the orange one that I wore to Jenny's wedding last summer. It's in the back of the closet." Audrey thought for a moment and then asked, "What color were you going with?"

"Well, you looked so good yesterday, we were thinking that champagne is a good color—something with a little sparkle and zip." Tami winked at Zain. "Unless you'd like something specific."

"If she's in it, I'll love it."

Diane dragged a "swooning" Tami from the store. Zain wrapped his arms around Audrey's waist and rested his chin on her shoulder. "Are we going to regret this?"

"Definitely." She turned her head and smiled at him. "But we'll love it too."

She should have anticipated the call. Had her mind not been occupied with chocolate, meeting her in-laws at last, and the new and delightful sensation of Zain's beard brushing her cheek, Audrey wouldn't have been taken by surprise. However, as the back door opened to admit Stacy, and her phone sang of wonderful times of the year, Audrey waved hello to her employee and answered the call. "Hey, Tami. Didja find it?"

"I found something else. What the heck is an air mattress doing on your living room floor? I'd say you were too lazy to put it away, but the house is otherwise spotless and his bag is open beside it. His stuff is in the downstairs—"

"Tami! I know exactly where everything is, thank-you-very-much!" Despite her confident-sounding protest, her heart sank. Zain gave her a questioning look and she covered the phone with her hand. "Tami discovered that you didn't sleep upstairs last night. She's demanding an—"

Zain pulled the phone from her hand and spoke with more firmness than Audrey had thought he possessed. "I wasn't aware that Audrey had to answer to you for our decisions regarding *our* marriage. I think I'm going to like you, Tami. But what happens or doesn't in our bedroom is really none of your business."

The wide-eyed look Stacy gave her sent Audrey's already spinning head into hyper-drive. She nudged Zain, trying to get him to stop, but he caught her hand in his and squeezed it. She read his meaning clearly. *Trust me.*

Lord, I do—I think. But he doesn't know my sist—

"I agree. But you assume that we are not praying and fasting about this. Give us a little credit and even more grace. Now go find that dress. I'm looking forward to seeing what you come up with—what?"

Audrey leaned closer to hear what her sister said but couldn't make out the words. Zain grinned, nodded, and said, "Got it. I'll take care of that and Barney. Well, unless Audrey thinks we should ask the local pastor. I'll get back to you on that—what? Oh. Right. Um, I'll do that too, and I mean, my brother could and I could call a couple of people, but I don't know if they could get here. I'll let you know by tomorrow morning. Is that okay?"

Audrey accepted the phone and listened to dead airspace. "Why—" she leaned closer and whispered, "You do realize that anyone in this shop could have heard that."

Zain glanced around him. "But only Stacy is here, and I doubt she plans to put on a sandwich board and walk around crying out, '"They're still virgins!'"

Stacy giggled. "Oh, man. I know a few people who would love to do that, but no. I'm not."

Before Audrey could recover from his outburst, Zain said. "Now, if you don't need me anymore, I'm off to find wedding rings, reserve a tuxedo or two or three, and try to find a sufficient number of groomsmen."

"How many?"

"Tami said I need two. I have Joe. I'll try to see if Mr. Ahmed can come, or if we use Pastor Allen, I'll see if Barney will do it."

"If you can get three, I'd love it," Audrey murmured, thinking.

"Why?"

"I'd like to ask Kelly." She squealed as he hugged her. "I take it you approve?"

"I'll approve more once you call her." His kiss, utterly unselfconscious in front of Stacy, sent a flutter of excitement through her. "And I've got an idea to go with your sister's objections. We'll talk later, though. What kind of ring do you want?"

"Anything."

He grinned. "Done."

As he waved and left, Audrey sighed. "That man is even more wonderful than I remembered."

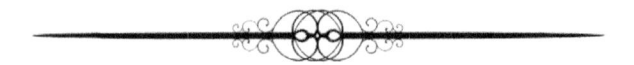

Kelly stared at the phone in her hand. Her sister stared at her. "What was that all about?"

But Kelly didn't answer. She moved to the couch and sat down, tears of relief flowing. "Mom, I didn't lose my job after all. Audrey forgave me. Even after I read her stuff." She mopped at her eyes, nervous laughter making her sound as ridiculous as she felt. "I still can't believe I did that. It made so much sense at the time. I actually thought I was helping in a warped way. I mean, my head knew it was wrong, but I didn't really believe it in my heart."

"Which is desperately sick. That's why you don't—"

Kelly laughed in spite of her tears. "—follow your heart. I know."

From the kitchen, her sisters Lila and Breanne began pelting her with questions. How could she do that? What made her think it was okay to do something she'd be furious if someone did to her? What would she do if *her* daughter did that?

"Whoa," her mother said after a few comments. "That's enough. Whatever happened to getting the plank out of your own eye and casting stones when you're without sin?"

"We're also supposed to call one another to repentance," Breanne retorted.

"Well, since Kelly has informed us that she actually *has* repented, *has* asked Audrey and Zain's forgiveness, and *has* received it. So—"

Lila threw up her hands. "That doesn't change that what she did was wrong."

"Stop." Dee glared at her girls. "If Jesus allowed Himself to be tortured and killed to forgive her, can't we at least have the decency to drop it now that she's repented?"

"Yeah," Lila murmured. "I'd want someone to do that too, I guess. Besides, the demon pregnancy hormones are probably to blame."

Kelly groaned and mouthed, *"Demon hormones? Seriously?"*

"Way to justify, Lila." Dee rolled her eyes. "So is this Zain staying?"

"Um, yeah. I just got invited to be a bridesmaid in a vow renewal ceremony Wednesday night." She groaned and shoved herself out of the couch, semi-waddling to the phone. "And I have no idea what I'm supposed to wear. I better call her back."

Chapter Thirty

Weariness had never brought with it such a delightful companion as anticipation. Add the scent of mouth-watering marinara sauce and the soulful sounds of Bach's cello suites, and Audrey decided that coming home after a long day at work might just prove to be the beginning of her day rather than the end of it. She paused in the kitchen just long enough to kiss Zain, taste his latest culinary creation, and kiss him once more, lingering this time longer than she had intended.

"Be back down in a minute. I'm filthy."

"Take your time. The bread won't be cool enough to cut for at least ten minutes, and it's not quite done baking."

At the bottom step, she turned and called out, "Where did you learn to cook like this?"

Without even a glance over his shoulder, Zain replied, "What else did I have to do when I got home? I could order take out every night, or I could learn to cook. I chose cooking."

And that is my gain, Audrey mused as she dug through her drawers and closet for something casual enough for home but less blasé than her usual yoga uniform. She found a sweater she loved and automatically reached for the camisole she wore with it. Undergarments, socks...but she hesitated between regular jeans and her one and only pair of "jeggings" that she usually saved for shorter dresses in winter.

*They're indecent to wear as regular pants **out** of the house, but here with my husband...*Audrey grabbed them and hurried into the bathroom. *Why not?*

That question surfaced again as she dressed minutes later. She pulled on the camisole and reached for the sweater. *Would it be too much or just exactly what he needs to know I'm trying. It's not like it's totally skanky. Most people wouldn't bother with the cami at all.*

Off it came. Audrey donned the sweater and stared critically at it until satisfied. "Looks just fine, and my necklace will look better without the cami breaking it up."

Her damp hair still dripped onto her sweater as she hurried out of the room, but Audrey found it a bit refreshing as she stepped into the over-warm kitchen. *Oh, boy. I might have to rethink winter clothes in the house. This guy needs long sleeves so we can turn down the thermostat.*

"Can I help?"

"You can sit there and look gorgeous." Zain smiled. "And you do. Nice sweater."

*Do I tell him I usually wear it with the cami? What's more embarrassing, him thinking I might show more skin than I do or me admitting I wanted to show a little **now?***

"Thanks."

"So, I got a lot done in a short amount of time." Zain passed her a plate of salad. "Want to hear?"

"Yeah. Can you pray first? I'm kind of starving over here."

Her phone rang mid-prayer. Audrey ignored it even after Zain concluded. "You going to get that?"

"Nah. After I eat."

"Okay then. So, my brother, Barney, and Mr. Ahmed are going to be groomsmen."

"He's coming! That's the teacher who taught you about Jesus, right?" Audrey jumped up to hug him. "I'm so excited! I've wanted to meet him since Vegas!"

"He's coming. I even managed to find a hotel room for him and the family in Ferndale. Note: rooms are easily found there and in Hillsdale—and nowhere else."

"A bit out of the way—Hillsdale—but hey." Audrey took a bite of her salad and moaned. "Oh, wow. This is amazing. What did you do to this dressing?"

"Sesame. I put it in almost everything. That stuff makes everything a bit nutty, and I like nuts." Zain continued as if uninterrupted. "So, I have my three guys for you. Tom Allen is going to officiate and has offered us the church fellowship hall for a 'reception.' Tami approves."

"Tami approves. Then we'll have to do it. Cake. What kind of cake do you like—oh, wait. Answer that after you're done with your news. Sorry."

He took a bite of his salad before continuing. "I think it needs cranberry juice. I meant to get some and forgot." His forehead furrowed as he thought. "What was I—oh. Cake. Probably something other than red velvet. My nephew shouldn't have that much red food dye. It makes him angry."

"Oh, but a velvet cake sounds good. I'll leave out the food dye. If anything, it just makes it a bit sweeter." Audrey pushed her empty plate aside, tempted to ask for more. *After whatever that pasta stuff is. If I'm still hungry.* "So what else do we have to do? I know they said they'd do it all, but we both know that isn't going to happen quite like they want us to think."

"I was going to suggest the guys just wear a dark suit from home in whatever color they had—"

"Sounds smart to me."

"But your dad insisted on paying for tux rentals so that no one had to take up luggage space with something so bulky."

"They called me," she murmured as he handed her a plate of steaming gnocchi. "Oh, wow. I'm thinking that you need to start a restaurant."

"No way. I love to cook and I want to keep it that

way. Doing it that much would kill it. Where was I?" Zain took a bite and chewed as he thought. "Oh, right. Tomorrow I get rings and meet with your dad. He wants to pray with me."

The moisture around Zain's eyes and the way his lower lip trembled tore at her heart. Audrey rose and skirted the island to hug him. "Are you okay?"

"It's just exactly the kind of thing I'd want my father to do, but of course, he won't. Your dad said he'd pray for their salvation."

"I have been all these years, but obviously I must not be very righteous or maybe my prayers would be more effectual."

His protest died almost as soon as he began. "Oh— James. Good one." He took her plate from the counter before her and carried it to the table. "I need to sit down. Feet are killing me; gotta get me some new shoes."

Audrey's phone rang again, but she still ignored it. "I bet it's Tami. She's not going to know what to do with me not answering the phone. Willow would be so proud."

"Willow?"

She couldn't stifle a smile. "Oh, Zain. Welcome to Fairbury. I'll take you out there Sunday. You've got to meet her."

How do I suggest it, Lord? Will she think I'm crazy? I know her sisters do. It's for less than a week, though. A time of getting to know and be comfortable with each other again. Is that so out of the box?

"I've been thinking about your sister's call all afternoon."

"Which one?"

Audrey snuggled closer, and Zain nearly lost his resolve in the realization that he could easily lead her exactly where he wanted with just the right words and necessary restraint at precise moments. *That's probably how unprincipled men seduce innocent girls, isn't it? Oh Lord, that's sick.* She shifted, giving him a perfect view that made his resolve weaken. *Lord, help!* "The one about my mattress."

"Oh?" the mischievousness in Audrey's tone once again tempted him away from the plan he'd devised.

"You are not making this easy, but you know how we said we shouldn't be in any rush—that we should take a few days?"

He couldn't pretend not to see disappointment in her eyes as she tilted her head back to look up at him. "Yeah..."

"I thought Tami's idea of taking a week off together—like the honeymoon we didn't have—sounded good, and then I thought—"

Audrey sat up and faced him, her legs criss-crossing on the couch. "You want to wait until after the renewal!" Before he could try to explain his reasoning, she nodded slowly. "I see where you're going with it." He held his breath, warring within himself as to whether he wanted her to agree or to protest. She toyed with the necklace as she considered the proposal. "Well," she said at last, "I think you should ask Dad. If he can't see a reason not to, I like it. I like knowing that I don't have to wonder if—well, I don't have to wonder."

"Deal." Anxious to change subjects, he brought up the week away. "I had an idea for the honeymoon too, but it's not exactly romantic. I just can't find anything that is remotely affordable in more traditional places—not at this late date."

"So what's the idea?" Audrey jumped up and retrieved a box of salted caramels from her purse. "I forgot about these."

I'm going to be obese inside a year at this rate. I think I better find a gym and get a membership. He stretched out, his feet resting on her coffee table, and pulled a throw pillow on his lap for her to rest her head against. "I thought I'd go home after you are back at the shop and close up everything, but then I thought maybe you'd want to see California—where I live. So instead, while you're off next week, we could go to my house, pack up what I want to keep, take it to Mom and Dad's, and maybe see a bit of the area."

"Disneyland?"

"You want to go to Disneyland?" He smiled down at her. "Yeah. We can do that." Shaking his head at the idea of Disneyland being the one thing she mentioned, Zain continued. "I'll put the condo on the market. It should sell fast. Most in my area do, and I've finally finished all the remodeling last year."

"You remodel too?"

He shook his head. "No, I don't do that kind of thing well. I had it done—one room at a time over the past five years. It should give me—well, us—a good profit too. I only paid one-fifty for it in '94. The one next door sold for five-fifty last year."

"Wait, are you saying you think you're going to make a four hundred thousand dollar profit?"

"Probably. Prices skyrocketed after I bought and it was a foreclosure when I got it." Confused at the evident dismay she showed, he asked, "What?"

"Do you know what kind of taxes you're going to have—we're going to have?"

"Well, even if it sells the day we list it, we'll have most of the year to figure it out. I'll talk to a tax attorney or something." He stroked her temple and relaxed a little. "So, you're okay with that idea? I thought we'd fly out, be there for a few days, and drive home to bring my car back."

"I like that this is home now. Is that horrible? I mean, you're giving up everything. I'm not sure that's right!"

"It's exactly what I want. It's what I should have done years ago, but I can't change that now." He closed his eyes and imagined a week at his condo, getting it ready to sell and showing her his favorite places near home. *Most of it is what I wanted to do twenty-five* years ago, although then I wanted to show her UCLA, not the condo.

She jumped up from the couch and grabbed his hand. "C'mon."

"Where—" He found himself stumbling up the stairs after her, confused. *I thought we agreed—*

Her "I want you to show me what to pack for a California January. I remember being so warm half the time in Las Vegas," amused him.

"And I got cold just standing near you."

As Audrey reached into her closet, she muttered, "That's not how I remember it. In fact, I think Christmas Adam proved the reverse."

Saturday, December 27th—Fairbury

Zain burst through the front door with a bag of Chinese food in one hand and a small gift bag in another. "Sorry I'm late. There shouldn't be that kind of traffic in Ferndale on a night like this."

"Did you go to China Station?" She inhaled the scent of sweet and sour sauce as she opened the bag.

"Yeah. Be right back. I've got stuff from Diane in the car. All she wants from you is a yes or no on it all."

Audrey stared at the closed door behind Zain and shook her head. *I swear; he's more into this than I am. I just want to start our life. I mean, I like the idea, Lord, but all I've ever wanted was just to be his wife. I am that. So who cares about all this?*

Despite her internal protests, she did find the little gift bag sitting on the coffee table a bit more intriguing than the coming "decisions" she'd have to make. *Is that our rings? So cool. That was the one thing about the Vegas wedding that I hated. No ring—especially when I had to come home without him. Now I'll have one. It'll say, "I'm taken" to the world.*

She dished up plates of still-steaming food and carried them to the coffee table. *If we eat here, maybe he won't get sidetracked.* A new thought discouraged her. *Unless he's saving them for the renewal. That would be just like him too. Ugh.*

Once more, Zain burst through the door carrying a bag of stuff. "She said she would have sent them to your phone, but you've developed a bad habit of ignoring calls lately, so she sent it all with me."

"I'm not going to stop making out with my husband so I can say yes or no to a shade of champagne that looks no different than the last one she showed me."

"Wise woman." Something came over him—an expression she'd learned meant he'd tuned out the world to focus solely on her. "Hey..."

"Evening, handsome." Audrey slipped her arms around his neck and allowed herself to revel in the moment—revel in the beauty that came with being his wife. *We're going to fight. I hate it, but I know it. We're both pretty stubborn people. I hate conflict and I'll avoid it as much as I can, but the day is going to come when neither of us backs down. Will this all go away then? Will we become distant in some warped sense of self-preservation? How do we avoid that?*

"What?"

Audrey blinked. "What, what?"

"I watched you go from happy to see me, and frankly, really happy to see me, to disturbed by something."

"Fights."

"What?" Zain's lips brushed her forehead. "I don't remember any fight."

"We'll have one someday, though. I don't want to lose this—this thing we have—to fights."

"From what I've heard, fights exist for the pleasure of making up." When she didn't laugh, he pulled her down to the couch and passed her the plate. "Eat. We'll deal with that when it comes. Right now, I want to enjoy this 'honeymoon phase' everyone keeps talking about."

She mulled his words while she ate. "So I'm just counting my fights before they erupt. Is that what you're saying?"

"Basically." He offered her his shrimp. "But, it's nice that you care. Just keep caring like that."

Audrey nudged the bag with her foot. "Is that what I think it is?"

"What do you think it is?"

"Our wedding bands? Do I get to see?" In an attempt to prove her ability to shake off the gloom that had tried to settle over her, Audrey grinned. "Or, do I not tell you what Tami bought me today?"

"What'd she buy you?"

"Nuh, uh. You show me, and I'll show you." Audrey snorted, sending rice flying from her nose. "Oh, ugh. That's classy." He reached for the bag and pulled out three ring boxes. Audrey's eyes widened. "Why three?"

After peeking into each one, he propped the first open. "This is mine. And I thank you. It's perfect. How did you know it is exactly what I would have picked out for myself?"

"I'm good. Let's face it. I'm just good."

"That you are." He propped open the second one. "This is yours. I hope you like it." Audrey reached for it, but he jerked it back, laughing. "Gotcha."

Audrey took the box from him and held it up to the light. "It's beautiful, Zain. Seriously. I couldn't have picked anything more *me.*"

"That's what Tami said. She was suitably impressed and demanded to know how many websites we perused so I'd know what to get."

"But—" Audrey laughed. "She really thought we did that, didn't she? Funny." She slipped the ring from the box and ran her finger over the etched surface. "How did you guess that I'd like a square band?"

"I looked for something that would work with your job. Got a chain for it too." He pulled out another box that held a chain with a clip on it. "So you can take it off easily."

Seconds ticked past as she waited for him to show her the final box. He didn't. He examined his band, compared it with hers, showed her how the clasp on the chain worked—everything else, but did not open that box. Audrey glared at him. He didn't seem to notice. She nudged him. He ignored her and took another bite of his food.

"Zain!"

"What?"

"Ahem." Audrey nudged the box. "I'm waiting to hear about *this* one."

"Oh... that one. Right. Well, I didn't get you an engagement ring—"

"For our twenty-four hour engagement," she agreed.

"Right. So I thought maybe since we have a few days this time—almost a week—I could get a re-engagement ring since we're engaged to be remarried." He winked. "So to speak."

Again she waited. When he didn't pick up the box, she grabbed his plate, set it atop hers, and rose as if to leave. However, as she passed the little box, she snatched it and raced to the kitchen. Zain wasn't far behind. "I let you do that."

"Ha!" Audrey tried holding the box over her head, but despite their almost identical heights, Zain's arms were most definitely longer. "Ugh. Mr. Monkey arms."

"First time in my life I am grateful for that. Now do you want to see this or not?"

"No duh, as we used to say." A weird sense of unease crept over her. *What if, after all this build up, I don't like it? It'll show. Don't let it show, Lord. There's got to be something good about it, right? He nailed the band.*

The lid opened slowly and Zain watched her as it came into view. Her eyes rose to meet his. "Perfect. I love it."

Chapter Thirty-One

Monday, December 29th—Fairbury

Zain burst into the shop at five minutes to six. "You ready?"

"What are you doing here? I'm going to go home and change!"

"We'll be late."

"They're not arriving until seven-thirty. By the time they get off the plane and to baggage, we'll be there." She untied her apron and tossed it in the laundry bin. "You got this, Stacy?"

"Yep. Get out of here. Make sure you bring the in-laws in tomorrow, though. I want to meet them."

As he shoved Audrey out the door, Zain called back to Stacy, "I will. Thanks!"

"You're crazy. You know that, don't you?" Audrey quipped. But she allowed herself to be ushered into Zain's rental car and driven home. Once inside, she rushed upstairs to change and do something with her hair. *Lord, I need a shower, but he'd probably have a heart attack if I did that. So please protect me from making an odorous nuisance of myself.*

"You ready?" Audrey jumped at the sound of Zain's voice in the doorway. She turned and watched him as he tried to recline calmly against the doorjamb, but his nervous fidgeting gave him away.

She threw her top at him, grateful she'd worn a

camisole under it. "What are you doing? Get out of here! I'm changing!"

"Well, it's not like we're not married. I'll change you myself if you don't hurry!"

"We both know that you wouldn't, so just go. I'll be down in a minute." Though tempted to take her sweet time to prove him crazy, Audrey found herself rushing in nervous anticipation of the coming introductions. *I know I'm going to love them, Lord. But I'm not so sure about them loving me. I'm taking away their son—Joe's brother. That's got to be hard to swallow. Oh, and while I'm begging for help here, I'd love it if you could make Tami show a little self-restraint while we're there. It'll be hard enough for them to meet all these new people at once. She's in over-drive right now, and it's making us all a little nuts. They don't need that too.*

Zain chattered all the way to the car, all the way through town, down the highway, onto the loop, and even as he rushed her through parking to the trams and into the airport. Half of what he said, she didn't follow. He talked about job opportunities and travel plans in the same breath, often mixing things into jumbled messes such as, "Called to see what kind of flight they offer with their employment package."

At baggage claim, where they'd agreed to meet his family, she pulled him into the most private place she could find—a half-corner near an empty carousel—and kissed him. Heretofore she'd kept her public affection to reaching for his hand or leaning close, but this time she concentrated on him rather than on where they stood. Seconds faded into the moment, until she pulled away and whispered, "Welcome back."

"I was—"

Applause thundered from a few feet away. Audrey flushed as she saw the Kadir family standing close and clapping. Several passers-by had stopped and added their approval as well. "Um…"

"Well, as you can see," Zain said, clearing his throat. "This is my wife, Audrey."

Introductions pelted her with names that she had trouble keeping straight. *What did he say his nephew's name is? Tariq is the dad, Sarah the mom, Aria—no, Aida the sister-in-law, Hana-with-one-n-and-no-h the niece, but what did he say—* The boy nodded and gave an awkward hug at his mother's bidding. Audrey winced. "I'm so sorry. I think your name starts with a T, but other than that, I can't remember and I didn't hear what Zain said." She leaned in a bit conspiratorially and murmured, "He's a bit nervous, I think."

"Tomas." The boy looked up at his uncle and back at Audrey. "Yeah. He's nervous."

"I think it's cute," Hana quipped. "I never thought I'd see Uncle Zain making out in an airport."

"You know how in movies sometimes men kiss women to shut them up?" Audrey laughed at Zain's groan. "Yeah, well, he's been talking nonsense since he picked me up from work, so I figured he needed a bit of grounding."

"A kiss like that would never ground any man," Tariq teased. "You just made things worse." His eyes, clear and reflecting a sharp, quick mind, searched her. "And that's exactly what you wanted. Smart girl. You will do well for him."

"Dad, the cars. We need to hurry before there's a line. Zain can help Mom and the kids get the bags. Let's go."

"You have bags?" Zain frowned. "Wha—"

"We decided to stay longer," Sarah explained. "You said we should see your town and where you will live."

"But I won't be here!"

"We'll be here when you get back. We can get around without your assistance, little boy." Sarah linked her arm in Audrey's and pulled the scarf from her head. "Oh, that was a long flight. So how far is it to your parents' house? Are we still going straight there?"

"If you're not too tired," Audrey agreed. "They're excited to meet you. My sisters and their husbands *and* their children will be there."

"And how far is the hotel from your house?"

"Just about a fifteen minute drive." A new idea occurred to her. "You know, you don't need to stay there the whole time. You're welcome at our house all the time, of course, but especially while we're gone next week. You'll have the house all to yourself. I have friends who would love to meet you—"

"Kelly? Can we meet Kelly? I know she hurt you," Sarah said quickly, "but without her, Zain might never have told us. We were so worried about him, but of course, you can't tell a son that."

"She'll be in the ceremony as a bridesmaid. She's going to walk with Mr. Ahmed."

Baggage began sliding down the chute to the carousel and distracted Sarah. Audrey stepped back and greeted Aida. "I didn't mean to ignore you."

"It's okay. Mama Kadir is so excited to meet you. I couldn't begrudge that." Aida leaned forward, "And thank you for that kiss."

"Well, I can't say I did it for your benefit, but I guess I'm glad you were—"

Aida's laughter echoed around them. "I meant for the kids' sake. They've taken it into their heads that you are just after Zain's 'money,' as if he has any to speak of." She rolled her eyes. "They've decided that you think all Saudis are oil magnates." Aida leaned close and whispered, "But Tomas said magnets."

"Well, I guess a magnate might draw people to him like a magnet," Audrey agreed.

"Mooom!" Tomas gave her a sheepish grin and went to find his father.

Sarah pointed to a suitcase sliding their way. "There's Tariq's. Grab it, Tomas!"

"He's gone, Mama. I'll get it." To Audrey, Aida muttered, "Welcome to the family."

Wednesday, December 31st—Fairbury

Audrey and Sarah shivered down the back steps

and to Audrey's car. Their mission: make the short drive to retrieve flowers from The Pettler and take them to the church, while Zain and the others went in different directions at Tami's bidding. As she buckled up in the already warm car, Audrey grinned at Sarah. "He's already adapted to being a gentleman in a colder climate—start the wife's car for her."

"He's a good man, our Zain." Sarah covered Audrey's hand with hers. "But he gives off a false impression sometimes. You should know this."

The words unsettled Audrey as she put the car in gear and crept down the alleyway. "What do you mean?"

"He's quiet and he defers to others. He's like me in that. Tariq and Yosef are direct, bold, assertive—always telling people what to do and how to do it." She smiled. "I sometimes have to remind them that they are not in the army and we are not their troops."

"I don't understand." Audrey kept her eyes split between Sarah and the road until she nearly sideswiped a car parked too far from the curb.

But Sarah's attention was diverted by the sudden display of Christmas lights all through the town. "That is just beautiful. I love Christmas lights, but there's something particularly charming about them here. Lovely."

Frustration mounted as she pulled up in front of the flower shop and parked, still clueless as to what Sarah could mean. She fed the meter and opened the door for Sarah, calling out for Wayne as she entered. "I'm here! Should I pull around back, or—"

Wayne appeared, smiling. "Hey, Audrey. Is this your mother-in-law?" He offered Sarah a flower before saying, "I'll just help carry things out front. No need to move the car. Sorry I couldn't deliver these with the ones for the church—too busy. I've never had such a busy New Year's Eve."

Sarah took two bouquet carriers and hurried outside. Audrey followed. It took a couple of trips to carry all the bouquet, corsage, and boutonniere packages—something Audrey suspected was Diane's doing. *She does love flowers. I hope Dad isn't regretting this yet.*

She'd hoped to hear more of Sarah's insights into Zain, but even as they unloaded the flowers into ice chests at the church, Sarah said nothing. Audrey tried several times to return the conversation to the original topic, but Sarah seemed fascinated with everything around her. "Can we see the church—where the altar is?"

Audrey didn't try to explain that First Church of Fairbury didn't actually have anything they called an "altar." She led Sarah upstairs to the sanctuary and flipped on the lights. "Ready?" *Are you? What if you hate it? Better know it now than let Tami and Diane see it later. Good call, Mama Kadir.*

She flung open the door, and Sarah's sigh of happiness would have made even the ugliest room seem gorgeous. But as her eyes took in every detail, Audrey couldn't help but notice that it was exactly as she would have wanted it had she had time to consider. "They did it. They made it *me.* I was so sure it would reflect Tami's tastes and she's a bit more—"

"Flamboyant?" Sarah laughed at Audrey's chagrin. "I like your sister. She is very loyal—very eager to invest in those she loves."

"And very good at being too pushy at all the wrong times."

"That comes with the good in her. We all have the negatives that walk hand-in-hand with our best traits. Hers is to be meddlesome and to fight for what she thinks will make those she loves happiest." Sarah turned happy eyes to Audrey. "I am so glad that Kelly did that too, but I think it is not her usual nature. Either that, or this experience has tempered her."

"It's not her. She might be tempted in her heart, but I think the shock of seeing something so unbelievable just made her go a little crazy. Either that, or she had an infusion of hormones that week and *they* did the crazy thing." Audrey hugged her mother-in-law and sighed. "But you're right. I'm glad she did, too—now. I wasn't so happy when it happened." The idea for how to drive the conversation back to Zain and his supposed faults presented itself and she accepted gratefully. "I was just as ticked at Zain as I was at her—or nearly so. And then he just kept apologizing for everything like saying 'sorry' meant it never happened. I don't like that."

"That is Zain," Sarah agreed. She fingered a silk flower at the end of the first pew before adding the words Audrey hoped to hear. "He is gentle that way. He has a firm will, though. People don't expect it, because he usually yields to others." The woman's eyes rose to Audrey's and her hands cupped Audrey's face. "He will surprise you, though. Someday, probably sooner than you expect, he will stand firm and bold in the face of something that he feels strongly about. And you might just feel a little betrayed." Sarah winked as she added, "I know this because that is what Tariq said after a few of my outbursts."

"He did that the other day," Audrey admitted. "I was surprised. He'd been so humble about everything with my family. They blasted him and he took it, but when my sister crossed a line he didn't like, he put her in her place."

"She will respect him for it, though. A woman like Tami would understand it better than him just changing the subject like he usually would."

Audrey nodded, thinking. "I think knowing that isn't a fluke is a good thing. I mean, in Vegas, he deferred to me all the time."

"He wanted to please, you and you didn't cross what he thought was right."

"He did that here too—on everything until that night at my parents' house." Audrey's mind replayed Christmas night on fast forward. "There he yielded to the family, but he led me. He took the brunt for me as much as he could, and then when he saw I couldn't take anymore, he just sent me home. I didn't even notice that he did it."

"That's exactly right!" Sarah beamed. "You understand him. Usually, that is how he will be firm and resolute. But sometimes it will come out as harsher— well, for him. Compared to Tariq or Yosef, he's still a kitten. But not at heart," Sarah said as she considered her words. "People mistake quiet for uncaring and gentle for weak. Zain is neither. He is strong."

"That he is." Audrey took her mother-in-law's hand and led the woman back through the foyer to the door. "Zain shows his strength by bearing the brunt of unpleasantness for others. That's a beautiful thing that I might not have realized for some time." As she opened the door for Sarah, she smiled into the woman's eyes. "I didn't know what an amazing man I married, but I'm beginning to see it more every day."

Sarah remained silent as they drove home. She rode with her neck craned to see every detail of Fairbury's last hurrah before setting aside its holiday finery for a more ordinary look. But as Audrey pulled into her parking space and shut off the engine, the woman turned to her. "You make him happy. Remember this when you want to throttle him or you think he might want to strangle you. You make him so happy. He loves you. You love him. Don't forget that when he acts like an idiot."

Chapter Thirty-Two

The junior high Sunday school room bustled with activity as four women dressed for the ceremony. While Kelly adjusted a dress she would never have purchased for any reason, Tami and Diane zipped each other into coordinating dresses. In the corner, Audrey opened a gift bag and smiled at the contents, her mind lost in Zain's words as he gave it to her.

"That night in Vegas, when I decided that I'd baited you and it was wrong of me, I remembered what you said about wanting to have something special for 'later.' So I rode a taxi everywhere until I found a store open and bought something to apologize. Funny," he'd mused, *"you bring out the gifter in me. I keep trying to show my feelings wrapped up in a pretty box. Anyway, I thought I'd finally give that to you—not that it's the same one, but still."*

A low whistle behind her made Audrey blush. "Look what we have here. Audrey's gone from sugar to spice."

Diane laughed at Tami's joke and added as she fingered the filmy lingerie, "Oh yeah, she's puttin' on everything nice."

Audrey stepped behind the makeshift screen to change. "Can someone get my dress? I'm not walking out wearing nothing but this—all girls or not."

The dress slipped over her head and Audrey backed out from behind the screen. Phyllis zipped her up and spun her slowly. "This is beautiful. When I saw the picture with all the crystals, I thought it would scream, 'Miss Country Music Pageant,' but it's just elegant. I love that chiffon."

The layers of chiffon settled around her knees and swept back to a waterfall skirt. Audrey adjusted the sleeves and reached for her jewelry boxes. Twice Tami tried to convince her to put her hair up, but she refused. "Zain likes it just like this, and I'm doing this for him, after all."

"Is he shaving off his beard?" Tami retorted.

"He better not be! I'd kill him."

"Overkill," Diane muttered. "Break the razor—oh, the photographer. He wants 'getting ready' pictures."

Wes Hartfield appeared in the doorway as Audrey asked, "We have a photographer? How'd we—whoa. How did you get him?"

"Is that a good or a bad 'him'?" Wes pressed the shutter release as he spoke. "Tom arranged it. I was in town, and how often do you get to say you shot a wedding, anniversary, and renewal all in one?"

"I wouldn't have even asked." Audrey bounced like a little girl. "Oh, shoes. I need shoes. I didn't bring—"

Tami shoved a box in her hand. "We've got this covered. If we forgot anything, I'll bake your anniversary cakes for life."

"Lord, please don't let her have forgotten anything," Audrey teased.

"Ha! Admit it, we did great."

That she couldn't argue with. Audrey hugged each of her sisters and both of her mothers. As she turned to Kelly, her heart constricted just a little. *Lord, there they blew it. Oh man, poor Kelly. It's the last thing she'd ever wear for any reason. Jon's gonna croak.*

The scarlet satin and chiffon dress sparkled with every movement. A single strap slung over one shoulder to keep the fitted bodice in place, something Audrey tried to remind herself to be thankful for, but one look at the handkerchief hem that barely skimmed Kelly's knees made her wince. She hugged her friend and murmured, "I am so sorry, Kelly. I should have thought that they'd try to go trendy."

"Don't worry about it. I'll save it for teasing Jon with when he's having a rough day. I'll stay out of as many pictures as I can, though."

"I'll tell Wes to position you to hide as much as possible."

"Isn't she cute!" Tami hugged both women and beamed at the picture Kelly made in her utterly hideous dress before rushing off to adjust Tanika's shoe straps.

"I consider it my penance." Kelly winked. "I've always wanted to say that, and this time, it fits."

Wes gathered them all together and stood Tanika in front of Kelly, winking at Audrey. "Let's get one quick one before I go get ready to grab the first look shot. It's nearly show time."

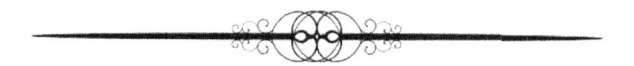

I wonder how she's doing? Does she like her dress? Will I? That thought made Zain grin. *Like I would care if she wore jeans and a t-shirt. It worked fine last time.*

Sitting alone at Tom Allen's desk, Zain wrote, oblivious to the conversation around him. He stopped, thought, and his pen scratched across the paper again as he tried to tell Audrey all he didn't know how to say in person. *Why did I think I'd be more eloquent with a pen? Writing was never my strong point. Still, it means something to her. Surely she'll see that I made the effort. That's what counts, isn't it?*

Once more, he tried to share his dreams for their marriage. He asked forgiveness for mistakes he knew he'd make. He assured her, repeatedly, of his determination to make serving her the goal of the rest of his life. *And Lord, please help me reach that goal. I'm a selfish man. I'll fail without Your help.*

Yosef pounced the minute Zain laid down his pen, folded the letter, and stowed it in his pocket. "Get yourself ready now. It's almost time!"

He rose and crossed the room. As he adjusted his bow tie, Zain stared into the mirror. "I think I should've shaved. Will someone go ask her if she wants me to—"

"No time, bro. Just go with it. She hasn't complained, has she?"

"We're not really at the stage to start criticizing appearance."

Yosef laughed. "Did you hear him? Zain says they're not at the 'stage to criticize appearance.'" He clapped a hand on Zain's shoulder and said, "You've been married for twenty-five years. You're through all stages by default."

"Leave him alone, Yosef. Your brother is enjoying the honeymoon stage that he never got." Tariq grinned at Nadir Ahmed. "Is there something in the Bible about bridegrooms?"

While Zain's brain whizzed in a dozen directions, trying to decide what scripture to share, Nadir tied his shoe and remarked in a deceptively calm voice, "In the Bible, most references to brides and bridegrooms are related to Jesus and His followers."

To Zain's astonishment, his father asked to hear the story—asked questions. He zipped a text to Audrey, warning that they might be late. I CAN'T JUST HUSH HIM WHILE HE'S INTERESTED. IT PROBABLY WON'T LAST, BUT I HAVE TO TRY. I HOPE YOU UNDERSTAND.

No answer came. *Is she upset? Did she get it? I—*

"Nadir, you must tell me more. I like your story, but we're going to make Zain late."

His heart sank. Of all the things his father could have said at that moment, "tell me later" hurt the most. *It feels like Felix being "almost persuaded." What do I do, Lord? Do I keep him talking—* That thought stopped him. *How is ignoring my father's courtesy to me "honoring him?" I can't bombard him with scripture just because he was interested. In Your time, Lord. Please give me another opportunity—another one at his request.*

A knock disrupted his thoughts. Wes opened the

door. "One last group shot and then you need to be waiting for her when she steps from the room. I want the reaction shot set up before she opens that door."

His groomsmen shuffled from the room, leaving Zain and his father alone. Unable to resist saying *something*, Zain hugged Tariq and murmured, "Thank you, Baba—for asking about our faith. I know you've let the lessons of the Qur'an go since you've lived in America. But you asked about my lessons today. It means a lot to me."

"Don't read too much into it, Zain," Tariq began.

Oh, Lord. I should have kept my mouth shut.

"—asked because I was interested, not for your sake."

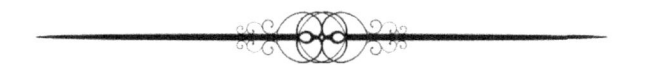

Zain's knock came just as Kelly thought Audrey would explode with anticipation. From her corner of the room, she could only see Zain's face, but the joy in the man's eyes radiated even across the room. *I'm so glad they did this, Lord. It'll be a treasured memory for all of us. What I did in curiosity and sin, You meant for good—used to reunite them. Thank you for that. I could have ruined things forever. Thank you for keeping hearts soft enough to forgive.*

The girls filed from the room and took their escorts' arms. Kelly held her bouquet of gardenias and roses in one hand and accepted Nadir's elbow with the other. They walked first, something Kelly hadn't known to be grateful for until she stood at the front of the sanctuary and watched the entire ceremony with a perfect view. The candlelit room sent soft shadows that she suspected would be a photography nightmare, but the effect couldn't have been more romantic. *Those Seevers know how to put on a rush wedding. This is exquisite.*

Tami stood next to her, nearly shaking with repressed excitement. Diane followed, looking her usual serene self. Kelly's eyes scanned the room. Walt and

Phyllis Seever sat next to their grandchildren. They'd aged, Audrey said, over the past week, but from Kelly's perspective, they looked happy. The Kadirs sat holding hands and grinning as they waited for Tanika to reach the front and stand in front of Diane.

The back doors remained open, but no one stood there. In the back of the room, Tabitha Allen sat alone, waiting for the last notes of "Londonderry Aire" to fade. As she played the first notes of "Barcarolle," Audrey and Zain stepped from the shadows, joined hands, and strolled down the aisle together.

Is Mr. Seever sorry he didn't get to give her away? I can see why he would be, but he just looks happy.

Tom Allen called the guests—almost a full church, much to Kelly's surprise—to prayer. "But first, who here agrees to help Audrey and Zain keep their vows?"

A collective "we will" rippled across the room. Audrey wiped at the corner of her eye, and Kelly could have sworn she saw a tear glistening on Zain's cheek as well. *What a cool variation on "who gives this bride." She's already given herself away. I wonder who thought of that. I would have liked to have that same question at my wedding.*

As Tom closed the prayer, Kelly glanced at the clock. *Ten minutes. Is that enough time? Too much? How do I not even know how long this should take? I just can't remember.*

To her astonishment, however, Tom began a wedding sermon. Her heart raced as panic set in. *He'll never get done in time. They're gonna miss that kiss.* Beside her, Tami shifted as if to confirm Kelly's unease.

Five minutes into the sermon, Kelly saw Tom glance up at the clock and back down at his notes. The story of the wedding feast lost detail as Tom stopped sharing cultural information and finished with, "I know this is a story of how we're brought into the church to be a part of the wedding feast, but look how this story works. The father provides for his son and their guests. He shows gracious hospitality, just as Zain's father has in providing us with a lovely reception downstairs."

Audrey and Zain exchanged glances before Zain turned and stared at his parents as Tom continued, "That's right, Walt explained that Tariq asked for something meaningful to Christians in relation to this ceremony. He wanted to do something that held meaning for his son, and Walt shared this story."

"Baba!"

Tariq chuckled and Sarah jabbed him in the ribs, hissing, "What?"

"Let's renew these vows, shall we?" Tom smiled at the couple and began reading, changing words to fit the occasion. "Zain do you hold fast to Audrey as your wedded wife? Will you now live with her in marriage? Do you promise to encompass all four loves in your marriage to her—agapae, phileo, storge, and eros —"

Kelly lost the rest of the words as she considered the three Greek words for love. *That's an interesting way to put it. To serve, be friends, show affection, and have passion—wrapped up in the general idea of love. I like that he separated them.*

The clock clicked to just over one minute left as Zain said, "I will."

Tom began with Audrey's, speaking a little faster now. Kelly's "I will" hit at the thirty second mark. "Now the rings. While I know the ring is 'but a symbol—'" Audrey and Zain snickered. Those around them waited for explanation, but Tom didn't have time for one. "Please repeat together. 'With these rings, we offer this reminder today of the vows we have made, and what God has put and kept together, may no one separate.'"

Somehow, as if to attest to the contrariness of time, ten seconds remained. Tom held up ten fingers. Dropped one. Another. The congregation began counting down in unison. "Seven, six, five—"

"Zain, you maaaaaaaaaaay kiss-your-wife."

Kelly found she'd been holding her breath as the air rushed from her lungs at exactly midnight. "Happy New Year," Tom called out. "Mr. and Mrs. Zain Kadir invite you to celebrate with them downstairs."

Zain slipped his hand into his jacket pocket and pulled out the letter. He glanced toward the bathroom where Audrey brushed her teeth behind a half-closed door, and crept from the room and down the hall to her office. He slid open the closet door, pulled box seven from the shelf, and retrieved the bundle of letters he'd read less than a week earlier. The rubber band broke as he pulled it from the stack and placed his on top. A fumble through her desk drawer eventually yielded a new one. As he replaced the bundle in the box, his eye scanned the opening words again.

—terrified that I'll fail you again, and then I realized. I will. What a humbling thought. I just hope that when it happens in the future, I'll see it, be swift to repent, and you will never tire of forgiving me.

That needs to be my daily prayer, Lord, Zain prayed as he closed the lid and stowed the box in the closet. *I need to pray that I don't fail her, that I recognize when I do, and that she forgives as I repent. Let it be, Lord. Please let it be.*

The light switch felt cool to his hand as Zain reached up to turn it off. Darkness fell over the room where the new chapter of their story began and the door to the office closed behind him. At Audrey's room, his hand rested on the knob as it stood ajar. He stepped in, his mind and heart filling with the wonder of the changes in his life. This time, as he closed the door behind him, another door opened and Audrey stepped into her room—their room.

"Hi."

Zain flipped off the overhead light, leaving only the small lamps on the bedside tables glowing, and murmured, "Hi."

Epilogue

Christmas Day—Fairbury

Audrey reached for box number three and dug through it, but no packet of letters appeared. After boxes four and eight, Audrey finally retrieved number seven. There on top lay her annual anniversary letters. She pulled the rubber band free and added this year's missive to the bottom of the stack, but Zain's handwriting caught her eye. She set the letters down and unfolded the paper dated New Year's Eve of the previous year. Tears blurred the words as she mulled over how many misunderstandings they'd already had in twelve short months. Job ideas, business opportunities, how to stay involved in missions while still running her business—the list seemed endless.

But it's been good, Lord. Even with the occasional "missing of the minds" as he calls it.

His voice called to her as he burst through the front door. "Audrey? Car's warm. Are you ready?"

"Coming!" She left the letters on the desk and hurried from the office. Above the front door in the entryway, an olive swag hung, and Audrey pulled him near it, availing herself of the unspoken invitation.

His chuckle melted her just as quickly and thoroughly as it had the previous year when she thought she wanted nothing more for him to go home. *He knows it too,* Audrey mused as she kissed him once more. "I love you."

"Is that a yes to the HearthLand investment or a yes to the foster kids? Maybe a yes to the baby idea? Or, I know!" Another kiss interrupted his questioning, but as he pulled her toward the back door, Zain asked one final question, "Or is it the best answer ever? Is it yes to all?"

Ignoring the rising panic that the idea of any of those changes brought, Audrey opted for a safe answer. "Yes."

"To one or to all?"

"One of those two," she agreed. "Now let's get out of here before we miss the present opening. You're always making me late."

Zain's laughter filled the backyard as they hurried to the carport. "A baby it is!"

"What?!"

"You said I'm making you late…"

Lord, give me the courage to say yes to any or all of them. She gazed up at her husband and rested her hand on his bearded cheek. "You definitely deserve all of them, but I don't know if I can handle that many changes in one year."

"One at a time then. You pick. It's all I want for Christmas."

"And here I thought that was me. You keep singing that song—"

Between a few more quick kisses, Zain said, "We're never going to get out of here if we don't stop this. We will also freeze. Thought you should know."

"So my kisses now leave you cold. I see—"

His lips proved once more that her words couldn't be any more untrue. They made it nearly to the rest stop between Fairbury and Rockland before she said, "Talk to Ralph again. If you're sure, go for it."

"And we'll talk family next year?" he asked.

"Sure." She waited another mile before she reached for his hand and squeezed it. "Of course, next year is only a week away…"

Episode 1: The Arrival

Chapter One

May 7th

Still lost in the anticipation of the fresh, sweet air of Walden Farm, Ralph Myner pushed his suitcases through the automatic doors of the Rockland airport and recoiled as the scent of exhaust from waiting taxis and belching busses filled his lungs. His phone vibrated in his pocket, and despite his intention of adapting to a lifestyle not ruled by electronics and the incessant demand of instant communication, his hand reached into his pocket, retrieved the phone, and tapped the screen before he realized what he'd done. Three words flashed across the screen. IT'S NOT TOO LATE.

A smile—not the first that day—filled his heart and rearranged his features into that trademarked grin that he knew had helped him through many business deals. *Now it just has to find me investors in my last business plan. Once I get that, I'll be retired. Wow.*

People jostled him—few pausing to mumble an apology—until he snapped out of his momentary reverie and joined the flow of people heading for the line of taxis just down from him. One after another, cars pulled up to the curb and harried travelers pushed their way into one. The next should have been his, but when a man staring more at his watch than where he walked or who he walked into stepped up behind him, Ralph backed out of the way. "You take it."

Without a word, the man opened the door, tossed a

small suitcase onto the seat beside him, and climbed in. Just as the car pulled away, his head stuck out the window. "Oh, thanks!"

Weariness—that sense of nervous exhaustion one only feels after a long flight and the knowledge that your day just began—slowly crept over Ralph as he stood waiting for the next one. After a minute or so, he realized that several had pulled up and been taken by passengers too impatient to point out his ride had arrived. A shuttle zipped around the traffic circle, a quiet announcement of its arrival. Ralph hesitated, only for a minute, and glanced around him for signs of the shuttle's intended stop. Minutes later, he collapsed in a seat beside a woman who looked ready for a marathon rather than a flight, and rested his eyes.

The thud of a suitcase at his feet jerked him from his impromptu catnap and out of his seat. "Thanks."

"Long flight?" The shuttle driver flashed him a bright smile that belonged in toothpaste commercials instead of on an airport shuttle and handed him his other bag.

"Long enough. Got a lot to do." He slipped her five dollars, stacked his suitcases, and wheeled them to the open shuttle doors.

"Thanks!"

He didn't make it far. The hub central led to underground trains for Amtrak, the Rockland Area Transit, Greyhound, and several of the smaller car rental companies. It also had a food court with scents that set his stomach rumbling. *Late lunch first. I want a steak sandwich.*

He used the top of his suitcase for a table as he unwrapped the first half of his beefsteak sandwich. The scent of bell peppers, onions, garlic sauce, and horseradish combined with the beef the moment the papers fell away. "Mmmm."

A woman passing smiled at him. "Those are good. Had half of one last week. Delicious."

Ralph nodded and offered the other half of his sandwich. "I see why half. I shouldn't have bought the full thing. Hungry?"

She hesitated, desire mingling with caution on her face before she nodded. "Thanks. Haven't eaten yet today." She held up a plastic trash bag—one that had seen a lot more use than the manufacturer probably intended—and shook the cans and bottles inside. "Slim pickings today. I think Harry got here before me."

Curious about her, Ralph scooted over to make room on the bench. "Well, take a break. Can I get you a bottle of water? Soda?"

"I've got enough for that now. Thanks." She strode away to a vending machine and popped in enough change for an overpriced bottle of water.

She shouldn't be spending her money here. Everything's twice as expensive in a place like this. That she eked out her existence off the rejects of others, Ralph had no doubt. However, the backpack slung over her shoulders and the clothes she wore were cleaner than he'd been accustomed to seeing in the homeless of LA. *Lost her job? Unemployed? Something's different about her.*

When she returned to the bench, Ralph tried to hide his surprise. He'd expected her to move along. In his experience, people in her situation didn't chat up strangers. "Too bad you can't go empty out the bottles at security. They get dozens. Every hour."

"I know, right? When the outside security guys are busy, I'll sometimes carry my bag around the doors. People drop 'em in then if I look like I'm working."

"Smart cookie." Ralph held out his hand and frowned. He wiped the horseradish off his fingers and extended it once more. "I'm Ralph, by the way."

There it was—that cautious look he knew and recognized. After a moment, she shook it and returned to her sandwich. "I shouldn't have shaken it. You're eating, and my hands aren't clean. Sorry."

The temptation to go wash his hands nearly drove him to the men's room, but he just scooched it down a bit, ensuring paper protected his sandwich, and tried not to let his mind imagine what she might have touched. "Paper'll protect me."

"I don't dig around in the cans," she reassured him. "If it's not right on top and covered with junk, I don't get it. I'm not quite that desperate yet." The woman gave him a smile—another pearly white flash that didn't belong to someone making her living by recycling other people's garbage. "I'm Annie."

"Nice to meet you." A piece of beef wedged itself between his teeth. *That crown still isn't right. I've got to find me a good dentist immediately. I shouldn't have left the floss in L.A. Now I—*

A new thought occurred to him. "Hey, can you do me a favor when you're done?"

"You've got a piece—"

"Yeah, it's a nuisance. Gotta get that tooth fixed. Anyway, I can't just leave these things here and I really don't want to wheel them all over the place. If I gave you the money, would you go into that shop and buy me a small thing of floss or one of those travel toiletry kits or something?"

Annie pulled out a plastic case. "I'd offer you some of mine, but I doubt you should take it. It's clean, but you have no way of knowing that."

As much as he wanted to show her he didn't consider her as something unwanted or unwelcome, this time he couldn't do it. "You'll need it. I can't take yours. But if you could..." He pulled out his wallet and passed her a twenty. "I'd appreciate it."

"I could just take off with it. How do you know I won't?"

Ralph shrugged. "I don't. But I'm kind of desperate and you seem honest enough, so I'm willing to risk it."

She started to grab the plastic bag and hesitated. "I'll leave my recycling. Keep an eye on it?"

The way she asked almost made him feel chivalrous as he nodded. "Sure."

A few minutes later, Annie returned and passed him his change, the receipt, and a small plastic bag. "They were out of just floss, so I got the kit like you said. Disgusting, the prices they charge."

Ralph pulled the floss from the clear, quart-sized zip-top bag and pulled a long string of it from the container. He zipped it all shut again and offered it to her. "I'll be buying everything I need in a few hours anyway. Take it."

Her eyes narrowed. "I don't ask people for their money or their stuff," she snapped.

"No, you didn't. And I didn't offer you any. I can offer this to someone else or you can take it, but I don't need a toothbrush half its normal size, and I don't like that brand of toothpaste. I just wanted some floss." He began working the floss between his teeth until the offending piece of meat broke free. The floss dropped into the paper bag from the sandwich place before he took another bite. The memory of shaking her hand combined with the more recent memory of sticking that hand in his mouth made him gag. He rolled up the sandwich, dropped it in the bag, and rolled it into a ball. "That was good."

"You didn't eat much."

Ralph shrugged as he stood. "Stupid tooth messes everything up. Have a good day, Annie. I'd offer to give you something for dinner, but I don't want to offend you."

Her laughter followed him across the wide circle and into the subway station.

"You can't expect to find a good vehicle and a trailer you like on your first day!"

Ralph's nephew's voice echoed in his mind as he spent a fortune in cab fare traveling from one dealership to the next in search of just the right truck. Newer vehicles seemed more like "Rancher's Cadillacs" than actual work vehicles and those that looked like they had actually done some work did little to impress him. *There's got to be some kind of balance here. It's one thing for Harlan to be right about the trailer, but I've bought cars in less time than dinner at a nice restaurant.*

While the latest salesman extolled the virtues of a Cummins engine, Ralph sent a text to the cab company he'd been working with, requesting what he and the dispatcher had begun calling an "extraction." The man must have come to a place where Ralph was expected to agree to some brilliant commentary about the suitability of the vehicle, but Ralph didn't know exactly what the man had said last. "Y'know," he murmured after a glance over the body of the truck. "I just don't think I can take a metallic, midnight blue truck seriously as a work vehicle. I think my problem is I just don't know what I want. All I know is what I *don't* want."

"That's okay. That's exactly my job—to help you find what you do want and get you on your way in it."

Ralph wondered if the potential of a cash sale would have produced the same amount of enthusiasm at the beginning of the day as it did near the end. With no financing approval to slow down the process, the salesman had a great chance to finish the day strong—if he could manage to find a truck that worked.

"I wonder..." Rob the salesman swept his eyes across the lot and pointed toward the mid-sized trucks. "Maybe you just need a smaller truck. I mean, this is one hunk of machinery and for most stuff; even a little Toyota could carry all you'd need. Why don't we look at these over here?"

The third truck from the end caught Ralph's attention. He paused, uncertain about something as flashy as a cherry red truck, but outside the color, it looked strong, in good condition, but not a luxury vehicle wrapped in a utilitarian body. *Harlan will definitely tell me I'm going through a late mid-life crisis, but it looks good.* "Let's test drive this one. It's the first one on this lot that I've even wanted to consider. He hesitated. "Wait, does it have a tow hitch? Can a smaller truck tow—"

"As long as you're not towing a big rig, you should be good. Travel-trailer, right? Not a fifth wheel?"

"Right—probably eighteen to twenty-one feet or so. There's a place over in Ferndale that refurbishes old ones. I'm planning on one of those, so the construction might be heavier than newer ones—or not." Ralph shrugged. "I'm not really sure, but hey."

By the time he got up to the speed limit on the Loop, Ralph was sold. Still, he asked questions, trying to keep a hint of skepticism in his tone. Rob the spent the drive commenting on the truck's best features, gas mileage, and mentioned the legroom at least three times.

Considering you're four inches taller than me, I can see why, but c'mon. I don't need something for an NBA player. "It'll be nice if Harlan ever drives it, I guess."

"Harlan your son?"

"Nephew," Ralph corrected. "I don't have any children." *Now what'd you say that for? He doesn't care. It's craziness.* Despite his internal blast, Ralph added, "He's not all that happy about me moving here."

"Work bring you to Rockland?"

A glance over his shoulder must have hidden the slow shake of his head, because Rob apologized for prying. Ralph shook his head again. "No, sorry. I'm retiring somewhere around the loop—starting a simple living community."

"Simple living? Like the Amish?" Rob gave Ralph a once over before adding, "You don't look like an Amish dude."

Was it worth it to explain? Ralph didn't know. Still, he had a responsibility to his retirement fund to talk up the idea. "Well, what we're doing is starting a community where people help one another be more self-sufficient. We'll be similar to the Amish in how we raise our own food or explore alternative energy ideas, but this is not a religious order but rather a cooperative of people who want to slow down their lives."

"Sounds right up my sister's alley. She's all into that 'green' stuff. Always saying, 'Make eco-friendly choices" or "that's not good for the planet.'"

I wish I had my business cards with me. I ordered them, but they're at the home of a friend outside Fairbury."

"There's that hippie place outside Ferndale... have you considered joining them? I mean, they're all about composting toilets and smaller footprints in housing and stuff like that. Over half of those places don't even have a kitchen—just a mini-fridge and bar sink. They have to do all their cooking in some big common area."

"Well, that's a different plan from what we're doing, but I'll have to look into it."

Ralph pulled into the lot, put the truck in gear, and hesitated. "Two years of free maintenance?"

"Our usual is one…"

He checked his watch. "I've got time to check out a couple more places. I may be back."

"Oh, no…" Rob laughed. "You're one of those. Lemme talk to Larry. I'll see what I can do."

"I want fifteen hundred off the top too. It's overpriced and you know it."

"I—" After a moment's pause, Rob frowned and sighed. "Can you give me five minutes before you go?"

"Sure." Ralph waited until Rob opened the truck door before he said, "It'll take that long for a cab to get here."

Printed in Great Britain
by Amazon